JUIN

IT ITAN F LOSS

'Kiran Desai is a terrific writer. This book richly fulfils the promise of her first' Salman Rushdie

'A wonderful writer of comic set-pieces. A novel that manages to be both warm-hearted about human nature and clear-sighted about humanity's flaws. Desai has a mature, compassionate voice' *Observer*

'Moving and bleakly comic . . . informed by wit' *Sunday Times*

'Desai brilliantly transports you to her novel's setting, making the characters' hopes and dreams feel as familiar as your own' *Glamour*

'Written with scintillating assurance and moral rigour' *Spectator*

'Desai weaves a rich tapestry of back stories and historical threads' *Metro*

'No subject is tired when tackled with the energy and intelligence of Kiran Desai's *The Inheritance of Loss*. Her Indian characters are exquisitely particular – funny but never quaint . . . Bittersweet, entertaining and just shy of tragic. Surprisingly wise' *Economist*

'Kiran Desai's extraordinary new novel manages to explore, with intimacy and insight, just about every contemporary international issue: globalization, multiculturalism, economic inequality, fundamentalism and terrorist violence . . . lit by a moral intelligence at once fierce and tender' *New York Times Book Review*

'Desai is wildly in love with the light and landscape and the characters who inhabit it. Summer comes alive with its sights and sounds and smells, and the rainy season seems to pour down with more force than in any other novel you've read . . . [She has] a love for language that few American writers her age seem able to rival. This story of exiles at home and abroad, of families broken and fixed, of love both bitter and bittersweet is one of the most

I predict you'll read it . . .

e, and the narrative inside

'A meditative look at the conflicting bonds of love and duty' *Vogue*

'Desai's assurance and energy keep the plot on track and bring her ambitious tale to a fittingly strong conclusion' *People*

'Seldom has an author offered so fearless a glimpse into how ordinary lives are caught up in the collision of modernity and cultural tradition, and in the schisms and fanaticism that all too often ensue' *Elle*

'With its razor insights and emotional scope, *The Inheritance of Loss* amplifies a developing and formidable voice' *Los Angeles Times*

'Desai's characters are so alive, the places so vivid, that we are always inside their lives. Her insights into human nature, rare for so young a writer, juggle timeless wisdom and twenty-first century self-doubt' *Boston Globe*

'Desai's strength lies in her ability to capture, with humor and grace, the nuanced complexities of the characters and their times' *Denver Post*

'The novel is finely accomplished in the way it makes connections between private lives and public events' *Seattle Times*

'Sweet and savoury, sometimes wise and desperately forlorn, this is an engaging second novel from a brave new talent' *Globe & Mail*

'With her second novel, Kiran Desai has written a sprawling and delicate book, like an ancient landscape glittering in the rain . . . Desai has a touch for alternating humor and impending tragedy that one associates with the greatest writers, and her prose is uncannily beautiful, a perfect balance of lyricism and plain speech' *O: The Oprah Magazine*

'Glorious . . . luminous' *San Francisco Chronicle*

'Stunning . . . In this alternately comical and contemplative novel, Desai deftly shuttles between first and third worlds, illuminating the pain of exile, the ambiguities of post-colonialism and the blinding desire for a "better life"' *Publishers Weekly* (starred review)

'Desai's *Hullabaloo in the Guava Orchard* introduced an astute observer of human nature and a delectably sensuous satirist. In her second novel, Desai is even more perceptive and bewitching . . . Desai is superbly insightful in her rendering of compelling characters, and in her wisdom regarding the perverse dynamics of society. Desai incisively and imaginatively dramatizes the wonders and tragedies of Himalayan life and, by extension, the fragility of peace and elusiveness of justice, albeit with her own powerful blend of tenderness and wit' *Booklist*

'The book's magic lies in [its] rich images' *Entertainment Weekly*

'A brilliant talent. Creating gorgeous pictures in the mind, Desai generously embellishes on colours, fragrances and evocative landscapes' *Asiana*

'Exquisite. Kiran Desai meets the complexity of our times with a language that is supple in its syntax and its rhythms. The story she tells is filled with patiently acquired insights about humanity, and every other page is a hymn to nature's abundance' Nadeem Aslam

'A remarkable book, funny and insightful – a showcase for the amazing range and depth of Kiran Desai's writing' Manil Suri

'*The Inheritance of Loss*, so moving, funny, unflinching, is the best novel I've yet read about the contemporary immigrant life and the on-going parallel world "left behind." And the writing is extraordinary: astonishingly observant and inventive, joyously alive. Really, it's just the best, sweetest, most delightful new novel I've read in ages!' Francisco Goldman, author of *The Divine Husband*

'If God is in the details, Ms. Desai has written a holy book. Page after page, from Harlem to the Himalayas, she captures the terror and exhilaration of being alive in this world' Gary Shteyngart, author of *The Russian Debutante's Handbook*

'*The Inheritance of Loss* is a revelation in the possibilities of the novel. It is vast in scope, from the peaks of the Himalayas to the immigrant quarters of New York; the gripping stories of people buffeted by the winds of history, personal and political. Kiran Desai's voice is fiercely funny – a humour born out of darkness, the laughter of the dispossessed. It is a remarkable novel because it is rich in that most elusive quality in fiction: wisdom' Suketu Mehta, author of *Maximum City: Bombay Lost and Found*

The Inheritance of Loss

Kiran Desai

PENGUIN BOOKS

To my mother with so much love

PENGUIN BOOKS

Published by the Penguin Group
Penguin Books Ltd, 80 Strand, London WC2R 0RL, England
Penguin Group (USA) Inc., 375 Hudson Street, New York, New York 10014, USA
Penguin Group (Canada), 90 Eglinton Avenue East, Suite 700, Toronto, Ontario, Canada M4P 2Y3
(a division of Pearson Penguin Canada Inc.)
Penguin Ireland, 25 St Stephen's Green, Dublin 2, Ireland (a division of Penguin Books Ltd)
Penguin Group (Australia), 250 Camberwell Road, Camberwell, Victoria 3124, Australia
(a division of Pearson Australia Group Pty Ltd)
Penguin Books India Pvt Ltd, 11 Community Centre, Panchsheel Park, New Delhi – 110 017, India
Penguin Group (NZ), 67 Apollo Drive, Rosedale, North Shore 0632, New Zealand
(a division of Pearson New Zealand Ltd)
Penguin Books (South Africa) (Pty) Ltd, 24 Sturdee Avenue, Rosebank, Johannesburg 2196, South Africa

Penguin Books Ltd, Registered Offices: 80 Strand, London WC2R 0RL, England

www.penguin.com

First published in the United States of America by Atlantic Monthly Press,
an imprint of Grove/Atlantic, Inc. 2006
First published in Great Britain by Hamish Hamilton 2006
Published in Penguin Books 2007
1

Printed in England by Clays Ltd, St Ives plc

ISBN: 978-0-141-02728-9

Boast of Quietness

Writings of light assault the darkness, more prodigious than meteors.
The tall unknowable city takes over the countryside.
Sure of my life and my death, I observe the ambitious and would like to
understand them.
Their day is greedy as a lariat in the air.
Their night is a rest from the rage within steel, quick to attack.
They speak of humanity.
My humanity is in feeling we are all voices of the same poverty.
They speak of homeland.
My homeland is the rhythm of a guitar, a few portraits, an old sword,
the willow grove's visible prayer as evening falls.
Time is living me.
More silent than my shadow, I pass through the loftily covetous multitude.
They are indispensable, singular, worthy of tomorrow.
My name is someone and anyone.
I walk slowly, like one who comes from so far away he doesn't expect to
arrive.

—Jorge Luis Borges

The Inheritance of Loss

One

All day, the colors had been those of dusk, mist moving like a water creature across the great flanks of mountains possessed of ocean shadows and depths. Briefly visible above the vapor, Kanchenjunga was a far peak whittled out of ice, gathering the last of the light, a plume of snow blown high by the storms at its summit.

Sai, sitting on the veranda, was reading an article about giant squid in an old *National Geographic.* Every now and then she looked up at Kanchenjunga, observed its wizard phosphorescence with a shiver. The judge sat at the far corner with his chessboard, playing against himself. Stuffed under his chair where she felt safe was Mutt the dog, snoring gently in her sleep. A single bald lightbulb dangled on a wire above. It was cold, but inside the house, it was still colder, the dark, the freeze, contained by stone walls several feet deep.

Here, at the back, inside the cavernous kitchen, was the cook, trying to light the damp wood. He fingered the kindling gingerly for fear of the community of scorpions living, loving, reproducing in the pile. Once he'd found a mother, plump with poison, fourteen babies on her back.

Eventually, the fire caught and he placed his kettle on top, as battered, as encrusted as something dug up by an archeological team, and waited for it to boil. The walls were singed and sodden, garlic hung by muddy stems from the charred beams, thickets of soot clumped batlike upon the ceiling. The flame cast a mosaic of shiny orange across the cook's face, and his top half grew hot, but a mean gust tortured his arthritic knees.

Up through the chimney and out, the smoke mingled with the mist that was gathering speed, sweeping in thicker and thicker, obscuring things in parts—half a hill, then the other half. The trees turned into silhouettes, loomed forth, were submerged again. Gradually the vapor replaced everything with itself, solid objects with shadow, and nothing remained that did not seem molded from or inspired by it. Sai's breath flew from her nostrils in drifts, and the diagram of a giant squid constructed from scraps of information, scientists' dreams, sank entirely into the murk.

She shut the magazine and walked out into the garden. The forest was old and thick at the edge of the lawn; the bamboo thickets rose thirty feet into the gloom; the trees were moss-slung giants, bunioned and misshapen, tentacled with the roots of orchids. The caress of the mist through her hair seemed human, and when she held her fingers out, the vapor took them gently into its mouth. She thought of Gyan, the mathematics tutor, who should have arrived an hour ago with his algebra book.

But it was 4:30 already and she excused him with the thickening mist.

When she looked back, the house was gone; when she climbed the steps back to the veranda, the garden vanished. The judge had fallen asleep and gravity acting upon the slack muscles, pulling on the line of his mouth, dragging on his cheeks, showed Sai exactly what he would look like if he were dead.

"Where is the tea?" he woke and demanded of her. "He's late," said the judge, meaning the cook with the tea, not Gyan.

"I'll get it," she offered.

The gray had permeated inside, as well, settling on the silverware, nosing the corners, turning the mirror in the passageway to cloud. Sai, walking to the kitchen, caught a glimpse of herself being smothered and reached forward to imprint her lips upon the surface, a perfectly formed film star kiss. "Hello," she said, half to herself and half to someone else.

No human had ever seen an adult giant squid alive, and though they had eyes as big as apples to scope the dark of the ocean, theirs was a solitude so profound they might never encounter another of their tribe. The melancholy of this situation washed over Sai.

Could fulfillment ever be felt as deeply as loss? Romantically she decided that love must surely reside in the gap between desire and fulfillment, in the lack, not the contentment. Love was the ache, the anticipation, the retreat, everything around it but the emotion itself.

The water boiled and the cook lifted the kettle and emptied it into the teapot.

"Terrible," he said. "My bones ache so badly, my joints hurt—I may as well be dead. If not for Biju. . . ." Biju was his son in America. He worked at Don Pollo—or was it The Hot Tomato? Or Ali Baba's Fried Chicken? His father could not remember or understand or pronounce the names, and Biju changed jobs so often, like a fugitive on the run—no papers.

"Yes, it's so foggy," Sai said. "I don't think the tutor will come." She jigsawed the cups, saucers, teapot, milk, sugar, strainer, Marie and Delite biscuits all to fit upon the tray.

"I'll take it," she offered.

"Careful, careful," he said scoldingly, following with an enamel basin of milk for Mutt. Seeing Sai swim forth, spoons making a jittery music upon the warped sheet of tin, Mutt raised her head. "Teatime?" said her eyes as her tail came alive.

"Why is there nothing to eat?" the judge asked, irritated, lifting his nose from a muddle of pawns in the center of the chessboard.

He looked, then, at the sugar in the pot: dirty, micalike glinting granules. The biscuits looked like cardboard and there were dark finger marks on the white of the saucers. Never ever was the tea served the way it should be, but he demanded at least a cake or scones, macaroons or cheese straws. Something sweet and something salty. This was a travesty and it undid the very concept of teatime.

"Only biscuits," said Sai to his expression. "The baker left for his daughter's wedding."

"I don't want biscuits."

Sai sighed.

"How dare he go for a wedding? Is that the way to run a business? The fool. Why can't the cook make something?"

"There's no more gas, no kerosene."

"Why the hell can't he make it over wood? All these old cooks can make cakes perfectly fine by building coals around a tin box. You think they used to have gas stoves, kerosene stoves, before? Just too lazy now."

The cook came hurrying out with the leftover chocolate pudding warmed on the fire in a frying pan, and the judge ate the lovely brown puddle and gradually his face took on an expression of grudging pudding contentment.

They sipped and ate, all of existence passed over by nonexistence, the gate leading nowhere, and they watched the tea spill copious ribbony curls of vapor, watched their breath join the mist slowly twisting and turning, twisting and turning.

Nobody noticed the boys creeping across the grass, not even Mutt, until they were practically up the steps. Not that it mattered, for there were no latches to keep them out and nobody within calling distance except Uncle Potty on the other side of the *jhora* ravine, who would be drunk on the floor by this hour, lying still but feeling himself pitch about—"Don't mind me, love," he always told Sai after a drinking bout, opening one eye like an owl, "I'll just lie down right here and take a little rest—"

They had come through the forest on foot, in leather jackets from the Kathmandu black market, khaki pants, bandanas—universal guerilla fashion. One of the boys carried a gun.

Later reports accused China, Pakistan, and Nepal, but in this part of the world, as in any other, there were enough weapons floating around for an impoverished movement with a ragtag army. They were looking for anything they could find—kukri sickles, axes, kitchen knives, spades, any kind of firearm.

They had come for the judge's hunting rifles.

Despite their mission and their clothes, they were unconvincing. The oldest of them looked under twenty, and at one yelp from Mutt, they screamed like a bunch of schoolgirls, retreated down the steps to cower behind the bushes blurred by mist. "Does she *bite,* Uncle? *My God!*"—shivering there in their camouflage.

Mutt began to do what she always did when she met strangers: she turned a furiously wagging bottom to the intruders and looked around from behind, smiling, conveying both shyness and hope.

Hating to see her degrade herself thus, the judge reached for her, whereupon she buried her nose in his arms.

The boys came back up the steps, embarrassed, and the judge became conscious of the fact that this embarrassment was dangerous for had the boys projected unwavering confidence, they might have been less inclined to flex their muscles.

The one with the rifle said something the judge could not understand.

"No Nepali?" he spat, his lips sneering to show what he thought of that, but he continued in Hindi. "Guns?"

"We have no guns here."

"Get them."

"You must be misinformed."

"Never mind with all this *nakhra*. Get them."

"I order you," said the judge, "to leave my property at once."

"Bring the weapons."

"I will call the police."

This was a ridiculous threat as there was no telephone.

They laughed a movie laugh, and then, also as if in a movie, the boy with the rifle pointed his gun at Mutt. "Go on, get them, or we will kill the dog first and you second, cook third, ladies last," he said, smiling at Sai.

"I'll get them," she said in terror and overturned the tea tray as she went.

The judge sat with Mutt in his lap. The guns dated from his days in the Indian Civil Service. A BSA five-shot barrel pump gun, a .30 Springfield rifle, and a double-barreled rifle, Holland & Holland. They weren't even locked away: they were mounted at the end of the hall above a dusty row of painted green and brown duck decoys.

"*Chtch*, all rusted. Why don't you take care of them?" But they were pleased and their bravado bloomed. "We will join you for tea."

"Tea?" asked Sai in numb terror.

"Tea and snacks. Is this how you treat guests? Sending us back out into the cold with nothing to warm us up." They looked at one another, at her, looked up, down, and winked.

She felt intensely, fearfully female.

Of course, all the boys were familiar with movie scenes where hero and heroine, befeathered in cosy winterwear, drank tea served in silver tea sets by polished servants. Then the mist would roll in, just as it did in reality, and they sang and danced, playing peekaboo in a nice resort hotel. This was classic cinema set in Kulu-Manali or, in preterrorist days, Kashmir, before gunmen came bounding out of the mist and a new kind of film had to be made.

The cook was hiding under the dining table and they dragged him out.

"*Ai aaa, ai aaa,*" he joined his palms together, begging them, "please, I'm a poor man, please." He held up his arms and cringed as if from an expected blow.

"He hasn't done anything, leave him," said Sai, hating to see him humiliated, hating even more to see that the only path open to him was to humiliate himself further.

"Please living only to see my son please don't kill me please *I'm a poor man spare me.*"

His lines had been honed over centuries, passed down through generations, for poor people needed certain lines; the script was always the same, and they had no option but to beg for mercy. The cook knew instinctively how to cry.

These familiar lines allowed the boys to ease still further into their role, which he had handed to them like a gift.

"Who wants to kill you?" they said to the cook. "We're just hungry, that's all. Here, your sahib will help you. Go on," they said to the judge, "you know how it should be done properly." The judge didn't move, so the boy pointed the gun at Mutt again.

The judge grabbed her and put her behind him.

"Too soft-hearted, sahib. You should show this kind side to your guests, also. Go on, prepare the table."

The judge found himself in the kitchen where he had never been, not once, Mutt wobbling about his toes, Sai and the cook too scared to look, averting their gaze.

It came to them that they might all die with the judge in the kitchen; the world was upside down and absolutely anything could happen.

"Nothing to eat?"

"Only biscuits," said Sai for the second time that day.

"La! What kind of sahib?" the leader asked the judge. "No snacks! Make something, then. Think we can continue on empty stomachs?"

Wailing and pleading for his life, the cook fried *pakoras,* batter hitting the hot oil, this sound of violence seeming an appropriate accompaniment to the situation.

The judge fumbled for a tablecloth in a drawer stuffed with yellowed curtains, sheets, and rags. Sai, her hands shaking, stewed tea in a pan and strained it, although she had no idea how to properly make tea this way, the Indian way. She only knew the English way.

The boys carried out a survey of the house with some interest. The atmosphere, they noted, was of intense solitude. A few bits of rickety furniture overlaid with a termite cuneiform stood isolated in the shadows along with some cheap metal-tube folding chairs. Their noses wrinkled from the gamy mouse stench of a small place, although the ceiling had the reach of a public monument and the rooms were spacious in the old manner of wealth, windows placed for snow views. They peered at a certificate issued by Cambridge University that had almost vanished into an overlay of brown stains blooming upon walls that had swelled with moisture and billowed forth like sails. The door had been closed forever on a storeroom where the floor had caved in. The storeroom supplies and what seemed like an unreasonable number of emptied tuna fish cans, had been piled on a broken Ping-Pong table in the kitchen, and only a corner of the kitchen was being used, since it was meant originally for the slaving minions, not the one leftover servant.

"House needs a lot of repairs," the boys advised.

"Tea is too weak," they said in the manner of mothers-in-law. "And not enough salt," they said of the *pakoras.* They dipped the Marie and Delite biscuits in the tea, drew up the hot liquid noisily. Two trunks they found in the bedrooms they filled with rice, lentils, sugar, tea, oil, matches, Lux soap, and Pond's Cold Cream. One of them assured Sai: "Only items necessary for the movement." A shout from another alerted the rest to a locked cabinet. "Give us the key."

The judge fetched the key hidden behind the *National Geographic*s that, as a young man, visualizing a different kind of life, he had taken to a shop to have bound in leather with the years in gold lettering.

They opened the cabinet and found bottles of Grand Marnier, amontillado sherry, and Talisker. Some of the bottles' contents had evaporated completely and some had turned to vinegar, but the boys put them in the trunk anyway.

"Cigarettes?"

There were none. This angered them, and although there was no water in the tanks, they defecated in the toilets and left them stinking. Then they were ready to go.

"Say, '*Jai* Gorkha,'" they said to the judge. "Gorkhaland for Gorkhas."

"*Jai* Gorkha."

"Say, 'I am a fool.'"

"I am a fool."

"Loudly. Can't hear you, *huzoor.* Say it louder."

He said it in the same empty voice.

"*Jai* Gorkha," said the cook, and "Gorkhaland for Gorkhas," said Sai, although they had not been asked to say anything.

"I am a fool," said the cook.

Chuckling, the boys stepped off the veranda and out into the fog carrying the two trunks. One trunk was painted with white letters on the black tin that read: "Mr. J. P. Patel, SS *Strathnaver.*" The other read: "Miss S. Mistry, St. Augustine's Convent." Then they were gone as abruptly as they had appeared.

"They've gone, they've gone," said Sai. Mutt tried to respond despite the fear that still inhabited her eyes, and she tried to wag her tail, although it kept folding back between her legs. The cook broke into a loud lament: "*Humara kya hoga, hai hai, humara kya hoga,*" he let his voice fly. "*Hai, hai,* what will become of us?"

"Shut up," said the judge and thought, These damn servants born and brought up to scream.

He himself sat bolt upright, his expression clenched to prevent its distortion, tightly clasping the arms of the chair to restrict a violent trembling, and although he knew he was trying to stop a motion that was inside him, it felt as if it were the world shaking with a ravaging force he was trying to hold himself against. On the dining table was the tablecloth he had spread out, white with a design of grapevines interrupted by a garnet stain where, many years ago, he had spilled a glass of port while trying to throw it at his wife for chewing in a way that disgusted him.

"So slow," the boys had taunted him. "You people! No shame. . . . Can't do one thing on your own."

Both Sai and the cook had averted their gaze from the judge and his humiliation, and even now their glances avoided the tablecloth and took the longer way across the room, for if the cloth were acknowledged, there was no telling how he might punish them. It was an awful thing, the downing of a proud man. He might kill the witness.

The cook drew the curtains; their vulnerability seemed highlighted by the glass and they appeared to be hanging exposed in the forest and the night, with the forest and the night hanging their dark shaggy cloaks upon them. Mutt saw her reflection before the cloth was drawn, mistook it for a jackal, and jumped. Then she turned, saw her shadow on the wall, and jumped once more.

It was February of 1986. Sai was seventeen, and her romance with Gyan the mathematics tutor was not even a year old.

9 ➛

When the newspapers next got through the road blocks, they read:

In Bombay a band named Hell No was going to perform at the Hyatt International.

In Delhi, a technology fair on cow dung gas stoves was being attended by delegates from all over the world.

In Kalimpong, high in the northeastern Himalayas where they lived—the retired judge and his cook, Sai, and Mutt—there was a report of new dissatisfaction in the hills, gathering insurgency, men and guns. It was the Indian-Nepalese this time, fed up with being treated like the minority in a place where they were the majority. They wanted their own country, or at least their own state, in which to manage their own affairs. Here, where India blurred into Bhutan and Sikkim, and the army did pull-ups and push-ups, maintaining their tanks with khaki paint in case the Chinese grew hungry for more territory than Tibet, it had always been a messy map. The papers sounded resigned. A great amount of warring, betraying, bartering had occurred; between Nepal, England, Tibet, India, Sikkim, Bhutan; Darjeeling stolen from here, Kalimpong plucked from there—despite, ah, despite the mist charging down like a dragon, dissolving, undoing, making ridiculous the drawing of borders.

Two

The judge sent the cook to the police station the next day although he protested, knowing from the same accumulated wisdom of the ages that had led him to plead before the intruders that this was not a sensible idea.

Always bad luck, the police, for if they were being paid off by the robbers, they would do nothing, and if, on the other hand, they were not, then it would be worse, for the boys who had come the evening before would take their revenge. They had guns now, which they might clean of rust, fill with bullets and . . . shoot! One way or the other, the police would try to extract a bribe. He thought of the 250 rupees from the sale to Uncle Potty of his own meticulously brewed *chhang*, which so successfully rendered the aging bachelor into flat-on-the-floor drunkenness. Last night he had hidden the money in a pocket of his extra shirt, but that didn't seem safe enough. He tied it up high on a beam of his mud and bamboo hut at the bottom of the judge's property, but then, seeing the mice running up and down the rafters, he worried they would eat it. Finally he put it in a tin and hid it in the garage, under the car that never went anywhere anymore. He thought of his son, Biju.

They at Cho Oyu needed a young man on their side.

In his trembling message, brought forward as if by the motion of his wringing hands, he tried to emphasize how he was just the messenger. He himself had nothing to do with anything and thought it was not worth it to bother the police; he would sooner ignore the robbery and, in fact, the whole conflict and anything else that might give offence. He was a powerless man, barely enough learning to read and write, had worked like a donkey all his life, hoped only to avoid trouble, lived on only to see his son.

Unfortunately the policemen seemed perturbed and questioned him harshly while also making their scorn for him clear. As a servant, he was far beneath them, but the robbery of guns from a retired member of the judiciary could not be ignored and they were forced to inform the superintendent.

That very afternoon the police arrived at Cho Oyu in a line of toad-colored jeeps that appeared through the moving static of a small anxious sleet. They left their opened umbrellas in a row on the veranda, but the wind undid them and they began to wheel about—mostly black ones that leaked a black dye, but also a pink, synthetic made-in-Taiwan one, abloom with flowers.

They interviewed the judge and wrote out a report to confirm a complaint of robbery and trespassing. "Any threats made, sir?"

"They asked him to set the table and bring the tea," said the cook in complete seriousness.

The policemen began to laugh.

The judge's mouth was a straight grim line: "Go sit in the kitchen. *Bar bar karta rehta hai.*"

The police dusted the surfaces with fingerprint-lifting powder and placed a melamine biscuit jar with greasy *pakora* thumbprints in a plastic bag.

They measured the footprints coming up the steps of the veranda and uncovered proof of several assorted sizes of feet: "One very big one, sir, in a Bata gym shoe."

Mostly, because the judge's residence had long been a matter of curiosity in the bazaar, they, like the gun robbers, took the opportunity to have a good nosy look around.

And, like the robbers, they were not impressed by what they saw. They surveyed the downfall of wealth with satisfaction, and one of the policemen kicked a shaky apparatus of pipes leading from the *jhora* stream, bandaged here and there with sopping rags. He shone his torch into the toilet tank and discovered the flushing contraption had been fixed with rubber bands and bamboo splints.

"What evidence are you going to find in the toilet?" asked Sai, following him around, feeling ashamed.

The house had been built long ago by a Scotsman, passionate reader of the accounts of that period: *The Indian Alps and How We Crossed Them*, by A Lady Pioneer. *Land of the Lama. The Phantom Rickshaw. My Mercara Home. Black Panther of Singrauli.* His true spirit had called to him, then, informed him that it, too, was wild and brave, and refused to be denied the right to adventure. As always, the price for such romance had been high and paid for by others. Porters had carried boulders from the riverbed—legs growing bandy, ribs curving into caves, backs into U's, faces being bent slowly to look always at the ground—up to this site chosen for a view that could raise the human heart to spiritual heights. Then the piping arrived, the tiling and tubing, the fancy wrought-iron gates to hang like lace between the banks, the dressmaker's dummy, which the police now stomped up to the attic and discovered—bom bom, the vigor of their movements causing the last remaining Meissen cup to gnash like a tooth on its saucer. A thousand deceased spiders lay scattered like dead blossoms on the attic floor, and above them, on the underside of the tin sieve roof, dodging drips, their offspring stared at the police as they did at their own ancestors—with a giant, saucer-sized lack of sympathy.

The police collected their umbrellas and went tramping across to the cook's hut, extra careful, extra suspicious. Everyone knew it was the servants when it came to robbery, more often than not.

They walked past the garage, car sunk low, nose to the ground, grass through the floor, its last groaning journey made to Darjeeling for the judge to see his only friend, Bose, long forgotten. They passed an oddly well maintained patch behind the water tank, where a saucer of milk and a pile of *mithai* had been spilled and pocked by the sleet. This weedless corner dated to the time when the cook, defeated by a rotten egg and made desperate, had defecated behind the house instead of at his usual place at the far end of the garden, thereby angering two snakes, *mia-bibi,* husband and wife, who lived in a hole nearby.

The cook told the policeman of the drama. "I wasn't bitten, but mysteriously my body swelled up to ten times my size. I went to the temple and they told me that I must ask forgiveness of the snakes. So I made a clay cobra and put it behind the water tank, made the area around it clean with cow dung, and did *puja*. Immediately the swelling went down."

The policemen approved of this. "Pray to them and they will always protect you, they will never bite you."

"Yes," the cook agreed, "they don't bite, the two of them, and they never steal chickens or eggs. In the winter you don't see them much, but otherwise they come out all the time and check if everything is all right. Do a round of the property. We were going to make this part a garden, but we left it to them. They go along the fence all around Cho Oyu and back to their home."

"What kind of snake?"

"Black cobras, thick as that," he said and pointed at the melamine biscuit jar that a policeman was carrying in a plastic bag. "Husband and wife."

But they had not protected them from the robbery . . . a policeman banished this irreligious thought from his mind, and they skirted the area respectfully, in case the snakes or their offended relatives came after them.

The respect on the policemen's faces collapsed instantly when they arrived at the cook's hut buried under a ferocious tangle of nightshade. Here they felt comfortable unleashing their scorn, and they overturned his narrow bed, left his few belongings in a heap.

It pained Sai's heart to see how little he had: a few clothes hung over a string, a single razor blade and a sliver of cheap brown soap, a Kulu blanket that had once been hers, a cardboard case with metal clasps that had belonged to the judge and now contained the cook's papers, the recommendations that had helped him procure his job with the judge, Biju's letters, papers from a court case fought in his village all the way in Uttar Pradesh over the matter of five mango trees that he had lost to his brother. And, in the sateen elastic pocket inside the case, there was a broken watch that would cost too much to mend, but was still too precious to throw away—he might be able to pawn the parts. They were collected in an envelope and the little wind-up knob skittered out into the grass when the police tore open the seal.

Two photographs hung on the wall—one of himself and his wife on their wedding day, one of Biju dressed to leave home. They were poor-people photographs, of those unable to risk wasting a picture, for while all over the world people were now posing with an abandon never experienced by the human race before, here they were still standing X-ray stiff.

Once, Sai had taken a picture of the cook with Uncle Potty's camera, snuck up on him as he minced an onion, and she had been surprised to see that he felt deeply betrayed. He ran to change into his best clothes, a clean shirt and trousers, then positioned himself before the *National Geographics* bound in leather, a backdrop he found suitable.

Sai wondered if he had loved his wife.

She had died seventeen years ago, when Biju was five, slipping from a tree while gathering leaves to feed the goat. An accident, they said, and there was nobody to blame—it was just fate in the way fate has of providing the destitute with a greater quota of accidents for which nobody can be blamed. Biju was their only child.

"What a naughty boy," the cook would always exclaim with joy. "But basically his nature was always good. In our village, most of the dogs bite, and some of them have teeth the size of sticks, but when Biju went by no animal would attack him. And no snake would bite him when he'd go out to cut grass for the cow. He has that personality," the cook said, brimming with pride. "He isn't scared of anything at all. Even when he was very small he would pick up mice by the tail, lift frogs by the neck. . . ." Biju in this picture did not look fearless but appeared frozen, like his parents. He stood between props of a tape player and a Campa Cola bottle, against a painted backdrop of a lake, and on the sides, beyond the painted screen, were brown fields and slivers of the neighbors, an arm and a toe, hair and a grin, a chicken tail frill, though the photographer had tried to shoo the extras out of the frame.

The police spilled all the letters from the case and began to read one of them that dated to three years ago. Biju had just arrived in New York. "Respected *Pitaji,* no need to worry. Everything is fine. The manager has offered me a full-time waiter position. Uniform and food will be given by them. *Angrezi khana* only, no Indian food, and the owner is not from India. He is from America itself."

"He works for the Americans," the cook had reported the contents of the letter to everyone in the market.

Three

All the way in America, Biju had spent his early days standing at a counter along with a row of men.

"Would you like a big one?" asked Biju's fellow server, Romy, lifting a sausage with his tongs, waving it full and fleshy, boing-boinging it against the side of the metal pan, whacking it up and down, elastic, before a sweet-faced girl, brought up to treat dark people like anyone else.

Gray's Papaya. Hot dogs, hot dogs, two and a soda for $1.95.

The spirit of these men he worked with amazed Biju, terrified him, overjoyed him, then terrified him again.

"Onions, mustard, pickles, ketchup?"

Dull thump thump.

"Chili dog?"

Thump Thump Wiggle Waggle. Like a pervert jumping from behind a tree—waggling the appropriate area of his anatomy—

"Big one? Small one?"

"Big one," said the sweet-faced girl.

"Orange drink? Pineapple drink?"

The shop had a festive air with paper chains, plastic oranges and bananas, but it was well over one hundred degrees in there and sweat dripped off their noses and splashed on their toes.

"You like Indian hot dog? You like American hot dog? *You like special one hot dog?*"

"Sir," said a lady from Bangladesh visiting her son in a New York university, "you run a very fine establishment. It is the best frankfurter I have ever tasted, but you should change the name. It is very strange—makes no sense at all!"

Biju waved his hot dog with the others, but he demurred when, after work, they visited the Dominican women in Washington Heights—only thirty-five dollars!

He covered his timidity with manufactured disgust: "How can you? Those, those women are dirty," he said primly. "Stinking bitches," sounding awkward. "Fucking bitches, fucking cheap women you'll get some disease . . . smell bad . . . *hubshi* . . . all black and ugly . . . they make me sick. . . ."

"By now," said Romy, "I could do it with a DOG!—*Aaaargh!*—" he howled, theatrically holding back his head. "*ArrrrghaAAAA . . .*"

The other men laughed.

They were men; he was a baby. He was nineteen, he looked and felt several years younger.

"Too hot," he said at the next occasion.

Then: "Too tired."

The season progressed: "Too cold."

Out of his depth, he was almost relieved when the manager of their branch received a memo instructing him to do a green card check on his employees.

"Nothing I can do," the manager said, pink from having to dole out humiliation to these men. A kind man. His name was Frank—funny for someone who managed frankfurters all day. "Just disappear quietly is my advice. . . ."

So they disappeared.

Four

Angrezi khana. The cook had thought of ham roll ejected from a can and fried in thick ruddy slices, of tuna fish soufflé, *khari* biscuit pie, and was sure that since his son was cooking English food, he had a higher position than if he were cooking Indian.

The police seemed intrigued by the first letter they had read and embarked on the others. To find what? Any sign of hanky panky? Money from the sale of guns? Or were they wondering about how to get to America themselves?

But although Biju's letters traced a string of jobs, they said more or less the same thing each time except for the name of the establishment he was working for. His repetition provided a coziness, and the cook's repetition of his son's repetition double-knit the coziness. "Excellent job," he told his acquaintances, "better even than the last." He imagined sofa TV bank account. Eventually Biju would make enough and the cook would retire. He would receive a daughter-in-law to serve him food, crick-crack his toes, grandchildren to swat like flies.

Time might have died in the house that sat on the mountain ledge, its lines grown indistinct with moss, its roof loaded with ferns, but with each letter, the cook trundled toward the future.

He wrote back carefully so his son would not think badly of his less educated father: "Just make sure you are saving money. Don't lend to anyone and be careful who you talk to. There are many people out there who will say one thing and do another. Liars and cheats. Remember also to take rest. Make sure you eat enough. Health is Wealth. Before you make any decisions talk them over with Nandu."

Nandu was another man from their village in the same city.

Once a coupon had arrived in the Cho Oyu post for a free *National Geographic* Inflatable Globe. Sai had filled it out and mailed it all the way to a PO box in Omaha, and when so much time had passed that they had forgotten about it, it arrived along with a certificate congratulating them for being adventure-loving members pushing the frontiers of human knowledge and daring for almost a full century. Sai and the cook had inflated the globe, attached it to the axis with the provided screws. Rarely was there something unexpected in the mail and never anything beautiful. They looked at the deserts, the mountains, the fresh spring colors of green and yellow, the snow at the poles; somewhere on this glorious orb was Biju. They searched out New York, and Sai attempted to explain to the cook why it was night there when it was day here, just as Sister Alice had demonstrated in St. Augustine's with an orange and a flashlight. The cook found it strange that India went first with the day, a funny back-to-front fact that didn't seem mirrored by any other circumstance involving the two nations.

Letters lay on the floor along with a few items of clothing; the worn mattress had been overturned, and the newspaper layers placed underneath to prevent the coils of the bed from piercing the meager mattress had been messily dispersed.

The police had exposed the cook's poverty, the fact that he was not looked after, that his dignity had no basis; they ruined the facade and threw it in his face.

Then policemen and their umbrellas—most black, one pink with flowers—retreated through the tangle of nightshade.

On his knees, the cook searched for the silver knob of the watch, but it had vanished.

"Well, they have to search everything," he said. "Naturally. How are they to know that I am innocent? Most of the time it is the servant that steals."

Sai felt embarrassed. She was rarely in the cook's hut, and when she did come searching for him and enter, he was ill at ease and so was she, something about their closeness being exposed in the end as fake, their friendship composed of shallow things conducted in a broken language, for she was an English-speaker and he was a Hindi-speaker. The brokenness made it easier never to go deep, never to enter into anything that required an intricate vocabulary, yet she always felt tender on seeing his crotchety face, on hearing him haggle in the market, felt pride that she lived with such a difficult man who nonetheless spoke to her with affection, calling her Babyji or Saibaby.

She had first met the cook when she had been delivered from St. Augustine's in Dehra Dun. Nine years ago now. The taxi had dropped her off and the moon had shone fluorescently enough to read the name of the house—Cho Oyu—as she had waited, a little stick figure at the gate, her smallness emphasizing the vastness of the landscape. A tin trunk was at her side. "Miss S. Mistry, St. Augustine's Convent." But the gate was locked. The driver rattled and shouted.

"Oi, koi hai? Khansama? Uth. Koi hai? Uth. Khansama?"

Kanchenjunga glowed macabre, trees stretched away on either side, trunks pale, leaves black, and beyond, between the pillars of the trees, a path led to the house.

It seemed a long while before they heard a whistle blowing and saw a lantern approaching, and there had come the cook, bandy-legged up the path, looking as leather-visaged, as weathered and soiled, as he did now, and as he would ten years later. A poverty stricken man growing into an ancient at fast-forward. Compressed childhood, lingering old age. A generation between him and the judge, but you wouldn't know it to look at them. There was age in his temperament, his kettle, his clothes, his kitchen, his voice, his face, in the undisturbed dirt, the undisturbed settled smell of a lifetime of cooking, smoke, and kerosene.

"How dare they behave this way to you," said Sai, trying to overcome the gap between them as they stood together surveying the mess the police had left in his hut.

"But what kind of investigation would it be, then?" the cook reasoned.

In their attempt to console his dignity in two different ways, they had merely highlighted its ruin.

They bent to collect his belongings, the cook careful to place the pages of the letters in the correct envelopes. One day he'd return them to Biju so his son would have a record of his journey and feel a sense of pride and achievement.

Five

Biju at the Baby Bistro.

Above, the restaurant was French, but below in the kitchen it was Mexican and Indian. And, when a Paki was hired, it was Mexican, Indian, Pakistani.

Biju at Le Colonial for the authentic colonial experience.

On top, rich colonial, and down below, poor native. Colombian, Tunisian, Ecuadorian, Gambian.

On to the Stars and Stripes Diner. All American flag on top, all Guatemalan flag below.

Plus one Indian flag when Biju arrived.

"Where is Guatemala?" he had to ask.

"Where is Guam?"

"Where is Madagascar?"

"Where is Guyana?"

"Don't you know?" the Guyanese man said. "Indians everywhere in Guyana, man."

"Indians in Guam. Everywhere you look, practically, Indians."

"Trinidad?"

"Trinidad full of Indians!! Saying—can you believe it?—'Open a caan of saalmon, maaan.'"

Madagascar—Indians Indians.

Chile—in the Zona Rosa duty-free of Tierra del Fuego, Indians, whiskey, electronics. Bitterness at the thought of Pakistanis up in the Areca used-car business. "Ah . . . forget it . . . let those *bhenchoots* make their quarter percent. . . ."

Kenya. South Africa. Saudi Arabia. Fiji. New Zealand. Surinam.

In Canada, a group of Sikhs came long ago; they went to remote areas and the women took off their *salwars* and wore their kurtas like dresses.

Indians, yes, in Alaska; a *desi* owned the last general store in the last town before the North Pole, canned foods mostly, fishing tackle, bags of salt, and shovels; his wife stayed back in Karnal with the children, where they could, on account of the husband's sacrifice, afford Little Angels Kindergarten.

On the Black Sea, yes, Indians, running a spice business.

Hong Kong. Singapore.

How had he learned nothing growing up? England he knew, and America, Dubai, Kuwait, but not much else.

There was a whole world in the basement kitchens of New York, but Biju was ill-equipped for it and almost relieved when the Pakistani arrived. At least he knew what to do. He wrote and told his father.

The cook was alarmed. What kind of place was he working in? He knew it was a country where people from everywhere journeyed to work, but oh, surely not Pakistanis! Surely they would not be hired. Surely Indians were better liked—

"Beware," the cook wrote to his son. "Beware. Beware. Keep away. Distrust."

His son had already done him proud. He found he could not talk straight to the man; every molecule of him felt fake, every hair on him went on alert.

Desis against Pakis.

Ah, old war, best war—

Where else did the words flow with an ease that came from centuries of practice? How else would the spirit of your father, your grandfather, rise from the dead?

Here in America, where every nationality confirmed its stereotype—

Biju felt he was entering a warm amniotic bath.

But then it grew cold. This war was not, after all, satisfying; it could never go deep enough, the crick was never cracked, the itch was never scratched; the irritation built on itself, and the combatants itched all the more.

"Pigs pigs, sons of pigs, *sooar ka baccha,*" Biju shouted.

"*Uloo ka patha,* son of an owl, low-down son-of-a-bitch Indian."

They drew the lines at crucial junctures. They threw cannonball cabbages at each other.

"***!!!!" said the Frenchman.

It sounded to their ears like an angry dandelion puff, but what he said was that they were a troublesome pair. The sound of their fight had traveled up the flight of steps and struck a clunky note, and they might upset the balance, perfectly first-world on top, perfectly third-world twenty-two steps below. Mix it up in a heap and then who would patronize his restaurant, *hm?* With its *coquilles Saint-Jacques à la vapeur* for $27.50 and the *blanquette de veau* for $23, and a duck that made an overture to the colonies, sitting like a pasha on a cushion of its own fat, exuding the scent of saffron.

What were they thinking? Do restaurants in Paris have cellars full of Mexicans, *desis,* and Pakis?

No, they do not. What are you thinking?

They have cellars full of Algerians, Senegalese, Moroccans. . . .

Good-bye, Baby Bistro. "Use the time off to take a bath," said the owner. He had been kind enough to hire Biju although he found him smelly.

Paki one way, Biju the other way. Rounding the corner, meeting each other again, turning away again.

Six

So, as Sai waited at the gate, the cook had come bandy-legged up the path with a lantern in his hand, blowing on a whistle to warn away jackals, the two cobras, and the local thief, Gobbo, who robbed all the residents of Kalimpong in rotation and had a brother in the police to protect him.

"Have you come from England?" the cook asked Sai, unlocking the gate with its fat lock and chain, although anyone could easily climb over the bank or come up the ravine.

She shook her head.

"America? No problem there with water or electricity," he said. Awe swelled his words, made them tick smug and fat as first-world money.

"No," she said.

"No? No? His disappointment was severe. "From Foreign." No question mark. Reiterating basic unquestionable fact. Nodding his head as if she'd said it, not he.

"No. From Dehra Dun."

"Dehra Dun!" Devastated, *"Kamaal hai,"* said the cook. "Here we have made so much fuss, thought you're coming from far away, and you've been in Dehra Dun all along. Why didn't you come before?

"Well," said the cook when she did not answer, "Where are your parents?"

"They're dead," she said.

"Dead." He dropped the lantern and the flame went out. "*Baap re!* I'm never told anything. What will happen to you, poor child?" he said with pity and hopelessness. "Where did they die?" With the lantern flame out, the scene became suffused with mysterious moonlight.

"Russia."

"Russia! But there aren't any jobs there." Words again became deflated currency, third-world, bad-luck money. "What were they doing?"

"My father was a space pilot."

"Space pilot, never heard of such a thing. . . ." He looked at her suspiciously. There was something wrong with this girl, he could tell, but here she was. "Just have to stay now," he mulled. "Nothing else for you . . . so sad . . . too bad. . . ." Children often made up stories or were told them so as to mask a terrible truth.

The cook and the driver struggled with the trunk as the driveway was too overgrown with weeds to accommodate a car; just a slim path had been stamped through.

The cook turned back: "How did they die?"

Somewhere above, there was the sound of an alarmed bird, of immense wings starting up like a propeller.

It had been a peaceful afternoon in Moscow, and Mr. and Mrs. Mistry were crossing the square to the Society for Interplanetary Travel. Here, Sai's father had been resident ever since he'd been picked from the Indian Air Force as a possible candidate for the Intercosmos Program. These were the last days of Indo-USSR romance and already there was a whiff of dried bouquet in the air, in the exchanges between the scientists that segued easily into tears and nostalgia for the red-rose years of courtship between the nations.

Mr. and Mrs. Mistry had grown up during those heady times when the affection had been cemented by weapons sales, sporting competitions, visiting dance troups, and illustrated books that introduced a generation of Indian schoolchildren to Baba Yaga, who lived in her house on chicken feet in the prehistoric dark of a Russian forest; to the troubles of Prince Ivan and Princess Ivanka before they resided happily ever after in an onion-domed palace.

The couple had met in a public park in Delhi. Mrs. Mistry, then a college student, would go from the ladies' dorm to study and to dry her hair in the shade and quiet of a neem tree where the matron had authorized her girls to go. Mr. Mistry had come jogging by, already in the air force, strong and tall, with a trim mustache, and the jogger found this student so astonishingly pretty, with an expression half tart, half sweet, that he stopped to stare. They became acquainted in this grassy acre, cows tethered to enormous rusty lawn mowers slowly grinding back and forth before a crumbling Mughal tomb. Before a year was up, in the deep cool center of the tomb, golden indirect light passing from alcove to hushed alcove, duskier, muskier through the carved panels each casting the light in a different lace pattern—flowers, stars—upon the floor, Mr. Mistry proposed. She thought quickly. This romance had allowed her to escape the sadness of her past and the tediousness of her current girlish life. There is a time when everyone wishes to be an adult, and she said yes. The pilot and the student, the Zoroastrian and the Hindu, emerged from the tomb of the Mughal prince knowing that nobody other than themselves would be impressed by their great secular romance. Still, they considered themselves lucky to have found each other, each one empty with the same loneliness, each one fascinating as a foreigner to the other, but both educated with an eye to the West, and so they could sing along quite tunefully while strumming a guitar. They felt free and brave, part of a modern nation in a modern world.

As early as 1955, Khrushchev had visited Kashmir and declared it forever part of India, and more recently, the Bolshoi had performed *Swan Lake* before a Delhi audience dressed for the occasion in their finest silk saris and largest jewels.

And, of course, these were the early days of space exploration. A dog named Laika had been whooshed up in *Sputnik II*. In 1961, a chimp named Ham had made the journey. After him, in the same year, Yuri Gagarin. As the years lumbered on, not only Americans and Soviets, dogs and chimps, but a Vietnamese, a Mongolian, a Cuban, a woman, and a black man went up. Satellites and shuttles were orbiting the earth and the moon; they had landed on Mars, been launched toward Venus, and had completed a flyby of Saturn. At this time, a visiting Soviet team of aeronautical and aviation experts who had been instructed by their government to find likely candidates to send to space had arrived in India.

Visiting an air force facility in the nation's capital, their attention had been caught by Mr. Mistry, not merely because of his competence but also because of the steely determination that shone from his eyes.

He had joined a few other candidates in Moscow, and six-year-old Sai had been hastily entrusted to the same convent her mother had attended.

The competition was fierce. Just as Mr. Mistry was confessing to his wife his certainty that he would be chosen over his colleagues to become the very first Indian beyond the control of gravity, the fates decided otherwise, and instead of blasting through the stratosphere, in this life, in this skin, to see the world as the gods might, he was delivered to another vision of the beyond when he and his wife were crushed by local bus wheels, weighted by thirty indomitable ladies from the provinces who had speeded two days to barter and sell their wares in the market.

Thus they had died under the wheels of foreigners, amid crates of babushka nesting dolls. If their last thoughts were of their daughter in St. Augustine's, she would never know.

Moscow was not part of the convent curriculum. Sai imagined a sullen bulky architecture, heavyset, solid-muscled, bulldog-jowled, in Soviet shades of gray, under gray Soviet skies, all around gray Soviet peoples eating gray Soviet foods. A masculine city, without frill or weakness, without crenellation, without a risky angle. An uncontrollable spill of scarlet now in this scene, unspooling.

"Very sorry," said Sister Caroline, "very sorry to hear the news, Sai. You must have courage."

"I'm an orphan," Sai whispered to herself, resting in the infirmary. "My parents are dead. I am an orphan."

She hated the convent, but there had never been anything else she could remember.

"Dear Sai," her mother would write, "well, another winter coming up and we have brought out the heavy woolens. Met Mr. and Mrs. Sharma for bridge and your papa cheated as usual. We enjoy eating herring, a pungent fish you must sample one day."

She responded during the supervised letter writing sessions:

"Dear Mummy and Papa, how are you? I am fine. It is very hot here. Yesterday we had our history exam and Arlene Macedo cheated as usual."

But the letters seemed like book exercises. Sai had not seen her parents in two whole years, and the emotional immediacy of their existence had long vanished. She tried to cry, but she couldn't.

In the conference room beneath a Jesus in a dhoti pinned onto two varnished sticks, the nuns conferred anxiously. This month there would be no Mistry bank draft in the convent coffers, no mandatory donations to the toilet renovation fund and bus fund, to fete days and feast days.

"Poor thing, but what can we do?" The nuns tsk-tsked because they knew Sai was a special problem. The older nuns remembered her mother and the fact that the judge paid for her keep but never visited. There were other parts of the tale that none of them would be able to piece together, of course, for some of the narrative had been lost, some of it had been purposely forgotten. All they knew of Sai's father was that he had been brought up in a Zoroastrian charity for orphans, and that he had been helped along by a generous donor from school to college and then finally into the air force. When Sai's parents eloped, the family in Gujarat, feeling disgraced, disowned her mother.

In a country so full of relatives, Sai suffered a dearth.

There was only a single listing in the register under "Please contact in case of emergency." It was the name of Sai's grandfather, the same man who had once paid the school fees:

Name: Justice Jemubhai Patel
Relation: Maternal Grandfather
Position: Chief Justice (Retd.)
Religion: Hindu
Caste: Patidar

Sai had never met this grandfather who, in 1957, had been introduced to the Scotsman who had built Cho Oyu and was now on his way back to Aberdeen.

"It is very isolated but the land has potential," the Scotsman had said, "quinine, sericulture, cardamom, orchids." The judge was not interested in agricultural possibilities of the land but went to see it, trusting the man's word—the famous word of a gentleman—despite all that had passed. He rode up on horseback, pushed open the door into that spare space lit with a monastic light, the quality of which altered with the sunlight outside. He had felt he was entering a sensibility rather than a house.

The floor was dark, almost black, wide planked; the ceiling resembled the rib cage of a whale, marks of an ax still in the timber. A fireplace made of silvery river stone sparkled like sand. Lush ferns butted into the windows, stiff seams of foliage felted with spores, curly nubs pelted with bronze fuzz. He knew he could become aware here of depth, width, height, and of a more elusive dimension. Outside, passionately colored birds swooped and whistled, and the Himalayas rose layer upon layer until those gleaming peaks proved a man to be so small that it made sense to give it all up, empty it all out. The judge could live here, in this shell, this skull, with the solace of being a foreigner in his own country, for this time he would not learn the language.

He never went back to court.

"Good-bye," said Sai, to the perversities of the convent, the sweet sweety pastel angels and the bloodied Christ, presented together in disturbing contrast. Good-bye to the uniforms so heavy for a little girl, manly shouldered blazer and tie, black cow-hoof shoes. Good-bye to her friend, Arlene Macedo, the only other student with an unconventional background. Arlene's father, Arlene claimed, was a Portuguese sailor who came and left. Not for the sea, whispered the other girls, but for a Chinese hairdresser in Claridge's Hotel in Delhi. Good-bye to four years of learning the weight of humiliation and fear, the art of subterfuge, of being uncovered by black-habited detectives and trembling before the rule of law that treated ordinary everyday slips and confusions with the seriousness of first-degree crime. Good-bye to:

a. standing in the rubbish bin with dunce cap on
b. getting heatstroke in the sun while on one leg and with hands up in the air
c. announcing your sins at the morning assembly
d. getting paddled red black blue and turmeric

"Shameless girl," Sister Caroline had told Sai, homeworkless, one day, and delivered her bottom bright as a baboon's, so that she without shame quickly acquired some.

The system might be obsessed with purity, but it excelled in defining the flavor of sin. There was a titillation to unearthing the forces of guilt and desire, needling and prodding the results. This Sai had learned. This underneath, and on top a flat creed: cake was better than *laddoos,* fork spoon knife better than hands, sipping the blood of Christ and consuming a wafer of his body was more civilized than garlanding a phallic symbol with marigolds. English was better than Hindi.

Any sense that Sai was taught had fallen between the contradictions, and the contradictions themselves had been absorbed. "Lochinvar" and Tagore, economics and moral science, highland fling in tartan and Punjabi harvest dance in *dhotis,* national anthem in Bengali and an impenetrable Latin motto emblazoned on banderoles across their blazer pockets and also on an arch over the entrance: *Pisci tisci episculum basculum.* Something of the sort.

She passed beneath this motto for the last time, accompanied by a visiting nun who was studying convent finance systems, on her way now to Darjeeling. Out of the window, from Dehra Dun to Delhi, Delhi to Siliguri, they viewed a panorama of village life and India looked as old as ever. Women walked by with firewood on their heads, too poor for blouses under their saris. "Shame shame, I know your name," said the nun, feeling jolly. Then she felt less jolly. It was early in the morning and the railway tracks were lined with rows of bare bottoms. Close up, they could see dozens of people defecating onto the tracks, rinsing their bottoms with water from a can. "Dirty people," she said, "poverty is no excuse, no it isn't, no don't try and tell me that. Why must they do such things here?"

"Because of the drop," said an earnest bespectacled scholar seated next to her, "the ground drops to the railway track, so it is a good place."

The nun didn't answer. And to the people who defecated, those on the train were so beside the point—not even the same species—that they didn't care if passersby saw their straining rears any more than if a sparrow were witness to them.

On and on.

Sai quiet . . . feeling her fate awaiting her. She could sense Cho Oyu.

"Don't worry, dear," said the nun.

Sai did not reply and the nun began to feel annoyed.

They transferred to a taxi and traversed through a wetter climate, a rusty green landscape, creaking and bobbing in the wind. They drove past tea stalls on stilts, chickens being sold in round cane baskets, and Durga Puja goddesses being constructed in shacks. They passed paddy fields and warehouses that looked decrepit but bore the names of famous tea companies: Rungli Rungliot, Ghoom, Goenkas.

"Don't you sit about feeling sorry for yourself. You don't think God sulked, do you? With all he had to do?"

Suddenly to the right, the Teesta River came leaping at them between white banks of sand. Space and sun crashed through the window. Reflections magnified and echoed the light, the river, each adding angles and colors to the other, and Sai became aware of the enormous space she was entering.

By the riverbank, wild water racing by, the late evening sun in polka dots through the trees, they parted company. To the east was Kalimpong, barely managing to stay on the saddle between the Deolo and the Ringkingpong hills. To the west was Darjeeling, skidding down the Singalila Mountains. The nun tried to offer a final counsel, but her voice was drowned out by the river roar so she pinched Sai's cheek in farewell. Off she went in a Sisters of Cluny jeep, six thousand feet up into tea growing country and to a town that was black and slimy, mushrooming with clusters of convents in the dripping fog.

Night fell quickly after the sun went down. With the car tilted back so its nose pointed to the sky, they corkscrewed on—the slightest wrong move and they would tumble. Death whispered into Sai's ear, life leaped in her pulse, her heart plummeted, up they twirled. There was not a streetlight anywhere in Kalimpong, and the lamps in houses were so dim you saw them only as you passed; they came up suddenly and disappeared immediately behind. The people who walked by in the black had neither torches nor lanterns, and the headlights caught them stepping off the road as the car passed. The driver turned from the tar road onto a dirt one, and finally the car stopped in the middle of the wilderness at a gate suspended between stone pillars. The sound of the engine faded; the headlights went dead. There was only the forest making *ssss tseu ts ts seuuu* sounds.

Seven

Oh, Grandfather more lizard than human.

Dog more human than dog.

Sai's face upside down in her soup spoon.

To welcome her, the cook had modeled the mashed potatoes into a motorcar, recollecting a long-forgotten skill from another age, when, using the same pleasant medium, he had fashioned celebratory castles decorated with paper flags, fish with bangle nose rings, porcupines with celery spines, chickens with real eggs placed behind for comic effect.

This motorcar had tomato slice wheels and decorations rolled out of ancient bits of tinfoil that the cook treated as a precious metal, washing, drying, using, and reusing them until they crumbled into tinselly scraps that he still couldn't bear to throw away.

The car sat in the middle of the table, along with paddle-shaped mutton cutlets, water-logged green beans, and a head of cauliflower under cheese sauce that looked like a shrouded brain. All the dishes were spinning steam furiously, and warm, food-scented clouds condensed on Sai's face. When the steam cleared a little, she had another look at her grandfather at the far end of the table and the dog on another chair by his side. Mutt was smiling—head inclined, thump thump went her tail against the seat—but the judge seemed not to have noticed Sai's arrival. He was a shriveled figure in a white shirt and black trousers with a buckle to the side. The clothes were frayed but clean, ironed by the cook, who still ironed everything—pajamas, towels, socks, underwear, and handkerchiefs. His face seemed distanced by what looked like white powder over dark skin—or was it just the vapor? And from him came a faint antibiotic whiff of cologne, a little too far from perfume, a little too close to a preserving liquid. There was more than a hint of reptile in the slope of his face, the wide hairless forehead, the introverted nose, the introverted chin, his lack of movement, his lack of lips, his fixed gaze. Like other elderly people, he seemed not to have traveled forward in time but far back. Harking to the prehistoric, in attendance upon infinity, he resembled a creature of the Galápagos staring over the ocean.

Finally, he looked up and fixed his gaze on Sai. "Well, what is your name?"

"Sai."

"Sai?" he said crossly, as if angered by an impudence.

The dog sneezed. It had an elegant snout, a bump of nobility at the top of its head, ruffly pantaloons, elaborately fringed tail—

Sai had never seen such a good-looking dog.

"Your dog is like a film star," said Sai.

"Maybe an Audrey Hepburn," said the judge, trying not to show how pleased he was at this remark, "but certainly not one of those lurid apparitions on the bazaar posters."

He picked up his spoon. "Where is the soup?"

The cook had forgotten it in his excitement over the mashed-potato car.

The judge brought down his fist. The soup after the main course? The routine had been upset.

The electricity fell abruptly to a lower strength as if in accordance with the judge's disapproval, and the bulb began to buzz like the beetle on its back skittering over the table, upset by this wishy-washy voltage that could not induce a kamikaze response. The cook had already turned off all other lamps in the house in order to gather the meager power into this one, and in this uneven lighting, they were four shadow puppets from a fairytale flickering on the lumpy plaster of the wall—a lizard man, a hunchbacked cook, a lush-lashed maiden, and a long-tailed wolf dog. . . .

"Must write to that fool of a subdivisional officer," said the judge, "but what good will it do!" He overturned the beetle on the table with his knife, it stopped buzzing, and Mutt, who had been staring at it with shock, gazed at him like an adoring spouse.

The cook carried in two bowls of sour and peppery tomato soup, muttering, "No thanks to me for anything. . . . See what I have to deal with and I'm not young and healthy anymore. . . . Terrible to be a poverty-stricken man, terrible, terrible, terrible. . . ."

The judge took a spoon from a bowl of cream and thwacked a white blob into the red.

"Well," he said to his granddaughter, "one must not disturb one another. One's had to hire a tutor for you—a lady down the hill, can't afford a convent school—why should one be in the business of fattening the church . . . ? Too far, anyway, and one doesn't have the luxury of transport anymore, does one? Can't send you to a government school, I suppose . . . you'd come out speaking with the wrong accent and picking your nose. . . ."

The light diminished now, to a filament, tender as Edison's first miracle held between delicate pincers of wire in the glass globe of the bulb. It glowed a last blue crescent, then failed.

"Damn it!" said the judge.

In her bed later that evening, Sai lay under a tablecloth, for the last sheets had long worn out. She could sense the swollen presence of the forest, hear the hollow-knuckled knocking of the bamboo, the sound of the *jhora* that ran deep in the décolleté of the mountain. Batted down by household sounds during the day, it rose at dusk, to sing pure-voiced into the windows. The structure of the house seemed fragile in the balance of this night—just a husk. The tin roof rattled in the wind. When Sai moved her foot, her toes went silently through the rotted fabric. She had a fearful feeling of having entered a space so big it reached both backward and forward.

Suddenly, as if a secret door had opened in her hearing, she became aware of the sound of microscopic jaws slow-milling the house to sawdust, a sound hard to detect for being so closely knit unto the air, but once identified, it grew monumental. In this climate, she would learn, untreated wood could be chewed up in a season.

Eight

Across the hall from Sai's room, the judge swallowed a Calmpose, for he found he was upset by his granddaughter's arrival. He lay awake in bed, Mutt at his side. "Little pet," he clucked over her. "What long curly ears, *hm?* Look at all these curls." Each night Mutt slept with her head on his pillow, and on cold nights she was wrapped in a shawl of angora rabbit wool. She was asleep, but even so, one of her ears cocked as she listened to the judge while she continued snoring.

The judge picked up a book and tried to read, but he couldn't. He realized, to his surprise, that he was thinking of his own journeys, of his own arrivals and departures, from places far in his past. He had first left home at the age of twenty, with a black tin trunk just like the one Sai had arrived with, on which white letters read "Mr. J. P. Patel, SS *Strathnaver.*" The year was 1939. The town he had left was his ancestral home of Piphit. From there he had journeyed to the Bombay dock and then sailed to Liverpool, and from Liverpool he had gone to Cambridge.

Many years had passed, and yet the day returned to him vividly, cruelly.

The future judge, then called only Jemubhai—or Jemu—had been serenaded at his departure by two retired members of a military band hired by his father-in-law. They had stood on the platform between benches labeled "Indians Only" and "Europeans Only," dressed in stained red coats with dull metallic ricrac unraveling about the sleeves and collars. As the train left the station, they played "Take Me Back to Dear Old Blighty," a tune they remembered was appropriate to the occasion of leaving.

The judge was accompanied by his father. At home, his mother was weeping because she had not estimated the imbalance between the finality of good-bye and the briefness of the last moment.

"Don't let him go. Don't let him go."

Her little son with his frail and comical mustache, with his love for her special *choorva* that he would never get in England and his hatred of cold that he would get too much of; with his sweater that she had knit in a pattern fanciful enough to express the extravagance of her affection; with his new *Oxford English Dictionary* and his decorated coconut to be tossed as an offering into the waves, so his journey might be blessed by the gods.

Father and son had rattled forth all through the morning and afternoon, the immensity of the landscape within which Jemu had unknowingly lived impressing itself upon him. The very fact that they were sitting in the train, the speed of it, rendered his world trivial, indicated through each window evidence of emptiness that stood eager to claim an unguarded heart. He felt a piercing fear, not for his future, but for his past, for the foolish faith with which he had lived in Piphit.

The malodor of Bombay duck drying on a scaffolding of sticks alongside the track snuffed his thoughts for a moment; passing into neutral air, his fears came up again.

He thought of his wife. He was a one-month-married man. He would return . . . many years from now . . . and then what . . . ? It was all very strange. She was fourteen years old and he had yet to properly examine her face.

They crossed the saltwater creek into Bombay, arrived at the Victoria Terminus, where they turned down hotel touts to stay with an acquaintance of his father-in-law's, and woke early to make their way to the Ballard Pier.

When Jemubhai had first learned that the ocean traveled around a globe, he had felt strengthened by this fact, but now when he stood on the confetti-strewn deck of the ship, looking out at the sea flexing its endless muscles, he felt this knowledge weaken him. Small waves subsided against the side of the ship in a parsimonious soda water fizz, over which the noise of the engine now exerted itself. As three siren blasts rent the air, Jemu's father, searching the deck, located his son.

"Don't worry," he shouted. "You'll do first class first." But his tone of terror undid the reassurance of the words.

"Throw the coconut!" he shrieked.

Jemubhai looked at his father, a barely educated man venturing where he should not be, and the love in Jemubhai's heart mingled with pity, the pity with shame. His father felt his own hand rise and cover his mouth: he had failed his son.

The ship moved, the water split and spilled, flying fish exploded silver above the unravelment, Tom Collinses were passed around, and the party atmosphere reached a crescendo. The crowd on the shore became flotsam churning at the tide's hem: scallops and starbursts, petticoat ruffles, rubbishy wrappings and saliva flecks, fish tails and tears. . . . Soon it vanished in the haze.

Jemu watched his father disappear. He didn't throw the coconut and he didn't cry. Never again would he know love for a human being that wasn't adulterated by another, contradictory emotion.

They sailed past the Colaba Lighthouse and out into the Indian Ocean until there was only the span of the sea whichever way he turned.

He was silly to be upset by Sai's arrival, to allow it to trigger this revisitation of his past. No doubt the trunks had jogged his memory.

Miss S. Mistry, St. Augustine's Convent.

Mr. J. P. Patel, SS *Strathnaver*.

But he continued to remember: when he located his cabin, he found he had a cabinmate who had grown up in Calcutta composing Latin sonnets in Catullan hendecasyllables, which he had inscribed into a gilded volume and brought along with him. The cabinmate's nose twitched at Jemu's lump of pickle wrapped in a bundle of puris; onions, green chilies, and salt in a twist of newspaper; a banana that in the course of the journey had been slain by heat. No fruit dies so vile and offensive a death as the banana, but it had been packed just in case. In case of *What?* Jemu shouted silently to his mother.

In case he was hungry along the way or it was a while before meals could be properly prepared or he lacked the courage to go to the dining salon on the ship, given that he couldn't eat with knife and fork—

He was furious that his mother had considered the possibility of his humiliation and thereby, he thought, precipitated it. In her attempt to cancel out one humiliation she had only succeeded in adding another.

Jemu picked up the package, fled to the deck, and threw it overboard. Didn't his mother think of the inappropriateness of her gesture? Undignified love, Indian love, stinking, unaesthetic love—the monsters of the ocean could have what she had so bravely packed getting up in that predawn mush.

The smell of dying bananas retreated, oh, but now that just left the stink of fear and loneliness perfectly exposed.

In his cabin bunk at night, the sea made indecent licking sounds about the ship's edge. He thought of how he had half undressed and hurriedly re-dressed his wife, of how he had only glimpsed her expression, just bits and pieces of it in the slipping of the *pallu* over her head. However in memory of the closeness of female flesh, his penis reached up in the dark and waved about, a simple blind sea creature but refusing to be refused. He found his own organ odd: insistent but cowardly; pleading but pompous.

They berthed at Liverpool and the band played "Land of Hope and Glory." His cabinmate, in Donegal tweeds, hailed a porter to help with his luggage—a white person to pick up a brown person's bags! Jemubhai carried his own bags, stumbled onto a train, and on his way to Cambridge, found himself shocked as they progressed through fields by the enormous difference between the (boxy) English and the (loopy) Indian cow.

He continued to be amazed by the sights that greeted him. The England in which he searched for a room to rent was formed of tiny gray houses in gray streets, stuck together and down as if on a glue trap. It took him by surprise because he'd expected only grandness, hadn't realized that here, too, people could be poor and live unaesthetic lives. While he was unimpressed, though, so too were the people who answered his knock, when they opened their doors to his face: "Just let," "All full," or even a curtain lifted and quickly dropped, a stillness as if all the inhabitants had, in that instant, died. He visited twenty-two homes before he arrived at the doorstep of Mrs. Rice on Thornton Road. She didn't want him either, but she needed the money and her house was so situated—on the other side of the train station from the university—she was concerned she wouldn't be able to find a lodger at all.

Twice a day she put out a tray at the foot of the stairs—boiled egg, bread, butter, jam, milk. After a spate of nights lying awake listening to the borborygmus of his half-empty stomach, thinking tearfully of his family in Piphit who thought him as worthy of a hot dinner as the queen of England, Jemubhai worked up the courage to ask for a proper evening meal. "We don't eat much of a supper ourselves, James," she said, "too heavy on the stomach for Father." She always called her husband Father and she had taken to calling Jemubhai James. But that evening, he found on his plate steaming baked beans on toast.

"Thank you. Absolutely delicious," he said as Mr. Rice sat looking steadily out of the window.

Later, he marveled at this act of courage, since he was soon to lose it all.

He had registered at Fitzwilliam with the help of an essay he penned for the entrance examination, "Similarities and Differences between the French and Russian Revolutions." Fitzwilliam was a bit of a joke in those days, more a tutoring place than a college, but he began immediately to study, because it was the only skill he could carry from one country to another. He worked twelve hours at a stretch, late into the night, and in thus withdrawing, he failed to make a courageous gesture outward at a crucial moment and found, instead, that his pusillanimity and his loneliness had found fertile soil. He retreated into a solitude that grew in weight day by day. The solitude became a habit, the habit became the man, and it crushed him into a shadow.

But shadows, after all, create their own unease, and despite his attempts to hide, he merely emphasized something that unsettled others. For entire days nobody spoke to him at all, his throat jammed with words unuttered, his heart and mind turned into blunt aching things, and elderly ladies, even the hapless—blue-haired, spotted, faces like collapsing pumpkins—moved over when he sat next to them in the bus, so he knew that whatever they had, they were secure in their conviction that it wasn't even remotely as bad as what *he* had. The young and beautiful were no kinder; girls held their noses and giggled, "Phew, he stinks of curry!"

Thus Jemubhai's mind had begun to warp; he grew stranger to himself than he was to those around him, found his own skin odd-colored, his own accent peculiar. He forgot how to laugh, could barely manage to lift his lips in a smile, and if he ever did, he held his hand over his mouth, because he couldn't bear anyone to see his gums, his teeth. They seemed too private. In fact, he could barely let any of himself peep out of his clothes for fear of giving offence. He began to wash obsessively, concerned he would be accused of smelling, and each morning he scrubbed off the thick milky scent of sleep, the barnyard smell that wreathed him when he woke and impregnated the fabric of his pajamas. To the end of his life, he would never be seen without socks and shoes and would prefer shadow to light, faded days to sunny, for he was suspicious that sunlight might reveal him, in his hideousness, all too clearly.

He saw nothing of the English countryside, missed the beauty of carved colleges and churches painted with gold leaf and angels, didn't hear the choir boys with the voices of girls, and didn't see the green river trembling with replications of the gardens that segued one into the other or the swans that sailed butterflied to their reflections.

Eventually he felt barely human at all, leaped when touched on the arm as if from an unbearable intimacy, dreaded and agonized over even a "How-do-you-do-lovely-day" with the fat woman dressed in friendly pinks who ran the corner store. "What can I get you? Say that again, duck . . ." she said to his mumble, leaned forward to scoop up his words, but his voice ran back and out as he dissolved into tears of self-pity at the casual affection. He began to walk farther across town to more anonymous shops, and when he bought a shaving brush and the shop girl said her husband owned the same item exactly, at the acknowledgment of their identical human needs, the intimacy of their connection, *shaving, husband,* he was overcome at the boldness of the suggestion.

The judge turned on the light and looked at the expiration date on the Calmpose package. No, the medicine was still valid: it should have worked. Yet, instead of putting him to sleep, it had caused him to dream a nightmare wide awake.

He lay there until the cows began to boom like foghorns through the mist and Uncle Potty's rooster, Kookar Raja, sent his *kukrookoo* up like a flag, sounding both silly and loud as if calling everyone to the circus. He had been healthy again ever since Uncle Potty had turned him upside down, stuck him headfirst into a tin can and eradicated the bluebottles in his bottom with a heavy spray of Flit.

Confronted yet again with his granddaughter, sitting at the breakfast table, the judge instructed the cook to take her to meet the tutor he had hired, a lady by the name of Noni who lived an hour's walk away.

Sai and cook trudged the long path that traveled thin and black as a rat snake up and down the hills, and the cook showed her the landmarks of her new home, pointed out the houses and told her who lived where. There was Uncle Potty, of course, their nearest neighbor, who had bought his land from the judge years ago, a gentleman farmer and a drunk; and his friend Father Booty of the Swiss dairy, who spent each evening drinking with Uncle Potty. The men had rabbit-red eyes, their teeth were browned by tobacco, their systems needed to be dredged, but their spirits were still nimble. "Hello Dolly," Uncle Potty said, waving to Sai from his veranda, which projected like a ship's deck over the steep incline. It was on this veranda that Sai would first hear the Beatles. And also: "All that MEAT and NO PERTATAS? Just ain't right, like GREEN TERMATAS!"

The cook pointed out the defunct pisciculture tanks, the army encampment, the monastery on top of Durpin hill, and down below, an orphanage and henhouse. Opposite the henhouse, so they could get their eggs easily, lived a pair of Afghan princesses whose father had gone to Brighton on holiday and returned to find the British had seated someone else on his throne. Eventually the princesses were given refuge by Nehru (such a gentleman!). In a small drab house lived Mrs. Sen, whose daughter, Mun Mun, had gone to America.

And finally there was Noni (Nonita), who lived with her sister Lola (Lalita) in a rose-covered cottage named Mon Ami. When Lola's husband had died of a heart attack, Noni, the spinster, had moved in with her sister, the widow. They lived on his pension, but still they needed more money, what with endless repairs being done to the house, the price of everything rising in the bazaar, and the wages of their maid, sweeper, watchman, and gardener.

So, in order to make her contribution to household finances, Noni had accepted the judge's request that she tutor Sai. Science to Shakespeare. It was only when Noni's abilities in mathematics and science began to falter when Sai was sixteen, that the judge was forced to hire Gyan to take over these subjects.

"Here is Saibaby," said the cook, presenting her to the sisters.

They had regarded her sadly, orphan child of India's failing romance with the Soviets.

"Stupidest thing India ever did, snuggling up to the wrong side. Do you remember when Chotu and Motu went to Russia? They said they had not seen the like," remarked Lola to Noni, "even in India. Inefficient beyond belief."

"And do you recall," said Noni back to Lola, "those Russians who lived next door to us in Calcutta? They'd go running out every morning and come back with mountains of food, remember? There they'd be, slicing, boiling, frying *mountains* of potatoes and onions. And then, by evening, they'd go running to the bazaar *again*, hair flying, coming back crazy with excitement and even *more* onions and potatoes for dinner. To them India was a land of plenty. They'd never seen *anything* like our markets."

But despite their opinion of Russia and Sai's parents, over the years they grew very fond of Sai.

Nine

"Oh my God," shrieked Lola, when she heard the judge's guns had been stolen from Cho Oyu. She was very much grayer now, but her personality was stronger than ever. "What if those hooligans come to Mon Ami? They're bound to come. But we have nothing. Not that *that* will deter them. They'll kill for fifty rupees."

"But you have a watchman," said Sai, absentminded, still trailing the thought of how Gyan hadn't arrived the day of the robbery. His affection was surely on the wane. . . .

"Budhoo? But he's Nepali. Who can trust him now? It's always the watchman in a case of robbery. They pass on the information and share the spoils. . . . Remember Mrs. Thondup? She used to have that Nepali fellow, returned from Calcutta one year to find the house wiped clean. *Wiped clean.* Cups plates beds chairs wiring light fixtures, every single thing—even the chains and floats in the toilets. One of the men had tried to steal the cables along the road and they found him electrocuted. Every bamboo had been cut and sold, every lime was off the tree. Holes had been bored into their water pipes so every hut on the hillside was drawing water from their supply—and no sign of the watchman, of course. Quick across the border, he'd disappeared back into Nepal. My God, Noni," she said, "we had better tell that Budhoo to go."

"Calm down. How can we?" said Noni. "He has given us no reason."

In fact, Budhoo had been a comforting presence for the two sisters who'd reached old age together at Mon Ami, its vegetable patch containing, as far as they knew, the country's only broccoli grown from seeds procured in England; its orchard providing enough fruit for stewed pears every day of pear season and enough leftover to experiment with wine making in the bathtub. Their washing line sagged under a load of Marks and Spencer panties, and through large leg portholes, they were favored with views of Kanchenjunga collared by cloud. At the entrance to the house hung a *thangkha* of a demon—with hungry fangs and skull necklaces, brandishing an angry penis—to dissuade the missionaries. In the drawing room was a trove of knickknacks. Tibetan *choksee* tables painted in jade and flame colors piled with books, including a volume of paintings by Nicholas Roerich, a Russian aristocrat who painted the Himalayas with such grave presence it made you shiver just to imagine all that grainy distilled cold, the lone traveler atop a yak, going—where? The immense vistas indicated an abstract destination. Also, Salim Ali's guide to birds and all of Jane Austen. There was Wedgwood in the dining room cabinet and a jam jar on the sideboard, saved for its prettiness. "By appointment to Her Majesty the queen jam and marmalade manufacturers," it read in gold under a coat of arms, supported by a crowned lion and a unicorn.

Then there was the cat, Mustafa, a sooty hirsute fellow demonstrating a perfection of containment no amount of love or science could penetrate. He was, at this moment, starting up like a lorry on Sai's lap, but his eyes looked blankly right into hers, warning her against mistaking this for intimacy.

To guard all this and their dignity, the sisters had hired Budhoo, a retired army man who had seen action against guerilla factions in Assam and had a big gun and an equally fierce mustache. He came each night at nine, ringing his bell as he rode up on his bicycle and lifting his bottom off the seat as he went over the bump in the garden.

"Budhoo?" the sisters would call from inside, sitting up in their beds, wrapped in Kulu shawls, sipping Sikkimese brandy, BBC news sputtering on the radio, falling over them in sparky explosions.

"Budhoo?"

"Huzoor!"

They would return to the BBC then, and later, sometimes, to their small black-and-white television, when Doordarshan provided the treat of *To the Manor Born* or *Yes, Minister,* featuring gentlemen with faces like moist, contented hams. With Budhoo on the roof fiddling with the aerial, the sisters shouted to him out of the window, "Right, left, no, back," as he swayed, poor fellow, amid the tree branches and moths, the outfall of messy Kalimpong weather.

At intervals through the night Budhoo also marched about Mon Ami, banging a stick and blowing a whistle so Lola and Noni could hear him and feel safe until the mountains once again shimmered in pure 24k and they woke to the powdery mist burning off in the sun.

But they had trusted Budhoo for no reason whatsoever. He might murder them in their nighties—

"But if we dismiss him," said Noni, "then he'll be angry and twice as likely to do something."

"I tell you, these Neps can't be trusted. And they don't just rob. They think absolutely nothing of murdering, as well."

"Well," sighed Lola, "it was bound to happen, really. Been brewing a long time. When has this been a peaceful area? When we moved to Mon Ami, the whole of Kalimpong was upside down, remember? Nobody knew who was a spy and who wasn't. Beijing had just named Kalimpong a hotbed of anti-Chinese activity. . . ."

Monks had streamed through the forests, garnet lines of fire pouring down the mountains, as they escaped from Tibet along the salt and wool trade routes. Aristocrats had arrived, too, Lhasa beauties dancing waltzes at the Gymkhana Ball, amazing the locals with their cosmopolitan style.

But for a long while there had been severe food shortages, as there always were when political trouble arrived on the hillside.

"We had better run to the market, Noni. It will empty out. And our library books! We must change them."

"I won't last the month," said Lola. "Almost through," she thumped *A Bend in the River,* "uphill task—"

"Superb writer," said Noni. "First-class. One of the best books I've ever read."

"Oh, I don't know," Lola said, "I think he's strange. Stuck in the past. . . . He has not progressed. Colonial neurosis, he's never freed himself from it. Quite a different thing now. In fact," she said, "chicken tikka masala has replaced fish and chips as the number one take-out dinner in Britain. It was just reported in the *Indian Express.*

"Tikka masala," she repeated. "Can you believe it?" She imagined the English countryside, castles, hedgerows, hedgehogs, etc., and tikka masala whizzing by on buses, bicycles, Rolls-Royces. Then she imagined a scene in *To the Manor Born*: "Oh Audrey. How perfectly lovely! Chicken tikka masala! Yes, and I got us some basmati as well. I do think it's the best rice, don't you?"

"Well, I don't like to agree with you, but maybe you have a point," Noni conceded. "After all, why isn't he writing of where he lives now? Why isn't he taking up, say, race riots in Manchester?"

"Also the new England, Noni. A completely cosmopolitan society. Pixie, for example, doesn't have a chip on her shoulder."

Pixie, Lola's daughter, was a BBC reporter, and now and then Lola visited her and came back making everyone sick, refusing to shut up: "Super play, and oh, the strawberries and cream. . . . And ah, the strawberries and cream. . . ."

"My! What strawberries and cream, my dear, and out in the *most lovely* garden," Noni mimicked her sister. "As if you can't get strawberries and cream in Kalimpong!" she said, then. "And you can eat without having to mince your words and behave like a pig on high heels."

"Dreadful legs those English girls have," said Uncle Potty, who had been present at the altercation. "Big pasty things. Good thing they've started wearing pants now."

But Lola was too dizzy to listen. Her suitcases were stuffed with Marmite, Oxo bouillon cubes, Knorr soup packets, After Eights, daffodil bulbs, and renewed supplies of Boots cucumber lotion and Marks and

Spencer underwear—the essence, quintessence, of Englishness as she understood it. Surely the queen donned this superior hosiery:

She was solid.	It was solid.
She was plain.	It was plain.
She was strong.	It was strong.
She was no-nonsense.	It was no-nonsense.

They prevailed.

It was Pixie who inspired the nightly ritual of listening to the radio.

"Budhoo?"

"Huzoor."

"Good evening . . . this is Piyali Bannerji with the BBC news."

All over India, people hearing the Indian name announced in pucca British accent laughed and laughed so hard their stomachs hurt.

Disease. War. Famine. Noni exclaimed and was outraged, but Lola purred with pride and heard nothing but the sanitized elegance of her daughter's voice, triumphant over any horrors the world might thrust upon others. "Better leave sooner rather than later," she had advised Pixie long ago, "India is a sinking ship. Don't want to be pushy, darling, sweetie, thinking of your happiness only, but *the doors won't stay open forever. . . .*"

Ten

Biju had started his second year in America at Pinocchio's Italian Restaurant, stirring vats of spluttering Bolognese, as over a speaker an opera singer sang of love and murder, revenge and heartbreak.

"He smells," said the owner's wife. "I think I'm allergic to his hair oil." She had hoped for men from the poorer parts of Europe—Bulgarians perhaps, or Czechoslovakians. At least they might have something in common with them like religion and skin color, grandfathers who ate cured sausages and looked like them, too, but they weren't coming in numbers great enough or they weren't coming desperate enough, she wasn't sure. . . .

The owner bought soap and toothpaste, toothbrush, shampoo plus conditioner, Q-tips, nail clippers, and most important of all, deodorant, and told Biju he'd picked up some things he might need.

They stood there embarrassed by the intimacy of the products that lay between them.

He tried another tactic: "What do they think of the pope in India?"

By showing his respect for Biju's mind he would raise Biju's self-respect, for the boy was clearly lacking in that department.

"You've tried," his wife said, comforting him a few days later when they couldn't detect any difference in Biju. "You even *bought* the soap," she said.

Biju approached Tom & Tomoko's—"No jobs."

McSweeney's Pub—"Not hiring."

Freddy's Wok—"Can you ride a bicycle?"

Yes, he could.

Szechuan wings and French fries, just $3.00. Fried rice $1.35 and $1.00 for pan-fried dumplings fat and tight as babies—slice them open and flood your plate with a run of luscious oil. In this country poor people eat like kings! General Tso's chicken, emperor's pork, and Biju on a bicycle with the delivery bag on his handlebars, a tremulous figure between heaving buses, regurgitating taxis—what growls, what sounds of flatulence came from this traffic. Biju pounded at the pedals, heckled by taxi drivers direct from Punjab—a man is not a caged thing, a man is wild *wild* and he must drive as such, in a bucking yodeling taxi. They harassed Biju with such blows from their horns as could split the world into whey and solids: paaaaaaWWW!

One evening, Biju was sent to deliver hot-and-sour soups and egg foo yong to three Indian girls, students, new additions to the neighborhood in an apartment just opened under reviewed city laws to raised rents. Banners reading "Antigentrification Day" had been hauled up over the street by the longtime residents for a festival earlier in the afternoon when they had played music, grilled hot dogs in the street, and sold all their gritty junk. One day the Indian girls hoped to be gentry, but right now, despite being unwelcome in the neighborhood, they were in the student stage of vehemently siding with the poor people who wished them gone.

The girl who answered the buzzer smiled, shiny teeth, shiny eyes through shiny glasses. She took the bag and went to collect the money. It was suffused with Indian femininity in there, abundant amounts of sweet newly washed hair, gold strung Kolhapuri slippers lying about. Heavyweight accounting books sat on the table along with a chunky Ganesh brought all the way from home despite its weight, for interior decoration plus luck in money and exams.

"Well," one of them continued with the conversation Biju had interrupted, discussing a fourth Indian girl not present, "why doesn't she just go for an Indian boy then, who'll understand all that temper tantrum stuff?"

"She won't look at an Indian boy, she doesn't want a nice Indian boy who's grown up chatting with his aunties in the kitchen."

"What does she want then?"

"She wants the Marlboro man with a Ph.D."

They had a self-righteousness common to many Indian women of the English-speaking upper-educated, went out to mimosa brunches, ate their Dadi's roti with adept fingers, donned a sari or smacked on elastic shorts for aerobics, could say "*Namaste,* Kusum Auntie, *aayiye, baethiye, khayiye!*" as easily as "Shit!" They took to short hair quickly, were eager for Western-style romance, and happy for a traditional ceremony with lots of jewelry: green set (meaning emerald), red set (meaning ruby), white set (meaning diamond). They considered themselves uniquely positioned to lecture everyone on a variety of topics: accounting professors on accounting, Vermonters on the fall foliage, Indians on America, Americans on India, Indians on India, Americans on America. They were poised; they were impressive; in the United States, where luckily it was still assumed that Indian women were downtrodden, they were lauded as extraordinary—which had the unfortunate result of making them even more of what they already were.

Fortune cookies, they checked, chili sauce, soy sauce, duck sauce, chopsticks, napkins, plastic spoons knives forks.

"*Dhanyawad. Shukria.* Thank you. Extra tip. You should buy topi-muffler-gloves to be ready for the winter."

The shiny-eyed girl said it many ways so that the meaning might be conveyed from every angle—that he might comprehend their friendliness completely in this meeting between Indians abroad of different classes and languages, rich and poor, north and south, top caste bottom caste.

Standing at that threshold, Biju felt a mixture of emotions: hunger, respect, loathing. He mounted the bicycle he had rested against the railings and was about to go on, but something made him stop and draw back. It was a ground-floor apartment with black security bars, and he put two fingers to his lips and whistled into the window at the girls dunking their spoons into the plastic containers where the brown liquid and foggy bits of egg looked horrible against the plastic, *twe tweeeeee twhoo,* and before he saw their response, he pedaled as fast as he could into the scowling howling traffic down Broadway, and as he pedaled, he sang loudly, *"O, yeh ladki zara si deewani lagti hai. . . ."*

Old songs, best songs.

But then, in a week, five people called up Freddy's Wok to complain that the food was cold. It had turned to winter.

The shadows drew in close, the night chomped more than its share of hours. Biju smelled the first of the snow and found it had the same pricking, difficult smell that existed inside the freezer; he felt the Thermocol scrunch of it underfoot. On the Hudson, the ice cracked loudly into pieces, and within the contours of this gray, broken river it seemed as if the city's inhabitants were being provided with a glimpse of something far and forlorn that they might use to consider their own loneliness.

Biju put a padding of newspapers down his shirt—leftover copies from kind Mr. Iype the newsagent—and sometimes he took the scallion pancakes and inserted them below the paper, inspired by the memory of an uncle who used to go out to the fields in winter with his lunchtime *parathas* down his vest. But even this did not seem to help, and once, on his bicycle, he began to weep from the cold, and the weeping unpicked a deeper vein of grief—such a terrible groan issued from between the whimpers that he was shocked his sadness was so profound.

When he returned home to the basement of a building at the bottom of Harlem, he fell straight into sleep.

The building belonged to an invisible management company that listed its address as One and a Quarter Street and owned tenements all over the neighborhood, the superintendent supplementing his income by illegally renting out basement quarters by the week, by the month, and even by the day, to fellow illegals. He spoke about as much English as Biju did, so between Spanish, Hindi, and wild mime, Jacinto's gold tooth flashing in the late evening sun, they had settled the terms of rental. Biju joined a shifting population of men camping out near the fuse box, behind the boiler, in the cubby holes, and in odd-shaped corners that once were pantries, maids' rooms, laundry rooms, and storage rooms at the bottom of what had been a single-family home, the entrance still adorned with a scrap of colored mosaic in the shape of a star. The men shared a yellow toilet; the sink was a tin laundry trough. There was one fuse box for the whole building, and if anyone turned on too many appliances or lights, *PHUT*, the entire electricity went, and the residents screamed to nobody, since there was nobody, of course, to hear them.

Biju had been nervous there from his very first day. "Howdy," a man on the steps of his new abode had said, holding out his hand and nodding, "my name's Joey, and I just had me some WHEES-KAY!" Power and hiss. This was the local homeless man at the edge of his hunting and gathering territory, which he sometimes marked by peeing a bright arc right across the road. He wintered here on a subway grate in a giant plastic-bag igloo that sagged, then blew taut with stale air each time a train passed. Biju had taken the sticky hand offered, the man had held tight, and Biju had broken free and run, a cackle of laughter following him.

"The food is cold," the customers complained. "Soup arrived cold! Again! The rice is cold each and every time."

"I'm also cold," Biju said losing his temper.

"Pedal faster," said the owner.

"I cannot."

It was a little after 1 A.M. when he left Freddy's Wok for the last time, the street lamps were haloes of light filled with starry scraps of frozen vapor, and he trudged between snow mountains adorned with empty take-out containers and solidified dog pee in surprised yellow. The streets were empty but for the homeless man who stood looking at an invisible watch on his wrist while talking into a dead pay phone. "Five! Four! Three! Two! One—TAKEOFF!!" he shouted, and then he hung up the phone and ran holding onto his hat as if it might get blown off by the rocket he had just launched into space.

Biju turned in mechanically at the sixth somber house with its tombstone facade, past the metal cans against which he could hear the unmistakable sound of rat claws, and went down the flight of steps to the basement.

"I am very tired," he said out loud.

A man near him was frying in bed, turning this way, that way. Someone else was grinding his teeth.

By the time he had found employment again, at a bakery on Broadway and La Salle, he had used up all the money in the savings envelope in his shoe.

It was spring, the ice was melting, the freed piss was flowing. All over, in city cafés and bistros, they took advantage of this delicate nutty sliver between the winter, cold as hell, and summer, hot as hell, and dined al fresco on the narrow pavement under the cherry blossoms. Women in baby-doll dresses, ribbons, and bows that didn't coincide with their personalities indulged themselves with the first fiddleheads of the season, and the fragrance of expensive cooking mingled with the eructation of taxis and the lascivious subway breath that went up the skirts of the spring-clad girls making them wonder if *this* was how Marilyn Monroe felt—somehow not, somehow not. . . .

The mayor found a rat in Gracie Mansion.

And Biju, at the Queen of Tarts bakery, met Saeed Saeed, who would become the man he admired most in the United States of America.

"I am from Zanzibar, *not* Tanzania," he said, introducing himself.

Biju knew neither one nor the other. "Where is that?"

"Don't you know?? Zanzibar full of Indians, man! My grandmother—she is Indian!"

In Stone Town they ate samosas and *chapatis, jalebis,* pilau rice. . . . Saeed Saeed could sing like Amitabh Bachhan and Hema Malini. He sang, *"Mera joota hai japani . . ."* and "Bombay *se aaya mera dost—Oi!"* He could gesture with his arms out and wiggle his hips, as could Kavafya from Kazakhstan and Omar from Malaysia, and together they assailed Biju with thrilling dance numbers. Biju felt so proud of his country's movies he almost fainted.

Eleven

Mondays, Wednesdays, and Fridays were the days Noni tutored Sai.

The cook dropped her off and collected her at Mon Ami, continuing to the market and the post office in the meantime, and selling his *chhang*.

He had first started a liquor business on the side for Biju's sake, because his salary had hardly been changed in years. His last raise had been twenty-five rupees.

"But sahib," he had begged, "how can I live on this?"

"All your expenses are paid for—housing, clothing, food, medicines. This is extra," growled the judge.

"What about Biju?"

"*What* about Biju? Biju must make his own way. What's wrong with him?"

The cook, known for the fine quality of his product, would buy millet, wash and cook it like rice, then, adding yeast, would leave it to ferment overnight in hot weather, longer in winter. A day or two in a gunny sack, and when it had that sour dry buzzing flavor, he would sell it at a shack restaurant called Gompu's. It filled him with pride to see men sitting in the steam and smoke with their bamboo mugs full of his grain topped with hot water. They sucked up the liquid, filtering out the millet with a bamboo stem for a straw—*aaaaah*. . . . The cook urged his customers to keep some *chhang* near their beds in case they felt thirsty at night, claiming it gave strength after illness. This venture led to another, even more lucrative one as the cook made contacts in the brand-name black market and became a crucial, if small, link in the underground business of subsidized army liquor and fuel rations. His shack was an easy jungle-camouflaged detour for military trucks on their way to the officers' mess. He stood in the bushes, waiting. The vehicles paused and quickly the crates were unloaded—Teacher's, Old Monk, Gilby's, Gymkhana; he carried them to his shack and later to certain merchants in town who sold the bottles. They all received a cut of the money, the cook a smidgen in the scheme of things, fifty rupees, a hundred rupees; the lorry drivers a bigger amount; the men at the mess even more; the biggest cut of all went to Major Aloo, friend of Lola and Noni, who procured for them, by similar means, their favorite Black Cat rum and cherry brandy from Sikkim.

This the cook had done for Biju, but also for himself, since the cook's desire was for modernity: toaster ovens, electric shavers, watches, cameras, cartoon colors. He dreamed at night not in the Freudian symbols that still enmeshed others but in modern codes, the digits of a telephone flying away before he could dial them, a garbled television.

He had found that there was nothing so awful as being in the service of a family you couldn't be proud of, that let you down, showed you up, and made you into a fool. How the other cooks and maids, watchmen and gardeners on the hillside laughed, boasting meanwhile how well *they* were treated by *their* employers—money, comfort, even pensions in special bank accounts. In fact, so beloved were some of these servants that they were actually *begged* not to work; their employers pleaded with them to eat cream and ghee, to look after their chilblains and sun themselves like monitor lizards on winter afternoons. The MetalBox watchman assured him that each morning he consumed a fried egg—with white toast, when white bread had been fashionable, and now that brown bread was most in vogue, with brown.

So serious was this rivalry that the cook found himself telling lies. Mostly about the past since the present could too easily be picked apart. He fanned a rumor of the judge's lost glory, and therefore of his own, so it flamed and prospered up and down the market. A great statesman, he told them, a wealthy landowner who gave his family property away, a freedom fighter who left a position of immense power in court as he did not wish to pass judgment on his fellow men—he could not, not with his brand of patriotic zest, jail congresswallahs, or stamp out demonstrations. A man so inspiring, but brought to his knees, to austerity and philosophy, by sorrow at his wife's death, the wife herself a martyred and religious mother of the kind that makes a Hindu weak in the knees. "That is why he sits by himself all day and every day."

The cook had never known the judge's wife, but he claimed that his information had been handed down from the older servants in the household, and eventually, he had grown to believe his own marvelous story. It gave him a feeling of self-respect even as he picked over the vegetables being sold cheap and considered rebate melons with caving pates.

"He was completely different," he told Sai, too, when she first came to Kalimpong. "You cannot believe. He was born a rich man."

"Where was he born?"

"Into one of the top families of Gujarat. Ahmedabad. Or was it Baroda? Huge *haveli* like a palace."

Sai liked to keep him company in the kitchen as he told her stories. He gave her bits of dough to roll into *chapatis* and showed her how to make them perfectly round, but hers came out in all kinds of shapes. "Map of India," he would say, dismissing one. "Oof ho, now you've made the map of Pakistan," he tossed out the next. Finally he'd let her put one of them on the fire to puff up and if it didn't, "Well, Dog Special Roti," he would say.

"But tell me more," she would ask, as he allowed her to spread jam on a tart or grate cheese into a sauce.

"They sent him to England and ten thousand people saw him off at the station. He went on top of an elephant! He had won, you see, a scholarship from the maharaja. . . ."

The sound of the cook talking reached the judge's ears as he sat over chess in the drawing room. When he thought of his past, he began, mysteriously, to itch. Every bit of him filled with a burning sensation. It roiled within until he could barely stand it.

Jemubhai Popatlal Patel had, in fact, been born to a family of the peasant caste, in a tentative structure under a palm roof scuffling with rats, at the outskirts of Piphit where the town took on the aspect of a village again. The year was 1919 and the Patels could still remember the time when Piphit had seemed ageless. First it had been owned by the Gaekwad kings of Baroda and then the British, but though the revenue headed for one owner and then another, the landscape had remained unaffected; a temple stood at its heart, and by its side, a several-legged banyan tree; in its pillared shade, white-bearded men regurgitated their memories; cows mooed *oo aaw, oo aaw;* women walked through the cotton fields to collect water at the mud-muddled river, a slow river, practically asleep.

But then tracks had been laid across the salt pans to bring steam trains from the docks at Surat and Bombay to transport cotton from the interior. Broad homes had come up in the civil lines, a courthouse with a clock tower to maintain the new, quick-moving time, and on the streets thronged all manner of people: Hindu, Christian, Jain, Muslim, clerks, army boys, tribal women. In the market, shopkeepers from the cubbyhole shops in which they perched conducted business that arced between Kobe and Panama, Port-au-Prince, Shanghai, Manila, and also to tin-roofed stalls too small to enter, many days' journey away by bullock cart. Here, in the market, upon a narrow parapet that jutted from a sweet-seller's establishment, Jemubhai's father owned a modest business procuring false witnesses to appear in court. (Who would think his son, so many years later, would become a judge?)

The usual stories: jealous husband cutting off wife's nose or falsified record claiming death of a widow who was still alive so her property might be divided among greedy descendants.

He trained the poor, the desperate, the scoundrels, rehearsed them strictly:

"What do you know about Manubhai's buffalo?"

"Manubhai, in fact, never had a buffalo at all."

He was proud of his ability to influence and corrupt the path of justice, exchange right for wrong or wrong for right; he felt no guilt. By the time a case of a stolen cow arrived at court, centuries of arguments had occurred between warring families, so many convolutions and tit-for-tats that there was no right or wrong anymore. Purity of answer was a false quest. How far back could you go, straightening things out?

The business succeeded. He bought a second-hand Hercules cycle for thirty-five rupees and became a familiar sight riding about town. When his first and only son was born his hopes were immediately buoyed. Baby Jemubhai wrapped five miniature fingers about a single one of his father's; his clutch was determined and slightly grim, but his father took the grip as proof of good health and could not shut his mustache over his smile. When his son was big enough, he sent him to the mission school.

Each weekday morning, Jemubhai's mother shook him awake in darkness so he might review his lessons.

"No, please no, little more time, little more." He wriggled from her grasp, eyes still closed, ready to drop back into sleep, for he had never grown used to this underground awakening, this time that belonged to dacoits and jackals, to strange sounds and shapes that weren't meant, he was sure, to be heard or seen by him, a mere junior student at the Bishop Cotton School. There was nothing but black against his eyes, though he knew it was really a cluttered scene, rows of opinionated relatives asleep outside, *kakas-kakis-masas-masis-phois-phuas,* bundles in various colors dangling from the thatched roof of the veranda, buffaloes tethered to the trees by rings in their noses.

His mother was a phantom in the dark courtyard, pouring cold well water over his invisible self, scrubbing viciously with the thick wrists of a farm woman, rubbing oil through his hair, and though he knew it would encourage his brains, it felt as if she were rubbing, rubbing them out.

Fed he was, to surfeit. Each day, he was given a tumbler of fresh milk sequined with golden fat. His mother held the tumbler to his lips, lowering it only when empty, so he reemerged like a whale from the sea, heaving for breath. Stomach full of cream, mind full of study, camphor hung in a tiny bag about his neck to divert illness; the entire package was prayed over and thumb-printed red and yellow with *tika* marks. He was taken to school on the back of his father's bicycle.

In the entrance to the school building was a portrait of Queen Victoria in a dress like a flouncy curtain, a fringed cape, and a peculiar hat with feathery arrows shooting out. Each morning as Jemubhai passed under, he found her froggy expression compelling and felt deeply impressed that a woman so plain could also have been so powerful. The more he pondered this oddity, the more his respect for her and the English grew.

It was there, under her warty presence, that he had finally risen to the promise of his gender. From their creaky Patel lineage appeared an intelligence that seemed modern in its alacrity. He could read a page, close the book, rat-a-tat it back, hold a dozen numbers in his head, work his mind like an unsnagging machine through a maze of calculations, roll forth the answer like a finished product shooting from a factory chute. Sometimes, when his father saw him, he forgot to recognize his son, so clearly in the X-ray flashes of his imagination did he see the fertile cauliflowering within his son's skull.

The daughters were promptly deprived to make sure he got the best of everything, from love to food. Years went by in a blur.

But Jemubhai's hopes remained fuzzy and it was his father who first mentioned the civil service.

When Jemu, aged fourteen, matriculated at the top of the class, the principal, Mr. McCooe, summoned his father and suggested his son take the local pleader's examination that would enable him to find employment in the courts of subordinate magistrates. "Bright boy . . . he might end up in the high court!"

The father walked out thinking, Well, if he could do that, he could do more. He could be the judge himself, couldn't he?

His son might, *might, could!* occupy the seat faced by the father, proud disrupter of the system, lowest in the hierarchy of the court. He might be a district commissioner or a high court judge. He might wear a silly white wig atop a dark face in the burning heat of summer and bring down his hammer on those phony rigged cases. Father below, son above, they'd be in charge of justice, complete.

He shared his dream with Jemubhai. So fantastic was their dreaming, it thrilled them like a fairy tale, and perhaps because this dream sailed too high in the sky to be tackled by logic, it took form, began to exert palpable pressure. Without naïveté, father and son would have been defeated; had they aimed lower, according to the logic of probability, they would have failed.

The recommended number of Indians in the ICS was 50 percent and the quota wasn't even close to being filled. Space at the top, space at the top. There certainly was no space at the bottom.

Jemubhai attended Bishop's College on a scholarship, and after, he left for Cambridge on the SS *Strathnaver*. When he returned, member of the ICS, he was put to work in a district far from his home in the state of Uttar Pradesh.

"So many servants then," the cook told Sai. "Now, of course, I am the only one." He had begun working at ten years old, at a salary half his age, five rupees, as the lowest all-purpose *chokra* boy in the kitchen of a club where his father was pudding cook.

At fourteen, he was hired by the judge at twelve rupees a month. Those were days when it was still pertinent to know that if you tied a pot of cream to the underside of a cow, as you walked to the next camp it would churn itself into butter by day's end. That a portable meat safe could be made with an upside-down open umbrella tied about with mosquito netting.

"We were always on tour," said the cook, "three weeks out of four. Only in the worst days of the monsoon did we stop. Your grandfather would drive in his car if he could, but the district was mostly without roads, and hardly any bridges spanned the rivers, so more often he had to ride out on horseback. Now and then, through jungly areas and through deeper, swifter currents, he crossed on elephant. We would travel before him in a train of bullock carts piled with the china, tents, furniture, carpets—everything. There were porters, orderlies, a stenographer. There was a thunder box for the bathroom tent and even a *murga-murgi* in a cage under the cart. They were a foreign breed and that hen laid more eggs than any other *murgi* I have known."

"Where did you sleep?" Sai asked.

"We would put up tents in villages all over the district: a big bedroom tent like a top for your grandfather, with an attached tent bathroom, dressing room, drawing room, and dining room. The tents were very grand, Kashmiri carpets, silver dishes, and your grandfather dressed for dinner even in the jungle, in black dinner jacket and bow tie.

"As I said, we went first, so that when your grandfather arrived, everything was set up exactly as it had been left in the old camp, the same files open at the same angle turned to the same page. If it was even a little bit different, he would lose his temper.

"The timetable was strictly enforced—we couldn't be late by even five minutes, so we all had to learn how to read a clock.

"At five-forty-five I would take the bed tea on a tray to your grandfather's tent. 'Bed tea,' I would call out as I lifted the tent flap.

"Bad tea," was how it sounded. *"Baaad teee. Baaad teeee."* Sai began to laugh.

The judge stared at his chessboard, but after the burning memory of his beginnings, he experienced the sweet relief now of recalling his life as a touring official in the civil service.

The tight calendar had calmed him, as did the constant exertion of authority. How he relished his power over the classes that had kept his family pinned under their heels for centuries—like the stenographer, for example, who was a Brahmin. There he was, crawling into a tiny tent to the side, and there was Jemubhai reclining like a king in a bed carved out of teak, hung with mosquito netting.

"Bed tea," the cook would shout. "Baaad tee."

He would sit up to drink.

6:30: he'd bathe in water that had been heated over the fire so it was redolent with the smell of wood smoke and flecked with ash. With a dusting of powder he graced his newly washed face, with a daub of pomade, his hair. Crunched up toast like charcoal from having been toasted upon the flame, with marmalade over the burn.

8:30: he rode into the fields with the local officials and everyone else in the village going along for fun. Followed by an orderly holding an umbrella over his head to shield him from the glare, he measured the fields and checked to make sure his yield estimate matched the headman's statement. Farms were growing less than ten maunds an acre of rice or wheat, and at two rupees a maund, every single man in a village, sometimes, was in debt to the *bania*. (Nobody knew that Jemubhai himself was noosed, of course, that long ago in the little town of Piphit in Gujarat, moneylenders had sniffed out in him a winning combination of ambition and poverty . . . that they still sat waiting cross-legged on a soiled mat in the market, snapping their toes, cracking their knuckles in anticipation of repayment. . . .)

2:00: after lunch, the judge sat at his desk under a tree to try cases, usually in a cross mood, for he disliked the informality, hated the splotch of leaf shadow on him imparting an untidy mongrel look. Also, there was a worse aspect of contamination and corruption: he heard cases in Hindi, but they were recorded in Urdu by the stenographer and translated by the judge into a second record in English, although his own command of Hindi and Urdu was tenuous; the witnesses who couldn't read at all put their thumbprints at the bottom of "Read Over and Acknowledged Correct," as instructed. Nobody could be sure how much of the truth had fallen between languages, between languages and illiteracy; the clarity that justice demanded was nonexistent. Still, despite the leaf shadow and language confusion, he acquired a fearsome reputation for his speech that seemed to belong to no language at all, and for his face like a mask that conveyed something beyond human fallibility. The expression and manner honed here would carry him, eventually, all the way to the high court in Lucknow where, annoyed by lawless pigeons shuttlecocking about those tall, shadowy halls, he would preside, white powdered wig over white powdered face, hammer in hand.

His photograph, thus attired, thus annoyed, was still up on the wall, in a parade of history glorifying the progress of Indian law and order.

4:30: tea had to be perfect: drop scones made in the frying pan. He would embark on them with forehead wrinkled, as if angrily mulling over something important, and then, as it would into his retirement, the draw of the sweet took over, and his stern work face would hatch an expression of tranquility.

5:30: out he went into the countryside with his fishing rod or gun. The countryside was full of game; lariats of migratory birds lassoed the sky in October; quail and partridge with lines of babies strung out behind whirred by like nursery toys that emit sound with movement; pheasant—fat foolish creatures, made to be shot—went scurrying through the bushes. The thunder of gunshot rolled away, the leaves shivered, and he experienced the profound silence that could come only after violence. One thing was always missing, though, the proof of the pudding, the prize of the action, the manliness in manhood, the partridge for the pot, because he returned with—

Nothing!

He was a terrible shot.

8:00: the cook saved his reputation, cooked a chicken, brought it forth, proclaimed it "roast bastard," just as in the Englishman's favorite joke book of natives using incorrect English. But sometimes, eating that roast bustard, the judge felt the joke might also be on him, and he called for another rum, took a big gulp, and kept eating feeling as if he were eating himself, since he, too, was (was he?) part of the fun. . . .

9:00: sipping Ovaltine, he filled out the registers with the day's gleanings. The Petromax lantern would be lit—what a noise it made—insects fording the black to dive-bomb him with soft flowers (moths), with iridescence (beetles). Lines, columns, and squares. He realized truth was best looked at in tiny aggregates, for many baby truths could yet add up to one big size unsavory lie. Last, in his diary also to be submitted to his superiors, he recorded the random observations of a cultured man, someone who was observant, schooled in literature as well as economics; and he made up hunting triumphs: two partridge . . . one deer with thirty-inch horns. . . .

11:00: he had a hot water bottle in winter, and, in all seasons, to the sound of the wind buffeting the trees and the cook's snoring, he fell asleep.

The cook had been disappointed to be working for Jemubhai. A severe comedown, he thought, from his father, who had served white men only.

The ICS was becoming Indianized and they didn't like it, some of these old servants, but what could you do? He'd even had a rival for the position, a man who appeared with tattered recommendations inherited from his father and grandfather to indicate a lineage of honesty and good service.

The cook's father, who had made his way through his career without such praise, had bought recommendations on the servant chittie exchange for his son, some so antiquated they mentioned expertise in the *dhobi* pie and country captain chicken.

The judge looked them over: "But his name is not Solomon Pappiah. It is not Sampson. It is not Thomas."

"They liked him so much, you see," said the cook's father, "that they gave him a name of their own people. Out of love they called him Thomas."

The judge was disbelieving.

"He needs to be trained," the father admitted finally and dropped his demand for twenty rupees for his son, "but that is why he will come cheap. And in puddings there is nobody to beat him. He can make a new pudding for each day of the year."

"What can he make?"

"Bananafritterpineapplefritterapplefritterapplesurpriseapple-charlotteapplebettybreadandbutterjamtartcaramelcustardtipsypudding rumtumpuddingjamrolypolygingersteamdatepuddinglemonpancakeegg custardorangecustardcoffeecustardstrawberrycustardtriflebakedalaska mangosoufflélemonsoufflécoffeesoufflechocolatesoufflégooseberrysoufflé hotchocolatepuddingcoldcoffeepuddingcoconutpuddingmilkpudding rumbabarumcakebrandysnappearstewguavastewplumstewapplestew peachstewapricotstewmangopiechocolatetartappletartgooseberrytart lemontartjamtartmarmaladetartbebincafloatingislandpineappleupside downappleupsidedowngooseberryupsidedownplumupsidedownpeach upsidedownraisinupsidedown—"

"All right. All right."

Twelve

So Sai's life had continued in Kalimpong—Lola and Noni, Uncle Potty and Father Booty, the judge and cook . . . until she met Gyan.

She met Gyan because one day, when Sai was sixteen, Noni found she could no longer teach her physics.

It had been an overhot summer afternoon and they sat on the Mon Ami veranda. All over the mountainside, the heat had reduced the townspeople to a stupor. Tin roofs sizzled, dozens of snakes lay roasting on the stones, and flowers bloomed as plushly and perfectly as on a summer outfit. Uncle Potty sat looking out on the warmth and sheen, the oil brought forth upon his nose, upon the salami, the cheese. A bite of cheese, a bite of salami, a gulp of icy Kingfisher. He leaned back so his face was in the shade and his toes were in the sun, and sighed: all was right with the world. The primary components were balanced, the hot and cold, the liquid and solid, the sun and shade.

Father Booty in his dairy found himself transported to a meditative state by the hum of his cows' chewing. What would yak-milk cheese taste like . . . ?

Nearby the Afghan princesses were sighing and deciding to eat their chicken cold.

Mrs. Sen, undefeated by the heat, started up the road to Mon Ami, propelled by the latest news from her daughter, Mun Mun, in America: she was to be hired by CNN. She reflected happily on how this would upset Lola. Hah, who did Lola Banerjee think *she* was? Putting on airs . . . always showing off about her daughter at the BBC. . . .

Unsuspecting of the approaching news, Lola was in the garden picking caterpillars off the English broccoli. The caterpillars were mottled green and white, with fake blue eyes, ridiculous fat feet, a tail, and an elephant nose. Magnificent creatures, she thought, studying one closely, but then she threw it to a waiting bird that pecked and a green stuffing squiggled out of the caterpillar like toothpaste from a punctured tube.

On the Mon Ami veranda, Noni and Sai sat before an open text book: neutrons . . . and protons . . . electrons. . . . So if—then—???

They were yet unable to grasp the question but were taunted by the sight, beyond the veranda, of a perfect sunlit illustration of the answer: speck insects suspended in a pod within which they jigged tirelessly, bound by a spell that could not be undone.

Noni felt a sudden exhaustion come over her; the answer seemed attainable via miracle not science. They put the book aside when the baker arrived at Mon Ami as he did each afternoon, lifting his trunk from his head and unlatching it. Outside the trunk was scuffed; inside it glowed like a treasure chest, with Swiss rolls, queen cakes, and, taught to him by missionaries on the hillside, peanut butter cookies evocative of, the ladies thought, cartoon America: gosh, golly, gee whiz, jeepers creepers.

They picked out pink and yellow queen cakes and began to chat.

"So, Sai, how old are you now? Fifteen?"

"Sixteen."

It was hard to tell, Noni thought. Sai looked far older in some ways, far younger in some.

Younger, no doubt, because she'd lived such a sheltered life and older, no doubt, because she spent all her time with retired people. She might always look like this, girlish even when she was old, old even when she was young. Noni looked her over critically. Sai was wearing khaki pants and a T-Shirt that said "Free Tibet." Her feet were bare and she wore her short hair in two untidy braids ending just before her shoulders. Noni and Lola had recently discussed how bad it was for Sai to continue to grow up like this: "She won't pick up social skills . . . nobody her own age . . . house full of men. . . ."

"Don't you find it difficult living like that with your grandfather?"

"The cook talks so much," said Sai, "that I don't mind."

The way she'd been abandoned to the cook for years. . . . If it wasn't for Lola and herself, Noni thought, Sai would have long ago fallen to the level of the servant class herself.

"What does he talk about?"

"Oh, stories about his village, how his wife died, his court case with his brother. . . . I hope Biju makes a lot of money," reflected Sai, "they are the poorest family in the village. Their house is still made of mud with a thatch roof."

Noni didn't think this was suitable information for the cook to share. It was important to draw the lines properly between classes or it harmed everyone on both sides of the great divide. Servants got all sorts of ideas, and then when they realized the world wasn't going to give them and their children what it gave to others, they got angry and resentful. Lola and Noni constantly had to discourage their maid, Kesang, from divulging personal information, but it was hard, Noni acknowledged, to keep it that way. Before one knew it one could slide into areas of the heart that should be referred to only between social equals. She thought of an episode not so long ago when the sisters had been too fascinated to stop their maid telling them of her romance with the milkman:

"I liked him so much," Kesang said. "I am a Sherpa, he is a Rai, but I lied and told my parents he was a Bhutia so they agreed to let us marry. It was a very nice wedding. His people, you have to give so much, pork, money, this and that, whatever they ask for you have to give, but we didn't have a wedding like that. He looked after my parents when they were ill and right from the beginning we made a vow that he wouldn't leave me and that I wouldn't leave him. Both things. Neither of us will leave each other. He will never die and leave me and I will never die and leave him. We made this vow. From before we got married we said this."

And she began to cry. Kesang with her crazy brown teeth going in different directions and her shabby stained clothes and funny topknot perched precariously on the nob of her head. Kesang, whom they had taken in untrained as a kindness and taught to make an Indonesian *saté* with peanut butter and soy sauce, a sweet-sour with ketchup and vinegar, and a Hungarian goulash with tomatoes and curd. Her love had shocked the sisters. Lola had always professed that servants didn't experience love in the same manner as people like themselves—"Their entire structure of relationships is different, it's economic, practical—far more sensible, I'm sure, if only one could manage it oneself." Even Lola was forced to wonder now if it were she who had never experienced the real thing; never had she and Joydeep had such a conversation of faith over the plunge—it wasn't rational, so they hadn't. But therefore might they not have had the love? She buried the thought.

Noni had never had love at all.

She had never sat in a hushed room and talked about such things as might make your soul tremble like a candle. She had never launched herself coquettishly at Calcutta parties, sari wrapped tightly over her hips, ice tonkling madly in her lime soda. She had never flown the brief glorious flag of romance, bright red, over her existence, not even as an episode of theater, a bit of pretense to raise her above her life. What did she have? Not even terrible hatreds; not even bitterness, grief. Merely irritations over small things: the way someone would *not* blow her nose but went *sur-sur-sur* in the library, laddering up the snot again and again.

She found, to her shock, that she had actually felt jealous of Kesang. The lines had blurred, luck had been misassigned.

And who would love Sai?

When Sai had first arrived, Noni had seen herself in her, in Sai's shyness. This was what came of committing a sensitive creature to a mean-spirited educational system, she thought. Noni, too, had been sent to such a school—you could only remain unsnared by going underground, remaining quiet when asked questions, expressing no opinion, hoping to be invisible—or they got you, ruined you.

Noni had recovered her confidence when it was too late. Life had passed her by and in those days things had to happen fast for a girl, or they didn't happen at all.

"Don't you want to meet people your own age?" she asked Sai.

But Sai was shy around her peers. Of one thing, though, she was sure: "I want to travel," she confessed.

Books were making her restless. She was beginning to read, faster, more, until she was inside the narrative and the narrative inside her, the pages going by so fast, her heart in her chest—she couldn't stop. In this way she had read *To Kill a Mockingbird, Cider with Rosie,* and *Life with Father* from the Gymkhana Club library. And pictures of the chocolaty Amazon, of stark Patagonia in the *National Geographic*s, a transparent butterfly snail in the sea, even of an old Japanese house slumbering in the snow. . . . —She found they affected her so much she could often hardly read the accompanying words—the feeling they created was so exquisite, the desire so painful. She remembered her parents, her father's hope of space travel. She studied the photographs taken via satellite of a storm blowing a red cloud off the sun's surface, felt a terrible desire for the father she did not know, and imagined that she, too, must surely have within her the same urge for something beyond the ordinary.

Cho Oyu and the judge's habits seemed curtailments to her then.

"Now and again, I wish I lived by the sea," sighed Noni. "At least the waves are never still."

A long while ago, when she was a young woman, she had gone to Digha and learned what it was to be lifted by the mysterious ocean. She stared out at the mountains, at the perfection of their stillness.

"The Himalayas were once underwater," Sai said. She knew this from her reading. "There are ammonite fossils on Mt. Everest."

Noni and Sai picked up the physics book again.

Then they put it down again.

"Listen to me," Noni told Sai, "if you get a chance in life, take it. Look at me, I should have thought about the future when I was young. Instead, only when it was too late did I realize what I should have done long ago. I used to dream about becoming an archaeologist. I'd go to the British Council and look at the books on King Tutankhamen. . . . But my parents were not the kind to understand, you know, my father was the old-fashioned type, a man brought up and educated only to give orders. . . . You must do it on your own, Sai."

Once more they tried physics, but Noni couldn't find an answer to the problem.

"I am afraid I have exhausted my abilities in science and mathematics.

Sai will require a tutor more qualified in these areas," said the note she sent home with Sai for the judge.

"Bloody irresponsible woman," said the judge, grumpy because the heat reminded him of his nationality. Later that evening he dictated to Sai a letter for the principal of the local college.

"If there is a teacher or an older student who provides tutoring, please let them know that we are looking for a mathematics and science instructor."

Thirteen

Not even a few sunshiny weeks had passed before the principal replied that he could recommend a promising student who had finished his bachelor's degree, but hadn't yet been able to find a job.

The student was Gyan, a quiet student of accounting who had thought the act of ordering numbers would soothe him; however, it hadn't turned out quite like that, and in fact, the more sums he did, the more columns of statistics he transcribed—well, it seemed simply to multiply the number of places at which solid knowledge took off and vanished to the moon. He enjoyed the walk to Cho Oyu and experienced a refreshing and simple happiness, although it took him two hours uphill, from Bong Busti where he lived, the light shining through thick bamboo in starry, jumping chinks, imparting the feeling of liquid shimmering.

Sai was unwilling at first to be forced from her immersion in *National Geographics* and be incarcerated in the dining room with Gyan. Before them, in a semicircle, were the instruments of study set out by the cook: ruler, pens, globe, graph paper, geometry set, pencil sharpener. The cook found they introduced a clinical atmosphere to the room similar to that which awed him at the chemist, at the clinic, and the path lab, where he enjoyed the hush guarded by the shelves of medicines, the weighing scale and thermometers, cupules, phials, pipettes, the tapeworm transformed into a specimen in formaldehyde, the measurements already inscribed on the bottle.

The cook would talk to the chemist, carefully, trying not to upset the delicate balances of the field, for he believed in superstition exactly as much as in science. "I see, yes, I understand," he said even if he didn't, and in a reasonable tone recorded his symptoms, resisting melodrama, to the doctor whom he revered, who studied him through her glasses: "No potty for five days, evil taste in the mouth, a thun thun in the legs and arms and sometimes a chun chun."

"What is a chun chun and what is a thun thun?"

"Chun chun is a tingling. Thun thun is when there is a pain going on and off."

"What do you have now? Chun chun?"

"No, THUN THUN."

The next visit. "Are you better?"

"Better, but still—"

"Thun thun?"

"No, doctor," he would say very seriously, "chun chun."

He emerged with his medicines feeling virtuous. Oh yes, he awaited modernity and knew that if you invested in it, it would inform you that you were worth something in this world.

But outside the clinic he would run into Kesang or the cleaner at the hospital or the MetalBox watchman, who would begin to declaim, "Now there is no hope, now you'll have to do *puja*, it will cost many thousands of rupees. . . ."

Or: "I knew someone who had exactly what you are describing, never walked again. . . ." By the time he had returned home he would have lost his faith in science and begun to howl: "*Hai hai, hamara kya hoga, hai hai, hamara kya hoga?*" And he'd have to go back to the clinic the next day to recover his good sense.

So, appreciating, desiring reasonableness, the cook brought in tea and fried cheese toast with chili pepper mixed into the cheese, and then sat on his stool just outside the door, keeping an eye on Sai and the new tutor, nodding approval at Gyan's careful tone, the deliberate words that led, calculation by calculation, to an exact, tidy answer that could be confirmed by a list at the back of the text.

Foolish cook. He had not realized that the deliberateness came not from faith in science, but from self-consciousness and doubt; that though they appeared to be engrossed in atoms, their eyes latched tightly to the numbers in that room where the walls swelled like sails, they were flailing; that like the evening hour opening to deeper depths outside, they would be swallowed into something more treacherous than the purpose for which Gyan had been hired; that though they were battling to build a firmness from all that was available to them, there was reason enough to worry it was not good enough to save them.

The small correct answer fell flat.

Gyan produced it apologetically. It was anticlimactic. It would not do. Flicking it aside, the tremendous anticipation that could no longer be pinned on the sum gathered strength and advanced, leaving them gasping by the time two hours were up and Gyan could flee without looking at Sai, who had produced such a powerful effect upon him.

"It is strange the tutor is Nepali," the cook remarked to Sai when he had left. A bit later he said, "I thought he would be Bengali."

"Hm?" asked Sai. How had she looked? she was thinking. How had she appeared to the tutor? The tutor himself had the aspect, she thought, of intense intelligence. His eyes were serious, his voice deep, but then his lips were too plump to have such a serious expression, and his hair was curly and stood up in a way that made him look comic. This seriousness combined with the comic she found compelling.

"Bengalis," said the cook, "are very intelligent."

"Don't be silly," said Sai. "Although they certainly would agree."

"It's the fish," said the cook. "Coastal people are more intelligent than inland people."

"Who says?"

"Everyone knows," said the cook. "Coastal people eat fish and see how much cleverer they are, Bengalis, Malayalis, Tamils. Inland they eat too much grain, and it slows the digestion—especially millet—forms a big heavy ball. The blood goes to the stomach and not to the head. Nepalis make good soldiers, coolies, but they are not so bright at their studies. Not their fault, poor things."

"Go and eat some fish yourself," Sai said. "One stupid thing after another from your mouth."

"Here I bring you up as my own child with so much love and just see how you are talking to me . . . ," he began.

That night Sai sat and stared into the mirror.

Sitting across from Gyan, she had felt so acutely aware of herself, she was certain it was because of his gaze on her, but every time she glanced up, he was looking in another direction.

She sometimes thought herself pretty, but as she began to make a proper investigation, she found it was a changeable thing, beauty. No sooner did she locate it than it slipped from her grasp; instead of disciplining it, she was unable to refrain from exploiting its flexibility. She stuck her tongue out at herself and rolled her eyes, then smiled beguilingly. She transformed her expression from demon to queen. When she brushed her teeth, she noticed her breasts jiggle like two jellies being rushed to the table. She lowered her mouth to taste the flesh and found it both firm and yielding. This plumpness jiggliness firmness softness, all coupled together in an unlikely manner, must surely give her a certain amount of bartering power?

But if she continued forever in the company of two bandy-legged men, in this house in the middle of nowhere, this beauty, so brief she could barely hold it steady, would fade and expire, unsung, unrescued, and unrescuable.

She looked again and found her face tinged with sadness, and the image seemed faraway.

She'd have to propel herself into the future by whatever means possible or she'd be trapped forever in a place whose time had already passed.

Over the days, she found herself continually obsessed with her own face, aware that she was meanwhile whetting her appetite for something else.

But how did she appear? She searched in the stainless-steel pots, in the polished gompa butter lamps, in the merchants' vessels in the bazaar, in the images proffered by the spoons and knives on the dining table, in the green surface of the pond. Round and fat she was in the spoons, long and thin in the knives, pocked by insects and tiddlers in the pond; golden in one light, ashen in another; back then to the mirror; but the mirror, fickle as ever, showed one thing, then another and left her, as usual, without an answer.

Fourteen

At 4:25 A.M., Biju made his way to the Queen of Tarts bakery, watching for the cops who sometimes came leaping out: where are you going and what are you doing with whom at what time and why?

But Immigration operated independently of Police, the better, perhaps, to bake the morning bread, and Biju fell, again and again, through the cracks in the system.

Above the bakery the subway ran on a rawly sketched edifice upheld by metal stilts. The trains passed in a devilish screaming; their wheels sparked firework showers that at night threw a violent jagged brightness over the Harlem projects, where he could see a few lights on already and some others besides himself making a start on miniature lives. At the Queen of Tarts, the grill went zipping up, the light flickered on, a rat moved into the shadow. Tap root tail, thick skulled, broad shouldered, it looked over its back sneering as it walked with a velvet crunch right over the trap too skimpy to detain it.

"*Namaste, babaji,*" said Saeed Saeed.

Biju considered his previous fight with a Pakistani, the usual attack on the man's religion that he'd grown up uttering: "Pigs, pigs, sons of pigs."

Now here was Saeed Saeed, and Biju's admiration for the man confounded him. Fate worked this way. Biju was overcome by the desire to be his friend, because Saeed Saeed wasn't drowning, he was bobbing in the tides. In fact, a large number of people wished to cling to him like a plank during a shipwreck—not only fellow Zanzibaris and fellow illegals but Americans, too; overweight confidence-leached citizens he teased when they lunched alone on a pizza slice; lonely middle-aged office workers who came by for conversation after nights of lying awake wondering if, in America—*in America!*—they were really getting the best of what was on offer. They told such secrets as perhaps might only be comfortably told to an illegal alien.

Saeed was kind and he was not Paki. Therefore he was OK?

The cow was not an Indian cow; therefore it was not holy?

Therefore he liked Muslims and hated only Pakis?

Therefore he liked Saeed, but hated the general lot of Muslims?

Therefore he liked Muslims and Pakis and India should see it was all wrong and hand over Kashmir?

No, no, how could that be and—

This was but a small portion of the dilemma. He remembered what they said about black people at home. Once a man from his village who worked in the city had said: "Be careful of the *hubshi*. Ha ha, in their own country they live like monkeys in the trees. They come to India and become men."

Biju had thought the man from his village was claiming that India was so far advanced that black men learned to dress and eat when they arrived, but what he had meant was that black men ran about attempting to impregnate every Indian girl they saw.

Therefore he hated all black people but liked Saeed?

Therefore there was nothing wrong with black people and Saeed?

Or Mexicans, Chinese, Japanese, or anyone else . . . ???

This habit of hate had accompanied Biju, and he found that he possessed an awe of white people, who arguably had done India great harm, and a lack of generosity regarding almost everyone else, who had never done a single harmful thing to India.

Presumably Saeed Saeed had encountered the same dilemma regarding Biju.

From other kitchens, he was learning what the world thought of Indians:

In Tanzania, if they could, they would throw them out like they did in Uganda.

In Madagascar, if they could, they would throw them out.

In Nigeria, if they could, they would throw them out.

In Fiji, if they could, they would throw them out.

In China, they hate them.

In Hong Kong.

In Germany.

In Italy.

In Japan.

In Guam.

In Singapore.

Burma.

South Africa.

They don't like them.

In Guadeloupe—they love us there?

No.

Presumably Saeed had been warned of Indians, but he didn't seem wracked by contradictions; a generosity buoyed him and dangled him above such dilemmas.

He had many girls.

"Oh myeee God!!" he said. "Oh myeee Gaaaawd! She keep calling me and calling me," he clutched at head, "*aaaiii* . . . I don't know *what* to do!!"

"You know what to do," said Omar sourly.

"Ha ha ha, ah ah, no, I am going crazeeeeee. Too much pooky pooky, man!"

"It's those dreadlocks, cut them off and the girls will go."

"But I don't want them to *go!*"

When pretty girls came to pick out their cinnamon buns with mine shafts of jeweled brown sugar and spice, Saeed described the beauty and the poverty of Zanzibar, and the girls' compassion rose like leavened loaf—how they wanted to save him, to take him home and lull him with good plumbing and TV; how they wanted to be seen down the road with a tall handsome man topped with dreadlocks. "He's *cute!* He's *cute!* He's *cute!*" they'd say, winding up tight and then wringing out their desire over the telephone to their friends.

Saeed's first job in America had been at the Ninety-sixth Street mosque, where the imam hired him to do the dawn call to prayer, since he did a fine rooster crow, but before he arrived at work, he took to stopping at the nightclubs along the way, it seeming a natural enough progression timewise. Disposable camera in his pocket, he stood at the door waiting to have snapshots of himself taken with the rich and famous: Mike Tyson, yes! He's my brother. Naomi Campbell, she's my girl. Hey, Bruce (Springsteen)! I am Saeed Saeed from Africa. But don't worry, man, we don't eat white people anymore.

There came a time when they began to let him inside.

He had an endless talent with doors, even though, two years ago during an INS raid, he had been unearthed and deported despite having been cheek-to-cheek, Kodak-proof, with the best of America. He went back to Zanzibar, where he was hailed as an American, ate kingfish cooked in coconut milk in the stripy shade of the palm trees, lazed on the sand sieved fine as semolina, and in the evening when the moon went gold and the night shone as if it were wet, he romanced the girls in Stone Town. Their fathers encouraged them to climb out of their windows at night; the girls climbed down the trees and onto Saeed's lap, and the fathers spied, hoping to catch the lovers in a compromising position. This boy who once had so long dawdled on the street corner—no work, all trouble, so much so that the neighbors had all contributed to his ticket out—now this boy was miraculously worth something. They prayed he would be forced to marry Fatma who was fat or Salma who was beautiful or Khadija with the gauzy gray eyes and the voice of a cat. The fathers tried and the girls tried, but Saeed escaped. They gave him *kangas* to remember them by, with slogans, "Memories are like diamonds," and "Your pleasant scent soothes my heart," so that when he was relaxing in NYC, he might throw off his clothes, wrap his *kanga* about him, air his balls, and think of the girls at home. In two months time, back he was—new passport, new name typed up with the help of a few greenbacks given to a clerk outside the government office. When he arrived at JFK as Rasheed Zulfickar, he saw the very same officer who had deported him waiting at the desk. His heart had beat like a fan in his ears, but the man had not remembered him: "Thank God, to them we all of us look the same!"

Saeed, he relished the whole game, the way the country flexed his wits and rewarded him; he charmed it, cajoled it, cheated it, felt great tenderness and loyalty toward it. When it came time, he who had jigged open every back door, he who had, with photocopier, Wite-Out, and paper cutter, spectacularly sabotaged the system (one skilled person at the photocopy machine, he assured Biju, could bring America to its knees), he would pledge emotional allegiance to the flag with tears in his eyes and conviction in his voice. The country recognized something in Saeed, he in it, and it was a mutual love affair. Ups and downs, sometimes more sour than sweet, maybe, but nonetheless, beyond anything the INS could imagine, it was an old-fashioned romance.

By 6 A.M. the bakery shelves were stocked with rye, oatmeal, and peasant bread, apricot and raspberry biscuits that broke open to a flood of lush amber or ruby jam. One such morning, Biju sat outside in a pale patch of sun, with a roll. He cracked the carapace of the crust and began to eat, plucking the tender fleece with his long thin fingers—

But in New York innocence never prevails: an ambulance passed, the NYPD, a fire engine; the subway went overhead and the jolting rhythm traveled up through his defenseless shoes; it shook his heart and sullied the roll. He stopped chewing, thought of his father—

Ill. Dead. Maimed.

He reminded himself his panicked thoughts were just the result of extra virile transport going by, and he searched for the bread in his mouth, but it had parted like an ethereal cloud about his tongue and disappeared.

In Kalimpong, the cook was writing, "Dear Biju, can you please help. . . ."

Last week the MetalBox watchman had paid him a formal visit to tell the cook about his son, big enough now to get a job, but there were no jobs. Could Biju help him across to America? The boy would be willing to start at a menial level but of course a job in an office would be best. Italy would also be all right, he added for good measure. A man from his village had gone to Italy and was making a good living as a tandoori cook.

At first the cook was agitated, upset by the request, felt a war in him between generosity and meanness, but then . . . : "Why not, I will ask him, very difficult, mind you, but there is no harm in trying."

And, he began to feel a tingle—the very fact the watchman had asked! It reestablished Biju in his father's eyes as a fine-suited-and-booted-success.

They sat outside his quarter and smoked; and it felt good to be two old men sitting together, talking of young men. The deadly nightshade was blooming, giant glowing bell flowers, white and starched, sinister and spotless. A star came forth and a lost cow wandered slowly by in the dusk.

So, the further to bolster his son and his own pride, the cook wrote on the blue airmail form: "Dear *beta*, please see if you can help the MetalBox watchman's son."

He went to bed snug and glad, only at one moment waking in terror at a thud, but it was just the lost cow that had come back up through the ravine and was trying to push her way in out of the rain. He chased her out, brought back the thought of his son, and thus reconnected with his peace, returned to sleep.

A petition improved your status.

The green card, the green card—

Saeed applied for the immigration lottery each year, but Indians were not allowed to apply. Bulgarians, Irish, Malagasys—on and on the list went, but no, no Indians. There were just too many jostling to get out, to pull everyone else down, to climb on one another's backs and run. The line would be stopped up for years, the quota was full, overfull, spilling over.

At the bakery, they called the immigration hotline as soon as the clock struck 8:30 and took turns holding the receiver for what might be an all-day activity of line holding.

"What is your status now, sir? I can't help you unless I know your current status."

They put down the phone hurriedly then, worried that immigration had a superduper zing bing beep peeping high-alert electronic supersonic space speed machine that could

transfer

connect

dial

read

trace the number through to their—

Illegality.

Oh the green card, the green card, the—

Biju was so restless sometimes, he could barely stand to stay in his skin. After work, he crossed to the river, not to the part where the dogs played madly in hanky-sized squares, with their owners in the fracas picking up feces, but to where, after singles night at the synagogue, long-skirted-and-sleeved girls walked in an old-fashioned manner with old-fashioned-looking men wearing black suits and hats as if they had to keep their past with them at all times so as not to lose it. He walked to the far end where the homeless man often slept in a dense chamber of green that seemed to grow not so much from soil as from a fertile city crud. A homeless chicken also lived in the park. Every now and then Biju saw it scratching in a homey manner in the dirt and felt a pang for village life.

"Chkchkchk," he called to it, but it ran away immediately, flustered

in the endearing way of a plain girl, shy and convinced of the attractions of virtue.

He walked to where the green ran out into a tail of pilings and where men like himself often sat on the rocks and looked out onto a dull stretch of New Jersey. Peculiar boats went by: garbage barges, pug-nosed tugboats with their snoots pushing big-bottomed coal carriers; others whose purpose was not obvious—all rusty cranes, cogs, black smoke flaring out.

Biju couldn't help but feel a flash of anger at his father for sending him alone to this country, but he knew he wouldn't have forgiven his father for not trying to send him, either.

Fifteen

In Kalimpong, the plum tree outside the clinic, watered with rotted blood from the path lab, produced so many flowers, that newlyweds had their pictures taken on a bench underneath. Disregarding one couple's entreaties to remove himself from their photo shoot, the cook settled down at the end of the bench, donning his spectacles to read the letter from Biju that had just arrived.

"I have a new job in a bakery and the boss leaves us in complete charge. . . ."

It was *haat* day in Kalimpong and a festive crowd thronged to the market in a high pitch of excitement, everyone in their best clothes.

The cook folded up the letter and put it in his shirt pocket. Feeling joyful, he descended steeply into the *haat,* pushing his way between bent and bowed Nepali ladies with golden nose rings dangling and Tibetan women with braids and prayer beads, between those who had walked from faraway villages to sell muddy mushrooms covered with brackish leaves or greenery, already half cooked in the sun. Powders, oils, and ganglions of roots were proffered by Lepcha medicine men; other stalls offered yak hair, untidy and rough as the hair of demons, and sacks of miniature dried shrimp with oversized whiskers; there were smuggled foreign goods from Nepal, perfumes, jean jackets, electronics; there were kukri sickles, sheets of plastic rainproofing, and false teeth.

When the cook and judge had first arrived in Kalimpong, wool caravans were still coming through, chaperoned by Tibetan muleteers in furry boots, earrings swinging, and the earthy smell of men and beasts had run a hot current against that exquisite scent of pine that people like Lola and Noni came from Calcutta to sample. The cook remembered yaks carrying over two hundred pounds of salt and, balanced on the top, rosy babies stuffed in cooking pots, chewing on squares of dried *churbi* cheese.

"My son works in New York," the cook boasted to everyone he met. "He is the manager of a restaurant business.

"New York. Very big city," he explained. "The cars and buildings are nothing like here. In that country, there is enough food for everybody."

"When are you going, Babaji?"

"One day," he laughed. "One day soon my son will take me."

Dried azalea and juniper lay bundled in newspaper packages. He remembered the day the Dalai and Panchen Lamas came to Kalimpong, and they had burnt this incense all along the path. The cook had been in the crowd. He was not Buddhist, of course, but had gone in a secular spirit. The muffled thunder of prayer rumbled down the mountain as the mules and horses stepped pom-pommed out of the fog, bells singing, prayer flags flying from the saddles. The cook had prayed for Biju and gone to bed feeling pious, so sparkily so that he felt clean although he knew he was dirty.

Now he walked through the greasy bus station with its choking smell of exhaust and past the dark cubbyhole where, behind a soiled red curtain, you could pay to watch on a shaking screen such films as *Rape of Erotic Virgin* and *SHE: The Secrets of Married Life*.

Nobody here would be interested in the cook's son.

At the Snow Lion Travel Agency, the cook waited to claim the manager's attention. Tashi was busy chatting up a tourist—he was famous for charming the Patagonia pants off foreign women and giving them an opportunity to write home with the requisite tale of amorous adventure with a sherpa. All around were brochures for the monastery trips Tashi organized, photographs of hotels built in the traditional style, furnished with antiques, many of which had been taken from the monasteries themselves. Of course he omitted the fact that the centuries-old structures were all being modernized with concrete, fluorescent lighting, and bathroom tiling.

"When you go to America, take me along also," said Tashi after he had sold the tourist a trip to Sikkim.

"Yes, yes. I will take us all. Why not? That country has lots of room. It's this country that is so crowded."

"Do not worry, I am saving my money to buy a ticket, and how are you, how is your health?" Biju had written. One day his son would accomplish all that Sai's parents had failed to do, all the judge had failed to do.

The cook walked by the Apollo Deaf Tailors. No point saying anything there, since they would literally turn a deaf ear just as they did to customer complaints after they'd made a hash of everything, stripes horizontal instead of vertical, the judge's clothes made in Sai's size and Sai's clothes made in the judge's size.

He went into Lark's Store for Tosh's tea, egg noodles, and Milkmaid condensed milk. He told the doctor, who had come in to collect the vaccines that she stored in the Lark's fridge, "My son has a new job in U.S.A." Her son was there as well. He shared this with a doctor! The most distinguished personage in town.

Walking home in the dusk, he told those catching their breath from carrying heavy loads uphill, resting right on the road, where mud and grass wouldn't spoil their good clothes. When a car came by they got up; when it passed they settled back again.

He told Mrs. Sen, who, of course, also had a child in America: "Best country in the world. All these people who went to England are now feeling sorry. . . ." Her hand gestured significantly to the house of her neighbors at Mon Ami. The cook then went and told Lola, who hated a challenge to England but was kind to him, because he was poor; it was only Mrs. Sen's daughter who was a threat to be lopped off at the neck. He told the Afghan princesses, who paid him to deliver them a chicken each time he went to the market. They boiled the chicken the same day, since they had no fridge, and each day until it was gone, they recooked a portion in a different style—curried, in soy sauce, in cheese sauce, and, at that blissful time when, overnight, gardens all over Kalimpong came up in mushrooms, in mushroom sauce with a bottlecapful of brandy.

He told the monks playing football outside the *gompa,* hitching up their robes. He told Uncle Potty and Father Booty. They were dancing on the veranda, Uncle Potty at the light switch turning it on off on off on off. "What did you say?" they said, turning down the music to listen. "Good for him!" They raised their glasses and turned up the music again: "Jambalaya . . . pumpkin pie-a . . . *mio maio*. . . ."

Then the cook stopped at the last stall for potatoes. He always bought them here so he didn't have to carry them all the way, and he found the daughter of the owner at the counter dressed in a long nightie, as had become the fashion. You saw women everywhere in nighties, daughters, wives, grandmothers, nieces, walking to the shops, collecting water in broad daylight as if on their way to bed, long hair, ruffly garments, making a beautiful dream scene in daylight.

She was a lovely girl, small and plump, a glimpse through the nightie placket of breasts so buttery that even women who saw them were captivated. And she seemed sensible in the shop. Surely Biju would like her? The girl's father was making money, so they said. . . .

"Three kilos potatoes," he told the girl in a voice unusually gentle for him. "What about rice? Is it clean?"

"No, Uncle," she said. "What we have is very dirty. It's so full of little stones you'll crack your teeth if you eat it."

"What about the *atta?*"

"The *atta* is better."

Anyway, he said to himself, money wasn't everything. There was that simple happiness of looking after someone and having someone look after you.

Sixteen

When Sai became interested in love, she became interested in other people's love affairs, and she pestered the cook about the judge and his wife.

The cook said: "When I joined the household, all the old servants told me that the death of your grandmother made a cruel man out of your grandfather. She was a great lady, never raised her voice to the servants. How much he loved her! In fact, it was such a deep attachment, it turned one's stomach, for it was too much for anybody else to look upon."

"Did he really love her so very much?" Sai was astonished.

"Must have," said the cook. "But they said he didn't show it."

"Maybe he didn't?" she then suggested.

"Bite your tongue, you evil girl. Take your words back!" shouted the cook. "Of course he loved her."

"How did the servants know, then?"

The cook thought a bit, thought of his own wife. "True," he said. "Nobody really knew, but no one said anything in those days, for there are many ways of showing love, not just the way of the movies—which is all you know. You are a very foolish girl. The greatest love is love that's never shown."

"You say anything that suits you."

"Yes, I've found it's the best way," said the cook after thinking some more.

"So? Did he or didn't he?"

The cook and Sai were sitting with Mutt on the steps leading to the garden, picking the ticks off her, and this was always an hour of contentment for them. The large khaki-bag ones were easy to dispatch, but the tiny brown ticks were hard to kill; they flattened against the depressions in the rock, so when you hit them with a stone, they didn't die but in a flash were up and running.

Sai chased them up and down. "Don't run away, don't you dare climb back on Mutt."

Then they tried to drown them in a can of water, but they were tough, swam about, climbed on one another's backs and crawled out. Sai chased them down again, put them back in the can, rushed to the toilet, and flushed them, but even then they resurfaced, doing a mad-scrabble swim in the toilet bowl.

Remembrance, now authentic, shone from the cook's eyes.

"Oh no," said the cook. "He didn't like her at all. She went mad."

"She did?!"

"Yes, they said she was a very mad lady."

"Who was she?"

"I've forgotten the name, but she was the daughter of a rich man and the family was of much higher standing than your grandfather, of a particular branch of a caste that in itself was not high, of course, as you know, but within this group, they had distinguished themselves. You could tell from her features, which were delicate; her toes, nose, ears, and fingers were all very fine and small, and she was very fair—just like milk. Complexion-wise, they said, you could have mistaken her for a foreigner. Her family only married among fifteen families, but an exception was made for your grandfather because he was in the ICS. But more than that I do not know."

"Who was my grandmother?" Sai then asked the judge sitting poised like a heron over his chessboard. "Did she come from a very fancy family?"

He said: "I'm playing chess, can't you see?"

He looked back at the board, and then he got up and walked into the garden. Flying squirrels chased one another through the circination of ferns and mist; the mountains were like ibex horns piercing through. He returned to his chessboard and made his move, but it felt like an old move in an old game.

He didn't want to think of her, but the picture that came to mind was surprisingly gentle.

The Patels had been dreaming of sending their son to England, but there wasn't enough money no matter how much Jemu's father worked, so they visited the moneylenders, who surveyed father and son with the sleepiness of crocodiles and then pounced with an offer of ten thousand rupees. At 22 percent interest.

There still wasn't enough, though, and they began to search for a bride.

Jemu would be the first boy of their community to go to an English university. The dowry bids poured in and his father began an exhilarated weighing and tallying: ugly face—a little more gold, a pale skin—a little less. A dark and ugly daughter of a rich man seemed their best bet.

On the other side of Piphit, by the military cantonment, lived a short man with a rhinocerous-like nose that seemed to travel up, not down, who carried a malacca cane, wore a long coat of brocade, and lived in a *haveli* carved so delicately it seemed weightless. This was Bomanbhai Patel. It was his father who had discreetly helped the right side in a certain skirmish between the English and the Gaekwads, and he was repaid by the regimental quartermaster with a contract to be the official supplier of horse feed to the British military encampment at Piphit. Eventually, the family had monopolized the delivery of all dry goods to the army, and when Bomanbhai succeeded his father, he saw the way to greater profit yet by extending his business seamlessly into another. He offered soldiers unauthorized women in an unauthorized part of town on whom they might spend their aggrandizement of manhood; returned them to their barracks strewn about with black hairs, and smelling like rabbits from a rabbit hutch.

Bomanbhai's own wife and daughters, however, were kept carefully locked up behind the high walls of the *haveli* outside which a plaque read:

"Residence of Bomanbhai Patel, Military Purveyor, Financier, Merchant." Here they lived an idle existence inside the women's quarters, the strictness of this purdah enforcement increasing Bomanbhai's honor in the community, and he began to acquire little fancies and foibles, to cultivate certain eccentricities that, just as he plotted, reiterated the security of his wealth and reinforced his honor all over again. He displayed his purchases, his habits casually but planned them with exactitude—acquired his trademark coat of brocade, his polished cane and kept a pet pangolin, since he had an affinity with all big-nosed creatures. He ordered a set of stained-glass panes that flooded the *haveli* with luscious multi-fruit-colored light under which the children played, entertained by how they might look orange or purple or half orange and half green.

Traveling Chinamen selling lace and silk waited outside as their wares were taken to the women for inspection. Jewelers brought rare pieces for the daughters' dowries, heirlooms being sold by a bankrupt raja. Bomanbhai's wife's earlobes lengthened with the weight of South African diamonds, so great, so heavy, that one day, from one ear, an earring ripped through, a meteor disappearing with a bloody clonk into her bowl of *srikhand*.

But the zenith of triumph came when he, nothing but a tin shack shopkeeper by origin, but richer than all the Brahmins in town, hired a Brahmin cook who upheld the laws of pollution so strictly that should you even utter *"eendoo,"* egg, in the kitchen, every pot and pan, every spoon would have to be washed, all the food thrown away.

One day a group of men almost quacking in their excitement, crowded in to see Bomanbhai and told him of Jemu's imminent departure for England. Bomanbhai's eyebrows drew together as he mulled over the information, but he said nothing, sipped a little Exshaw No. 1 brandy with hot water in a Venetian goblet.

Ambition still gnawed at him, and Brahmin cook he might have, but he knew that there was a wider world and only very rarely did history provide a chink allowing an acrobatic feat. A week later, he got into his landau drawn by two white mares, drove past the British Club on Thornton Road he could never join no matter how much money he had in his pocket, all the way to the other side of town, and there, he stunned the residents of the Patel warren with the offer of Bela, his most beautiful daughter, who lay with her sisters in their big bed complaining of boredom under a crystal chandelier that provided the luxurious look of ice in the summer heat.

If Jemu succeeded in his endeavor, she would be the wife of one of the most powerful men in India.

The wedding party lasted a week and was so opulent that nobody in Piphit could doubt but the family lived a life awash in ghee and gold, so when Bomanbhai bent over with a *namaste* and begged his guests to eat and drink, they knew his modesty was false—and of the best kind, therefore. The bride was a polished light-reflecting hillock of jewels, barely able to walk under the gem and metal weight she carried. The dowry included cash, gold, emeralds from Venezuela, rubies from Burma, uncut *kundun* diamonds, a watch on a watch chain, lengths of woolen cloth for her new husband to make into suits in which to travel to England, and in a crisp envelope, a ticket for passage on the SS *Strathnaver* from Bombay to Liverpool.

When she married, her name was changed into the one chosen by Jemubhai's family, and in a few hours, Bela became Nimi Patel.

Jemubhai, made brave by alcohol and the thought of his ticket, attempted to pull off his wife's sari, as much gold as silk, as she sat on the edge of the bed, just as his younger uncles had advised him, smacking him on the back.

He was almost surprised to discover a face beneath the gilded lump. It was strung with baubles, but even they could not entirely disguise the fourteen-year-old crying in terror: "Save me," she wept.

He himself was immediately terrified, frightened by her fright. The spell of arrogance broken, he retreated to his meek self. "Don't cry," he said in a panic, trying to undo the damage. "Listen, I'm not looking, I'm not even looking at you." He returned the heavy fabric to her, bundled it back over her head, but she continued to sob.

Next morning, the uncles laughed. "What happened? Nothing?" They gestured at the bed.

More laughter the next day.

The third day, worry.

"Force her," the uncles urged him. "Insist. Don't let her behave badly."

"Other families would not be so patient," they warned Nimi.

"Chase her and pin her down," the uncles ordered Jemubhai.

Though he felt provoked, and sometimes recognized a focused and defined urge in himself, in front of his wife, the desire vanished.

"Spoiled," they said to Nimi. "Putting on airs."

How could she not be happy with their brainy Jemu, the first boy from their community to go to England?

But Jemubhai began to feel sorry for her, as well as for himself, as they shared this ordeal of inaction through one night and another.

While the family was out selling the jewels for extra money, he offered her a ride on his father's Hercules cycle. She shook her head, but when he rode up, a child's curiosity conquered her commitment to tears and she climbed on sideways. "Stick your legs out," he instructed and worked away at the pedals. They went faster and faster, between the trees and cows, whizzing through the cow pats.

Jemubhai turned, caught quick sight of her eyes—oh, no man had eyes like these or looked out on the world this way. . . .

He pedaled harder. The ground sloped, and as they flew down the incline, their hearts were left behind for an instant, levitating amid green leaves, blue sky.

The judge looked up from his chess. Sai had climbed up a tree at the garden's edge. From its branches you could look onto the road curving down below and she would be able to catch Gyan's approach.

Each succeeding week of mathematics tutoring, the suspense was growing until they could barely sit in the same room without desiring to flee. She had a headache. He had to leave early. They made excuses, but the minute they left each other's company, they were restless and curiously angry, and they waited again for the following Tuesday, anticipation rising unbearably.

The judge walked over.

"Get down."

"Why?"

"It's making Mutt nervous to see you up there."

Mutt looked up at Sai, wagged, not a shadow crossed her eyes.

"Really?" said Sai.

"I hope that tutor of yours doesn't get any funny ideas," said the judge, then.

"What funny ideas?"

"Get down at once."

Sai got down and went indoors and shut herself up in her room. One day she would leave this place.

"Time should move," Noni had told her. "Don't go in for a life where time doesn't pass, the way I did. That is the single biggest bit of advice I can give you."

Seventeen

Saeed Saeed caught a mouse at the Queen of Tarts, kicked it up with his shoe, dribbled it, tried to exchange it with Biju, who ran away, tossed it up, and as it came down, kicked it squeaking up again, laughing, "So it is *you* who has been eating eating the bread, eh, it is *you* eating the sugar?" It went hysterically up until it came down dead. Fun over. Back to work.

In Kalimpong, the cook was writing on an airmail form. He wrote in Hindi and then copied out the address in awkward English letters.

He was being besieged by requests for help. The more they asked the more they came the more they asked—Lamsang, Mr. Lobsang Phuntsok, Oni, Mr. Shezoon of the *Lepcha Quarterly*, Kesang, the hospital cleaner, the lab technician responsible for the tapeworm in formaldehyde, the man who plugged the holes in rusting pots, everyone with sons in the queue ready to be sent. They brought him chickens as gifts, little packets of nuts or raisins, offered him a drink at Ex-Army Thapa's Canteen, and he was beginning to feel as if he were a politician, a bestower of favors, a receiver of thanks.

The more pampered you are the more pampered you will be the more presents you receive the more presents you will get the more presents you receive the more you are admired the more you will be admired the more you are admired the more presents you will get the more pampered you will be—

"Bhai, dekho, aesa hai . . ." he would begin to lecture them. "Look, you have to have some luck, it is almost impossible to get a visa. . . ." It was superhumanly difficult, but he would write to his son. "Let's see, let's see, perhaps you will get lucky. . . ."

"Biju beta," he wrote, "you have been fortunate enough to get there, please do something for the others. . . ."

Then he applied a homemade mucilage of flour and water to glue down the sides of the airmail forms, sent them finning their way over the Atlantic, a whole shoal of letters. . . .

They would never know how many of them went astray in all the rickety connections made along the way, between the temperamental postman in the pouring rain, the temperamental van across the landslides on the way to Siliguri, the lightning and thunder, the befogged airport, the journey from Calcutta all the way to the post office on 125th street in Harlem that was barricaded like an Israeli army outpost in Gaza. The mailman abandoned the letters atop the boxes of legal residents, and sometimes the letters fell, were trampled, and tracked back outdoors.

But enough came through that Biju felt he might drown.

"Very bright boy, family very poor, please look after him, he already has a visa, will be arriving. . . . Please find a job for Poresh. In fact, even his brother is ready to go. Help them. Sanjeeb Thom Karma Ponchu, and remember Budhoo, watchman at Mon Ami, his son. . . ."

"I know, man, I know how you feel," Saeed said.

Saeed Saeed's mother was dispensing his phone number and address freely to half of Stone Town. They arrived at the airport with one dollar in their pocket and his phone number, seeking admittance to an apartment that was bursting with men already, every scrap rented out: Rashid Ahmed Jaffer Abdullah Hassan Musa Lutfi Ali and a whole lot of others sharing beds in shifts.

"More tribes, more tribes. I wake up, go to the window, and there—MORE TRIBES. Every time I look—ANOTHER TRIBE. Everybody saying, 'Oh, no visas anymore, they are getting very strict, it so hard,' and in the meantime everybody who apply, EVERYBODY is getting a visa. Why they do this to me? That American Embassy in Dar—WHY??!! Nobody would give that Dooli a visa. Nobody. One look and you would say OK, something wrong here—but they give it to *him!*"

Saeed cooked cow peas and kingfish from the Price Chopper to cheer himself up, and plantains in sugar and coconut milk. This goo mixture smelling of hope so ripe he slathered on French bread and offered to the others.

The sweetest fruit in all of Stone Town grew in the graveyard, and the finest bananas grew from the grandfather's grave of that same wayward Dooli whom the American Embassy in Dar es Salaam had so severely misjudged as to give him a visa—so Saeed was telling them when he glanced out of the window—

And in a second he was under the counter.

"Oh myeeee God!" Whispering. "Tribes, man, *it's the tribes.* Please God. Tell them I don't work here. *How they get this address!* My mother! I told her, 'No more!' *Please!* Omar, Go! Go! *Go tell them to leave."*

Outside the bakery stood a group of men, looking weary as if they'd been traveling several lifetimes, scratching their heads and staring at the Queen of Tarts.

"Why do you help?" asked Omar. "I stopped helping and now they all know I won't help and nobody comes to me."

"This is not the *time* to give a lecture."

Omar went out. "Who? *Saaeed?* No, no. What name? *Soyad?* No, no one of that name. Just me, Kavafya, and Biju."

"But he work here. His mother tell us."

"No. No. You all get moving. Nobody here who you want to see and if you make trouble WE get into trouble so now I ask you nicely, GO."

"Very good," said Saeed, "thank you. They have gone?"

"No."

"What are they doing?"

"They are still standing and looking," said Biju feeling brave and excited by someone else's misfortune. He was almost hopping.

The men were shaking their heads unwilling to believe what they'd heard.

Biju went out and came back in. "They say they will try your home address now." He felt a measure of pride in delivering this vital news. Realized he missed playing this sort of role that was common in India. One's involvement in other peoples' lives gave one numerous small opportunities for importance.

"They will come back. *I know them*. They will try many more times, or one will stay and the others will go. Close the door, close the window. . . ."

"We can't close the shop. Too hot, can't close the window."

"Close it!"

"No. What if Mr. Bocher visit us?" He was the owner who dropped by at odd moments hoping to surprise them doing something against the rules.

"No sweati, bossi," Saeed would tell him. "We do everything you tell us just like you tell us. . . ."

But now. . . .

"It's my life we're talking about, man, not little hot here and little hot there, boss or no boss. . . ."

They closed the window and the door, and from the floor he telephoned his apartment. "Hey Ahmed, don't answer the phone, man, that Dooli and all them boys have come from the airport! Lock up, stay down, don't stand, and don't go near the window."

"Hah! Why they give them a visa? How they buy the ticket!" They could hear the voice at the other end. Then it vanished into Swahili in a potent dungform, a rich, steaming animal evacuation.

The phone rang in the bakery.

"Don't answer," he said to Biju who was reaching for it.

When the answering machine came on, it went off.

"The tribes! They always *scared* of the answering machine!"

It rang again and then again. *Tring tring tring tring*. Answering machine. Phone down.

Again: *tring tring*.

"Saeed, you have to talk to them." Biju's heart was suddenly pulsing with the anguish of the ringing. It could be the boss, it could be India on the line, his father his father—

Dead? Dying? Diseased?

Kavafya picked it up and a voice projected into the room raw and insistent with panic. "Emergency! Emergency! We are coming from airport. *Emergency! Emergency! Saaeed S-aa-eed?*"

He put it down and unplugged it.

Saeed: "Those boys, let them in, they will *never* leave. They are desperate. *Desperate.* Once you let them in, once you hear their story, you can't say no, you know their aunty, you know their cousin, you have to help the *whole* family, and once they begin, they will take *everything.* You can't say this is my food, like Americans, and only I will eat it. Ask Thea"—she was the latest pooky pooky interest in the bakery—"where she live with three *friends,* everyone go shopping *separately, separately* they cook their dinner, *together* they eat their *separate* food. The fridge they divide up, and into their own place—*their own place!*—they put what is left in a *separate box.* One of the roommates, she put her *name on the box so it say who it belong to!*" His finger went up in uncharacteristic sternness. "In Zanzibar what one person have *he have to share with everyone,* that is *good,* that is the *right way—*

"But then everyone have nothing, man! That is why I leave Zanzibar."

Silence.

Biju's sympathy for Saeed leaked into sympathy for himself, then Saeed's shame into his own shame that he would never help all those people praying for his help, waiting daily, *hourly,* for his response. He, too, had arrived at the airport with a few dollar bills bought on the Kathmandu black market in his pocket and an address for his father's friend, Nandu, who lived with twenty-two taxi drivers in Queens. Nandu had also not answered the phone and had tried to hide when Biju arrived on his doorstep, and then when he thought Biju had left, had opened the door and to his distress found Biju still standing there two hours later.

"No jobs here anymore," he said. "If I were a young man I would go back to India, more opportunities there now, too late for me to make a change, but you should listen to what I'm saying. Everyone says you *have* to stay, this is where you'll make a good life, but much better for you to *go back.*"

Nandu met someone at his work who told him of the basement in

Harlem and ever since he had deposited Biju there, Biju had never seen him again.

He had been abandoned among foreigners: Jacinto the superintendent, the homeless man, a stiff bow-legged coke runner, who walked as if his balls were too big for normal walking, with his stiff yellow bow-legged dog, who also walked as if his balls were too big for normal walking. In the summer, families moved out of cramped quarters and sat on the sidewalk with boom boxes; women of great weight and heft appeared in shorts with shaven legs, stippled with tiny black dots, and groups of deflated men sat at cards on boards balanced atop garbage cans, swigged their beer from bottles held in brown paper bags. They nodded kindly at him, sometimes they even offered him a beer, but Biju did not know what to say to them, even his tiny brief "Hello" came out wrong: too softly, so they did not hear, or just as they had turned away.

The green card the green card. The. . . .

Without it he couldn't leave. To leave he wanted a green card. This was the absurdity. How he desired the triumphant After The Green Card Return Home, thirsted for it—to be able to buy a ticket with the air of someone who could return if he wished, or not, if he didn't wish. . . . He watched the legalized foreigners with envy as they shopped at discount baggage stores for the miraculous, expandable third-world suitcase, accordion-pleated, filled with pockets and zippers to unhook further crannies, the whole structure unfolding into a giant space that could fit in enough to set up an entire life in another country.

Then, of course, there were those who lived and died illegal in America and never saw their families, not for ten years, twenty, thirty, never again.

How did one do it? At the Queen of Tarts, they watched the TV shows on Sunday mornings on the Indian channel that showcased an immigration lawyer fielding questions.

A taxi driver appeared on the screen: watching bootleg copies of American movies he had been inspired to come to America, but how to move into the mainstream? He was illegal, his taxi was illegal, the yellow paint was illegal, his whole family was here, and all the men in his village were here, perfectly infiltrated and working within the cab system of the city. But how to get their papers? Would any viewer out there wish to marry him? Even a disabled or mentally retarded green card holder would be fine—

It was, of course, Saeed Saeed who found out about the van and took Omar, Kavafya, and Biju to Washington Heights, and there they waited on a street corner. All the shops had grills, even the little chewing gum and cigarette places. The pharmacies and liquor stores had buzzers; he saw people ringing, gaining admittance into a cage set into the shop from where you could survey the shelves and point to what you wanted, and after money had been placed in the revolving tray set into a little hole carved out of the grill and the bullet proof glass, purchased objects would be sent grudgingly around. Even in the Jamaican patty place, the lady, the patties, the callaloo and rotis, the Drinks Nice Every Time—sat behind a high-security barricade.

Still, it was jolly. Many people thronged by. Outside the Church of Zion, a preacher baptized a whole line of people in the spray of a fire hydrant. A man emerged in a Florida hibiscus shorts-and-shirt combo, thin knobby knees, crinkly pomaded hair, little square Charlie Chaplin–Hitler mustache, carrying a tape player, *"Guantanamera . . . guajira Guantanamera. . . ."* A pair of saucy women hailed him from the windows: "Oooo BABY! Look at them l e g s! *Oooooooo weeee!* You free tonight?"

Another lady was giving advice to a younger woman who accompanied her: "Life is short, sweetheart—Put him out with the garbage! You are young, you should be happy! Poot! heem! out! weeth! de! gar-baje!"

Saeed was at home here. He lived two streets up and many people hailed him on the street.

"Saeed!"

A boy with a gold chain as fat as a bathtub attachment, his prosperity flashing out, slapped Saeed on the back. . . .

"What does he do?" Biju asked about the boy.

Saeed laughed. "Hustling."

To further chili-pepper the occasion, Saeed regaled them with a story of how he had been helping one of the tribes move; and a car stopped while they were struggling with boxes of patched clothes, an alarm clock, shoes, a blackened pot all the way from Zanzibar thrown into the suitcase by a tearful mother—and a gun came out of the car window and a voice said:

"Put it in the back, boys." The trunk opened, and "That's all?" the voice behind the gun said in disgust. Then the car had driven off.

They waited at the corner, sweating away, my God, my God. . . . Finally a battered van came by and they paid into the cracked open door, handed over their photographs taken according to INS requirements showing a single bared ear and a three-quarter profile, and were thumbprinted through the crack. Two weeks later, they waited once more—

they waited—

and waited—

and. . . . The van did not come back. The cost of this endeavor once again emptied Biju's savings envelope.

Omar suggested they console themselves since they were in the neighborhood.

Kavafya said he would join him.

Only thirty-five dollars.

Prices not raised.

Biju blushed to remember what he had said in his hot dog days. "Smell awful . . . black women. . . . *Hubshi hubshi*."

"It's too hot," he said, "for me to go."

They laughed.

"Saeed?"

But Saeed didn't have to go to whores.

He was meeting a new pooky pooky.

"What happened to Thea?" asked Biju.

"She has gone for hiking outside the city. I told her, 'AFRICAN MEN don't look at leaves!!' Anyway, man, I still have one or two pooky pookies that Thea don't know about."

"You better watch out," said Omar. "White women, they look good when they're young, but wait, they fall apart fast, by forty they look so ugly, hair falling out, lines everywhere, and those spots and those veins, you know what I'm talking about. . . ."

Saeed said, "Ah ah ah ha ha, I know, I know." He understood their jealousy.

At the bakery a customer found an entire mouse baked inside a sunflower loaf. It must have gone after the seeds. . . .

A team of health inspectors arrived. They entered in the style of U.S. Marines, the FBI, the CIA, the NYPD; burst in: HANDS UP!

They found a burst sewage pipe, a hiccuping black drain, knives stored behind the toilet, rat droppings in the flour, and in a forgotten basin of eggs, single-celled organisms so comfortable they were reproducing on their own without inspiration from another.

The boss, Mr. Bocher, was called.

"The friggin' electricity blew," said Mr. Bocher, "it's hot outside, what the fuck are we supposed to do?"

But the same episode had occurred twice, in the days before Biju, Saeed, Omar, and Kavafya when there had been Karim, Nedim, and Jesus. The Queen of Tarts would be closed in favor of a Russian establishment.

"Fucking Russians! Crazy borscht and shit!" shouted Mr. Bocher in anger, but to no avail, and abruptly, it was all over again. "Fuck you, you fuckers," he yelled at the men who had worked for him.

"Come and visit uptown sometime, Biju man." Saeed quickly found employment at a Banana Republic, where he would sell to urban sophisticates the black turtleneck of the season, in a shop whose name was synonymous with colonial exploitation and the rapacious ruin of the third world.

Biju knew he probably wouldn't see him again. This was what happened, he had learned by now. You lived intensely with others, only to have them disappear overnight, since the shadow class was condemned to movement. The men left for other jobs, towns, got deported, returned home, changed names. Sometimes someone came popping around a corner again, or on the subway, then they vanished again. Adresses, phone numbers did not hold. The emptiness Biju felt returned to him over and over, until eventually he made sure not to let friendships sink deep anymore.

Lying on his basement shelf that night, he thought of his village where he had lived with his grandmother on the money his father sent each month. The village was buried in silver grasses that were taller than a man and made a sound, *shuu shuuuu*, *shu shuuu*, as the wind turned them this way and that. Down a dry gully through the grasses, you reached a tributary of the Jamuna where you could watch men traveling downstream on inflated buffalo skins, the creatures' very dead legs, all four, sticking straight up as they sailed along, and where the river scalloped shallow over the stones, they got out and dragged their buffalo skin boats over. Here, at this shallow place, Biju and his grandmother would cross on market trips into town and back, his grandmother with her sari tucked up, sometimes a sack of rice on her head. Fishing eagles hovered above the water, changed their horizontal glide within a single moment, plunged, rose sometimes with a thrashing muscle of silver. A hermit also lived on this bank, positioned like a stork, waiting, oh waiting, for the glint of another, an elusive mystical fish; when it surfaced he must pounce lest it be lost again and never return. . . . On Diwali the holy man lit lamps and put them in the branches of the *peepul* tree and sent them down the river on rafts with marigolds—how beautiful the sight of those lights bobbing in that young dark. When he had visited his father in Kalimpong, they had sat outside in the evenings and his father had reminisced: "How peaceful our village is. How good the roti tastes there! It is because the *atta* is ground by hand, not by machine . . . and because it is made on a *choolah*, better than anything cooked on a gas or a kerosene stove. . . . Fresh roti, fresh butter, fresh milk still warm from the buffalo. . . ." They had stayed up late. They hadn't noticed Sai, then aged thirteen, staring from her bedroom window, jealous of the cook's love for his son. Small red-mouthed bats drinking from the *jhora* had swept over again and again in a witch flap of black wings.

Eighteen

"Oh, bat, bat," said Lola, panicking, as one swooped by her ear with its high-pitched *choo choo.*

"What does it matter, just a bit of shoe leather flying about," said Noni, looking, in her pale summer sari, as if she were a blob of melting vanilla ice cream. . . .

"Oh shut up," said Lola.

"It's too hot and stuffy," Lola said then, by way of apology to her sister. The monsoon must be on its way.

It was just two months after Gyan had arrived to teach Sai, and Sai had at first confused the tension in the air with his presence.

But now everyone was complaining. Uncle Potty sat limply. "It's building. Early this year. Better get me rum in, dolly, before the old boy is marooooooned."

Lola sipped a Disprin that fizzed and hopped in the water.

When the papers, too, reported the approach of storm clouds, she became quite merry: "I *told* you. I can always *tell.* I've always been very sensitive. You know how I am—the princess and the pea—my dear, what can I say—the princess and the pea."

At Cho Oyu, the judge and Sai sat out on the lawn. Mutt, catching sight of the shadow of her own tail, leapt and caught it, began to whizz around and around, confused as to whose tail it was. She would not let go, but her eyes expressed confusion and beseeching—how could she stop? what should she do?—she had caught a strange beast and didn't know it was herself. She went skittering helplessly about the garden.

"Silly girl," said Sai.

"Little pearl," said the judge when Sai left, in case Mutt's feelings had been bruised.

Then, in a flash, it was upon them. An anxious sound came from the banana trees as they began to flap their great ears for they were always the first to sound the alarm. The masts of bamboo were flung together and rang with the sound of an ancient martial art.

In the kitchen, the cook's calendar of gods began to kick on the wall as if it were alive, a plethora of arms, legs, demonic heads, blazing eyes.

The cook clamped everything shut, doors and windows, but then Sai opened the door just as he was sifting the flour to get rid of the weevils, and up the flour gusted and covered them both.

"Ooof ho. Look what you've done." Little burrowing insects ran free and overexcitedly on the floor and walls. Looking at each other covered with white, they began to laugh.

"*Angrez ke tarah*. Like the English."

"*Angrez ke tarah. Angrez jaise.*"

Sai put her head out. "Look," she said, feeling jolly, "just like English people."

The judge began to cough as an acrid mix of smoke and chili spread into the drawing room. "Stupid fool," he said to his granddaughter. "Shut the door!"

But the door shut itself along with all the doors in the house. Bang bang bang. The sky gaped, lit by flame; blue fire ensnared the pine tree that sizzled to an instant death leaving a charcoal stump, a singed smell, a crosshatch of branches over the lawn. An unending rain broke on them and Mutt turned into a primitive life form, an amoebic creature, slithering about the floor.

A lightning conductor atop Cho Oyu ran a wire into an underground pit of salt, which would save them, but Mutt couldn't understand. With renewed thunder and a blast upon the tin roof, she sought refuge behind the curtains, under the beds. But either her behind was left vulnerable, or her nose, and she was frightened by the wind making ghost sounds in the empty soda bottles: *whoo hoooo hooo.*

"Don't be scared, puppy dog, little frog, little duck, duckie dog. It's just rain."

She tried to smile, but her tail kept folding under and her eyes were those of a soldier in war, finished with caring for silly myths of courage. Her ears strained beyond the horizon, anticipating what didn't fail to arrive, yet another wave of bombardment, the sound of civilization crumbling—she had never known it was so big—cities and monuments fell—and she fled again.

This aqueous season would last three months, four, maybe five. In Cho Oyu, a leak dripping into the toilet played a honky-tonk, until it was interrupted by Sai, who held an umbrella over herself when she went inside the bathroom. Condensation fogged the glass of clocks, and clothes hanging to dry in the attic remained wet for a week. A white scurf sifted down from the beams, a fungus spun a shaggy age over everything. Bits of color, though, defined this muffled scene: insects flew in carnival gear; bread, in a day, turned green as grass; Sai, pulling open her underwear drawer, found a bright pink jelly scalloping the layers of dreary cotton; and the bound volumes of *National Geographic* fell open to pages bruised with flamboyant disease, purple-yellow molds rivaling the bower birds of Papua New Guinea, the residents of New Orleans, and the advertisements—"It's better in the Bahamas!"—that it showcased.

Sai had always been calm and cheerful during these months, the only time when her life in Kalimpong was granted perfect sense and she could experience the peace of knowing that communication with anyone was near impossible. She sat on the veranda, riding the moods of the season, thinking how intelligent it was to succumb as all over Kalimpong modernity began to fail. Phones emitted a death rattle, televisions tuned into yet another view of the downpour. And in this wet diarrheal season floated the feeling, loose and light, of life being a moving, dissipating thing, chilly and solitary—not anything you could grasp. The world vanished, the gate opened onto nothing—no Gyan around the bend of the mountain—and that terrible feeling of waiting released its stranglehold. Even Uncle Potty was impossible to visit for the *jhora* had overflowed its banks and carried the bridge downstream.

At Mon Ami, Lola, fiddling the knob of the radio, had to relinquish proof that her daughter Pixie still prevailed in a dry place amid news of bursting rivers, cholera, crocodile attacks, and Bangladeshis up in their trees again. "Oh well," Lola sighed, "perhaps it will wash out the hooligans in the bazaar."

Recently a series of strikes and processions had indicated growing political discontent. And now a three-day strike and a *raasta roko* roadblock endeavor were postponed because of the weather. What was the point of preventing rations from getting through if they weren't getting through anyway? How to force offices to close when they were going to remain closed? How to shut down streets when the streets had gone? Even the main road into Kalimpong from Teesta Bazaar had simply slipped off the incline and lay in pieces down in the gorge below.

Between storms, a grub-white sun appeared and everything began to sour and steam as people rushed to market.

Gyan, though, walked in the other direction, to Cho Oyu.

He was worried about the tuition and worried his payment might be denied him, that he and Sai had fallen far behind in the syllabus. So he told himself, slipping about the slopes, clutching onto plants.

Really, though, he walked in this direction because the rain's pause had brought forth, once again, that unbearable feeling of anticipation, and under its influence he couldn't sit still. He found Sai among the newspapers that had arrived on the Siliguri bus, two weeks' worth bunched together. Each leaf had been ironed dry separately by the cook. Several species of ferns were bushy about the veranda, frilled with drops; elephant ears held trembling clutches of rain spawn; and all the hundreds of invisible spiderwebs in the bushes around the house had become visible, lined in silver, caught with trailing tissues of cloud. Sai was wearing her kimono, a present from Uncle Potty, who had found it in a chest of his mother's, a souvenir of her voyage to Japan to see the cherry blossoms. It was made of scarlet silk, gilded with dragons, and thus Sai sat, mysterious and highlighted in gold, an empress of a wild kingdom, glowing against its lush scene.

The country, Sai noted, was coming apart at the seams: police unearthing militants in Assam, Nagaland, and Mizoram; Punjab on fire with Indira Gandhi dead and gone in October of last year; and those Sikhs with their Kanga, Kachha, etc., still wishing to add a sixth *K*, Khalistan, their own country in which to live with the other five *K*s.

In Delhi the government had unveiled its new financial plan after much secrecy and debate. It had seen fit to reduce taxes on condensed milk and ladies' undergarments, and raise them on wheat, rice, and kerosene.

"Our darling Piu," an obituary outlined in black had a photo of a smiling child—"seven years have passed since you left for your heavenly abode, and the pain has not gone. Why were you so cruelly snatched away before your time? Mummy keeps crying to think of your sweet smile. We cannot make sense of our lives. Anxiously awaiting your reincarnation."

"Good afternoon," said Gyan.

She looked up and he felt a deep pang.

Back at the dining table, the mathematics books between them, tortured by graphs, by decimal points of perfect measurement, Gyan was conscious of the fact that a being so splendid should not be seated before a shabby textbook; it was wrong of him to have forced this ordinariness upon her—the bisection and rebisection of the bisection of an angle. Then, as if to reiterate the fact that he should have remained at home, it began to pour again and he was forced to shout over the sound of rain on the tin roof, which imparted an epic quality to geometry that was clearly ridiculous.

An hour later, it was still hammering down. "I had better go," he said desperately.

"Don't," she squeaked, "you might get killed by lightning."

It began to hail.

"I really must," he said.

"Don't," warned the cook, "In my village a man stuck his head out of the door in a hailstorm, a big *goli* fell on him and he died right away."

The storm's grip intensified, then weakened as night fell, but it was far too dark by this time for Gyan to pick his way home through a hillside of ice eggs.

The judge looked irritably across the chops at Gyan. His presence, he felt, was an insolence, a liberty driven if not by intent then certainly by foolishness. "What made you come out in such weather, Charlie?" he said. "You might be adept at mathematics, but common sense appears to have eluded you."

No answer. Gyan seemed ensnared by his own thoughts.

The judge studied him.

He detected an obvious lack of familiarity, a hesitance with the cutlery and the food, yet he sensed Gyan was someone with plans. He carried an unmistakable whiff of journey, of ambition—and an old emotion came back to the judge, a recognition of weakness that was not merely a feeling, but also a taste, like fever. He could tell Gyan had never eaten such food in such a manner. Bitterness flooded the judge's mouth.

"So," he said, slicing the meat expertly off the bone, "so, what poets are you reading these days, young man?" He felt a sinister urge to catch the boy off guard.

"He is a science student," said Sai.

"So what of that? Scientists are not barred from poetry, or are they?

"Whatever happened to the well-rounded education?" he said into the continuing silence.

Gyan racked his brains. He never read any poets. "Tagore?" he answered uncertainly, sure that was safe and respectable.

"Tagore!" The judge speared a bit of meat with his fork, dunked it in the gravy, piled on a bit of potato and mashed on a few peas, put the whole thing into his mouth with the fork held in his left hand.

"Overrated," he said after he had chewed well and swallowed, but despite this dismissal, he gestured an order with his knife: "Recite us something, won't you?"

"Where the head is held high, Where knowledge is free, Where the world has not been broken up into fragments by narrow domestic walls. . . . Into that heaven of freedom, my Father, let me and my country awake." Every schoolchild in India knew at least this.

The judge began to laugh in a cheerless and horrible manner.

How he hated this dingy season. It angered him for reasons beyond

Mutt's unhappiness; it made a mockery of him, his ideals. When he looked about he saw he was not in charge: mold in his toothbrush, snakes slithering unafraid right over the patio, furniture gaining weight, and Cho Oyu also soaking up water, crumbling like a mealy loaf. With each storm's bashing, less of it was habitable.

The judge felt old, very old, and as the house crumbled about him, his mind, too, seemed to be giving way, doors he had kept firmly closed between one thought and the next, dissolving. It was now forty years since he had been a student of poetry.

The library had never been open long enough.

He arrived as it opened, departed when it closed, for it was the rescuer of foreign students, proffered privacy and a lack of thugs.

He read a book entitled *Expedition to Goozerat*: "The Malabar coast undulates in the shape of a wave up the western flank of India, and then, in a graceful motion, gestures toward the Arabian sea. This is Goozerat. At the river deltas and along the malarial coasts lie towns configured for trade. . . ."

What on earth was all of this? It had nothing to do with what he remembered of his home, of the Patels and their life in the Patel warren, and yet, when he unfolded the map, he found Piphit. There it was—a mosquito speck by the side of a sulky river.

With amazement, he read on, of scurvied sailors arriving, the British, the French, the Dutch, the Portuguese. In their care the tomato traveled to India, and also the cashew nut. He read that the East India Company had rented Bombay at ten pounds a year from Charles II who came by it, a jujube in his dowry bag upon his wedding to Catherine of Braganza, and by the middle of the nineteenth century, he learned that mock turtle soup was being trawled on ships through the Suez to feed those who might be pining for it in rice and dal country. An Englishman might sit against a tropical background, yellow yolk of sun, shine spun into the palms, and consume a Yarmouth herring, a Breton oyster. This was all news to him and he felt greedy for a country that was already his.

Mid morning he rose from his books, went to the lavatory for the daily trial of his digestion, where he sat straining upon the pot with pained and prolonged effort. As he heard others shuffling outside, waiting for their turn, he stuck a finger up the hole and excavated within, allowing a backed up load of scropulated goat pellets to rattle down loudly. Had they heard him outside? He tried to catch them before they bulleted the water. His finger emerged covered in excrement and blood, and he washed his hands repeatedly, but the smell persisted, faintly trailing him through his studies. As time went on, Jemubhai worked harder. He measured out a reading calendar, listed each book, each chapter in a complex chart. Topham's *Law of Property*, Aristotle, *Indian Criminal Procedure*, the *Penal Code* and the *Evidence Act*.

He worked late into the night back in his rented room, still tailed by the persistent smell of shit, falling from his chair directly into bed, rising in terror a few hours later, and rolling up onto the chair again. He worked eighteen hours a day, over a hundred hours a week, sometimes stopping to feed his landlady's dog when she begged for a share of pork pie dinner, drooling damp patches onto his lap, raking an insistent paw across his knees and wrecking the pleat of his corduroys. This was his first friendship with an animal, for in Piphit the personalities of dogs were not investigated or encouraged. Three nights before the Probation Finals, he did not sleep at all, but read aloud to himself, rocking back and forth to the rhythm, repeating, repeating.

A journey once begun, has no end. The memory of his ocean trip shone between the words. Below and beyond, the monsters of his unconscious prowled, awaiting the time when they would rise and be proven real and he wondered if he'd dreamt of the drowning power of the sea before his first sight of it.

His landlady brought his dinner tray right to his door. A treat: a quadruplet of handsome oily sausages, confident, gleaming, whizzing with life. Ready already for the age when food would sing on television to advertise itself.

"Don't work too hard."

"One must, Mrs. Rice."

He had learned to take refuge in the third person and to keep everyone at bay, to keep even himself away from himself like the Queen.

Open Competitive Examination, June 1942

He sat before a row of twelve examiners and the first question was put to him by a professor of London University—Could he tell them how a steam train worked?

Jemubhai's mind drew a blank.

"Not interested in trains?" The man looked personally disappointed.

"A fascinating field, sir, but one's been too busy studying the recommended subjects."

"No idea of how a train works?"

Jemu stretched his brain as far as he could—what powered what?—but he had never seen the inside of a railway engine.

"No, sir."

Could he describe then, the burial customs of the ancient Chinese.

He was from the same part of the country as Gandhi. What of the noncooperation movement? What was his opinion of the Congress?

The room was silent. BUY BRITISH—Jemubahi had seen the posters the day of his arrival in England, and it had struck him that if he'd yelled BUY INDIAN in the streets of India, he would be clapped into jail. And all the way back in 1930, when Jemubhai was still a child, Gandhi had marched from Sabarmati ashram to Dandi where, at the ocean's maw, he had performed the subversive activity of harvesting salt.

"—Where will that get him? Phtoo! His heart may be in the right place but his brain has fallen out of his head"—Jemu's father had said although the jails were full of Gandhi's supporters. On the SS *Strathnaver*, the sea spray had come flying at Jemubhai and dried in taunting dots of salt upon his face and arms. . . . It *did* seem ridiculous to tax it. . . .

"If one was not committed to the current administration, sir, there would be no question of appearing here today."

Lastly, who was his favorite writer?

A bit nervously for he had none, he replied that one was fond of Sir Walter Scott.

"What have you read?"

"All the printed works, sir."

"Can you recite one of your favorite poems for us?" asked a professor of social anthropology.

Oh! Young Lochinvar is come out of the west,
Through all the wide Border his steed was the best

By the time they stood for the ICS, most of the candidates had crisp-ironed their speech, but Jemubhai had barely opened his mouth for whole years and his English still had the rhythm and the form of Gujerati.

But ere he alighted at Netherby gate
The bride had consented, the gallant came late:
For a laggard in love and a dastard in war
Was to wed the fair Ellen of brave Lochinvar. . . .

When he looked up, he saw they were all chuckling.

While her mother did fret, and her father did fume,
And the bridegroom stood dangling his bonnet and plume. . . .

The judge shook himself. “Damn fool,” he said out loud, pushed his chair back, stood up, brought his fork and knife down in devastating judgment upon himself and left the table. His strength, that mental steel, was weakening. His memory seemed triggered by the tiniest thing—Gyan’s unease, his reciting that absurd poem. . . . Soon all the judge had worked so hard to separate would soften and envelop him in its nightmare, and the barrier between this life and eternity would in the end, no doubt, be just another such failing construct.

Mutt followed him to his room. As he sat brooding, she leaned against him with the ease that children have when leaning against their parents.

“I am sorry,” said Sai, hot with shame. “It’s impossible to tell how my grandfather will behave.”

Gyan didn’t appear to hear her.

“Sorry,” said Sai again, mortified, but again he didn’t appear to have heard. For the first time his eyes rested directly upon her as if he were eating her alive in an orgy of the imagination—aha! At last the proof.

The cook cleared away the dirty dishes and shut the quarter cup of leftover peas into the cupboard. The cupboard looked like a coop, with its wire netting around a wooden frame and its four feet standing in bowls of water to deter ants and other vermin. He topped the water in these bowls from one of the buckets placed under the leaks, emptied the other buckets out of the window, and returned them to their appointed spots.

He made up the bed in an extra room, which was actually filled with rubbish but contained a bed placed in the very center, and he fixed pale virginal candles into saucers for Sai and Gyan to take to their rooms. "Your bed is ready for you, *masterji,*" he said and sniffed:

Was there a strange atmosphere in the room?

But Sai and Gyan seemed immersed in the newspapers again, and he confused their sense of ripening anticipation with his own, because that morning, two letters from Biju had arrived in the post. They were lying under an empty tuna fish tin by his bed, saved for the end of the day, and all evening he'd been savoring the thought of them. He rolled up his pants and departed with an umbrella as it had begun to pour again.

In the drawing room, sitting with the newspapers, Sai and Gyan were left alone, quite alone, for the first time.

Kiki De Costa's recipe column: marvels with potatoes. Tasty treat with meat. Noodles with doodles and doodles of sauce and oodles and oodles of cheese.

Fleur Hussein's beauty tips.

The handsome baldy competition at the Calcutta Gymkhana Club had given out prizes to Mr. Sunshine, Mr. Moonshine, and Mr. Will Shine.

Their eyes read on industriously, but their thoughts didn't cleave to such discipline, and finally Gyan, unable to bear this any longer, this tightrope tension between them, put down his paper with a crashing sound, turned abruptly toward her, and blurted:

"Do you put oil in your hair?"

"No," she said, startled. "I never do."

After a bit of silence, "Why?" she asked. Was there something wrong with her hair?

"I can't hear you—the rain is so loud," he said, moving closer. "What?"

"Why?"

"It looks so shiny I thought you might."

"No."

"It looks very soft," he observed. "Do you wash it with shampoo?"

"Yes."

"What kind?"

"Sunsilk."

Oh, the unbearable intimacy of brand names, the boldness of the questions.

"What soap?"

"Lux."

"Beauty bar of the film stars?"

But they were too scared to laugh.

More silence.

"You?"

"Whatever is in the house. It doesn't matter for boys."

He couldn't admit that his mother bought the homemade brown soap that was sold in large rectangles in the market, blocks sliced off and sold cheap.

The questions grew worse: "Let me see your hands. They are so small."

"Are they?"

"Yes." He held his own out by hers. "See?"

Fingers. Nails.

"*Hm.* What long fingers. Little nails. But look, you bite them."

He weighed her hand.

"Light as a sparrow. The bones must be hollow."

These words that took direct aim at something elusive had the deliberateness of previous consideration, she realized with a thud of joy.

Rainy season beetles flew by in many colors. From each hole in the floor came a mouse as if tailored for size, tiny mice from the tiny holes, big mice from big holes, and the termites came teeming forth from the furniture, so many of them that when you looked, the furniture, the floor, the ceiling, all seemed to be wobbling.

But Gyan did not see them. His gaze itself was a mouse; it disappeared into the belladonna sleeve of Sai's kimono and spotted her elbow.

"A sharp point," he commented. "You could do some harm with that."

Arms they measured and legs. Catching sight of her foot—

"Let me see."

He took off his own shoe and then the threadbare sock of which he immediately felt ashamed and which he bundled into his pocket. They examined the nakedness side by side of those little tubers in the semidark.

Her eyes, he noted, were extraordinarily glamorous: huge, wet, full of theater, capturing all the light in the room.

But he couldn't bring himself to mention them; it was easier to stick to what moved him less, to a more scientific approach.

With the palm of his hand, he cupped her head. . . .

"Is it flat or is it curved?"

With an unsteady finger, he embarked on the arch of an eyebrow. . . .

Oh, he could not believe his bravery; it drove him on and wouldn't heed the fear that called him back; he was brave despite himself. His finger moved down her nose.

The sound of water came from every direction: fat upon the window, a popgun off the bananas and the tin roof, lighter and messier on the patio stones, a low-throated gurgle in the gutter that surrounded the house like a moat. There was the sound of the *jhora* rushing and of water drowning itself in this water, of drainpipes disgorging into the rain barrels, the rain barrels brimming over, little sipping sounds from the moss.

The growing impossibility of speech would make other intimacies easier.

As his finger was about to leap from the tip of Sai's nose to her perfectly arched lips—

Up she jumped.

"Owwaaa," she shouted.

He thought it was a mouse.

It wasn't. She was used to mice.

"Oooph," she said. She couldn't stand a moment longer, that peppery feeling of being traced by another's finger and all that green romance burgeoning forth. Wiping her face bluntly with her hands, she shook out her kimono, as if to rid the evening of this trembling delicacy.

"Well, good night," she said formally, taking Gyan by surprise. Placing her feet one before the other with the deliberateness of a drunk, she made her way toward the door, reached the rectangle of the doorway, and dove into the merciful dark with Gyan's bereft eyes following her.

She didn't return.

But the mice did. It was quite extraordinary how tenacious they were—you'd think their fragile hearts would shatter, but their timidity was misleading; their fear was without memory.

In his bed slung like a hammock on broken springs, leaks all around, the judge lay pinned by layers of fusty blankets. His underwear lay on top of the lamp to dry and his watch sat below so the mist under the dial might lift—a sad state for the civilized man. The air was spiked with pinpricks of moisture that made it feel as if it were raining indoors as well, yet this didn't freshen it. It bore down thick enough to smother, an odiferous yeasty mix of spore and fungi, wood smoke and mice droppings, kerosene and chill. He got out of bed to search for a pair of socks and a woolen skull cap. As he was putting them on, he saw the unmistakable silhouette of a scorpion, bold against the dingy wall, and lurched at it with a fly swatter, but it sensed his presence, bristled, the tail went up, and it began to run. It vanished into the crack between the bottom of the wall and the floorboard. "Drat!" he said. His false teeth leered at him with a skeleton grin from a jar of water. He rummaged about for a Calmpose and swallowed it with a gulp of water from thc top of the jar, so cold, always cold—the water in Kalimpong was directly from Himalayan snow—and it transformed his gums to pure pain. "Good night, my darling mutton chop," he said to Mutt when he could manipulate his tongue again. She was already dreaming, but oh the weakness of an aged man, even the pill could not chase the unpleasant thoughts unleashed at dinner back into their holes.

When the results of the viva voce had been posted, he found his performance had earned him one hundred out of three hundred, the lowest qualifying mark. The written portion of the test had brought up his score and he was listed at forty-eight, but only the top forty-two had been included for admission to the ICS. Shaking, almost fainting, he was about to stumble away when a man came out with a supplementary announcement: a new list had been conceived in accordance with attempts to Indianize the service. The crowd of students rushed forward, and in between the lurching, he caught sight of the name, Jemubhai Popatlal Patel, at the very bottom of the page.

Looking neither right nor left, the newest member, practically unwelcome, of the heaven-born, ran home with his arms folded and got immediately into bed, all his clothes on, even his shoes, and soaked his pillow with his weeping. Tears sheeted his cheeks, eddied about his nose, cascaded into his neck, and he found he was quite unable to control his tormented ragged nerves. He lay there crying for three days and three nights.

"James," rattled the landlady. "Are you all right?"

"Just tired. Not to worry."

"James?"

"Mrs. Rice," he said. "One is done. One is finally through."

"Good for you, James," she said generously, and told herself she was glad. How progressive, how bold and brave the world was. It would always surprise her.

Not the first position, nor the second. But there he was. He sent a telegram home.

"Result unequivocal."

"What," asked everyone, "does that mean?" It sounded as if there was a problem, because "un" words were negative words, those basically competent in English agreed. But then, Jemubhai's father consulted the assistant magistrate and they exploded with joy, his father transformed into a king holding court, as neighbors, acquaintances, even strangers, streamed by to eat syrup-soaked sweets and offer congratulations in envy-soaked voices.

Not long after the results were declared, Jemubhai with his trunk that read "Mr. J. P. Patel, SS *Strathnaver*," drove in a hired cab away from the house on Thornton Road and turned back to wave for the sake of the dog with pork pies in its eyes. It was watching him out of a window and he felt an echo of the old heartbreak of leaving Piphit.

Jemubhai, who had lived on ten pounds a month, could now expect to be paid three hundred pounds a year by the secretary of state for India for the two years of probation. He had found more expensive lodgings which he could now afford, closer to the university.

The new boardinghouse boasted several rooms for rent, and here, among the other lodgers, he was to find his only friend in England: Bose.

They had similar inadequate clothes, similar forlornly empty rooms, similar poor native's trunks. A look of recognition had passed between them at first sight, but also the assurance that they wouldn't reveal one another's secrets, not even to each other.

Bose was different from the judge in one crucial aspect, though. He was an optimist. There was only one way to go now and that was forward. He was further along in the process: "Cheeri-o, right-o, tickety boo, simply smashing, chin-chin, no siree, how's that, bottom's up, I say!" he liked to say. Together they punted clumsily down the glacéed river to Grantchester and had tea among the jam-sozzled wasps just as you were supposed to, enjoying themselves (but not really) as the heavy wasps fell from flight into their laps with a low-battery buzz.

They had better luck in London, where they watched the changing of the guard at Buckingham Palace, avoided the other Indian students at Veeraswamy's, ate shepherd's pie instead, and agreed on the train home that Trafalgar Square was not quite up to British standards of hygiene—all those defecating pigeons, one of which had done a masala-colored doodle on Bose. It was Bose who showed Jemubhai what records to buy for his new gramophone: Caruso and Gigli. He also corrected his pronunciation: *Jheelee*, not *Giggly*. York*sher*. Edin*burrah*. Jane *Aae*, a word let loose and lost like the wind on the Brönte heath, never to be found and ended; not Jane *Aiyer* like a South Indian. Together they read *A Brief History of Western Art*, *A Brief History of Philosophy*, *A Brief History of France*, etc., a whole series. An essay on how a sonnet was constructed, the variations on the form. A book on china and glass: Waterford, Salviati, Spode, Meissen, and Limoges. Crumpets they investigated and scones, jams, and preserves.

Thus it was that the judge eventually took revenge on his early confusions, his embarrassments gloved in something called "keeping up standards," his accent behind a mask of a quiet. He found he began to be mistaken for something he wasn't—a man of dignity This accidental poise became more important than any other thing. He envied the English. He loathed Indians. He worked at being English with the passion of hatred and for what he would become, he would be despised by absolutely everyone, English and Indians, both.

At the end of their probation, the judge and Bose signed the covenant of service, swore to obey His Majesty and the viceroy, collected circulars giving up-to-date information on snakebites and tents, and received the list of supplies they were required to purchase: breeches, riding boots, tennis racket, twelve-bore gun. It made them feel as if they were embarking on a giant Boy Scout expedition.

On board the *Strathnaver* on his way back, the judge sipped beef tea and read *How to Speak Hindustani*, since he had been posted to a part of India where he did not speak the language. He sat alone because he still felt ill at ease in the company of the English.

His granddaughter walked by his door, went into her bathroom, and he heard the eery whistle of half water–half air in the tap.

Sai washed her feet with whatever piddled into the bucket, but she forgot her face, wandered out, remembered her face, went back in and wondered why, remembered her teeth, put the toothbrush into her pocket, came out again, remembered her face *and* her teeth, went back, rewashed her feet, reemerged—

Paced up and down, bit off her fingernails—

She prided herself on being able to take anything—

Anything but gentleness.

Had she washed her face? She went back into the bathroom and washed her feet again.

The cook sat with a letter in front of him; blue ink waves lapped the paper and every word had vanished, as so often happened in the monsoon season.

He opened the second letter to find the same basic fact reiterated: there was literally an ocean between him and his son. Then, once again, he shifted the burden of hope from this day to the next and got into his bed, hooked onto his pillow—he had recently had the cotton replaced—and he mistook its softness for serenity.

In the spare room, Gyan was wondering what he had done—had he done the right thing or the wrong, what courage had entered his foolish heart and enticed him beyond the boundaries of propriety? It was the bit of rum he had drunk, it was the strange food. It couldn't be real, but incredibly, it was. He felt frightened but also a little proud. *"Ai yai yai ai yai yai,"* he said to himself.

All four inhabitants lay awake as outside the rain and wind whooshed and banged, the trees heaved and sighed, and the lightning shamelessly unzipped the sky over Cho Oyu.

Nineteen

"Biju! Hey man." It was Saeed Saeed oddly wearing a white *kurta* pajama with sunglasses, gold chain, and platform shoes, his dreadlocks tied in a ponytail. He had left the Banana Republic. "My boss, I swear he keep grabbing my ass. Anyway," he continued, "I got married."

"You're married?!"

"That's it, man."

"Who did you marry???"

"Toys."

"Toys?"

"Toys."

"All of a sudden they ask for my green card, say they forget to look when I apply, so I ask her, 'Will you marry me for papers?'"

"Flakey," they had all said, in the restaurant where they worked, he in the kitchen, she as a waitress. "She's a flake."

Sweet flake. Heart like a cake. She went to city hall with Saeed—rented tuxedo, flowery dress—said "I do," under the red white and blue.

Now they were practicing for the INS interview:

"What kind of underwear does your husband wear, what toothpaste does your wife favor?"

If they were suspicious, they would separate you, husband in one room, wife in another, asking the same questions, trying to catch you out. Some said they sent out spies to double-check; others said no—the INS didn't have the time or money.

"Who buys the toilet paper?"

"I do, man, I do, Softy, and you should see how *much* she use. Every two days I am going to the Rite Aid."

"But her parents are letting her?" asked Biju, incredulous.

"But they LOVE me! Her mother, she LOVE me, she LOVE me."

He had been to visit them and found a family of long-haired Vermont hippies feeding on pita bread spread with garlic and baba ghanoush. They pitied anyone who didn't eat their food brown, co-op organic, in bulk, and unprocessed. Saeed, who enjoyed his basics white—white rice, white bread, and white sugar—had to join their dog, who shared his disdain for the burdock burger, the nettle soup, the soy milk, and Tofutti—"She's a fast-food junkie!"—in the backseat of Grandma's car painted in rainbow colors putt-putting down to the Burger'n Bun. And there they were, Saeed and Buckeroo Bonzai, two BigBoyBurgers spilling from two big grins, in the picture taken for the INS photo album. He showed it to Biju, taking it from his new briefcase specially bought to carry these important documents.

"I like the pictures very much," Biju assured him.

There was also Saeed with the family at the Bread & Puppet theater festival posing with the evil insurance-man puppet; Saeed touring the Grafton cheese factory; Saeed by the compost heap with his arm around Grandma, braless in her summer muumuu, salt-and-pepper armpit hair shooting off in several directions.

Oh, the United States, it's a wonderful country. A wonderful country. And its people are the most delightful in the world. The more he told them about his family in Zanzibar, his faked-up papers, of how he had one passport for Saeed Saeed and one for Zulfikar—the happier they got. Stayed up late into the zany Vermont night, stars coming down coming down, cheering him on. Any subversion against the U.S. government—they would be happy to help.

Grandma wrote a letter to the INS to assure them Zulfikar of Zanzibar was a welcome—no, more than that—a cherished new member of the ancient clan of the *Mayflower* Williams.

He slapped Biju on the back. "See you around," he said and he left to practice kissing for the interview. "Have to look right or they will suspect."

Biju continued on his way, tried to smile at female American citizens: "Hi. Hi." But they barely looked at him.

The cook went back to the post office. "You are getting the letters wet. Taking no care."

"*Babaji,* just look outside—how are we to keep them dry? It is humanly impossible, they are getting wet as we transfer them from van to office."

Next day: "Post came?"

"No, no, roads closed. Nothing today. Maybe the road will open in the afternoon. Come back later."

Lola was hysterically trying to make a phone call from the STD booth because it was Pixie's birthday: "What do you mean it doesn't work, for a week it hasn't worked!"

"For a month it hasn't worked," a young man who had also been in line corrected her, but he seemed content. "The microwave is down," he explained.

"What?"

"The microwave." He turned for affirmation to the others in the office. "Yes," they said, nodding; they were all men and women of the future. He turned back. "Yes, the satellite in the sky," he indicated, pointing up, "it's fallen down." And he pointed at the plebeian floor, gray concrete all stamped about with local mud.

No way to telephone, no way for letters to get through. She and the cook, running into each other, commiserated a moment and then he went on sadly to the butcher and she went to get some Baygon spray and swatters, for the insects. Each day of this fecund season scores of tiny souls lost their brief lives to Lola's poisons. Mosquitoes, ants, termites, millipedes, centipedes, spiders, woodworms, beetles. Yet, what did it matter? Each day a thousand new ones were born. . . . Entire nations appeared boldly overnight.

Twenty

Gyan and Sai. At subsequent pauses in the rain they measured ears, shoulders, and the span of their rib cages.

Collar bones, eyelashes, and chins.

Knees, heels, arch of the feet.

Flexibility of fingers and toes.

Cheekbones, necks, muscles of the upper arm, the small complexities of the hinge bones.

The green and purple of their veins.

The world's most astonishing tongue display: Sai, tutored by her friend Arlene in the convent, could touch her nose with her tongue and showed Gyan.

He could wiggle his eyebrows, slide his head off his neck from left to right to left like a Bharat Natyam dancer, and he could stand on his head.

Now and then, she recalled certain delicate observations she had made during her own explorations before the mirror that had been overlooked by Gyan, on account of the newness of landscape between them. It was, she knew herself, a matter of education to learn how to look at a woman, and worried that Gyan wasn't entirely aware of how lucky he was.

Ear lobes downy as tobacco leaves, the tender substance of her hair, the transparent skin of the inner wrist. . . .

She brought up the omissions at his next visit, proffered her hair with the zeal of a shawl merchant: "See—feel. Like silk?"

"Like silk," he confirmed.

Her ears she displayed like items taken from under the counter and put before a discerning customer in one of the town's curio shops, but when he tried to test the depth of her eyes with his, her glance proved too slippery to hold; he picked it up and dropped it, retrieved it, dropped it again until it slid away and hid.

So they played the game of courtship, reaching, retreating, teasing, fleeing—how delicious the pretense of objective study, miraculous how it could eat up the hours. But as they eliminated the easily revealable and exhausted propriety, the unexamined portions of their anatomies exerted a more severely distilled potential, and once again the situation was driven to the same desperate pitch of the days when they sat forcing geometry.

Up the bones of the spine.

Stomach and belly button—

"*Kiss me!*" he pleaded.

"No," she said, delighted and terrified.

She would hold herself ransom.

Oh, but she had never been able to stand suspense.

A fine drizzle spelled an ellipsis on the tin roof. . . .

Moments clocked by precisely, and finally she couldn't bear it—she closed her eyes and felt the terrified measure of his lips on hers, trying to match one shape with the other.

Just a week or two later, they were shameless as beggars, pleading for more.

"Nose?" He kissed it.

"Eyes?" Eyes.

"Ears?" Ears.

"Cheek?" Cheek.

"Fingers." One, two, three, four, five.

"The other hand, please." Ten kisses.

"Toes?"

They linked word, object, and affection in a recovery of childhood, a confirmation of wholeness, as at the beginning—

Arms legs heart—

All their parts, they reassured each other, were where they should be.

Gyan was twenty and Sai sixteen, and at the beginning they had not paid very much attention to the events on the hillside, the new posters in the market referring to old discontents, the slogans scratched and painted on the side of government offices and shops. "We are stateless," they read. "It is better to die than live as slaves," "We are constitutionally tortured. Return our land from Bengal." Down the other way, the slogans persisted and multiplied along the landslide reinforcements, jostled for place between the "Better late than never" slogans, the "If married don't flirt with speed," "Drinking whisky is risky," that flashed by as you drove toward the Teesta.

The call was repeated along the road to the army cantonment area; began to pop up in less obvious places; the big rocks along thin paths that veined the mountains, the trunks of trees amid huts made of bamboo and mud, corn drying in bunches under the veranda roofs, prayer flags flying overhead, pigs snorting in pens behind. Climbing perpendicular to the sky, arriving breathless at the top of Ringkingpong hill, you'd see "LIBERATION!" scrawled across the waterworks. Still, for a while nobody knew which way it would go, and it was dismissed as nothing more serious than the usual handful of students and agitators. But then one day fifty boys, members of the youth wing of the GNLF, gathered to swear an oath at Mahakaldara to fight to the death for the formation of a homeland, Gorkhaland. Then they marched down the streets of Darjeeling, took a turn around the market and the mall. "Gorkhaland for Gorkhas. We are the liberation army." They were watched by the pony men and their ponies, by the proprietors of souvenir shops, by the waiters of Glenary's, the Planter's Club, the Gymkhana, and the Windamere as they waved their unsheathed kukris, sliced the fierce blades through the tender mist under the watery sun. Quite suddenly, everyone was using the word *insurgency.*

Twenty-one

"They have a point," said Noni, "maybe not their whole point, but I'd say half to three-quarters of their point."

"Nonsense." Lola waved her sister's opinion away. "Those Neps will be after all outsiders now, but especially us Bongs. They've been plotting this a long while. Dream come true. All kinds of atrocities will go on—then they can skip merrily over the border to hide in Nepal. Very convenient."

In her mind she pictured their watchman, Budhoo, with her BBC radio and her silver cake knife, living it up in Kathmandu along with various other Kanchas and Kanchis with their respective loot.

They were sitting in the Mon Ami drawing room having tea after Sai's lesson.

An opaque scene through the window resembled something from folk art: flat gray mountain and sky, flat white row of Father Booty's cows on the crest of the hill, sky showing through their legs in squarish shapes. Indoors, the lamp was on, and a plate of cream horns lay in the tawny light and there were tuberoses in a vase. Mustafa climbed onto Sai's lap and she thought of how, since her romance with Gyan, she had a new understanding of cats. Uncaring of the troubles in the market, Mustafa was wringing forth ecstasies, pushing against her ribs to find a bone to ribble his chin against.

"This state-making," Lola continued, "biggest mistake that fool Nehru made. Under his rules any group of idiots can stand up demanding a new state and get it, too. How many new ones keep appearing? From fifteen we went to sixteen, sixteen to seventeen, seventeen to twenty-two. . . ." Lola made a line with a finger from above her ear and drew noodles in the air to demonstrate her opinion of such madness.

"And here, if you ask me," she said, "it all started with Sikkim. The Neps played such a dirty trick and began to get grand ideas—now they think they can do the same thing again—you know, Sai?"

Mustafa's bones seemed to be dissolving under Sai's stroking, and he twirled on her knees in a trance, eyes closed, a mystic knowing neither one religion nor another, neither one country nor another, just this *feeling*.

"Yes," she said absentmindedly, she had heard the story so many times before: Indira Gandhi had maneuvered a plebiscite and all the Nepalis who had flooded Sikkim voted against the king. India had swallowed the jewel-colored kingdom, whose blue hills they could see in the distance, where the wonderful oranges came from and the Black Cat rum that was smuggled to them by Major Aloo. Where monasteries dangled like spiders before Kanchenjunga, so close you'd think the monks could reach out and touch the snow. The country had seemed unreal—so full of fairy tales, of travelers seeking Shangri-la—it had proved all the easier to destroy, therefore.

"But you have to take it from their point of view," said Noni. "First the Neps were thrown out of Assam and then Meghalaya, then there's the king of Bhutan growling against—"

"Illegal immigration," said Lola. She reached for a cream horn. "*Naughty* girl," she said to herself, her voice replete with gloating.

"Obviously the Nepalis are worried," said Noni. "They've been here, most of them, several generations. Why shouldn't Nepali be taught in schools?"

"Because on that basis they can start statehood demands. Separatist movement here, separatist movement there, terrorists, guerillas, insurgents, rebels, agitators, instigators, and they all learn from one another, of course—the Neps have been encouraged by the Sikhs and their Khalistan, by ULFA, NEFA, PLA; Jharkhand, Bodoland, Gorkhaland; Tripura, Mizoram, Manipur, Kashmir, Punjab, Assam. . . ."

Sai thought of how she turned to water under Gyan's hands, her skin catching the movement of his fingers up her and down, until finally she couldn't tell the difference between her skin and his touch.

The nasal whine of the gate:

"Hello, hello," said Mrs. Sen, hooking her beaky nose around the open door. "Hope I'm not disturbing—was just going by, heard your voices—oh look, pastries and all—" In her happiness she made small bird and mouse sounds.

Lola: "You saw that letter they sent to the queen of England? Gorbachev and Reagan? Apartheid, genocide, looking after Pakistan, forgetting us, colonial subjugation, vivisected Nepal. . . . When did Darjeeling and Kalimpong belong to Nepal? Darjeeling, in fact, was annexed from Sikkim and Kalimpong from Bhutan."

Noni: "Very unskilled at drawing borders, those bloody Brits."

Mrs. Sen, diving right into the conversation: "No practice, na, water all around them, ha ha."

When they would finally attempt to rise from those indolent afternoons they spent together, Gyan and Sai would have melted into each other like pats of butter—how difficult it was to cool and compose themselves back into their individual beings.

"Pakistan! There is the problem," said Mrs. Sen, jumping to one of her favorite topics, her thoughts and opinions ready-made, polished over the years, rolled out wherever they might be stuffed somehow into a conversation. "First heart attack to our country, no, that has never been healed—"

Lola: "It's an issue of a porous border is what. You can't tell one from the other, Indian Nepali from Nepali Nepali. And then, *baba*, the way these Neps multiply."

Mrs. Sen: "Like Muslims."

Lola: "Not the Muslims *here*."

Mrs. Sen: "No self-control, those people. Disgusting."

Noni: "Everyone is multiplying. Everywhere. You cannot blame one group over another."

Lola: "Lepchas are not multiplying, they are disappearing. In fact, they have the first right to this land and nobody is even mentioning them." Then, reconsidering her support for Lepchas, she said, "Not that they are so wonderful either, of course. Look at those government loans to Lepchas to start piggeries—"Traditional Occupation Resurrection Plan"—and not a single piggery to be seen, although, of course, they all handed in beautifully written petitions, showing trough measurements and the cost of pig feed and antibiotics—collected the money all right, smart and prompt. . . ."

Mrs. Sen: "More Muslims in India than in Pakistan. They prefer to multiply over here. You know, that Jinnah, he ate bacon and eggs for breakfast every morning and drank whiskey every evening. What sort of Muslim nation they have? And five times a day bums up to God. Mind you," she put her sticky finger in her mouth and then pulled it out with a pop, "With that Koran, who can be surprised? They have no option but to be two-faced."

The reasoning, they all knew from having heard this before, formed a central pillar of Hindu belief and it went like this: so strict was the Koran that its teachings were beyond human capability. Therefore Muslims were forced to pretend one thing, do another; they drank, smoked, ate pork, visited prostitutes, and then denied it.

Unlike Hindus, who needn't deny.

Lola was uneasy and drank her tea too hot. This complaining about Muslim birth rates was vulgar and incorrect among the class that reads Jane Austen, and she sensed Mrs. Sen's talk revealed her own position on Nepalis, where there was not so easy a stereotype, to be not so very different a prejudice.

"It's quite another matter with Muslims," she said stiffly. "They were already here. The Nepalis have come and taken over and it's not a religious issue."

Mrs. Sen: "Same thing with the Muslim cultural issue. . . . They also came from somewhere else, Babar and all. . . . And stayed here to breed. Not that it's the fault of the women—poor things—it's the men—marrying three, four wives—no shame." She began to giggle. "They have nothing better to do, you know. Without TV and electricity, there will always be this problem—"

Lola: "Oh, Mrs. Sen, again you are derailing the conversation. We aren't talking about that!"

Mrs. Sen: "Ah-hah-ha," she sang airily, putting another cream horn on her plate with a flourish.

Noni: "How is Mun Mun?" But as soon as she said it, she wished she hadn't, for this would rile Lola and she would have to spend all evening undoing the harm.

Mrs. Sen: "Oh, they keep begging her and *begging her* to take a green card. She says, 'No, no.' I told her, 'Don't be silly, take it, what harm is there? If they're *offering* it, pushing it on you. . . .' How many people would kill for one. . . . Silly goose, isn't it so? What a bee-oo-tee-ful country and so well organized."

The sisters had always looked down on Mrs. Sen as a low-caliber person. Her inferiority was clear to them long before her daughter settled in a country where the jam said Smuckers instead of "By appointment to Her Majesty the queen," and before she got a job with CNN placing her in direct opposition to Pixie at BBC. This was because Mrs. Sen pronounced potato "*POE*tatto," and tomato "*TOE*matto," and because of the rumor that she had once made a living going door to door in a scooter selling confiscated items from the customs at Dum Dum Airport, peddling the goods to mothers collecting dowries of black-market items, the better to increase their daughters' chances.

Lola: "But don't you find them very simple people?"

Mrs. Sen: "No hang-ups, na, very friendly."

"But a fake friendliness I've heard, hi-bye and no meaning to it."

"Better than England, *ji,* where they laugh at you behind your back—"

Perhaps England and America didn't know they were in a fight to the death, but it was being fought on their behalf, anyway, by these two spirited widows of Kalimpong.

"Mun Mun has no hassles in America, nobody cares where you're from—"

"Well, if you're going to call ignorance freedom! And don't tell me that nobody cares. Everybody knows," Lola said bitterly as if it actually mattered to her, "how they treat the Negroes."

"At least they believe you can be happy, *baba.*"

"And the kind of patriotism they go in for turns monkey into donkey *phata-phat*—just give them a hot dog on a stick, they begin to wave it at the flag and—"

"So, what's wrong with enjoying yourself—"

"Tell us your news, Sai," pleaded Noni, desperate to change the topic again. "Come on, cheer us up, that much you young people should be good for."

"No news," Sai lied and went red thinking of herself and Gyan. Companionship had increased the sensation of fluidity she'd felt before the mirror, that reduction to malleable form, the endless possibility for reinvention.

The three ladies gave her a hard look. She seemed out of focus, they couldn't read her expression clearly, and she was squirming oddly in her chair.

"So," said Lola, redirecting her frustration with Mrs. Sen, "no boyfriends yet? Why not, why not? We used to be so adventurous in the old days. Always giving Mummy-Daddy the slip."

"Let her be. She's a good girl," said Noni.

"Better do it now," said Mrs. Sen, making a mysterious expression. "Wait too long and the craze will go. That's what I told Mun Mun."

"Perhaps you have worms," said Lola.

Noni rummaged in a jumble-filled bowl and came up with a strip of medicine. "Here—take a deworming pill. We got some for Mustafa. Caught him rubbing his bottom on the floor. Sure sign."

Mrs. Sen looked at the tuberoses on the table. "You know," she said, "just put a few drops of food coloring and you can make your flowers any color you like, red, blue, orange. Years ago we used to have fun in parties like that."

Sai stopped petting Mustafa and that spiteful cat bit her.

"Mustafa!" Lola warned, "if you don't behave yourself, we'll turn you into katty kebabs!"

Twenty-two

Brigitte's, in New York's financial district, was a restaurant all of mirrors so the diners might observe exactly how enviable they were as they ate. It was named for the owners' dog, the tallest, flattest creature you ever saw; like paper, you could see her properly only from the side.

In the morning, as Biju and the rest of the staff began bustling about, the owners, Odessa and Baz, drank Tailors of Harrowgate darjeeling at a corner table. Colonial India, free India—the tea was the same, but the romance was gone, and it was best sold on the word of the past. They drank tea and diligently they read the *New York Times* together, including the international news. It was overwhelming.

Former slaves and natives. Eskimos and Hiroshima people, Amazonian Indians and Chiapas Indians and Chilean Indians and American Indians and Indian Indians. Australian aborigines, Guatemalans and Colombians and Brazilians and Argentineans, Nigerians, Burmese, Angolans, Peruvians, Ecuadorians, Bolivians, Afghans, Cambodians, Rwandans, Filipinos, Indonesians, Liberians, Borneoans, Papua New Guineans, South Africans, Iraqis, Iranians, Turks, Armenians, Palestinians, French Guyanese, Dutch Guyanese, Surinamese, Sierra Leonese, Malagasys, Senegalese, Maldivians, Sri Lankans, Malaysians, Kenyans, Panamanians,

Mexicans, Haitians, Dominicans, Costa Ricans, Congoans, Mauritanians, Marshall Islanders, Tahitians, Gabonese, Beninese, Malians, Jamaicans, Botswanans, Burundians, Sudanese, Eritreans, Uruguayans, Nicaraguans, Ugandans, Ivory Coastians, Zambians, Guinea-Bissauans, Cameroonians, Laotians, Zaireans coming at you screaming colonialism, screaming slavery, screaming mining companies screaming banana companies oil companies screaming CIA spy among the missionaries screaming it was Kissinger who killed their father and why don't you forgive third-world debt; Lumumba, they shouted, and Allende; on the other side, Pinochet, they said, Mobutu; contaminated milk from Nestlé, they said; Agent Orange; dirty dealings by Xerox. World Bank, UN, IMF, everything run by white people. Every day in the papers another thing!

Nestlé and Xerox were fine upstanding companies, the backbone of the economy, and Kissinger was at least a patriot. The United States was a young country built on the finest principles, and how could it possibly owe so many bills?

Enough was enough.

Business was business. Your bread might as well be left unbuttered were the butter to be spread so thin. The fittest one wins and gets the butter.

"Rule of nature," said Odessa to Baz. "Imagine if we were sitting around saying, 'So-and-so-score years ago, Neanderthals came out of the woods, attacked my family with a big dinosaur bone, and now you give back.' Two of the very first iron pots, my friend, and one toothsome toothy daughter from the first days of agriculture, when humans had larger molars, and four samples of an early version of the potato claimed, incidentally, by both Chile and Peru."

She was very witty, Odessa. Baz was proud of her cosmopolitan style, loved the sight of her in her little wire-rimmed glasses. Once he had been shocked to overhear some of their friends say she was black-hearted, but he had put it out of his mind.

"These white people!" said Achootan, a fellow dishwasher, to Biju in the kitchen. "Shit! But at least this country is better than England," he said. "At least they have some hypocrisy here. They believe they are good people and you get some relief. There they shout at you openly on the street, 'Go back to where you came from.'" He had spent eight years in Canterbury, and he had responded by shouting a line Biju was to hear many times over, for he repeated it several times a week: "Your father came to *my* country and took *my* bread and now I have come to *your* country to get *my* bread back."

Achootan didn't want a green card in the same way as Saeed did. He wanted it in the way of revenge.

"Why do you want it if you hate it here?" Odessa had said angrily to Achootan when he asked for sponsorship.

Well, he wanted it. Everyone wanted it whether you liked it or you hated it. The more you hated it sometimes, the more you wanted it.

This they didn't understand.

The restaurant served only one menu: steak, salad, fries. It assumed a certain pride in simplicity among the wealthy classes.

Holy cow. Unholy cow. Biju knew the reasoning he should keep by his side. At lunch and dinner the space filled with young uniformed businesspeople in their twenties and thirties.

"How would you like that, ma'am?"

"Rare."

"And you, sir?"

"Still mooin'."

Only the fools said, "Well done, please." Odessa could barely conceal her scorn. "Sure about that? Well, all right, but it's going to be tough."

She sat at the corner table where she had her morning tea and aroused the men by tearing into her steak.

"You know, Biju," she said, laughing, "isn't it ironic, nobody eats beef in India and just look at it—it's the shape of a big T-bone."

But here there were Indians eating beef. Indian bankers. Chomp chomp. He fixed them with a concentrated look of meaning as he cleared the plates. They saw it. They knew. He knew. They knew he knew. They pretended they didn't know he knew. They looked away. He took on a sneering look. But they could afford not to notice.

"I'll have the steak," they said with practiced nonchalance, with an ease like a signature that's a thoughtless scribble that you *know* has been practiced page after page.

Holy cow unholy cow.

Job no job.

One should not give up one's religion, the principles of one's parents and their parents before them. No, no matter what.

You had to live according to something. You had to find your dignity. The meat charred on the grill, the blood beaded on the surface, and then the blood also began to bubble and boil.

Those who could see a difference between a holy cow and an unholy cow would win.

Those who couldn't see it would lose.

So Biju was learning to sear steaks.

Blood, meat, salt, and the cannon directed at the plates: "Would you like freshly ground pepper on that, sir?"

"You know we may be poor in India, but there only a dog would eat meat cooked like this," said Achootan.

"We need to get aggressive about Asia," the businessmen said to each other. "It's opening up, new frontier, millions of potential consumers, big buying power in the middle classes, China, India, potential for cigarettes, diapers, Kentucky Fried, life insurance, water management, cell phones—big family people, always on the phone, all those men calling their mothers, all those mothers calling all their many, many children; this country is done, Europe done, Latin America done, Africa is a basket case except for oil; Asia is the next frontier. Is there oil anywhere there? They don't have oil, do they? They must. . . ."

The talk was basic. If anyone dared to call them *Fool!* they could just point at their bank accounts and let the numbers refute the accusation.

Biju thought of Saeed Saeed who still refused to eat a pig, "They dirty, man, they messy. *First* I am Muslim, then I am Zanzibari, *then* I *will BE* American." Once he'd shown Biju his new purchase of a model of a mosque with a quartz clock set into the bottom that was programmed, at the five correct hours, to start agitating: *"Allah hu Akbar, la ilhaha illullah, wal lah hu akbar. . . ."* Through the crackle of the tape from the top of the minaret came ancient sand-weathered words, that keening cry from the desert offering sustenance to create a man's strength, his faith in an empty-bellied morning and all through the day, that he might not fall through the filthy differences between nations. The lights came on encouragingly, flashing in the mosque in disco green and white.

"Why do you want to leave?" Odessa was shocked. A chance like they had given him! He surely didn't know how lucky he was.

"He'll never make it in America with that kind of attitude," said Baz hopefully.

Biju left as a new person, a man full to the brim with a wish to live within a narrow purity.

"Do you cook with beef?" he asked a prospective employer.

"We have a Philly steak sandwich."

"Sorry. I can't work here."

"They worship the cow," he heard the owner of the establishment tell someone in the kitchen, and he felt tribal and astonishing.

Smoky Joe's.

"Beef?"

"Honey," said the lady, "Ah don't mean to ahffend you, but Ah'm a steak eater and Ah AAHM beef."

Marilyn. Blown-up photographs of Marilyn Monroe on the wall, Indian owner at the desk!

The owner was on the speakerphone.

"Rajnibhai, *Kem chho?*"

"What?"

"Rajnibhai?"

"Who aez thees?" Very Indian-trying-to-be-American accent.

"Kem chho? Saaru chho? Teme samjo chho?"

"WHAAT?"

"Don't speak Gujerati, sir?"

"No."

"You are Gujerati, no?"

"No."

"But your name is Gujerati??"

"Who are you??!!"

"You are *not* Gujerati?"

"Who are you??!!"

"AT&T, sir, offering special rates to India."

"Don't know anyone in India."

"Don't know anyone???? You must have some relative?"

"Yeah," American accent growing more pronounced, "but I don' taaalk to my relateev. . . ."

Shocked silence.

"Don't talk to your relative?"

Then, "We are offering forty-seven cents per minute."

"Vhaat deeference does that make? I haeve aalready taaald you," he spoke s l o w as if to an idiot, "no taleephone caalls to Eeendya."

"But you are from Gujerat?" Anxious voice.

"Veea Kampala, Uganda, Teepton, England, and Roanoke state of Vaergeenia! One time I went to Eeendya and, laet me tell you, you canaat pay me to go to that caantreey agaen!"

Slipping out and back on the street. It was horrible what happened to Indians abroad and nobody knew but other Indians abroad. It was a dirty little rodent secret. But, no, Biju wasn't done. His country called him again. He smelled his fate. Drawn, despite himself, by his nose, around a corner, he saw the first letter of the sign, *G*, then an *AN*. His soul anticipated the rest: *DHI*. As he approached the Gandhi Café, the air gradually grew solid. It was always unbudgeable here, with the smell of a thousand and one meals accumulated, no matter the winter storms that howled around the corner, the rain, the melting heat. Though the restaurant was dark, when Biju tested the door, it swung open.

There in the dim space, at the back, amid lentils splattered about and spreading grease transparencies on the cloths of abandoned tables yet uncleared, sat Harish-Harry, who, with his brothers Gaurish-Gary and Dhansukh-Danny, ran a triplet of Gandhi Cafés in New York, New Jersey, and Connecticut. He didn't look up as Biju entered. He had his pen hovering over a request for a donation sent by a cow shelter outside Edison, New Jersey.

If you gave a hundred dollars, in addition to such bonus miles as would be totted up to your balance sheet for lives to come, "We will send you a free gift; please check the box to indicate your preference":

1. A preframed decorative painting of Krishna-Lila: "She longs for her lord and laments."
2. A copy of the *Bhagavad Gita* accompanied by commentary by Pandit so-and-so (B.A., MPhil., Ph.D., President of the Hindu Heritage Center), who has just completed a lecture tour in sixty-six countries.
3. A CD of devotional music beloved by Mahatma Gandhi.
4. A gift-coupon to the Indiagiftmart: "Surprise the special lady in your life with our special *choli* in the colors of onion and tender pink, coupled with a butter *lehnga*. For the woman who makes your house a home, a set of twenty-five spice jars with vacuum lids. Stock up on Haldiram's Premium Nagpur Chana Nuts that you must have been missing. . . ."

His pen hovered. Pounced.

To Biju he said: "Beef? Are you crazy? We are an all-Hindu establishment. No Pakistanis, no Bangladeshis, those people don't know how to cook, have you been to those restaurants on Sixth Street? *Bilkul bekaar. . . .*"

One week later, Biju was in the kitchen and Gandhi's favorite tunes were being sung over the sound system.

Twenty-three

Gyan and Sai's romance was flourishing and the political trouble continued to remain in the background for them.

Eating *momos* dipped in chutney, Gyan said: "You're my *momo.*"

Sai said: "No you're mine."

Ah, dumpling stage of love—it had set them off on a tumble of endearments and nicknames. They thought of them in quiet moments and placed them before each other like gifts. The *momo,* mutton in dough, one thing plump and cozy within the other—it connoted protection, affection.

But during the time they ate together at Gompu's, Gyan had used his hands without a thought and Sai ate with the only implement on the table—a tablespoon, rolling up her roti on the side and nudging the food onto the spoon with it. Noticing this difference, they had become embarrassed and put the observation aside.

"Kishmish," he called her to cover it up, and *"Kaju"* she called him, raisin and cashew, sweet, nutty, and expensive. Because new love makes sightseers out of couples even in their own town, they went on excursions to the Mong Pong Nature Reserve, to Delo Lake; they picnicked by the Teesta and the Relli. They went to the sericulture institute from which

came a smell of boiling worms. The manager gave them a tour of the piles of yellowy cocoons moving subtly in a corner, machines that tested water-proofing, flexibility; and he shared his dream of the future, of the water-proof and drip-dry sari, stain-proof, prepleated, zippable, reversible, super duper new millennium sari, named for timeless Bollywood hits like *Disco Dancer.* They took the toy train and went to the Darjeeling zoo and viewed in their free, self-righteous, modern love, the unfree and ancient bars, behind which lived a red panda, ridiculously solemn for being such a madly beautiful thing, chewing his bamboo leaves as carefully as a bank clerk doing numbers. They visited the Zang Dog Palri Fo Brang Monastery on Durpin Dara, where little monks were being entertained by the gray-haired ones, running up and down pulling the children on rice sacks, sailing them over the polished monastery floor, before the murals of demons and Guru Padmasambhava with his wrathful smile ensconced in a curly mustache, his carmine cloak, diamond scepter, lotus hat with a vulture feather; before a ghost riding a snow lion and a green Tara on a yak; sailing the children before the doors that opened like bird wings onto the scene of mountains all around.

From Durpin Dara, where you could see so far and high, the world resembled a map from a divine perspective. One could see the landscape stretching below and beyond, rivers and plateaus. Gyan asked Sai about her family, but she felt uncertain about what she should say, because she thought if she told him about the space program, he might feel inferior and ashamed. "My parents eloped and nobody spoke to them again. They died in Russia where my father was a scientist."

But his own family story also led overseas, he told Sai, quite proudly. They had more in common than they thought.

The story went like this:

In the 1800s his ancestors had left their village in Nepal and arrived in Darjeeling, lured by promises of work on a tea plantation. There, in a small hamlet bordering one of the remoter tea estates, they had owned a buffalo renowned for its astonishingly creamy milk. By and by along came the Imperial Army, measuring potential soldiers in villages all over the hills with a measuring tape and ruler, and they had happened upon the impressive shoulders of Gyan's great-grandfather, who had grown so strong on the milk of their buffalo that he had beaten the village sweet-seller's son in a wrestling match, an exceptionally glossy and healthy boy. An earlier recruit from their village reported soldiers were kept in ladylike comfort—warm and dry with blankets and socks, butter and ghee, mutton twice a week, an egg each day, water always in the taps, medicine for every ailment, every whim and scuff. You could solicit help for an itch on the bottom or a bee sting without shame, all for no more work than to march up and down the Grand Trunk Road. The army offered far more money to this boy grown strong on buffalo milk than his father had ever earned, for his father labored as a runner for the plantation; left before dawn with a big conical basket divided into sections on his back and strove to return by sundown, struggling uphill. The basket would now be filled with a vegetable layer and a live chicken pecking at the weave; eggs, toilet paper, soap, hairpins, and letter paper on top for the memsahib to write: "My darling daughter, it is wildly beautiful here and the beauty almost, almost makes up for the loneliness. . . ."

So he swore allegiance to the Crown, and off he went, the beginning of over a hundred years of family commitment to the wars of the English.

At the beginning, the promise had held true—all Gyan's great-grandfather did was march for many prosperous years, and he acquired a wife and three sons. But then they sent him to Mesopotamia where Turkish bullets made a sieve of his heart and he leaked to death on the battlefield. As a kindness to the family, that they might not lose their income, the army employed his eldest son, although the famous buffalo, by now, was dead, and the new recruit was spindly. Indian soldiers fought in Burma, in Gibraltar, in Egypt, in Italy.

Two months short of his twenty-third birthday, in 1943, the spindly soldier was killed in Burma, shakily defending the British against the Japanese. His brother was offered a job and this boy died, too, in Italy, outside Florence, not fighting at all, but making jam from apricots for the major of the battalion in a villa housing British troops. Six lemons, he had been instructed, and four cups of sugar. He stirred the pot in the unthreatening Italian countryside, pheasants whirring over the olives and the vines, the resistance army unearthing truffles in the woods. It was a particularly bountiful spring, and then, they were bombed—

When Gyan was quite small, the last family recruit had one day climbed off the bus in Kalimpong's bus station and arrived missing a toe. There was nobody who could remember him, but finally, their father's childhood memories were resurrected and the man was recognized as an uncle. He had lived with Gyan's family until he died, but they never discovered where he traveled to, or which countries he had fought against. He came of a generation, all over the world, for whom it was easier to forget than to remember, and the more their children pressed, the more their memory dissipated. Once Gyan had asked: "Uncle, but what is England *like?*"

And he said: "I don't know. . . ."

"How can you not know???"

"But I have never been."

All these years in the British army and he had never been to England! How could this be? They thought he had prospered and forgotten them, living like a London lord. . . .

Where *had* he been, then?

The uncle wouldn't say. Once every four weeks he went to the post office to collect his seven-pound-a-month pension. Mostly he sat on a folding chair, silently moving an expressionless face like a sunflower, a blank handicapped insistence following the sun, the only goal left in his life to match the two, the orb of his face and the orb of light.

The family had since invested their fortunes in schoolteaching and Gyan's father taught in a tea plantation school beyond Darjeeling.

Then the story stopped. "What about your father? What is he like?" Sai asked, but she didn't press him. After all, she knew about stories having to stop.

The nights were turning chilly already, and it grew dark earlier. Sai, returning late and fumbling for the road beneath her feet, stopped at Uncle Potty's for a torch. "Where's that handsome fellow . . . ?" Uncle Potty and Father Booty teased her. "Goodness. Those Nepali boys, high cheekbones, arm muscles, broad shoulders. Men who can *do* things, Sai, cut down trees, build fences, carry heavy boxes . . . *mmm mmm.*"

The cook was waiting at the gate with a lantern when she finally reached Cho Oyu. His bad-tempered wrinkled face peered from an assortment of mufflers and sweaters. "I've been waiting, waiting. . . . In this darkness you have not come home!" he complained, waddling in front of her along the path from gate to house, looking round and womanish.

"Why don't you leave me alone?" she said, conscious for the first time of the unbearable stickiness of family and friends when she had found freedom and space in love.

The cook felt hurt to his chutney core. "I'll give you one smack," he shouted. "From childhood I have brought you up! With so much love! Is this any way to talk? Soon I'll die and then who will you turn to? Yes, yes, soon I'll be dead. Maybe then you'll be happy. Here I am, so worried, and there you are, having fun, don't care. . . ."

"Ohhoho." As usual she ended by attempting to placate him. He wouldn't be placated and then he was, just a little.

Twenty-four

In the Gandhi Café, the lights were kept low, the better to hide the stains. It was a long journey from here to the fusion trend, the goat cheese and basil samosa, the mango margarita. This was the real thing, generic Indian, and it could be ordered complete, one stop on the subway line or even on the phone: gilt and red chairs, plastic roses on the table with synthetic dewdrops, cloth paintings portraying—

Oh no, not again—

Yes again—

Krishna and the gopis, village belle at the well. . . .

And the menu—

Oh no, not again—

Yes, again—

Tikka masala, tandoori grill, navrattan vegetable curry, dal makhni, pappadum. Said Harish-Harry: "Find your market. Study your market. Cater to your market." Demand-supply. Indian-American point of agreement. This is why we make good immigrants. Perfect match. (In fact, dear sirs, madams, we were practicing a highly evolved form of capitalism long before America was America; yes, you may think it's your success, but all civilization comes from India, yes).

But was he underestimating his market? He didn't care.

The customers—poor students, untenured professors—filled up at the lunch buffet, "ALL YOU CAN EAT FOR $5.99," tottered out overcome by the tipsy snake charmer music and the heaviness of the meal.

To add up the new numbers that came clinking in, Harish-Harry's wife arrived on Sunday mornings after she had washed her hair. A horsetail of sopping tresses, bound loosely in a gold ribbon from a Diwali fruit-and-nut box, dripped onto the floor behind.

"*Arre,* Biju . . . *to sunao kahani,*" she always said, "*batao* . . . what's the story?"

But it didn't matter that he had no story to tell, because she went immediately to the ledgers kept under a row of gods and incense sticks.

"Hae hae," her husband laughed with pleasure, diamond and gold glints coming forth on the black velvet of his pupils, "You can't make a fool of Malini. She get on the phone, she get the best deal of anybody."

It had been Malini who had suggested the staff live down below in the kitchen.

"Free housing," Harish-Harry told Biju.

By offering a reprieve from NYC rents, they could cut the pay to a quarter of the minimum wage, reclaim the tips for the establishment, keep an eye on the workers, and drive them to work fifteen-, sixteen-, seventeen-hour donkey days. Saran, Jeev, Rishi, Mr. Lalkaka, and now Biju. All illegal. "We are a happy family here," she said, energetically slapping vegetable oil on her arms and face, "no need for lotions-potions, *baba,* this works just as well."

Biju had left the basement in Harlem one early morning when the leaves of the scraggly tree outside were an orange surprise, supple and luminous. He had one bag with him and his mattress—a rectangle of foam with egg crate marking rolled into a bundle and tied with string. Before he packed, he took one more look at his parents' wedding photo that he had brought from India, the color leaching out; it was, by now, a picture of two serious ghosts. Just as he was about to go, Jacinto, who always appeared for his rent at the right moment, came around the corner: "Adios adios," gold tooth flashing a miner's delight.

Biju looked back for the last time at that facade of former respectability deteriorating. In the distance stood Grant's tomb like a round gray funeral cake with barbarous trim. Closer, the projects were a dense series of bar graphs against the horizon.

At the Gandhi Café, amid oversized pots and sawdusty sacks of masalas, he set up his new existence. The men washed their faces and rinsed their mouths over the kitchen sink, combed their hair in the postage stamp mirror tacked above, hung their trousers on a rope strung across the room, along with the dishtowels. At night they unrolled their bedding wherever there was room.

The rats of his earlier jobs had not forsaken Biju. They were here, too, exulting in the garbage, clawing through wood, making holes that Harish-Harry stuffed with steel wool and covered with bricks, but they moved such petty obstructions aside. They were drinking milk just like the billboards told them, eating protein; vitamins and minerals spilled out of their invincible ears and claws, their gums and fur. Kwarshikov, beri beri, goiter (that in Kalimpong had caused a population of mad toad throated dwarves to roam the hillside), such deficiency disorders were unknown to such a population.

One chewed Biju's hair at night.

"For its nest," said Jeev. "It's expecting, I think."

They took to creeping up and sleeping on the tables. At daybreak they shuffled back down before Harish arrived, "*Chalo*, *chalo*, another day, another dollar."

Toward his staff Harish-Harry was avuncular, jocular, but he could suddenly become angry and disciplinary. "Shuddap, keep shut," he'd say, and he wasn't above smacking their heads. But when an American patron walked through the door, his manner changed instantly and drastically into another thing and a panic seemed to overcome him.

"Hallo Hallo," he said to a pink satin child smearing food all over the chair legs, "Ya givin your mom too much trouble, ha ha? But one day ya make her feel proud, right? Gointa be a beeeg man, reech man, vhat you say? Ya vanna nice cheekan karry?" He smiled and genuflected.

Harish-Harry—the two names, Biju was learning, indicated a deep rift that he hadn't suspected when he first walked in and found him, a manifestation of that clarity of principle which Biju was seeking. That support for a cow shelter was in case the Hindu version of the afterlife turned out to be true and that, when he died, he was put through the

Hindu machinations of the beyond. What, though, if other gods sat upon the throne? He tried to keep on the right side of power, tried to be loyal to so many things that he himself couldn't tell which one of his selves was the authentic, if any.

It wasn't just Harish-Harry. Confusion was rampant among the *"haalf 'n' haf"* crowd, the Indian students coming in with American friends, one accent one side of the mouth, another the other side; muddling it up, wobbling then, downgrading sometimes all the way to Hindi to show one another: Who? No, no, it was not they pretending to be other than who and what they were. They weren't the ones turning their back on the greatest culture the world has ever seen. . . .

And the romances—the Indian-White combination, in particular, was a special problem.

The *desis* entered feeling very ill at ease and the waiters began to smirk and sneer, raising their eyebrows to show them what they thought.

"Hot, medium, or mild?" they asked. "Hot," the patrons said invariably, showing off, informing their date they were the unadulterated exotic product, and in the kitchen they laughed, "Ha ha," then suddenly the unadulterated anger came out, *"sala!"*

The evildoers bit into the vindaloo—

And that vindaloo—it bit them back.

Faces smarting, ears and eyes burning, tongues becoming numb, they whimpered for yogurt, explaining to the table, "That is what we do in India, we always eat yogurt for the balance. . . ."

The balance, you know. . . .

You know, you know—

Hot cool, sweet sour, bitter pungent, the ancient wisdom of the Ayurveda that can grant a person complete poise. . . .

"Too hot?" Biju would ask, grinning.

Weeping, "No, no."

There was no purity in this venture. And no pride. He had come home to no clarity of vision.

Harish-Harry blamed his daughter for rattling his commitment. The girl was becoming American. Nose ring she found compatible with combat boots and clothes in camouflage print from the army-navy surplus.

His wife said, "All this nonsense, what is this, give her two tight slaps, that's what. . . ."

"Good you did like that," he had said, but slaps had not worked. "You go, girl!" he said, trying to rise, instead, to the occasion of his daughter being American. "You GO, gurlllll!!!" But that didn't work either. "I didn't ask to be born," she said. "You had me for your own selfish reasons, wanted a servant, didn't you? But in this country, Dad, nobody's going to wipe your ass for free."

Not even *bottom! * Wipe your *ass! Dad!* Not even *Papaji.* No wipe your bottom, *Papaji.* Dad and ass. Harish-Harry got drunk in an episode that would become familiar and tedious; he sat at the cash register and wouldn't go home, though the kitchen staff were anxiously waiting so they could get up on the tables and sleep wrapped in the tablecloths. "And they think we admire them!" He began to laugh. "Every time one enters my shop I smile"—he showed his skeleton grin—"'Hi, how ya doin,' but all I want is to break their necks. I can't, but maybe my son will, and that is my great hope. One day Jayant-Jay will smile and get his hands about their sons' necks and he will choke them dead."

"See, Biju, see what this world is," he said and began to weep with his arm on Biju's shoulder.

It was only the recollection of the money he was making that calmed him. Within this thought he found a perfectly reasonable reason for being here, a morality to agree on, a bridge over the split—and this single fact that didn't seem a contradiction between nations he blazoned forth.

"Another day another dollar, penny saved is penny earned, no pain no gain, business is business, gotta do what ya gotta do." These axioms were a luxury unavailable to Biju, of course, but he repeated them anyway, enjoying the cheerful words and the moment of camaraderie.

"Have to make a living, what can you do?" Biju would say.

"You are right, Biju. What can I do? Here we are," he ruminated, "for more opportunity. How can we help it?"

He hoped for a big house, then he hoped for a bigger house even if he had to leave it unfurnished for a while, like his nemesis Mr. Shah who owned seven rooms, all empty except for TV, couch, and carpeting in white. Even the TV was a white TV for white symbolized success out of India for the community. "Hae hae, we will take our time with the furniture," said Mr. Shah, "but house is there." Photos of the exterior had been sent to all the relatives in Gujarat, a white car parked in front. A Lexus, that premier luxury vehicle. On top of it sat his wife looking self-satisfied. She had left India a meek bride, scrolled and spattered with henna, so much gold in her sari she set off every metal detector in the airport—and now here she was—white pantsuit, bobbed hair, vanity case, and capable of doing the macarena.

Twenty-five

They took Mutt to the Apollo Deaf Tailors to be measured for a winter coat that would be cut out of a blanket, since the days had passed into winter, and while it didn't snow in Kalimpong, just turned dull, all around the snow line dipped, and the high mountains around town were brindled white. In the morning, they found frost in the runnels, frost on the crest, and frost in the crotch of the hills.

Through cracks and holes in Cho Oyu, came a sterile smell of winter. The bathroom taps and switches threw off shocks. Sweaters and shawls bristled with aroused fibers, shedding lightning. "Ow ow," Sai said. Her skin was a squamous pattern of drought. When she took off her clothes, dry skin fell like salt from a salt cellar and her hair, ridiculing gravity, rose in crackling radio antennae above her skull. When she smiled, her lips split and spilled blood.

Vaselined shiny and supple for Christmas, she joined Father Booty and Uncle Potty at Mon Ami, where, in addition to the Vaseline smell, there was an odor of wet sheep—but it was only their damp sweaters. A thatch of tinsel on a potted fir glinted in the light of the fire that razzmatazzed and popped, the cold smarting beyond.

Father Booty and Uncle Potty sang together:

Who threw the overalls in Mrs. Murphy's chowder?
When nobody answered, they shouted all the louder—
WHO THREW THE OVERALLS IN MRS. MURPHY'S
CHOWDER??

And they all joined in, drunk and wild.

Oh, beautiful evening—

Oh, beautiful soup in the copper Gyako pot, a moat of broth around the chimney of coals, mutton steam in their hair, rollicking shimmer of golden fat, dried mushrooms growing so slippery they'd slither down scalding before you could chomp upon their muscle. "What's for PUDS?" Lola, when she said this in England, had been unsettled to find that the English didn't understand. . . . Even Pixie had pretended to be bewildered. . . .

But here they comprehended perfectly, and Kesang lugged out a weighty pudding that united via brandy its fraternity of fruit and nut, and they made the pudding holy with a sanctifying crown of brandy flame.

Mustafa climbed to his favorite place again, on Sai's lap, turning first his face to the fire, then his behind, slowly softening, until his bottom began to dribble down the chair and he leaped up with a startled yowl, glaring at Sai as if she had been responsible for this indecency.

For the occasion, the sisters had brought out their ornaments from England—various things that looked as if they might taste of mints—snowflakes, snowmen, icicles, stars. There were little trolls, and elf shoemakers (why were cobblers, trolls, and elves, Christmasy? Sai wondered) that were stored the rest of the year inside a Bata shoe box up in the attic along with the story of the English ghost in a flouncy nightie with whom they used to scare Sai when she first arrived:

"What does she say?"

"Hmm, I think she makes a *whoo hoo* like an owl, whistling low, *whoo hooo,* sweet and serious. And now and then she says, 'Care for a drop of sh-e-rr-y, mye dee-a-r?' In an unsteady, but highly cultivated voice."

And there were presents of knitted socks from the Tibetan refugee village, the wool still with bits of straw and burrs that provided authenticity and aroused extra sympathy for refugees even while it irritated the toes. There were amber and coral earrings, bottles of homemade apricot brandy made by Father Booty, books to write in with translucent sheets of rice paper, and ribbed bamboo spines made in Bong Busti by a tableful of chatty lady employees sharing the tasty things in their tiffins at lunch, who sometimes dropped a pickle . . . and sometimes the pages had a festive yellow splotch. . . .

More rum. Deeper into Lola's intoxication, when the fire died low, she became serene, drew a pure memory from the depths:

"In those old days, in the fifties and sixties," she said, "it was still a long journey into Sikkim or Bhutan, for there were hardly any roads. We used to travel on horseback, carrying sacks of peas for the ponies, maps, hip flasks of whiskey. In the rainy season, leeches would free-fall from the trees onto us, timing precisely the perfect acrobat moment. We would wash in saltwater to keep them off, salt our shoes and socks, even our hair. The storms would wash the salt off and we'd have to stop and salt ourselves again. The forests at that time were fierce and enormous—if you were told a magical beast lived there, you'd believe it. We'd emerge to the tops of mountains where monasteries limpet to the sides of rock, surrounded by chortens and prayer flags, the white facades catching the light of the sunset, all straw gold, the mountains rugged lines of indigo. We'd stand and rest until the leeches began working into our socks. Buddhism was ancient here, more ancient than it was anywhere else, and we went to a monastery that had been built, they said, when a flying lama had flown from one mountaintop to another, from Menak Hill to Enchey, and another that had been built when a rainbow connected Kanchenjunga to the crest of the hill. Often the gompas were deserted for the monks were also farmers; they were away at their fields and gathered only a few times a year for *pujas* and all you could hear was the wind in the bamboo. Clouds came through the doors and mingled with paintings of clouds. The interiors were dark, smoke-stained, and we'd try to make out the murals by the light of butter lamps. . . .

"It took two weeks of rough trekking to get to Thimpu. On the way, through the jungle, we would stay in those shiplike fortresses called *dzongs*, built without a single nail. We'd send a man ahead with news of our arrival, and they'd send along a gift to welcome us at some midpoint. A hundred years ago it would have been Tibetan tea, saffron rice, silk robes from China lined with the fleece of unborn lambs, that kind of thing; by then, for us, it would be a picnic hamper of ham sandwiches and Gymkhana beer. The *dzongs* were completely self-contained, with their own armies, peasants, aristocrats, and prisoners in the dungeons—murderers and men caught fishing with dynamite all thrown in together. When they needed a new cook or gardener, they put down a rope and pulled a man out. We'd arrive to find, in lantern-lit halls, cheese cauliflower and pigs in blankets. This one man, in for violent murder, had such a hand for pastry—Whatever it takes, he had it. The best gooseberry tart I've ever tasted."

"And the baths," Father Booty joined in, "remember the baths? Once, when I was on a dairy outreach program, I stayed with the mother of the king, sister of Jigme Dorji, the Bhutanese agent and ruler of the province of Ha, who lived next to you, Sai, at Tashiding—he became so powerful that the king's assassins killed him even though he was brother of the queen. The baths in their *dzong* were made of hollowed-out tree trunks, a carved slot underneath for heated rocks to keep the water steaming, and as you soaked, the servants came in and out to replace the hot stones and give you a scrub. And if we were camping, they would dig a pit by the river, fill it with water, lower hot stones into it; thus you splashed about with all the Himalayan snows around and forests of rhododendrons.

"Years later, when I returned to Bhutan, the queen insisted I visit the bathroom. 'But I don't need to go.'

"'No, but you must.'

"'But I don't NEED to go.'

"'Oh, but you MUST.'

"So I went, and the bathrooms had been redone, all modern piping, pink tiles, pink showers, and pink flush loos.

"When I came out again, the queen was waiting, pink as the bathroom with pride, 'See how nice it is? Did you SEE?'

"Why don't we all go again," said Noni. "Let's plan a trip. Why not?"

Sai got into bed that night in her new socks, the same three-layered design that sherpas used in mountaineering expeditions, that Tenzing had worn to climb Everest.

Sai and Gyan had recently made an excursion to see these socks of Tenzing, spread-eagled in the Darjeeling museum adjoining his memorial, and they had taken a good look at them. They had also studied his hat, ice pick, rucksack, samples of dehydrated foods that he might have taken along, Horlicks, torches, and samples of moths and bats of the high Himalayas.

"He was the real hero, Tenzing," Gyan had said. "Hilary couldn't have made it without sherpas carrying his bags." Everyone around had agreed. Tenzing was certainly first, or else he was made to wait with the bags so Hilary could take the first step on behalf of that colonial enterprise of sticking your flag on what was not yours.

Sai had wondered, Should humans conquer the mountain or should they wish for the mountain to possess them? Sherpas went up and down, ten times, fifteen times in some cases, without glory, without claim of ownership, and there were those who said it was sacred and shouldn't be sullied at all.

Twenty-six

It was after the new year when Gyan happened to be buying rice in the market that he heard people shouting as his rice was being weighed. When he emerged from the shop, he was gathered up by a procession coming panting up Mintri Road led by young men holding their kukris aloft and shouting, "*Jai* Gorkha." In the mess of faces he saw college friends whom he'd ignored since he started his romance with Sai. Padam, Jungi, Dawa, Dilip.

"Chhang, Bhang, Owl, Donkey," he called his friends by their nick-names—

They were shouting, "Victory to the Gorkha Liberation Army," and didn't hear him. On the strength of those pushing behind, and with the momentum of those who went before, they melded into a single being. Without any effort at all, Gyan found himself sliding along the street of Marwari merchants sitting cross-legged on white mattress platforms. They flowed by the antique shops with the *thangkhas* that grew more an-tique with each blast of exhaust from passing traffic; past the Newari silversmiths; a Parsi homeopathic doctor; the deaf tailors who were all looking shocked, feeling the vibrations of what was being said but unable to make sense of it. A mad lady with tin cans hanging from her ears and dressed in tailor scraps, who had been roasting a dead bird on some coals by the side of the road, waved to the procession like a queen.

As he floated through the market, Gyan had a feeling of history being wrought, its wheels churning under him, for the men were behaving as if they were being featured in a documentary of war, and Gyan could not help but look on the scene already from the angle of nostalgia, the position of a revolutionary. But then he was pulled out of the feeling, by the ancient and usual scene, the worried shopkeepers watching from their monsoon-stained grottos. Then he shouted along with the crowd, and the very mingling of his voice with largeness and lustiness seemed to create a relevancy, an affirmation he'd never felt before, and he was pulled back into the making of history.

Then, looking at the hills, he fell out of the experience again. How can the ordinary be changed?

Were these men entirely committed to the importance of the procession or was there a disconnected quality to what they did? Were they taking their cues from old protest stories or from the hope of telling a new story? Did their hearts rise and fall to something true? Once they shouted, marched, was the feeling authentic? Did they see themselves from a perspective beyond this moment, these unleashed Bruce Lee fans in their American T-shirts made-in-China-coming-in-via-Kathmandu?

He thought of how often he wished he might line up at the American embassy or the British, and leave. "Listen Momo," he had said to a delighted Sai, "let's go to Australia." Fly away, bye-bye, ta-ta. Free from history. Free from family demands and the built-up debt of centuries. The patriotism was false, he suddenly felt as he marched; it was surely just frustration—the leaders harnessing the natural irritations and disdain of adolescence for cynical ends; for their own hope in attaining the same power as government officials held now, the same ability to award local businessmen deals in exchange for bribes, for the ability to give jobs to their relatives, places to their children in schools, cooking gas connections. . . .

But the men were shouting, and he saw from their faces that they didn't have his cynicism. They meant what they were saying; they felt a lack of justice. They moved past the godowns dating from when Kalimpong was the center of the wool trade, past the Snow Lion travel agency, the STD telephone booth, Ferrazzini's Pioneer in Fast Food, the two Tibetan sisters at the Warm Heart Shawl Shop; past the comics lending library and the broken umbrellas hanging oddly like injured birds around the man who mended them. They came to a stop outside the police station, where the policemen who could usually be found gossiping outside had vanished indoors and locked the door.

Gyan remembered the stirring stories of when citizens had risen up in their millions and demanded that the British leave. There was the nobility of it, the daring of it, the glorious fire of it—"India for Indians. No taxation without representation. No help for the wars. Not a man, not a rupee. British Raj Murdabad!" If a nation had such a climax in its history, its heart, would it not hunger for it again?

A man clambered up on the bench:

"In 1947, brothers and sisters, the British left granting India her freedom, granting the Muslims Pakistan, granting special provisions for the scheduled castes and tribes, leaving everything taken care of, brothers and sisters——

"Except us. EXCEPT US. The Nepalis of India. At that time, in April of 1947, the Communist Party of India demanded a Gorkhasthan, but the request was ignored. . . . We are laborers on the tea plantations, coolies dragging heavy loads, soldiers. And are we allowed to become doctors and government workers, owners of the tea plantations? *No!* We are kept at the level of servants. We fought on behalf of the British for two hundred years. We fought in World War One. We went to East Africa, to Egypt, to the Persian Gulf. We were moved from here to there as it suited them. We fought in World War Two. In Europe, Syria, Persia, Malaya, and Burma. Where would they be without the courage of our people? We are still fighting for them. When the regiments were divided at independence, some to go to England, some to stay, those of us who remained here fought in the same way for India. We are soldiers, loyal, brave. India or England, they never had cause to doubt our loyalty. In the wars with Pakistan we fought our former comrades on the other side of the border. How our spirit cried. But we are Gorkhas. We are soldiers. Our character has never been in doubt. And have we been rewarded?? Have we been given compensation?? Are we given respect??

"*No!* They spit on us."

Gyan recalled his last job interview well over a year ago, when he had traveled all the way to Calcutta by overnight bus to an office buried in the heart of a concrete block lit with the shudder of a fluorescent tube that had never resolved into steady light.

Everyone looked hopeless, the men in the room and the interviewer who had finally turned the shuddering light off—"Voltage low"—and conducted the interview in darkness. "Very good, we will let you know if you are successful." Gyan, feeling his way out through the maze and stepping into the unforgiving summer light, knew he would never be hired.

"Here we are eighty percent of the population, ninety tea gardens in the district, but is even one Nepali-owned?" asked the man.

"No."

"Can our children learn our language in school?"

"No."

"Can we compete for jobs when they have already been promised to others?"

"No."

"In our own country, the country we fight for, we are treated like slaves. Every day the lorries leave bearing away our forests, sold by foreigners to fill the pockets of foreigners. Every day our stones are carried from the riverbed of the Teesta to build their houses and cities. We are laborers working barefoot in all weather, thin as sticks, as they sit fat in managers' houses with their fat wives, with their fat bank accounts and their fat children going abroad. Even their chairs are fat. We must fight, brothers and sisters, to manage our own affairs. We must unite under the banner of the GNLF, Gorkha National Liberation Front. We will build hospitals and schools. We will provide jobs for our sons. We will give dignity to our daughters carrying heavy loads, breaking stone on the roads. We will defend our own homeland. This is where we were born, where our parents were born, where our grandparents were born. We will run our own affairs in our own language. If necessary, we will wash our bloody kukris in the mother waters of the Teesta. *Jai* Gorkha." The speech giver waved his kukri and then pierced his thumb, raised the gory sight for all to see.

"*Jai* Gorkha! *Jai* Gorkha! *Jai* Gorkha!" the crowd screamed, their own blood thrumming, pulsing, surging forth at the sight of the speech giver's hand. Thirty supporters stepped forward and also drew blood from their thumbs with their kukris to write a poster demanding Gorkhaland, in blood.

"Brave Gorkha soldiers protecting India—hear the call," said the leaflets flooding the hillsides. "Please quit the army at once. For when you will be retired then you may be treated as a foreigner."

The GNLF would offer jobs to its own, and a 40,000 strong Gorkha army, universities, and hospitals.

Later, Chhang, Bhang, Owl, Donkey, and many others sat in the cramped shack of Ex-Army Thapa's Canteen on Ringkingpong Road. A small handwritten sign painted on the side said "Broiler Chicken." A carom game board was balanced on an oil barrel outside and two creaky tattered soldiers, on bowlegs, originally of the Eighth Gurkha Rifles, played as the clouds shifted and billowed through their knees. The mountains sliced sharply and tumbled down at either side to bamboo thickets gray with distilled vapor.

The air grew colder and the evening progressed. Gyan, who had been gathered up accidentally in the procession, who had shouted half facetiously, half in earnest, who had half played, half lived a part, found the fervor had affected him. His sarcasm and his embarrassment were gone. Fired by alcohol, he finally submitted to the compelling pull of history and found his pulse leaping to something that felt entirely authentic.

He told the story of his great grandfather, his great uncles, "And do you think they got the same pension as the English of equal rank? They fought to death, but did they earn the same salary?"

All the other anger in the canteen greeted his, clapped his anger on the back. It suddenly became clear why he had no money and no real job had come his way, why he couldn't fly to college in America, why he was ashamed to let anyone see his home. He thought of how he had kept Sai away the day she had suggested visiting his family. Most of all, he realized why his father's meekness infuriated him, and why he found himself unable to speak of him, he who had so modest an idea of happiness that even the daily irritant of fifty-two screaming boys in his plantation schoolroom, even the distance of his own family, the loneliness of his work, didn't upset him. Gyan wanted to shake him, but what satisfaction could be received from shaking a sock? To accost such a person—it just came back to frustrate you twice over. . . .

For a moment all the different pretences he had indulged in, the shames he had suffered, the future that wouldn't accept him—all these things joined together to form a single truth.

The men sat unbedding their rage, learning, as everyone does in this country, at one time or another, that old hatreds are endlessly retrievable.

And when they had disinterred it, they found the hate pure, purer than it could ever have been before, because the grief of the past was gone. Just the fury remained, distilled, liberating. It was theirs by birthright, it could take them so high, it was a drug. They sat feeling elevated, there on the narrow wood benches, stamping their cold feet on the earth floor.

It was a masculine atmosphere and Gyan felt a moment of shame remembering his tea parties with Sai on the veranda, the cheese toast, queen cakes from the baker, and even worse, the small warm space they inhabited together, the nursery talk—

It suddenly seemed against the requirements of his adulthood.

He voiced an adamant opinion that the Gorkha movement take the harshest route possible.

Twenty-seven

Moody and restless, Gyan arrived at Cho Oyu the next day, upset at having to undertake that long walk in the cold for the small amount of money the judge paid him. It maddened him that people lived here in this enormous house and property, taking hot baths, sleeping alone in spacious rooms, and he suddenly remembered the cutlets and boiled peas dinner with Sai and the judge, the judge's "Common sense seems to have evaded you, young man."

"How late you are," said Sai when she saw him, and he was angry in a different way from the night before when, indignant in war paint, he had stuck his bottom out one way and his chest the other way and discovered a self-righteous posturing, a new way of talking. This was a petty anger that pulled him back, curtailed his spirit, made him feel peevish. The annoyance was different from any he'd felt with Sai before.

To cheer him up, Sai told him of the Christmas party—

You know, three times we tried to light the soup ladle full of brandy and pour it over the pudding—

Gyan ignored her, opened up the physics book. Oh, if only she would shut up—that bright silliness he had not noticed in her before—he was too irritated to stand it.

She turned reluctantly to its pages; it was a long time since they had properly looked at physics.

"If two objects, one weighing . . . and the other weighing . . . are dropped from the leaning tower of Pisa, at which time and at what speed will they fall to the ground?"

"You're in an unpleasant mood," she said and yawned with luxury to indicate other, better, options.

He pretended he hadn't heard her.

Then he yawned, too, despite himself.

She yawned again, elaborately like a lion, letting it bloom forward.

Then he did also, a meager yawn he tried to curb and swallow.

She did—

He did.

"Bored by physics?" she asked, encouraged by the apparent reconciliation.

"No. Not at all."

"Why are you yawning then?"

"BECAUSE I'M BORED TO DEATH BY YOU, THAT'S WHY."

Stunned silence.

"I am not interested in Christmas!" he shouted. "Why do you celebrate Christmas? You're Hindus and you don't celebrate Id or Guru Nanak's birthday or even Durga Puja or Dussehra or Tibetan New Year."

She considered it: Why? She always had. Not because of the convent, her hatred of it was so deep, but. . . .

"You are like slaves, that's what you are, running after the West, embarrassing yourself. It's because of people like you we never get anywhere."

Stung by his unexpected venom, "No," she said, "that's not it."

"Then what?"

"If I want to celebrate Christmas, I will, and if I don't want to celebrate Diwali then I won't. Nothing wrong in a bit of fun and Christmas is an Indian holiday as much as any other."

This tagged on to make him feel antisecular and anti-Gandhian.

"Do what you will," he shrugged, "it's nothing to me—it only shows to the whole world that you are a FOOL."

He uttered the words deliberately, eager to see that hurt cross her face.

"Well, why don't you go home then, if I'm such a fool? What *is* the point of teaching me?"

"All right, I will. You're right. What *is* the point of teaching you? It's clear all you want to do is copy. Can't think for yourself. *Copycat, copycat.* Don't you know, these people you copy like a copycat, THEY DON'T WANT YOU!!!!"

"I'm not copying anyone!"

"You think you are the original person celebrating Christmas? Come on, don't tell me you're as stupid as that?"

"Well, if you're so clever," she said, "how come you can't even find a proper job? Fail, fail, fail. Every single interview."

"Because of people like you!"

"Oh, because of me . . . and you're telling me that I am stupid? Who's stupid? Go put it before a judge and we'll see who he says is the stupid one."

She picked up her glass and the water in it sloshed over before it reached her lips, she was trembling so.

Twenty-eight

The judge was thinking of his hate.

When he returned from England, he had been greeted by the same geriatric brass band that had seen him off on his journey, but it was invisible this time because of the billows of smoke and dust raised by the fireworks that had been thrown on the railway track, exploding as the train drew into the station. Whistles and whoops went up from the two thousand people who had gathered to witness this historic event, the first son of the community to join the ICS. He was smothered with garlands; flower petals settled on the brim of his hat. And there, standing in a knife's width of shade at the end of the station, was someone else who looked vaguely familiar; not a sister, not a cousin; it was Nimi, his wife, who had been returned from her father's house, where she'd spent the intervening time. Except for exchanges with landladies and "How do you do?" in shops, he hadn't spoken to a woman in years.

She came toward him with a garland. They didn't look at each other as she lifted it over his head. Up went his eyes, down went hers. He was twenty-five, she was nineteen.

"So shy, so shy"—the delighted crowd was sure of having

witnessed the terror of love. (What amazing hope the audience has—always refusing to believe the nonexistence of romance.)

What would he do with her?

He had forgotten he had a wife.

Well, he knew, of course, but she had drifted away like everything in his past, a series of facts that no longer had relevance. This one, though, it would follow him as wives in those days followed their husbands.

All these past five years Nimi had remembered their bicycle ride and her levitating heart—how lovely she must have appeared to him. . . . He had found her desirable and she was willing to appreciate anyone who would think so. She rummaged in the toilet case Jemubhai had brought back from Cambridge and found a jar of green salve, a hairbrush and comb set in silver, a pom-pom with a loop of silk in a round container of powder—and, coming at her exquisitely, her first whiff of lavender. The crisp light scents that rose from his new possessions were all of a foreign place. Piphit smelled of dust and once in a while there was the startling fragrance of rain. Piphit's perfumes were intoxicants, rich and dizzying. She didn't know much about the English, and whatever she did know was based on a few snatches of talk that had reached them in the seclusion of the women's quarters, such as the fact that Englishwomen at the club played tennis dressed only in their underwear.

"Shorts!" said a young uncle.

"Underwear," the ladies insisted.

Among underwear-clad ladies wielding tennis rackets, how would she manage?

She picked up the judge's powder puff, unbuttoned her blouse, and powdered her breasts. She hooked up her blouse again and that puff, so foreign, so silken, she stuffed inside; she was too grown-up for childish thieving, she knew, but she was filled with greed.

The afternoons in Piphit lasted so long, the Patels were resting, trying to efface the fear that time would never move again, all except for Jemubhai who had grown unused to such surrender.

He sat up, fidgeted, looked at the winged dinosaur, purple-beaked banana tree with the eye of one seeing it for the first time. He was a foreigner—*a foreigner*—every bit of him screamed. Only his digestion dissented and told him he was home: squatting painfully in that cramped outhouse, his gentleman's knees creaking, swearing "Bloody hell," he felt his digestion work as super efficient as—as *Western transportation.*

Idly deciding to check on his belongings, he uncovered the loss.

"Where is my powder puff?" shouted Jemubhai at the Patel ladies spread-eagled on mats in the veranda shade.

"What?" they asked, raising their heads, shielding their eyes against the detonating light.

"Someone has been through my belongings."

Actually, by then, almost everyone in the house had been through his belongings and they failed to see why this was a problem. His new ideas of privacy were unfathomable; why did he mind and how did this coincide with stealing?

"But what is missing?"

"My puff."

"What is that?"

He tried to explain.

"But what on earth is it for, *baba?*" They looked at him bemused.

"Pink and white what? That you put on your skin? Why?"

"Pink?"

His mother began to worry. "Is anything wrong with your skin?" she asked, concerned.

But, "Ha ha," laughed a sister who was listening carefully, "we sent you abroad to become a gentleman, and instead you have become a lady!"

The excitement spread, and from farther houses in the Patel clan, relatives began to arrive. The *kakas kakis masas masis phuas phois.* Children horrible all together, a clump that could not be separated child into child, for they resembled a composite monster with multiple arms and legs that came cartwheeling in, raising the dust, screaming; hundreds of hands were held over the monster's hundreds of giggling mouths. Who had stolen what?

"His powder puff is missing," said Jemubhai's father, who seemed to think this thing must be crucial to his son's work.

They all said *powder puff* in English, for, naturally, there was no Gujarati word for this invention. Their very accents rankled the judge. "Pauvdar Paaf," sounding like some Parsi dish.

They pulled out all the items in the cupboard, turned them upside down, exclaiming over and examining each one, his suits, his underwear, his opera glasses, through which he had viewed the tutus of ballerinas dancing a delicate sideways scuttle in *Giselle,* unfolding in pastry patterns and cake decorations.

But no, it wasn't there. It wasn't in the kitchen either, or in the veranda. It wasn't anywhere.

His mother questioned the naughtiest cousins.

"Did you see it?"

"What?"

"The paudar paaf."

"What is a paudur poff? Paudaar paaf?"

"To protect the skin."

"To protect the skin from what?"

And the entire embarrassment of explaining had to be gone through again.

"Pink and white? What for?"

"What the hell do all of you know?" said Jemubhai. Thieving, ignorant people.

He had thought they would have the good taste to be impressed and even a little awed by what he had become, but instead they were laughing.

"You must know something," the judge finally accused Nimi.

"I haven't seen it. Why should I pay it any attention?" she said. Her heart pounded beneath her two lavender-powdered pink and white breasts, beneath her husband's England-returned puff.

He did not like his wife's face, searched for his hatred, found beauty, dismissed it. Once it had been a terrifying beckoning thing that had made his heart turn to water, but now it seemed beside the point. An Indian girl could never be as beautiful as an English one.

Just then, as he was turning away, he saw it—

Sticking out between the hooks, a few thin and tender filaments.

"You filth!" he shouted and, from between her sad breasts, pulled forth, like a ridiculous flower, or else a bursting ruined heart—

His dandy puff.

"Break the bed," shouted an ancient aunt, hearing the scuffle inside the room, and they all began to giggle and nod in satisfaction.

"Now she will settle down," said another medicine-voiced hag. "That girl has too much spirit."

Inside the room, specially vacated of all who normally slept there, Jemubhai, his face apuff with anger, grabbed at his wife.

She slipped from his grasp and his anger flew.

She who had stolen. She who had made them *laugh at him*. This illiterate village girl. He grabbed at her again.

She was running and he was chasing her.

She ran to the door.

But the door was locked.

She tried again.

It didn't budge.

The aunt had locked it—just in case. All the stories of brides trying to escape—now and then even an account of a husband sidling out. Shameshameshameshame to the family.

He came at her with a look of murder.

She ran for the window.

He blocked her.

Without thinking, she picked up the powder container from the table near the door and threw it at his face, terrified of what she was doing, but the terror had joined irreversibly with the gesture, and in a second it was done—

The container broke apart, the powder lurched up

filtered down.

Ghoulishly sugared in sweet candy pigment, he clamped down on her, tussled her to the floor, and as more of that perfect rose complexion, blasted into a million motes, came filtering down, in a dense frustration of lust and fury—penis uncoiling, mottled purple-black as if with rage, blundering, uncovering the chute he had heard rumor of—he stuffed his way ungracefully into her.

An aging uncle, wizened bird man in dhoti and spectacles, watching through a crack in the wall outside, felt his own lust ripen and—pop—it sent him hopping about the courtyard.

Jemubhai was glad he could disguise his inexpertness, his crudity, with hatred and fury—this was a trick that would serve him well throughout his life in a variety of areas—but, my God, the grotesqueness of it all shocked him: the meeting of reaching, suckering organs in an awful attack and consumption; maimed, bruise-colored kicking, cringing forms of life; sour, hair-fringed gullet; agitating snake muscled malevolency; the stench of urine and shit mixed up with the smell of sex; the squelch, the marine squirt, that uncontrollable run—it turned his civilized stomach.

Yet he repeated the gutter act again and again. Even in tedium, on and on, a habit he could not stand in himself. This distaste and his persistence made him angrier than ever and any cruelty to her became irresistible. He would teach her the same lessons of loneliness and shame he had learned himself. In public, he never spoke to or looked in her direction.

She grew accustomed to his detached expression as he pushed into her, that gaze off into middle distance, entirely involved with itself, the same blank look of a dog or monkey humping in the bazaar; until all of a sudden he seemed to skid from control and his expression slid right off his face. A moment later, before anything was revealed, it settled back again and he withdrew to spend a long fiddly time in the bathroom with soap, hot water, and Dettol. He followed his ablutions with a clinical measure of whiskey, as if consuming a disinfectant.

The judge and Nimi traveled two days by train and by car, and when they arrived in Bonda, the judge rented a bungalow at the edge of the civil lines for thirty-five rupees a month, without water or electricity. He could afford nothing better until he repaid his debts, but still, he kept money aside to hire a companion for Nimi. A Miss Enid Pott who looked like a bulldog with a hat on top. Her previous employment had been governess to the children of Mr. Singh, the commissioner, and she had brought up her charges to call their mother Mam, their father Fa, had given them cod-liver oil for their collywobbles, and taught them to recite "Nellie Bly." A photograph in her purse showed her with two dark little girls in sailor frocks; their socks were sharp but their faces drooped.

Nimi learned no English, and it was out of stubbornness, the judge thought.

"What is this?" he questioned her angrily, holding aloft a pear.

"What is this?"—pointing at the gravy boat bought in a secondhand shop, sold by a family whose monogram had happily matched, *JPP*, in an extravagance of flourishes. He had bought it secretly and hidden it within another bag, so his painful pretension and his thrift would not be detected. *James Peter Peterson or Jemubhai Popatlal Patel.* IF you please.

"What is this?" he asked holding up the bread roll.

Silence.

"If you can't say the word, you can't eat it."

More silence.

He removed it from her plate.

Later that evening, he snatched the Ovaltine from her tentative sipping: "And if you don't like it, don't drink it."

He couldn't take her anywhere and squirmed when Mrs. Singh waggled her finger at him and said, "Where is your wife, Mr. Patel? None of that purdah business, I hope?" In playing her part in her husband's career, Mrs. Singh had attempted to mimic what she considered a typical Englishwoman's balance between briskly pleasant and firmly no-nonsense, and had thus succeeded in quashing the spirits of so many of the locals who prided themselves on being mostly nonsense.

Nimi did not accompany her husband on tour, unlike the other wives, who went along on horseback or elephantback or camelback or in *palkis* upheld by porters (all of whom would, because of the ladies' fat bottoms, die young), as rattling behind came the pots and pans and the bottle of whiskey and the bottle of port, Geiger counter and Scintillometre, the tuna fish tin and the mad-with-anxiety live chicken. Nobody had ever told it, but it knew; it was in its soul, that anticipation of the hatchet.

Nimi was left to sit alone in Bonda; three weeks out of four, she paced the house, the garden. She had spent nineteen years within the confines of her father's compound and she was still unable to contemplate the idea of walking through the gate. The way it stood open for her to come and go—the sight filled her with loneliness. She was uncared for, her freedom useless, her husband disregarded his duty.

She climbed up the stairs to the flat roof in the slow civility of summer dusks, and watched the Jamuna flowing through a scene tenderly cocooned in dust. Cows were on their way home; bells were ringing in the temple; she could see birds testing first one tree as a roost for the night, then another, all the while making an overexcited noise like women in a sari shop. Across the river, in the distance, she could see the ruins of a hunting lodge that dated to the Mughal emperor Jehangir: just a few pale arches still upholding carvings of irises. The Mughals had descended from the mountains to invade India but, despite their talent in waging war, were softhearted enough to weep for the loss of this flower in the heat; the persistent dream of the iris was carved everywhere, by craftsman who felt the nostalgia, saw the beauty of what they had made and never known.

The sight of this scene, of history passing and continuing, touched Nimi in a desolate way. She had fallen out of life altogether. Weeks went by and she spoke to nobody, the servants thumped their own leftovers on the table for her to eat, stole the supplies without fear, allowed the house to grow filthy without guilt until the day before Jemubhai's arrival when suddenly it was brought to luster again, the clock set to a timetable, water to a twenty-minute boil, fruit soaked for the prescribed number of minutes in solutions of potassium permanganate. Finally Jemubhai's new second-hand car—that looked more like a friendly stout cow than an automobile—would come belching through the gate.

He entered the house briskly, and when he found his wife rudely contradicting his ambition—

Well, his irritation was too much to bear.

Even her expressions annoyed him, but as they were gradually replaced by a blankness, he became upset by their absence.

What would he do with her? She without enterprise, unable to entertain herself, made of nothing, yet with a disruptive presence.

She had been abandoned by Miss Enid Pott who said, "Nimi seems to have made up her mind not to learn. You have a *swaraji* right under your nose, Mr. Patel. She will not argue—that way one might respond and have a dialogue—she just goes limp."

Then there was her typically Indian bum—lazy, wide as a buffalo. The pungency of her red hair oil that he experienced as a physical touch.

"Take those absurd trinkets off," he instructed her, riled by the tinkle-tonk of her bangles.

"Why do you have to dress in such a gaudy manner? Yellow and pink? Are you mad?" He threw the hair oil bottles away and her long hairs escaped no matter how tidily she made her bun. The judge found them winging their way across the room, treading air; he found one strangling a mushroom in his cream of mushroom soup.

One day he found footprints on the toilet seat—*she was squatting on it, she was squatting on it!*—he could barely contain his outrage, took her head and pushed it into the toilet bowl, and after a point, Nimi, made invalid by her misery, grew very dull, began to fall asleep in heliographic sunshine and wake in the middle of the night. She peered out at the world but could not focus on it, never went to the mirror, because she couldn't see herself in it, and anyway she couldn't bear to spend a moment in dressing and combing, activities that were only for the happy and the loved.

When Jemubhai saw her, cheeks erupting in pustules, he took her fallen beauty as a further affront and felt concerned the skin disease would infect him as well. He instructed the servants to wipe everything with Dettol to kill germs. He powdered himself extra carefully with his new puff, each time remembering the one that had been cushioned between his wife's obscene, clown-nosed breasts.

"Don't show your face outside," he said to her. "People might run from you screaming." By year's end the dread they had for each other was so severe it was as if they had tapped into a limitless bitterness carrying them beyond the parameters of what any individual is normally capable of feeling. They belonged to this emotion more than to themselves, experienced rage with enough muscle in it for entire nations coupled in hate.

Twenty-nine

"Christmas!" said Gyan. "You little fool!"

As he left he could hear Sai beginning to sob. "You dirty bastard," she shouted through her weeping, "you get back here. Behave so badly and then run away??"

The sight of the wreck they'd made was alarming and his anger began to scare him as he saw her face through the bars of distorting emotion. He realized Sai could not be the cause of what he felt, but as he left he slammed the gate shut.

Christmas had never bothered him before—

She was defining his hatred, he thought. Through her, he caught sight of it—oh—and then he couldn't resist sharpening it, if only for clarity's sake.

Don't you have any pride? Trying to be so Westernized. They don't want you!!!! Go there and see if they will welcome you with open arms. You will be trying to clean their toilets and even then they won't want you.

Gyan returned to Cho Oyu.

"Look," he said, "I'm sorry."

It took some coaxing.

"Behaving so badly!" said Sai.

"Sorry."

But in the end she accepted his apology, because she was relieved to turn away from the realization that, for him, she was not the center of their romance. She had been mistaken—she was only the center to herself, as always, and a small player playing her part in someone else's story.

She turned from this thought into his kisses.

"I can't resist you, that's the problem. . . ." Gyan said.

She, the temptress, laughed.

But human nature is what it is. The kisses were too soppy. A few moments more, the apology turned from sincere to insincere, and he was angry at himself for giving in.

Gyan went on to the canteen, sunset doing a mad Kali as he walked, and once again he felt the stir of purity. He would have to sacrifice silly kisses for his adulthood. A feeling of martyrdom crept over him, and with purity for a cause came ever more acute worries of pollution. He was sullied by the romance, unnerved by how easily she gave herself. It wasn't the way one was supposed to do things. It was unsavory.

He remembered the center of the Buddhist wheel of life clasped in a demon's fangs and talons to indicate the hell that traps us: rooster-snake-pig; lust-anger-foolishness; each chasing, each feeding on, each consumed by the other.

Sai at Cho Oyu also sat contemplating desire, fury, and stupidity. She tried to suppress her anger, but it kept bubbling up; she tried to compromise her own feelings, but they wouldn't bend.

What on earth was wrong with an excuse for a party? After all, one could then logically continue the argument and make a case against speaking English, as well, or eating a patty at the Hasty Tasty—all matters against which Gyan could hardly defend himself. She spent some time developing her thoughts against his to show up all the cracks.

"You bastard," she said to the emptiness. "My dignity is worth a thousand of you."

"Where did he go so soon?" asked the cook later that evening.

"Who knows?" she said. "But you're right about the fish and Nepalis.

He isn't very intelligent. The more we study, the less he seems to know, and the fact that he doesn't know and that I can tell—it makes him furious."

"Yes," said the cook sympathetically, having forecast the boy's stupidity himself.

At Thapa's Canteen, Gyan told Chhang and Bhang, Owl and Donkey, of how he was forced to tutor in order to earn money. How glad he would be if he could get a proper job and leave that fussy pair, Sai and her grandfather with the fake English accent and the face powdered pink and white over dark brown. Everyone in the canteen laughed as he mimicked the accent: "What poets are they reading these days, young man?" And, encouraged by their "Ha ha," tongue tingling and supple with alcohol, he leaped smoothly to a description of the house, the guns on the wall, and a certificate from Cambridge that they didn't even know to be ashamed of.

Why should he not betray Sai?

She who could speak no language but English and pidgin Hindi, she who could not converse with anyone outside her tiny social stratum.

She who could not eat with her hands; could not squat down on the ground on her haunches to wait for a bus; who had never been to a temple but for architectural interest; never chewed a *paan* and had not tried most sweets in the *mithaishop,* for they made her retch; she who left a Bollywood film so exhausted from emotional wear and tear that she walked home like a sick person and lay in pieces on the sofa; she who thought it vulgar to put oil in your hair and used paper to clean her bottom; felt happier with so-called English vegetables, snap peas, French beans, spring onions, and feared—*feared*—*loki, tinda, kathal, kaddu, patrel,* and the local *saag* in the market.

Eating together they had always felt embarrassed—he, unsettled by her finickiness and her curbed enjoyment, and she, revolted by his energy and his fingers working the dal, his slurps and smacks. The judge ate even his chapatis, his puris and *parathas,* with knife and fork. Insisted that Sai, in his presence, do the same.

Still, Gyan was absolutely sure that she was proud of her behavior; masqueraded it about as shame at her lack of Indianness, maybe, but it marked her status. Oh yes. It allowed her that perverse luxury, the titillation of putting yourself down, criticizing yourself and having the opposite happen—*you did not fall, you mystically rose.*

So, in the excitement of the moment, he told. Of the guns and the well-stocked kitchen, the liquor in the cabinet, the lack of a phone and there being nobody to call for help.

Next morning, when he woke, though, he felt guilty all over again. He thought of lying entangled in the garden last year, on the rough grass under high trees jigsawing the sky, spidery stars through the prehistoric ferns.

But so fluid a thing was love. It wasn't firm, he was learning, it wasn't a scripture; it was a wobbliness that lent itself to betrayal, taking the mold of whatever he poured it into. And in fact, it was difficult to keep from pouring it into numerous vessels. It could be used for all kinds of purposes. . . . He wished it were a constraint. It was truly beginning to frighten him.

Thirty

Worried about growing problems in the market and the disruption of supplies due to strikes, the cook was putting some buffalo meat that was growing harder and harder to buy into Mutt's stew. He unwrapped the flank from its newspaper wrapping soaked in blood, and suddenly he had the overwhelming thought that he held two kilos of his son's body there, dead like that.

Years ago when the cook's wife had been killed falling from a tree while gathering leaves for their goat, everyone in his village had said her ghost was threatening to take Biju with her, since she had died violently. The priests claimed that a spirit passing on in such a way remained angry. His wife had been a mild person—in fact he had little memory of her speaking at all—but they had insisted it was true, that Biju had seen his mother, a transparent apparition in the night, trying to claw at him. The extended family walked all the way to the post office in the nearest town to send a barrage of telegrams to the judge's address. The telegrams in those days had arrived via postal runner who ran shaking a spear from village to village. "In the name of Queen Victoria let me pass," he sang in a high voice, although he neither knew nor cared that she was long gone.

"The priest has said the *balli* must be done at *amavas,* darkest no-moon night of the month. You must sacrifice a chicken."

The judge refused to let the cook go. "Superstition. You fool! Why aren't there ghosts here? Wouldn't they be here as well as in your village?"

"Because there is electricity here," said the cook. "They get a scare from electricity and in our village there is no electricity, that's why. . . ."

"What has your life been for?" said the judge, "You live with me, go to a proper doctor, you have even learned to read and write a little, sometimes you read the newspaper, and all to no purpose! Still the priests make a fool of you, rob you of your money."

All the other servants set up a chorus advising the cook to disregard their employer's opinions and save his son instead, for there certainly were ghosts: "*Hota hai hota hai,* you have to do it."

The cook went to the judge with a made-up story of the roof of his village hut having blown off again in the latest storm. The judge gave up and the cook traveled to the village.

He became worried now, all these years later, that the sacrifice hadn't really worked, that its effect had been undone by the lie he told the judge, that his wife's spirit hadn't actually been appeased, that the offering hadn't been properly recorded, or wasn't big enough. He had sacrificed a goat and a chicken, but what if the spirit still had a hunger for Biju?

The cook had first made the effort to send his son abroad four years ago when a recruiting agent for a cruise ship line appeared in Kalimpong to solicit applications for waiters, vegetable choppers, toilet cleaners—basic drudge staff, all of whom would appear at the final gala dinner in suits and bow ties, skating on ice, standing on one another's shoulders, with pineapples on their heads, and flambéing crepes.

"Will procure legal employment in the USA!!!!" said the advertisements that appeared in the local paper and were pasted on the walls in various locations around town.

The man set up a temporary office in his room at Sinclair's Hotel.

The line that formed outside circled the hotel and came all the way back around, at which point the head of the line got mixed up with the tail and there was some foul play.

Pleased to get in sooner than he had expected was Biju, who had been summoned from their home to Kalimpong for this interview, despite the judge's objection. Why couldn't Biju plan to work for him when the cook retired?

Biju took some of the cook's fake recommendations with him to the interview to prove he came from an honest family, and a letter from Father Booty to say he was of sound moral character and one from Uncle Potty to say he made the best damn roast bar none, though Uncle Potty had never eaten anything cooked by this boy who had also never eaten anything cooked by himself, since he had simply never cooked. His grandmother had fed and spoiled him all his life, though they were one of the poorest families in a poor village.

Nevertheless—the interview was a success.

"I can make any kind of pudding. Continental or Indian."

"But that is excellent. We have a buffet of seventeen sweets each night."

In a wonderful moment Biju was accepted and he signed on the dotted line of the proffered form.

The cook was so proud: "It was because of all the puddings I told the boy about. . . . They have a big buffet in the ship every night, the ship is like a hotel, you see, run just like the clubs in the past. The interviewer asked him what he could make and he said, 'I can make this and that, anything you require. Baked Alaska, floating island, brandy snap.'"

"Are you sure he seemed legitimate?" asked the MetalBox watchman.

"Completely legitimate," the cook said, defending the man who had so appreciated his son.

They went back to the hotel the next evening with a completed medical form and a bank draft of eight thousand rupees to cover his processing fee and the cost of the training camp that was to be held in Kathmandu, since it made sense to them all to pay to get a job. The recruiter made out a receipt for the bank draft, checked the medical forms that had been completed free by the bazaar doctor, who had been kind enough to show Biju's blood pressure as being lower than it was, his weight as greater, and she had filled up the inoculations column with dates that would have been the correct time to have inoculations had he had them.

"Have to look perfect or the embassy people will make trouble and then what will you do?" She knew this because she'd sent her own son off on this journey some years ago. In return for the favor, Biju promised to take a packet of dried *churbi* cheese to the U.S. and mail it to her son doing a medical residency in Ohio, for the boy had been a boarder in a Darjeeling school and acquired the habit of chewing it as he studied.

Two weeks later, Biju traveled to Kathmandu by bus for a week of training at the recruiting agency's main office.

Kathmandu was a carved wooden city of temples and palaces, caught in a disintegrating tangle of modern concrete that stretched into the dust and climbed into the sky.

He looked in vain for the mountains; Mt. Everest—where was it? He traversed along flat main roads into a knot of medieval passages full of the sounds of long ago, a street of metal workers, a street of potters melding clay, straw, sand, with their bare feet; rats in a Ganesh temple eating sweets. At one point a crooked shutter etched with stars opened and a face from a fairy tale looked out, pure among the muck, but when he looked back the young girl was gone; a wrinkled old crone had taken her place to talk to another old crone on her way with a *puja* tray of offerings; and then he was back out among the blocks of concrete, scooters, and buses. A billboard was painted with an underwear advertisement showing a giant, bulging underwear placket; across the bulge was a black crisscross. "No Pickpocket," it warned. Some laughing foreigners were having their picture taken in front of it. Down a lane, around a corner, behind a cinema, there was a small butcher's shop, with a row of yellow chicken feet in a decorative fringe over the door. A man stood outside, his hands dripping with meat juices over a basin of water tinged rust with blood, and the number inscribed on the side of the door matched the address Biju had in his pocket: 223 A block, ground floor, behind Pun Cinema House.

"Another one!" the man in front shouted to the back room. Several other men were there wrestling with an unwilling goat that had caught sight of a fellow grazer's heart lying discarded on the floor.

"You've been cheated," the butcher laughed. "So many people have been asking to go the USA."

The men trussed up the goat and came out grinning, all with bloody vests. "Ah, idiot. Who goes and gives money like that? Where do you come from? What do you think the world is made of? Criminals! Criminals! Go file a report at the police station. Not that they will do anything. . . ."

Before the butcher slit the goat's throat, Biju could hear him working up his disdain, yelling *"Bitch, whore, cunt, sali,"* at her, dragging her forward then, and killing her.

You have to swear at a creature to be able to destroy it.

As Biju stood dazed outside, wondering what to do, they skinned her, slung her upside down to drain.

His second attempt at America was a simple, straightforward application for a tourist visa.

A man from his village had made fifteen tries and recently, on the sixteenth, he got the visa.

"Never give up," he'd advised the boys in the village, "at some point your lucky day will come."

"Is this the Amriken embassy?" Biju asked a watchman outside the formidable exterior.

"*Amreeka nehi, bephkuph*. This is U.S. embassy!"

He walked on: "Where is the Amriken embassy?"

"It is there." The man pointed back at the same building.

"That is U.S."

"It is the same thing," said the man impatiently. "Better get it straight before you get on the plane, *bhai*."

Outside, a crowd of shabby people had been camping, it appeared, for days on end. Whole families that had traveled from distant villages, eating food packed and brought with them; some individuals with no shoes, some with cracked plastic ones; all smelling already of the ancient sweat of a never-ending journey. Once you got inside, it was air-conditioned and you could wait in rows of orange bucket chairs that shook if anyone along the length began to bop their knees up and down.

First name: Balwinder

Last name: Singh

Other names:———

What would those be??

Pet names, someone said, and trustfully they wrote: "Guddu, Dumpy, Plumpy, Cherry, Ruby, Pinky, Chicky, Micky, Vicky, Dicky, Sunny, Bunny, Honey, Lucky. . . ."

After thinking a bit, Biju wrote "Baba."

"Demand draft? Demand draft?" said the touts going by in the auto rickshaws. "Passport photo *chahiye?* Passport photo? Campa Cola *chahiye*, Campa Cola?"

Sometimes every single paper the applicants brought with them was fake: birth certificates, vaccination records from doctors, offers of monetary support. There was a lovely place you could go, clerks by the hundreds sitting cross-legged before typewriters, ready to help with stamps and the correct legal language for every conceivable requirement. . . .

"How do you find so much money?" Someone in the line was worried he would be refused for the small size of his bank account.

"*Ooph,* you cannot show so little," laughed another, looking over his shoulder with frank appraisal. "Don't you know how to do it?"

"How?"

"My whole family," he explained, "uncles from all over, Dubai–New Zealand–Singapore, wired money into my cousin's account in Tulsa, the bank printed the statement, my cousin sent a notarized letter of support, and then he sent the money back to where it had come from. How else can you find enough to please them!"

An announcement was made from the invisible loudspeaker: "Will all visa applicants line up at window number seven to collect a number for visa processing."

"What what, what did they say?" Biju, like half the room, didn't understand, but he saw from the ones who did, who were running, pleased to be given a head start, what they should do. Stink and spit and scream and charge; they jumped toward the window, tried to splat themselves against it hard enough that they would just stick and not scrape off; young men mowing through, tossing aside toothless grannies, trampling babies underfoot. This was no place for manners and this is how the line was formed: wolf-faced single men first, men with families second, women on their own and Biju, and last, the decrepit. Biggest pusher, first place; how self-contented and smiling he was; he dusted himself off, presenting himself with the exquisite manners of a cat. I'm civilized, sir, ready for the U.S., I'm civilized, mam. Biju noticed that his eyes, so alive to the foreigners, looked back at his own countrymen and women, immediately glazed over, and went dead.

Some would be chosen, others refused, and there was no question of fair or not. What would make the decision? It was a whim; it was not liking your face, forty-five degrees centigrade outside and impatience with all Indians, therefore; or perhaps merely the fact that you were in line after a yes, so you were likely to be the no. He trembled to think of what might make these people unsympathetic. Presumably, though, they would start off kind and relaxed, and then, faced with all the fools and annoying people, with their lies and crazy stories, and their desire to stay barely concealed under fervent promises to return, they would respond with an indiscriminate machine-gun-fire of NO!NO!NO!NO!NO!

On the other hand, it occurred to those who now stood in the front, that at the beginning, fresh and alert, they might be more inclined to check their papers more carefully and find gaps in their arguments. . . . Or perversely start out by refusing, as if for practice.

There was no way to fathom the minds and hearts of these great Americans, and Biju watched the windows carefully, trying to uncover a pattern he might learn from. Some officers seemed more amiable than others, some scornful, some thorough, some were certain misfortune, turning everyone away empty-handed.

He would have to approach his fate soon enough. He stood there telling himself, Look unafraid as if you have nothing to hide. Be clear and firm when answering questions and look straight into the eyes of the officer to show you are honest. But when you are on the verge of hysteria, so full of anxiety and pent-up violence, you could only appear honest and calm by being dishonest. So, whether honest or dishonest, dishonestly honest-looking, he would have to stand before the bulletproof glass, still rehearsing answers to the questions he knew were coming up, questions to which he had to have perfectly made-up replies.

"How much money do you have?"

"Can you prove to us you won't stay?"

Biju watched as the words were put forward to others with complete bluntness, with a fixed and unembarrassed eye—odd when asking such rude questions. Standing there, feeling the enormous measure of just how despised he was, he would have to reply in a smart yet humble manner. If he bumbled, tried too hard, seemed too cocky, became confused, if they didn't get what they wanted quickly and easily, he would be out. In this room it was a fact accepted by all that Indians were willing to undergo any kind of humiliation to get into the States. You could heap rubbish on their heads and yet they would be begging to come crawling in. . . .

"And what is the purpose of your visit?"

"What should we say, what should we say?" they discussed in the line. "We'll say a *hubshi* broke into the shop and killed our sister-in-law and now we have to go to the funeral."

"Don't say that." An engineering student who was already studying at the University of North Carolina, here for the renewal of his visa, knew this would not sound right.

But he was shouted down. He was unpopular.

"Why not?"

"You are going too far. It's a stereotype. They'll suspect."

But they insisted. It was a fact known to all mankind: "It's black men who do all of this."

"Yes, yes," several others in the line agreed. "Yes, yes." Black people, living like monkeys in the trees, not like us, so civilized. . . .

They were, then, shocked to see the African-American lady behind the counter. (God, if the Americans accepted them, surely they would welcome Indians with open arms? Won't they be happy to see us!)

But . . . already some ahead were being turned away. Biju's worry grew as he saw a woman begin to shriek and throw herself about in an epilepsy of grief. "These people won't let me go, my daughter has just had a baby, these people won't let me go, I can't even look at my own grandchild, these people. . . . I am ready to die . . . they won't even let me see the face of my grandchild. . . ." And the security guards came rushing forward to drag her away down the sanitized corridor rinsed with germ killers.

The man with the *hubshi* story of murder—he was sent to the window of the *hubshi*. *Hubshi hubshi bandar bandar,* trying to do some quick thinking—oh no, normal Indian prejudice would not work here, distaste and rudeness—story falling to pieces in his head.

"Mexican, say Mexican," hissed someone else.

"Mexican?"

He arrived at the window, retreating under threat, to his best behavior. "Good morning, ma'am." (Better not make that *hubshi* angry, *yaar*—so much he wished to immigrate to the U.S. of A., he could even be polite to black people.) "Yes ma'am, something like this, Mexican-Texican, I don't know exactly," he said to the woman who pinned him with a lepidopterist's gaze. (Mexican-Texican??) "I don't know, madam," squirming, "something or the other like this my brother was saying, but he is so upset, you know, don't want to ask all the details."

"No, we cannot give you a visa."

"Why ma'am, please ma'am, I already have bought the ticket ma'am. . . ."

And those who waited for visas who had spacious homes, ease-filled lives, jeans, English, driver-driven cars waiting outside to convey them back to shady streets, and cooks missing their naps to wait late with lunch (something light—cheese macaroni . . .), all this time they had been trying to separate themselves from the vast shabby crowd. By their manner, dress, and accent, they tried to convey to the officials that they were a preselected, numerically restricted, perfect-for-foreign-travel group, skilled in the use of knife and fork, no loud burping, no getting up on the toilet seat to squat as many of the village women were doing at just this moment never having seen the sight of such a toilet before, pouring water from on high to clean their bottoms and flooding the floor with bits of soggy shit.

"I have been abroad before and I have always returned. You can see from my passport." England. Switzerland. America. Even New Zealand. Looking forward, when in New York, to the latest movie, to pizza, to Californian wine, also Chilean—very good, you know, and reasonably priced. If you were lucky already you would be lucky again.

Biju approached his assigned window that framed a clean young man with glasses. White people looked clean because they were whiter; the darker you were, Biju thought, the dirtier you looked.

"Why are you going?"

"I would like to go as a tourist."

"How do we know you will come back?"

"My family, wife, and son are here. And my shop."

"What shop?"

"Camera shop." Could the man really believe this?

"Where are you going to stay?"

"With my friend in New York. Nandu is his name and here is his address if you would like to see."

"How long?"

"Two weeks, if that is suitable to you." (Oh, please, just a day, a day. That will be enough to serve my purpose. . . .)

"Do you have funds to cover your trip?"

He showed a fake bank statement procured by the cook from a corrupt state bank clerk in exchange for two bottles of Black Label.

"Pay at the window around the corner and you can collect your visa after five P.M."

How could this be?

A man he had spoken to, still in the line behind him, called out in a piercing tone:

"Were you successful, Biju? Biju, were you successful? *Biju? Biju!*"

In that passionate peacock cry, Biju felt this man was willing to die for him, but his desperation was for himself, of course.

"Yes, I was successful."

"You are the luckiest boy in the whole world," the man said.

The luckiest boy in the whole world. He walked through a park to luxuriate in the news alone. Raw sewage was being used to water a patch of grass that was lush and stinking, grinning brilliantly in the dusk. Out of the sewage Biju chased a line of pigs with black watermarks across their bellies, ran after them in jubilation. "Hup hup," he shouted. The crows that had been sitting on the pigs' backs scrambled into indignant flight, having to start up backward. A jogger in a tracksuit stopped to stare, the chauffeur waiting for the jogger and brushing his teeth with a neem twig, meanwhile, also stopped and stared. Biju ran after a cow. "Hup hup." He hopped over the ornamental plants and he jumped on the exercise bars, did pull-ups and push-ups.

The next day, he sent a telegram to his father, "the luckiest boy in the whole wide world," and when it arrived he knew his father would be the happiest father in the world. He didn't know, of course, that Sai, too, would be overjoyed. That when he had visited Kalimpong for that doomed interview with the cruise ship, she had found her heart shaken by the realization that the cook had his own family and thought of them first. If his son were around, he would pay only the most cursory attention to her. She was just the alternative, the one to whom he gave his affection if he could not have Biju, the real thing.

"Yipeee," she had shouted when she heard of his visa. "Hip hip hooray."

In the Gandhi Café, a little after three years from the day he'd received his visa, the luckiest boy in the whole world skidded on some rotten spinach in Harish-Harry's kitchen, streaked forward in a slime green track and fell with a loud popping sound. It was his knee. He couldn't get up.

"Can you get a doctor?" he said to Harish-Harry after Saran and Jeev had helped him to his mattress between the vegetables.

"Doctor!! Do you know what is medical expense in this country?!"

"It happened here. Your responsibility."

"My responsibility!" Harish-Harry stood over Biju, enraged. "*You* slip in the kitchen. If you slip on the road, then who would you ask, *hm?*" He had given this boy the wrong impression. He had been too kind and Biju had misunderstood those nights of holding his boss's divided soul in his lap, gluing it together with Harish-Harry's favorite axioms. "I take you in. I hire you with no papers, treat you like my own son and now this is how you repay me! Living here rent-free. In India would they pay you? What right do you have? Is it my fault you don't even clean the floor? YOU should have to pay ME for not cleaning, living like a pig. Am I telling YOU to live like a pig?"

"Biju's throbbing knee made him brave, reduced him to animal directness. He glared at Harish-Harry, the pretence was gone; in this moment of physical pain, his own feelings were strained clear.

"Without us living like pigs," said Biju, "what business would you have? This is how you make your money, paying us nothing because you know we can't do anything, making us work day and night because we are illegal. Why don't you sponsor us for our green cards?"

Volcanic explosion.

"How can I sponsor you?! If I sponsor *you* I have to sponsor *Rishi*, and if I sponsor *Rishi*, then I have to sponsor *Saran*, and if *him* then *Jeev*, and then *Mr. Lalkaka* will come and say, but I have been here for longest, I am the most distinguished, and I should be first in line. How can I make an exception? I have to go to the INS and say that no American citizen can do the job. I have to prove it. I have to prove I advertised it. They will look into my restaurant. They will study and ask questions. And the way they have it, it's the owner who gets put in jail for hiring illegal staff. If you are not happy, then go right now. Go find someone to sponsor you. Know how easily I can replace you? *Know how lucky you are!!!* You think there aren't thousands of people in this city looking for a job? I can replace you like this," he snapped his fingers, "I'll snap my fingers and in one second hundreds of people will appear. *Get out of my face!*"

But since Biju couldn't walk, it was Harish-Harry who had to leave. He went back up and then he came back down, because his temper had changed in a flash—it was always like that with him, a thunder squall that moved on fast.

"Look," he said more kindly, "when have I treated you badly? I am not a bad man, am I? Why are you attacking me? As it is, I stick out my neck for you, Biju, tell me, how much more can you ask? These risky things I cannot do." He counted out fifty dollars from his wallet. "Here. Why not take some rest? You can help cutting the vegetables while lying down and if you are not better, go home. Doctors are very cheap and good in India. Get the best medical attention and later on you can always return."

A modest geometry of morning light lay on the floor, a small rhombus falling through the grate. "Naaty boy," Harish-Harry waggled his finger like a joke. The geometrical shape began to leak light, became shifty, exited slithering up the walls.

Return.

Come back.

Somebody in one of the kitchens of Biju's past had said: "It could not be so hard or there would not be so many of you here."

But it *WAS* so hard and *YET* there were so many here. It was terribly, terribly hard. Millions risked death, were humiliated, hated, lost their families—YET there were so many here.

But Harish-Harry knew this. How could he say "Return–come back," in that easy oiled way?

"Naaty boy . . ." he said again when he brought Biju *prasad* from the temple in Queens. "Giving so much worry and trouble."

And in that *prasad* Biju knew not to expect anything else. It was a decoy, an old Indian trick of master to servant, the benevolent patriarch garnering the loyalty of staff; offering slave wages, but now and then a box of sweets, a lavish gift. . . .

So Biju lay on his mattress and watched the movement of the sun through the grate on the row of buildings opposite. From every angle that you looked at this city without a horizon, you saw more buildings going up like jungle creepers, starved for light, holding a perpetual half darkness congealed at the bottom, the day shafting through the maze, slivering into apartments at precise and fleeting times, a cuprous segment visiting between 10 and 12 perhaps, or between 10 and 10:45, between 2:30 and 3:45. As in places of poverty where luxury is rented out, shared, and passed along from neighbor to neighbor, its time of arrival was noted and anticipated by cats, plants, elderly people who might sit with it briefly across their knees. But this light was too brief for real succor and it seemed more the visitation of a beautiful memory than the real thing.

After two weeks, Biju could walk with the aid of a stick. Two more weeks and the pain left him, but not, of course, the underlying green card problem. That continued to make him ill.

His papers, his papers. The green card, green card, the *machoot sala oloo ka patha chaar sau bees* green card that was not even green. It roosted heavily, clumsily, pinkishly on his brain day and night; he could think of nothing else, and he threw up sometimes, embracing the toilet, emptying his gullet into its gullet, lying over it like a drunk. The post brought more letters from his father, and as he picked them up, he cried. Then he read them and he grew violently angry.

"Please help Oni. . . . I asked you in my previous letter but you have not replied. . . . He went to the embassy and the Americans were very impressed with him. He will be arriving in one month's time. . . . Maybe he can stay with you until he finds something. . . ." Biju began to grind his teeth through his nightmares, woke one morning with a tooth that had cracked across.

"You sound like a cement mixer," complained Jeev, "I just can't sleep myself, what with you grinding and the rats running."

One night, Jeev woke and trapped a rat in the metal garbage can where it was foraging.

He poured in lighter fluid and set the rat aflame.

"Shut the fuck up, motherfucker," men shouted from up above. "Shithead. What the fuck. For fuck's sake. Asshole. Fuck you." A rain of beer bottles crashed around them.

"Ask me the price of any shoes all over Manhattan and I'll tell you where to get the best price."

Saeed Saeed again. How did he come popping up all over the city?

"Come on, ask me."

"I don't know."

"Pay attention, man," he said with strict kindness. "Now you are here, you are not back home. Anything you want, you try and you can do." His English was good enough now that he was reading two books, *Stop Worrying and Start Living* and *How to Share Your Life with Another Person.*

He owned twenty-five pairs of shoes at this point; some were the wrong size, but he had bought them anyway, just for the exquisite beauty of them.

Biju's leg had mended.

What if it hadn't?

Well, it had.

Maybe, though, maybe he would return. Why not? To spite himself, spite his fate, give joy to his enemies, those who wanted him gone from here and those who would gloat to see him back—maybe he *would* go home.

While Saeed was collecting shoes, Biju had been cultivating self-pity. Looking at a dead insect in the sack of basmati that had come all the way from Dehra Dun, he almost wept in sorrow and marvel at its journey, which was tenderness for his own journey. In India almost nobody would be able to afford this rice, and you had to travel around the world to be able to eat such things where they were cheap enough that you could gobble them down without being rich; and when you got home to the place where they grew, you couldn't afford them anymore.

"Stay there as long as you can," the cook had said. "Stay there. Make money. Don't come back here."

Thirty-one

In the month of March, Father Booty, Uncle Potty, Lola, Noni, and Sai sat in the Swiss Dairy jeep on their way to the Darjeeling Gymkhana to exchange their library books before the trouble on the hillside got any worse.

It was some weeks after the gun robbery at Cho Oyu and a program of action newly drawn up in Ghoom, threatened:

Roadblocks to bring economic activity to a standstill and to prevent the trees of the hills, the boulders of the river valleys, from leaving for the plains. All vehicles would be stopped.

Black flag day on April 13.

A seventy-two-hour strike in May.

No national celebrations. No Republic Day, Independence Day, or Gandhi's birthday.

Boycott of elections with the slogan "We will not stay in other people's state of West Bengal."

Nonpayment of taxes and loans (very clever).

Burning of the Indo-Nepal treaty of 1950.

Nepali or not, everyone was encouraged (required) to contribute to funds and to purchase calendars and cassette tapes of speeches made by Ghising, the top GNLF man in Darjeeling, and by Pradhan, top man in Kalimpong.

It was requested (required) that every family—Bengali, Lepcha, Tibetan, Sikkimese, Bihari, Marwari, Nepali, or whatever else in the mess—send a male representative to every procession, and they were also to show up at the burning of the Indo-Nepal treaty.

If you didn't, they would know and . . . well, nobody wanted them to finish the sentence.

"Where is your bum?" said Uncle Potty to Father Booty as he got into the jeep.

He studied his friend severely. A bout of flu had rendered Father Booty so thin his clothes seemed to be hanging on a concavity. "Your bum has gone!"

The priest sat on an inflatable swimming ring, for his gaunt rear ached from riding in that rough jeep running on diesel, just a few skeleton bars and sheets of metal and a basic engine attached, the windscreen spider-webbed with cracks delivered by stones flying up off the broken roads. It was twenty-three years old, but it still worked and Father Booty claimed no other vehicle on the market could touch it.

In the back were the umbrellas, books, ladies, and several wheels of cheese for Father Booty to deliver to the Windamere Hotel and Loreto Convent, where they ate it on toast in the mornings, and an extra cheese for Glenary's Restaurant in case he could persuade them to switch from Amul, but they wouldn't. The manager believed that when something came in a factory tin with a name stamped on it, when it was showcased in a national advertising campaign, naturally it was better than anything made by the farmer next door, some dubious Thapa with one dubious cow living down the lane.

"But this is made by local farmers, don't you wish to support them?" Father Booty would plead.

"Quality control, Father," he countered, "all-India reputation, name brand, customer respect, international standards of hygiene."

Father Booty was with hope, anyway, whizzing through the spring, every flower, every creature preening, flinging forth its pheromones.

The garden at St. Joseph's Convent was abuzz with such fecundity that Sai wondered, as they drove by in the jeep, if it discomfited the nuns. Huge, spread-open Easter lilies were sticky with spilling anthers; insects chased each other madly through the sky, zip zip; and amorous butterflies, cucumber green, tumbled past the jeep windows into the deep`marine valleys; the delicacy of love and courtliness apparent even between the lesser beasts.

Gyan and Sai—she thought of the two of them together, of their fight over Christmas; it was ugly, and how badly it contrasted with the past. She remembered her face in his neck, arms and legs over and under, bellies, fingers, here then there, so much so that at times she kissed him and found instead that she'd kissed herself.

"Jesus is coming," read a sign on the landslide reinforcements as they nose-dived to the Teesta.

"To become a Hindu," someone had added in chalk underneath.

This struck Father Booty as very funny, but he stopped laughing when they passed the Amul billboard.

Utterly Butterly Delicious—

"Plastic! How can they call it butter and cheese? It's *not. You could use it for waterproofing!"*

Lola and Noni were waving out of the jeep window. "Hello, Mrs. Thondup." Mrs. Thondup, from an aristocratic Tibetan family, was sitting out with her daughters Pem Pem and Doma in jewel-colored *bakus* and pale silk blouses woven subtly with the eight propitious Buddhist signs. These daughters, who attended Loreto Convent, were supposed to make friends with Sai—once, long ago, so the adults had conspired—but they didn't want to be her friends. They had friends already. All full up. No room for oddness.

"What an elegant lady," Lola and Noni always said when they saw her, for they liked aristocrats and they liked peasants; it was just what lay between that was distasteful: the middle class bounding over the horizon in an endless phalanx.

Thus, they did not wave to Mrs. Sen emerging from the post office. "They keep begging and begging my daughter to *please just* take a green card," Lola mimicked her neighbor. Liar, liar, pants on fire. . . .

They waved again as they passed the Afghan princesses sitting on cane chairs among white azaleas in flower, virginal yet provocative like a good underwear trick. From their house came the unmistakable smell of chicken.

"Soup?" shouted Uncle Potty, already hungry, nose trembling with excitement. He had missed his usual leftovers-inside-an-omelet breakfast.

"Soup!"

Waving, then, at the Graham's School orphans in the playground—they were so angelically beautiful, they looked as if they had already died and gone to heaven.

The army came jogging along overlaid by courting butterflies and the colorful dashes—blue, red, orange—of dragonflies, hinged in the severely cricked geometric angles of their mating. The men puffed and panted, their spindly legs protruding from comically wide shorts: how would they defend India against the Chinese so close over the mountains at Nathu-La?

From the army mess kitchens came rumors of increasing vegetarianism.

Lola often encountered young officers who were not only vegetarian, but also teetotalers. Even the top command.

"I think to be in the army you should eat fish at least," she said.

"Why?" asked Sai.

"To kill you must be carnivorous or otherwise you're the hunted. Just look at nature—the deer, the cow. We are animals after all and to triumph you must taste blood." But the army was retreating from being a British-type army and was becoming a true Indian army. Even in choice of paint. They passed the Striking Lion's Club that was painted a bridal pink.

"Well," said Noni, "they must be tired of that mud color over every single thing."

"FLOWERS," it read on a grand sign nearby as part of the Army Beautification Program, though it was the only spot on the hill where there were none.

They stopped for a pair of young monks crossing to the gates of a mansion recently bought by their order.

"Hollywood money," Lola said. "And once upon a time the monks used to be grateful to Indians, the only country to take them in! Now they despise us. Waiting for Americans to take them to Disneyland. Fat chance!"

"God, they're so handsome," said Uncle Potty, "who wants them to leave?"

He remembered the time he and Father Booty had first met . . . their admiring eyes on the same monk in the market . . . the start of a grand friendship. . . .

"Everyone says poor Tibetans—poor Tibetans," Lola continued, "but what brutal people, barely a Dalai Lama survived—they were all popped off before their time. That Potala Palace—the Dalai Lama must be thanking his lucky stars to be in India instead, better climate, and let's be honest, better food. Good fat mutton *momos.*"

Noni: "But *he* must be vegetarian, no?"

"These monks are not vegetarian. What fresh vegetables grow in Tibet? And in fact, Buddha died of greed for pork."

"What a situation," said Uncle Potty. "The army is vegetarian and the monks are gobbling down meat. . . ."

Down they hurtled through the *sal* trees and the *pani saaj,* Kiri te Kanawa on the cassette player, her voice soaring from valley level to hover around the five peaks of Kanchenjunga.

Lola: "But give me Maria Callas any day. Nothing like the old lot. Caruso over Pavarotti."

In an hour, they had descended into the tropical density of air thick and hot over the river and into even greater concentrations of butterflies, beetles, dragonflies. "Wouldn't it be nice to live there?" Sai pointed at the government rest house with its view over the sand banks, through the grasses to the impatient Teesta—

Then they rose up again into the pine and ether amid little snips of gold rain. "Blossom rain, *metok-chharp,*" said Father Booty. "Very auspicious in Tibet, rain and sunshine at the same time." He beamed at the sunny buds through the broken windows as he sat on his swimming ring.

In order to accommodate the population boom, the government had recently passed legislation that allowed an extra story to be built on each home in Darjeeling; the weight of more concrete pressing downward had spurred the town's lopsided descent and caused more landslides than ever. As you approached it, it looked like a garbage heap rearing above and sliding below, so it seemed caught in a photostill, a frozen moment of its tumble. "Darjeeling has really gone downhill," the ladies said with satisfaction, and meant it not just literally. "Remember how lovely it used to be?"

By the time they found a parking space half in a drain behind the bazaar, the point had been too well proven and their smugness had changed to sourness as they dismounted between cows quaffing fruit peels, made their way past nefarious liquid pouring down the streets, and through traffic jams on the market road. To add to the confusion and noise, monkeys loped over the tin roofs overhead, making a crashing sound. But then, just as Lola was going to make another remark about Darjeeling's demise, suddenly the clouds broke and Kanchenjunga came looming—it was astonishing; it was *right there;* close enough to lick: 28,168 feet high. In the distance, you could see Mt. Everest, a coy triangle.

A tourist began generously to scream as if she had caught sight of a pop star.

Uncle Potty departed. He wasn't in Darjeeling for the sake of books but to procure enough alcohol to last him through civil unrest. He'd already bought up the entire supply of rum in the Kalimpong shops and with the addition of a few more cartons here, he would be prepared for curfew and a disruption of liquor supplies during strikes and roadblocks.

"Not a reader," said Lola, disapproving.

"Comics," corrected Sai. He was an appreciative consumer of *Asterix, Tin Tin,* and also *Believe It or Not* in the loo, didn't consider himself above such literature though he had studied languages at Oxford. Because of his education, the ladies put up with him, and also because he came from a well-known Lucknow family and had called his parents Mater and Pater. Mater had been such the belle in her day that a mango was named for her: Haseena. "She was a notorious flirt," said Lola who had heard from someone who had heard from someone of a sari slipping off the shoulder, low-cut blouse and all. . . . After packing in as much fun as she possibly could, she'd married a diplomat named Alphonso (also, of course, the name of a distinguished mango). Haseena and Alphonso, they celebrated their wedding with the purchase of two racehorses, Chengiz Khan and Tamerlane, who once made front page of the *Times of India.* They had been sold along with a home off Marble Arch in London, and defeated by bad luck and changing times, Mater and Pater finally became reconciled to India, went like mice into an ashram, but this sad end to their fabulous spirit their son refused to accept.

"What kind of ashram?" Lola and Noni had asked him. "What are their teachings?"

"Starvation, sleep deprivation," mourned Uncle Potty, "followed by donation. Proper dampening of the spirits so you howl out to God to save you." He liked to tell the story of when, into strict vegetarian surroundings—no garlic or onions, even, to heat the blood—he'd smuggled a portion of roast *jungli* boar that he had caught rooting in his garlic field and shot. The meat was redolent with the creature's last meal. "Licked up every scrap, they did, Mater and Pater!"

They made a plan to meet for lunch, and Uncle Potty, with the dregs of his family fortune in his pocket, went to the liquor shop while the rest continued to the library.

The Gymkhana library was a dim morguelike room suffused with the musk, almost too sweet and potent to bear, of aging books. The books had titles long faded into the buckled covers; some of them had not been touched in fifty years and they broke apart in one's hands, shedding glue like chitinous bits of insect. Their pages were stenciled with the shapes of long disintegrated fern collections and bored by termites into what looked like maps of plumbing. The yellowed paper imparted a faint acidic tingle and fell easily into mosaic pieces, barely perceptible between the fingers—moth wings at the brink of eternity and dust.

There were bound copies of the *Himalayan Times*, "the only English weekly serving Tibet, Bhutan, Sikkim, the Darjeeling tea gardens, and Dooars," and the *Illustrated Weekly*, which had once printed a poem on a cow by Father Booty.

Of course they had *The Far Pavilions* and *The Raj Quartet*—but Lola, Noni, Sai, and Father Booty were unanimous in the opinion that they didn't like English writers writing about India; it turned the stomach; delirium and fever somehow went with temples and snakes and perverse romance, spilled blood, and miscarriage; it didn't correspond to the truth. English writers writing of England was what was nice: P. G. Wodehouse, Agatha Christie, countryside England where they remarked on the crocuses being early that year and best of all, the manor house novels. Reading them you felt as if you were watching those movies in the air-conditioned

British council in Calcutta where Lola and Noni had often been taken as girls, the liquid violin music swimming you up the driveway; the door of the manor opening and a butler coming out with an umbrella, for, of course, it was always raining; and the first sight you got of the lady of the manor was of her shoe, stuck out of the open door; from the look of the foot you could already delightedly foresee the snooty nature of her expression.

There were endless accounts of travel in India and over and over, in book after book, there was the scene of late arrival at a *dak* bungalow, the cook cooking in a black kitchen, and Sai realized that her own delivery to Kalimpong in such a manner was merely part of the monotony, not the original. The repetition had willed her, anticipated her, cursed her, and certain moves made long ago had produced all of them: Sai, judge, Mutt, cook, and even the mashed-potato car.

Browsing the shelves, Sai had not only located herself but read *My Vanishing Tribe,* revealing to her that she meanwhile knew nothing of the people who had belonged here first. Lepchas, the Rong pa, people of the ravine who followed Bon and believed the original Lepchas, Fodongthing, and Nuzongnyue were created from sacred Kanchenjunga snow.

There was also James Herriot that funny vet, Gerald Durrell, Sam Pig and Ann Pig, Paddington Bear, and Scratchkin Patchkin who lived like a leaf in the apple tree.

And:

> The Indian gentleman, with all self-respect to himself, should not enter into a compartment reserved for Europeans, any more than he should enter a carriage set apart for ladies. Although you may have acquired the habits and manners of the European, have the courage to show that you are not ashamed of being an Indian, and in all such cases, identify yourself with the race to which you belong.
>
> —H. Hardless, *The Indian Gentleman's Guide to Etiquette*

A rush of anger surprised her. It was unwise to read old books; the fury they ignited wasn't old; it was new. If she couldn't get the pompous fart himself, she wanted to search out the descendants of H. Hardless and stab the life out of them. But the child shouldn't be blamed for a father's crime, she tried to reason with herself, then. But should the child therefore also enjoy the father's illicit gain?

Sai eavesdropped instead on Noni talking to the librarian about *Crime and Punishment*: "Half awed I was by the writing, but half I was bewildered," said Noni, "by these Christian ideas of confession and forgiveness—they place the burden of the crime on the victim! If nothing can undo the misdeed, then why should sin be undone?"

The whole system seemed to favor, in fact, the criminal over the righteous. You could behave badly, say you were sorry, you would get extra fun and be reinstated in the same position as the one who had done nothing, who now had both to suffer the crime and the difficulty of forgiving, with no goodies in addition at all. And, of course, you would feel freer than ever to sin if you were aware of such a safety net: sorry, sorry, oh so so sorry.

Like soft birds flying you could let the words free.

The librarian who was the sister-in-law of the doctor they all went to in Kalimpong, said: "We Hindus have a better system. You get what you deserve and you cannot escape your deeds. And at least our gods look like gods, no? Like Raja Rani. Not like this Buddha, Jesus—beggar types."

Noni: "But we, too, have wriggled out! Not in this lifetime, we say, in others, perhaps. . . ."

Added Sai: "Worst are those who think the poor should starve because it's their own misdeeds in past lives that are causing problems for them. . . ."

The fact was that one was left empty-handed. There was no system to soothe the unfairness of things; justice was without scope; it might snag the stealer of chickens, but great evasive crimes would have to be dismissed because, if identified and netted, they would bring down the entire structure of so-called civilization. For crimes that took place in the monstrous dealings between nations, for crimes that took place in those intimate spaces between two people without a witness, for these crimes the guilty would never pay. There was no religion and no government that would relieve the hell.

For a moment their conversation was drowned out by the sounds of a procession in the street. "What are they saying?" asked Noni. "They're shouting something in Nepali."

They watched from the window as a group of boys went by with signs.

"Must be the Gorkha lot again."

"But what are they saying?"

"It's not as if it's being said for anyone to understand. It's just noise, *tamasha*," said Lola.

"Ha, yes, they keep on going up and down, something or the other . . . ," the librarian said. "It just takes a few degenerate people and they drum up the illiterates, all the no-gooders hanging about with nothing to do. . . ."

Uncle Potty had joined them now, having delivered his rum supply to the jeep, and Father Booty emerged from the mysticism stacks.

"Should we eat here?"

They went into the dining room, but it seemed deserted, the tables with overturned plates and glasses to signal it was not open for business.

The manager came out of his office, looking harried.

"So sorry, ladies. We're having cash flow problems and we've had to close the dining hall. Getting more and more difficult to maintain things."

He paused to wave at some foreigners. "Going for sightseeing. Yes? At one time all the rajas came to Darjeeling, the Cooch Behar raja, the raja of Burdwan, the Purnia raja. . . . Don't miss the Ghoom Monastery. . . ."

"You must get money from these tourists?"

The Gymkhana had begun to rent out rooms to keep the club going.

"Hah! What money? They are so scared they'll get taken advantage of because of their wealth, they try and bargain down on the cheapest room. . . . And yet, just see." He showed them a postcard the couple had left for the front desk to post: "Had a great dinner for $4.50. We can't believe how cheap this country is!!! We're having a great time, but we'll be glad to get home, where, let's be honest (sorry, we've never been the PC types!) there is widespread availability of deodorant. . . ."

"And these are the last of the tourists. We're lucky to have them. This political trouble will drive them away."

Thirty-two

In this Gymkhana dining hall, in one of the corners slung about with antlers and moth eaten hides, hovered the ghost of the last conversation between the judge and his only friend, Bose.

It had been the last time they ever met. The last time the judge had ever driven his car out of the Cho Oyu gates.

They had not seen each other in thirty-three years.

Bose lifted his glass. "To old times," he had said, and drank. "Ahhh. Mother's milk."

He had brought a bottle of Talisker for them to share, and it was he, as was expected, who had instigated this meeting. It was a month before Sai had arrived in Kalimpong. He had written to the judge that he would stay at the Gymkhana. Why did the judge go? Out of some vain hope of putting his memories to sleep? Out of curiosity? He told himself he went because if he did not go to the Gymkhana, Bose would come to Cho Oyu instead.

"You have to say we have the best mountains in the world," said Bose. "Have you ever trekked up Sandak Fu? That Micky went—remember him? Stupid fellow? Wore new shoes and by the time he arrived at the base, he had developed such blisters he had to sit at the bottom, and his wife Mithu—remember her? lot of spirit? great girl?—she ran all the way to the top in her Hawaii *chappals*.

"Remember Dickie, that one with a tweed coat and cherry pipe pretending to be an English lord, saying things like, 'Look upon this hoary . . . hoary . . . winter's . . . light . . . et cetera?' Had a retarded child and couldn't take it . . . he killed himself.

"Remember Subramanium? Wife, a dumpy woman, four feet by four feet? Cheered himself up with the Anglo secretary, but that wife of his, she booted him out of the house and took all the money . . . and once the money vanished so did the Anglo. Found some other bugger. . . ."

Bose threw back his head to laugh and his dentures came gnashing down. He hurriedly lowered his head and gobbled them up again. The judge was pained by the scene of them before they'd even properly embarked on the evening—two white-haired Fitzbillies in the corner of the club, water-stained *durries*, the grimacing head of a stuffed bear slipping low, half the stuffing fallen out. Wasps lived in the creature's teeth, and moths lived in its fur, which also fooled some ticks that had burrowed in, confident of finding blood, and died of hunger. Above the fireplace, where a portrait of the king and queen of England in coronation attire had once hung, there was now one of Gandhi, thin and with ribs showing. Hardly conducive to appetite or comfort in a club, the judge thought.

Still, you could imagine what it must have been like, planters in boiled shirts riding for miles through the mist, coattails in their pockets to meet for tomato soup. Had the contrast excited them, the playing of tiny tunes with fork and spoon, the dancing against a backdrop that celebrated blood-sports and brutality? In the guest registers, the volumes of which were kept in the library, massacres were recorded in handwriting that had a feminine delicacy and perfect balance, seeming to convey sensitivity and good sense. Fishing expeditions to the Teesta had brought back, just forty years ago, a hundred pounds of *mahaseer*. Twain had shot thirteen tigers on the road between Calcutta and Darjeeling. But the mice hadn't been shot out and they were chewing the matting and scurrying about as the two men talked.

"Remember how I took you to buy the coat in London? Remember that awful bloody thing you had? Looking like a real *gow wallah?* Remember how you used to pronounce *Jheelee* as *Giggly?* Remember? Ha ha."

The judge's heart filled with a surge of venomous emotion: how *dare* this man! Is this why he had made the journey, to raise himself up, put the judge down, establish a past position of power so as to be able to respect himself in the present?

"Remember Granchester? *And is there honey still for tea?*"

He and Bose in the boat, holding themselves apart in case they brush against the others and offend them with brown skin.

The judge looked for the waiter. They should order dinner, get this over with, make it an early night. He thought of Mutt waiting for him.

She would be at the window, her eyes hooked on the gate, tail uncurled between her legs, her body tense with waiting, her brows furrowed.

When he returned, he would pick up a stick.

"I could throw it? You could catch it? Should I?" he would ask her.

Yes yes yes yes—she would leap and jump, unable to bear the anticipation for a moment longer.

So he tried to ignore Bose, but hysterically, once he had begun, Bose accelerated the pace and tone of his invasiveness.

He had been one of the ICS men, the judge knew, who had mounted a court case to win a pension equal to that of a white ICS man, and they had lost, of course, and somehow the light had gone out of Bose.

Despite letter after letter typed on Bose's portable Olivetti, the judge had refused to become involved. He'd already learned his cynicism by then and how Bose had kept his naïveté alive—well, it was miraculous. Even stranger, his naïveté had clearly been inherited by his son, for years later, the judge heard that the son, too, had fought a case against his employer, Shell Oil, and he, too, had lost. The son had reasoned that it was a different age with different rules, but it had turned out to be only a different version of the same old.

"It costs less to live in India," they responded.

But what if they wished to have a holiday in France? Buy a bottle at the duty-free? Send a child to college in America? Who could afford it? If they were paid less, how would India not keep being poor? How could Indians travel in the world and live in the world the same way Westerners did? These differences Bose found unbearable.

But profit could only be harvested in the gap between nations, working one against the other. They were damning the third world to being third-world. They were forcing Bose and his son into an inferior position—thus far and no further—and he couldn't take it. Not after believing he was their friend. He thought of how the English government and its civil servants had sailed away throwing their *topis* overboard, leaving behind only those ridiculous Indians who couldn't rid themselves of what they had broken their souls to learn.

Again they went to court and again they would go to court with their unshakable belief in the system of justice. Again they lost. Again they would lose.

The man with the white curly wig and a dark face covered in powder, bringing down his hammer, always against the native, in a world that was still colonial.

In England they had a great good laugh, no doubt, but in India, too, everyone laughed with the joy of seeing people like Bose cheated. There they had thought they were superior, putting on airs, and they were just the same—weren't they?—as the rest.

The more the judge's mouth tightened, the more Bose seemed determined to drive the conversation until it broke.

"Best days of my life," he said. "Remember? Punting by King's, Trinity, what a view, my God, and then what was it? Ah yes, Corpus Christi. . . . No, I'm getting it wrong, aren't I? First Trinity, then St. John's. No. First Clare, then Trinity, then some ladies' thing, Primrose . . . Primrose?"

"No, that's not the order at all," the judge heard himself saying in tight-wound offended tones like an adolescent. "It was Trinity then Clare."

"No, no, what are you saying. King's, Corpus Christi, Clare, then St. John. Memory going, old chap. . . ."

"I think *your* memory may be failing *you!*"

Bose was drinking peg after peg, desperate to wrangle something—a common memory, an establishment of truth that had, at least, a commitment from two people—

"No, no. King's! Trinity!" he pounded his glass on the table. "Jesus! Clare! Gonville! And then on to tea at Granchester!"

The judge could no longer bear it, he raised his hand into the air, counted fingers:

1. St. John's!
2. Trinity!
3. Clare!
4. King's!

Bose fell silent. He seemed relieved by the challenge.

"Should we order some dinner?" asked the judge.

But Bose swung rapidly to another position—satisfaction either way—but depth, resolution. Still a question for Bose: should he damn the past or find some sense in it? Drunk, eyes aswim with tears, "Bastards!" he said with such bitterness. "What bastards they were!" raising his voice as if attempting to grant himself conviction. "*Goras*—get away with everything don't they? *Bloody white people.* They're responsible for all the crimes of the century!"

Silence.

"Well," he said then, to the disapproving silence, trying to reconcile with it, "one thing we're lucky for, *baap re,* is that they didn't stay, thank God. At least they left. . . ."

Still nothing from the judge.

"Not like in Africa—still making trouble over there. . . ."

Silence.

"Well, I suppose it doesn't matter too much—now they can just do their dirty work from far away. . . ."

Jaw clenched unclenched hands clenched unclenched clenched.

"Oh, they weren't all bad, I suppose. . . . Not all. . . ."

Jaw clenched unclenched hands clenched unclenched clenched unclenched—

Then the judge burst out, despite himself:

"YES! YES! YES! They were bad. They were part of it. And we were part of the problem, Bose, exactly as much as you could argue that we were part of the solution."

And:

"Waiter!

"Waiter!

"Waiter?

"Waiter!!

"WAITER!!!" shouted the judge, in utter desperation.

"Probably gone chasing the hen," said Bose weakly. "I don't think they were expecting anyone."

The judge walked into the kitchen and found two green chilis looking ridiculous in a tin cup on a wooden stand that read "Best Potato Exhibit 1933."

Nothing else.

He went to the front desk. "Nobody in the kitchen."

The man at the reception was half asleep. "It is very late, sir. Go next door to Glenary's. They have a full restaurant and bar."

"We have come here for dinner. Should I report you to the management?" Resentfully the man went around to the back, and eventually a reluctant waiter arrived at their table; dried lentil scabs on his blue jacket made yellow dabs. He had been having a snooze in an empty room—ubiquitous old-fashioned waiter that he was, functioning like a communist employee, existing comfortably away from horrible capitalist ideas of serving monied people politely.

"Roast mutton with mint sauce. Is the mutton tender?" asked the judge imperiously.

The waiter remained unintimidated: "Who can get tender mutton?" he said scornfully.

"Tomato soup?"

He considered this option but lacked the conviction to break free of the considering. After several undecided minutes had passed, Bose broke the spell by asking, "*Rissoles*?" That might salvage the evening.

"Oh no," the waiter said, shaking his head and smiling insolently. "No, *that* you *cannot* get."

"Well, what do you have then?"

"Muttoncurrymuttonpulaovegetablecurryvegetablepulao. . . ."

"But you said the mutton wasn't tender."

"Yes, I already told you, didn't I?"

The food arrived. Bose made a valiant effort to retract and start over: "Just found a new cook myself," he said. "That Sheru kicked the bucket after thirty years of service. The new one is untrained, but he came cheap because of that. I got out the recipe books and read them aloud as he copied it all down in Bengali. 'Look,' I told him, 'keep it basic, nothing fancy. Just learn a brown sauce and a white sauce—shove the bloody white sauce on the fish and shove the bloody brown sauce on the mutton.'"

But he couldn't manage to keep this up.

He now pleaded directly with the judge: "We're friends, aren't we?

"Aren't we? Aren't we friends?"

"Time passes, things change," said the judge, feeling claustrophobia and embarrassment.

"But what is in the past remains unchanged, doesn't it?"

"I think it does change. The present changes the past. Looking back you do not find what you left behind, Bose."

The judge knew that he would never communicate with Bose again. He wanted neither to pretend he had been the Englishman's friend (all those pathetic Indians who glorified a friendship that was later proclaimed by the other [white] party to be nonexistent!), nor did he wish to allow himself to be dragged through the dirt. He had kept up an immaculate silence and he wasn't about to have Bose destroy it. He wouldn't tumble his pride to melodrama at the end of his life and he knew the danger of confession—it would cancel any hope of dignity forever. People pounced on what you gave them like a raw heart and gobbled it up.

The judge called for the bill, once, twice, but even the bill was unimportant to the waiter. He was forced to walk back into the kitchen.

Bose and the judge shook a soggy handshake, and the judge wiped his hands on his pants when they were done, but still, Bose's eye on him was like mucous.

"Good night. Good-bye. So long"—not Indian sentences, English sentences. Perhaps that's why they had been so happy to learn a new tongue in the first place: the self-consciousness of it, the effort of it, the grammar of it, pulled you up; a new language provided distance and kept the heart intact.

The mist was hooked tightly into the tea bushes on either side of the road as he left Darjeeling, and the judge could barely see. He drove slowly, no other cars, nothing around, and then, damn it—

A memory of—

Six little boys at a bus stop.

"Why is the Chinaman yellow? He pees against the wind, HA HA. Why is the Indian brown? He shits upside down, HA HA HA."

Taunting him in the street, throwing stones, jeering, making monkey faces. How strange it was: he had feared children, been scared of these human beings half his size.

Then he remembered a worse incident. Another Indian, a boy he didn't know, but no doubt someone just like himself, just like Bose, was being kicked and beaten behind the pub at the corner. One of the boy's attackers had unzipped his pants and was pissing on him, surrounded by a crowd of jeering red-faced men. And the future judge, walking by, on his way home with a pork pie for his dinner—what had he done? He hadn't said anything. He hadn't done anything. He hadn't called for help. He'd turned and fled, run up to his rented room and sat there.

Without thinking, the judge made the calibrated gestures, the familiar turns back to Cho Oyu, instead of over the edge of the mountainside.

Close to home, he almost ran into an army jeep parked by the side of the road, lights off. The cook and a couple of soldiers were hiding boxes of liquor in the bushes. The judge swore but continued on. He knew about this side business of the cook's and ignored it. It was his habit to be a master and the cook's to be a servant, but something had changed in their relationship within a system that kept servant and master both under an illusion of security.

Mutt was waiting for him at the gate, and the judge's expression softened—he blew his horn to signal his arrival. In a second she went from being the unhappiest dog in the world to the happiest and Jemubhai's heart grew young with pleasure.

The cook opened the gate, Mutt jumped into the seat next to him, and they rode together from the gate to the garage—this was her treat and even when he stopped driving anywhere, he gave her rides about the property to entertain her. As soon as she'd get in, she would acquire a regal air, angling her expression and smiling graciously right and left.

On the table, when the judge got in, he found the telegram waiting. "To Justice Patel from St. Augustine's: regarding your granddaughter, Sai Mistry."

The judge had considered the convent's request in the brief interlude of weakness he experienced after Bose's visit, when he was forced to confront the fact that he had tolerated certain artificial constructs to uphold his existence. When you build on lies, you build strong and solid. It was the truth that undid you. He couldn't knock down the lies or else the past would crumble, and therefore the present. . . . But he now acquiesced to something in the past that had survived, returned, that might, without his paying too much attention, redeem him—

Sai could look after Mutt, he reasoned. The cook was growing decrepit. It would be good to have an unpaid somebody in the house to help with things as the years went by. Sai arrived, and he was worried that she would incite a dormant hatred in his nature, that he would wish to rid himself of her or treat her as he had her mother, her grandmother. But Sai, it had turned out, was more his kin than he had thought imaginable. There was something familiar about her; she had the same accent and manners. She was a westernized Indian brought up by English nuns, an estranged Indian living in India. The journey he had started so long ago had continued in his descendants. Perhaps he had made a mistake in cutting off his daughter . . . he'd condemned her before he knew her. Despite himself, he felt, in the backwaters of his unconscious, an imbalance in his deeds balancing itself out.

This granddaughter whom he didn't hate was perhaps the only miracle fate had thrown his way.

Thirty-three

Six months after Sai, Lola and Noni, Uncle Potty and Father Booty made a library trip to the Gymkhana Club, it was taken over by the Gorkha National Liberation Front, who camped out in the ballroom and the skating rink, ridiculing even further whatever pretensions the club might still harbor despite having already been brought low by the staff.

Men with guns rested in the ladies' powder room, enjoyed the spacious plumbing that was still stamped BARHEAD SCOTLAND, PATENTEES in mulberry letters and dawdled before the long mirror, because like most of the towns' residents, they rarely had the opportunity to see themselves from top to bottom.

The dining room was filled with men in khaki, posing for pictures, feet on the stuffed head of a leopard, whiskey in hand, fire in the fireplace still with rosette tiles. They drank up the entire bar, and on chilly nights they took down the skins from the walls and slept in the musty folds.

Later evidence proved they also stockpiled guns, drew maps, plotted the bombing of bridges, hatched plans that grew in daring as managers fled from the tea plantations that stretched in waves over the Singalila Mountains all around the Gymkhana, from Happy Valley, Makaibari, Chonglu, Pershok.

Then, when it was all over, and the men had signed a peace treaty and moved out—here at this very spot in the Gymkhana Club, on these dining tables placed side by side in a row—they had staged a public surrender of arms.

On October 2, 1988, Gandhi Jayanti Day, seven thousand men surrendered more than five thousand pipe guns, country-made revolvers, pistols, double- and single-barrel guns, Sten guns. They gave up thousands of rounds of ammunition, thirty-five hundred bombs, gelatine sticks, detonators and land mines, kilograms of explosives, mortar shells, cannons. Ghising's men alone had more than twenty-four thousand pieces. In the pile was the judge's BSA pump gun, the Springfield rifle, the double-barreled Holland & Holland with which he had roamed, after teatime, in the countryside surrounding Bonda.

But when Lola, Noni, Father Booty, Uncle Potty, and Sai were turned away from the Gymkhana dining room, they didn't expect things to go so badly with the club. They mistook the gloom for present trouble, just as the manager had suggested, and not for a premonition of the dining hall's future.

Where should they lunch, then?

"That new place, Let's B Veg?" asked Father Booty.

"No *ghas phoos*, no twigs and leaves!" said Uncle Potty firmly. He never ate anything green if he could help it.

"Lung Fung?" It was a shabby Chinese establishment with slain-looking paper dragons dangling from the ceiling.

"Not very nice to sit in."

"Windamere?"

"Too expensive, only for foreigners. Anyway, it's their tea that's good, lunch is the missionary boardinghouse type of thing . . . *thunda khitchri* . . . blubbery collar of mutton . . . salt and pepper, if you're very lucky. . . .

In the end it was Glenary's, as usual.

"Lots of options, at least—everybody can get what they want."

So they trooped across. At a table in the corner sat Father Peter Lingdamoo, Father Pius Marcus, and Father Bonniface D'Souza eating apple strudel. "Good afternoon, Monsignor," they said to Father Booty, bringing a whiff of Europe to them. So elegant: *Monsignor* . . .

As always, the room was mostly crowded with schoolchildren

squirming with joy on their lunch out, boarding schools being one of Darjeeling's great economic ventures along with tea. There were older children celebrating birthdays on their own without supervision, younger ones accompanied by parents visiting from Calcutta or even Bhutan and Sikkim, or Bangladesh, Nepal, or from the surrounding tea gardens. Several patriarchs in a generous mood were also questioning their children about their studies, but the mothers were protesting, "Let them be for once, *baba*," piling up plates and stroking hair, looking at their children in the way their children were looking at the food, trying to stuff in all they could.

They knew the menu by heart from years of special meals at Glenary's. Indian, Continental, or Chinese; sizzlers, chicken and sweet corn soup, ice cream with hot chocolate sauce. Taking swift advantage of parents' melting eyes—almost time to say good-bye—another ice cream with hot chocolate sauce? "Please, Ma, please, Ammi, please, Mummy," mother's eyes turned toward father, "Priti, no, it is quite enough, don't spoil him now," then giving in, knowing Ma, Ammi, or Mummy would be weeping all the lonely road back to the plantation or airport or train station. Had her mother been like this? And her father? Sai felt suddenly bereft and jealous of these children. There was one Tibetan woman so intensely pretty in her sky-colored *baku* and apron with those disjointed bands of jolly color that made one feel cozy and loved right away. "Oh, such sweet sweet cheeks," the family were all saying, laughing as they pretended to eat the baby, somehow kindly and gently, and the baby was laughing hardest of all. Why couldn't she be part of that family? Rent a room in someone else's life?

The ladies polished their cutlery on the paper napkins, wiped their plates and glasses, returned one that looked cloudy.

"How about a wee drink, ladies?" said Uncle Potty.

"Oh Potty, starting so early."

"Suit yourselves. Gin tonic," he ordered and dipped his bread stick directly into the butter dish. Came up with a cheerful golden berg. "I do like a bit of bread with my butter," he proclaimed.

"They do a good fish and chips with tartar sauce," said Father Booty with a flutter of hope, thinking of river fish in crisp gold uniforms of bread crumbs.

"Is the fish fresh?" Lola demanded of the waiter. "From the Teesta?"

"Why not?" said the waiter.

"Why not???!! I don't know! You know *WHY* if NOT!!!"

"Better not risk it. How about chicken in cheese sauce?"

"What cheese?" asked Father Booty.

Everyone froze . . . chilled silence.

They knew the insult was coming—

Utterly butterly delicious. . . . All India Cheese Champ—

"AMUL!!"

"WATERPROOFING!!" cried Father Booty.

As always they pondered their options and picked Chinese.

"It's not like real Chinese food, of course," Lola reminded everyone that Joydeep, her now dead husband, had once visited China and reported that Chinese food in China was quite another matter. A much worse matter, in fact. He described the hundred-day-old egg (and sometimes he said it was a two-hundred-day) buried and dug up as a delicacy, and everyone groaned with horrified delight. He had been a great success at cocktail parties upon his return. "Don't much care for their looks, either," he said, "*chapta* features. Much better, Indian women, Indian antiquities, Indian music, Indian Chinese—"

And in all India, nothing better than Calcutta Chinese! Remember Ta Fa Shun? Where ladies out shopping met for hot-and-acrid soup and accompanied it with hot-and-acrid gossip—

"So what should we have?" asked Uncle Potty who had finished all the bread sticks now.

"Chicken or pork?"

"Chee Chee. Don't trust the pork, full of tapeworms. Who knows what pig it comes from?"

"Chili chicken, then?"

From outside came the noise of the parading boys going by again.

"God, what a racket. All this do-or-die stuff."

The chili chicken arrived and, after depositing it on their table, the waiter wiped his nose on the curtain. "Just take a look at that," said Lola. "No wonder we Indians never progress." They began to eat. "But food here is good." Chomping.

As they were exiting the restaurant, the same procession that had disturbed them while they were eating and while they were at the library came back up the road after having traversed all of Darjeeling.

"Gorkhaland for Gorkhas."

"Gorkhaland for Gorkhas."

They stood back to let them pass and who should almost stamp on Sai's toes?—

Gyan!!!

In his tomato red sweater, yelling lustily in a way she couldn't recognize.

What would he be doing in Darjeeling?! Why would he be at a GNLF rally rallying on behalf of independence for Nepali-Indians?

She opened her mouth to shout to him, but at that moment he caught sight of her, too, and the dismay on his face was followed by a slight ferocious gesture of his head and a cold narrow look in his eye that was a warning not to approach. She shut her mouth like a fish, and astonishment flooded over her gills.

By that time he had passed on.

"Isn't that your mathematics tutor?" asked Noni.

"I don't think so," she said, scrabbling for dignity, scrabbling for sense. "Looked just like him, I thought it was him myself, but it wasn't. . . ."

On their steep way back down to the Teesta, they noticed Sai had turned green.

"Are you all right?" asked Father Booty.

"Travel sick."

"Look at the horizon, that always helps."

She fixed her eyes on the highest ridge of the Himalayas, on the unmoving stillness. But this didn't make any difference. There was a whirl in Sai's brain and she couldn't register what her eyes saw. Finally, a mordant bile rose up her throat, frizzling her system, burning her mouth, corroding her teeth—she could feel them turn to chalk as they were attacked by a resurgence of the chili chicken.

"Stop the car, stop the car," said Lola. "Let her out."

Sai began to retch into the grass, vomiting up a sort of mulligatawny, giving them another unfortunate look at their lunch now so much the worse for wear. Noni poured her a cup of icy water from the space-age silver capsule of the thermos flask, and Sai rested on a rock in the sunshine by the beautiful transparent Teesta. "Take some deep breaths, dear, that food was very greasy, they've really gone downhill—dirty kitchen—oh, just the sight of that waiter should have been enough to warn us."

At the other end of the bridge the checkpoint guards were inspecting some vehicles going through. Careful in this time of trouble, they had opened the bundles and cases of everyone in a bus and turned their belongings inside out. The passengers waited impassively inside; poor people, their faces squashed against the windows, hundreds of pairs of eyes half dead, like animals on their way to death; as if the journey had been so exhausting, their spirits had already been extinguished. The bus had vomit-strewn sides, great banners of brown flared back by the wind. Several other vehicles waited in line after the bus for the same treatment, barred from going on by a metal pole across the road.

The afternoon sun lay thick and golden on the trees, and with the light so bright, the shadows in the foliage, by the car, and between the blades of grass and the rocks were black as night. It was hot here in the valley, but the river, when Sai dipped her hand in, was icy enough to numb her veins.

"Take your time, Sai, long wait anyway, the cars are backed up."

Father Booty got out himself, walked up and down, stretching his limbs, glad of the rest to his aching behind, when he spotted a remarkable butterfly.

The Teesta valley was renowned for its butterflies, and specialists came from around the world to paint and record them. Rare and spectacular creatures depicted in the library volume *Marvelous Butterflies of the North-Eastern Himalayas* were flying about before their eyes. One summer, when she was twelve, Sai had made up names for them—"Japanese mask butterfly, butterfly of the far mountain, Icarus falling from the sun butterfly, butterfly that a flute set free, kite festival butterfly"—and written them into a book labeled "My Butterfly Collection" and accompanied the names with illustrations.

"Astonishing." said Father Booty. "Just look at this one here." Peacock blue and long emerald streamer tails. "Oh goodness, and that one"—black with white spots and a pink flame at its heart. . . . "Oh my camera . . . Potty, can you just rummage in the glove compartment?"

Uncle Potty was reading *Asterix: Ave Gaul! By Toutatis!!!!#@***!!*, but he roused himself and handed the little Leica through the window.

As the butterfly fluttered beguilingly on a cable of the bridge, Father Booty snapped the photograph. "Oh dear, I think I shook, the picture might be blurry."

He was about to try again when the guards began to shout and one of them came racing up. "Photography strictly prohibited on the bridge." Didn't he know?

Oh dear, he did, he did, a mistake, he had forgotten in his excitement. "So sorry, officer." He knew, he knew. It was a very important bridge, this, India's contact with the north, with the border at which they might have to fight the Chinese again someday, and now, of course, there was the Gorkha insurgency as well.

It didn't help that he was a foreigner.

They took his camera and began to search the jeep.

A disturbing smell.

"What is that smell?"

"Cheese."

"Kya cheez?" said a fellow from Meerut.

They had never heard of cheese. They looked unconvinced. It smelled far too suspicious and one of them reported that he thought it smelled of bomb-making materials. "Gas *maar raha hai,*" said the Meerut boy.

"What did he say?" asked Father Booty.

"Something is *whacking* gas. Something is *firing* gas."

"Throw it out," they told Father Booty. "It's gone bad."

"No it hasn't."

"Yes, it has, the whole vehicle is smelling."

The checkpoint guards now began to examine the pile of books, regarding them with the same wrinkled noses as the unclaimed cheese that had been destined for Glenary's.

"What is this?" They hoped for literature of an antinational and inflammatory nature.

"Trollope," Lola said brightly, excited and aroused by the turn of events. "I always said," she turned to the others in a frivolous fashion, "that I would save Trollope for my dotage; I knew it would be a perfect slow indulgence when I had nothing much to do and, well, here I am. Old-fashioned books is what I like. Not the new kind of thing, no beginning, no middle, no end, just a thread of . . . free-floating plasma . . .

"English writer," she told the guard.

He flipped through: *The Last Chronicle of Barset: The Archdeacon goes to Framley, Mrs. Dobbs Broughton Piles her Fagots.*

"Did you know," Lola asked the others, "that he also invented the post box?"

"Why are you reading it?"

"To take my mind off all of this." She gestured vaguely and rudely at the scene in general and the guard himself. Who had his pride. Knew he was something. Knew his mother knew he was something. Not even an hour ago she had fed her belief and her son with *puri aloo* accompanied by a lemony-limy-luscious Limca, the fizz from which had made a mini excitement about his nose.

Angry at Lola's insolence, his face still awake from the soda spray, he gave orders for the book to be placed in the police jeep.

"You can't take it," she said, "it's a library book, you foolish little man. I'll get into trouble at the Gymkhana. You're not going to pay them to replace it."

"And this?" The guard examined another book.

Noni had picked a sad account of police brutality during the Naxalite movement by Mahashveta Devi, translated by Spivak who, she had recently read with interest in the *Indian Express,* was made cutting edge by a sari and combat boots wardrobe. She had also selected a book by Amit Chaudhuri that contained a description of electricity failure in Calcutta that caused people across India to soften with communal nostalgia for power shortage. She had read it before but returned every now and then to half drink, half drown in those beautiful images. Father Booty had a treatise on Buddhist esotericism, written by a scholar from one of the legendary monastic universities of Lhasa, and Agatha Christie's *Five Little Pigs.* And Sai had *Wuthering Heights* in her bag.

"We have to take these to the station for inspection."

"Why? Please sir," said Noni, trying to persuade him, "we've especially gone. . . . What will we read. . . . Stuck at home. . . . All those hours of curfew. . . ."

"But officer, you only have to look at us to know we're hardly the people to waste your time on," said Father Booty. "So many *goondas* around. . . ."

But they had no sympathy for bookworms, and Lola began to shout, "Thieves, that's what you police are. Everybody knows it. Hand in hand with *goondas*. I will go to the army major, I will go to the SDO. What kind of situation is this, bullying the population, you little men throwing your weight around. I'm not going to bribe you, if that's what you're hoping—forget about it. Let us go," she said grandly to the others.

"*Chalo yaar,*" said Uncle Potty and glanced at his bottles to indicate they might have one or two IF . . .

But the man said, "Serious trouble. Even five bottles will not be enough." And it became obvious what Kalimpong was in for.

"Calm down, madam," the policeman said to Lola, offending her still more. "If there is nothing in your books, we will return them."

The red-hot library books were taken carefully away. Father Booty's camera, too, was confiscated and delivered to their supervisor's desk; his case they would review separately.

———

Sai didn't notice much, for she was still thinking about Gyan ignoring her, and she didn't care the books were gone.

Why was he there? Why hadn't he wanted to acknowledge her? He had said: "I can't resist you . . . I have to keep coming back. . . ."

At home the cook was waiting, but she went to bed without her dinner, and this greatly offended the cook, who took it to mean that she had eaten fancily in a restaurant and now despised the offerings at home.

Sensitive to his jealousy, she usually came home and complained, "The spices were not ground properly—I almost broke my tooth on a peppercorn, and the meat was so tough, I had to swallow it without chewing, all in a big lump with glasses of water." He would laugh and laugh. "Ha ha, yes, nobody takes the time to clean and tenderize the meat properly anymore, to grind the spices, roast them. . . ." Then, growing suddenly serious, he would exclaim, holding up a finger to make his point like a politician: "And for this they charge a lot of money!" Nodding hard, wise to the horrors of the world. Now, in a spoiled mood, he banged the dishes.

"What is going on!" shouted the judge. A statement, not a question, that was to be responded to by silence.

"Nothing," he said, beyond caring, "what can be going on? Babyji went to sleep. She ate at the hotel."

Thirty-four

A week after the library trip, the books were returned, having been declared harmless, but the authorities didn't take a similar view of the photograph of the butterfly, which showed, beyond its beguiling wings of black, white and pink, the sentry post at the bridge, and the bridge itself, spanning the Teesta. In fact, it was focused, they noted, not on the butterfly, but on the bridge.

"I was in a hurry," said Father Booty, "I forgot to focus properly and then just as I was going to try again, I was nabbed."

But the police didn't listen and that evening they visited him at home, turned everything upside down; took away his alarm clock, his radio, some extra batteries, a package of nails he had bought to finish work on his cowshed, and a bottle of illegal Black Cat rum from Sikkim. They took all that away.

"Where are your papers?"

Father Booty was now found to be residing in India illegally. Oh dear, he had not expected contact with the authorities; he had allowed his residence permit to lapse in the back of a moldy drawer for to renew the permit was such bureaucratic hell, and never again did he plan to leave or to reenter India. . . . He knew he was a foreigner but had lost the notion that he was anything but an *Indian* foreigner. . . .

He had two weeks to leave Kalimpong.

"But I have lived here forty-five years."

"That is of no consequence. It was your privilege to be residing here, but we cannot tolerate abuse of privilege."

Then the messenger grew kinder, remembering that his own son was being taught by Jesuits, and he hoped to send the boy to England or America. Or even Switzerland would be all right. . . .

"Sorry, Father," he said, "but these days. . . . I myself will lose my job. Another time I could slip you through, maybe, but just now . . . please go at once to the Snow Lion Travel Agency and book your ticket. We will provide free passage on a government jeep to Siliguri. Think of it as a holiday, Father, and keep in touch. When this is finished, apply for the proper papers and return. No problem." How easy it was to say these words. He grew happier at being able to be so civilized and nice.

Return. No problem. Take rest. Have a holiday.

Father Booty went running to everyone he knew who might help him, the police chief and the SDO who made regular trips to the dairy for sweet curd, Major Aloo in the cantonment who enjoyed the chocolate cigars he made, the forest department officials who had given him oyster mushroom spawn so he might have mushrooms in his garden during fungus season. One year when the bamboo clump on his property bloomed and bees from the whole district descended whrooming upon the white flowers, the forest department had bought the seeds from him, because they were valuable—bamboo flowered only once in a hundred years. When the clump died after this extravagant effort, they gave him new bamboo to plant, young spears with their tips like braids.

But now, all those who in peaceful times had enjoyed his company and chatted about such things as curd, mushrooms, and bamboo were too busy or too scared to help.

"We cannot allow a threat to our national security."

"What about my home? What about my dairy, the cows?"

But they were as illegal as he was.

"Foreign nationals can't own property and you know that, Father. What business do you have owning all of this?"

The dairy was actually in the name of Uncle Potty, because long ago, when this tetchy little problem had come up, he had signed the papers on behalf of his friend. . . .

But empty property was a great risk, for Kalimpong had long ago been demarcated an "area of high sensitivity," and according to the laws, the army was entitled to appropriate any unoccupied land. They paid rock-bottom rent, slapped concrete about, and filled the homes they took over with a string of temporary people who didn't care and wrecked the place. That was the usual story.

Father Booty felt his heart fail at the thought of his cows being turned out in favor of army tanks; looked about at his craggy bit of mountainside—violet bamboo orchids and pale ginger lilies spicing the air; a glimpse of the Teesta far below that was no color at all right now, just a dark light shining on its way to join the Brahmaputra. Such wilderness could not incite a gentle love—he loved it fiercely, intensely.

But two days later, Father Booty received another visitor, a Nepali doctor who wished to open a private nursing home and without being invited to do so, walked through the gate to gaze at the same view Father Booty had looked out on and caressed it with his eyes. He examined the solidly constructed house that Father Booty had named *Sukhtara*. Star of Happiness. He knocked his knuckles against the cowsheds with the approval of ownership. Twenty-five rich patients in a row. . . . And then he made an offer to buy the Swiss dairy for practically nothing.

"That isn't even the cost of the shed, let alone the main house."

"You will not get any other offers."

"Why not?"

"I have arranged it and you have no choice. You are lucky to get what I am giving you. You are residing in this country unlawfully and you must sell or lose everything."

"I will look after the cows, Booty," said his friend Uncle Potty. "No worries. And when the trouble is over, you return and take up where you left off."

They sat together, Father Booty, Uncle Potty, and Sai. In the background, a tape of Abida Parveen was playing. *"Allah hoo, Allah hoo Allah hoo. . . ."* God was just wilderness and space, said the husky voice, careless with the loss of love. It took you to the edge of all you could bear and then—it let go, let go. . . . *"Mujhe jaaaane do. . . ."* All one should desire was freedom. But Father Booty wasn't comforted by Uncle Potty's assurance, for it had to be admitted that his friend was an alcoholic and undependable. In a drunken state he would allow anything to happen, he might sign on any line, but it was Father Booty's own fault: why hadn't he applied for an Indian passport? Because it was just as silly as NOT applying for an American or a Swiss? He felt a lack in himself, despised his conformity to the ideas of the world even as he disagreed with them.

A mongoose loped like water over the grass, matching the color of the evening, only its movement betraying it.

Anger strained against Sai's heart. This was Gyan's doing, she thought. This is what he had done and what people like him were doing in the name of decency and education, in the name of hospitals for Nepalis and management positions. In the end, Father Booty, lovable Father Booty who, frankly, had done much more for development in the hills than any of the locals, and without screaming or waving kukris, Father Booty was to be sacrificed.

In the valleys, it was already night, lamps coming on in the mossy, textured loam, the fresh-smelling darkness expanding, unfolding its foliage. The three of them drank Old Monk, watched as the black climbed all the way past their toes and their knees, the cabbage-leafed shadows reaching out and touching them on their cheeks, noses, enveloping their faces. The black climed over the tops of their heads and on to extinguish Kanchenjunga glowing a last brazen pornographic pink. . . . each of them separately remembered how many evenings they'd spent like this . . . how unimaginable it was that they would soon come to an end. Here Sai had learned how music, alcohol, and friendship together could create a grand civilization. "Nothing so sweet, dear friends—" Uncle Potty would say raising his glass before he drank.

There were concert halls in Europe to which Father Booty would soon return, opera houses where music molded entire audiences into a single grieving or celebrating heart, and where the applause rang like a downpour. . . .

But could they feel as they did here? Hanging over the mountain, hearts half empty–half full, longing for beauty, for innocence that now knows. With passion for the beloved or for the wide world or for worlds beyond this one. . . .

Sai thought of how it had been unclear to her what exactly she longed for in the early days at Cho Oyu, that only the longing itself found its echo in her aching soul. The longing was gone now, she thought, and the ache seemed to have found its substance.

Her mind returned to the day of the gun robbery at Cho Oyu—the start of everything going wrong.

Thirty-five

How foolishly those rifles had been left mounted on the wall, retired artifacts relegated to history, seen too often to notice or think about. Gyan was the last one to take them down and examine them—boys liked things like that. Even the Dalai Lama, Sai had read, had a collection of war games and toy soldiers. It hadn't occurred to her that they might be resurrected into use. Would there be crimes committed that would, when dot was linked to dot, be traced to their doorstep?

"My grandfather used to go hunting," Sai had told Gyan, trying to impress him, but why had she been proud? Of something that should be shaming?

The cook had told her the stories:

"A great shikari he was, Saibaby. He was very handsome, and he looked very brave and stylish on his horse. The villagers would call him if there was ever a man-eater around."

"Was there often one?" Goose pimples.

"Oh, all the time. *Rrrr-rrrr,* you would hear them, and the sound was of wood being sawed. I can remember waking up and listening. In the morning you could see pug marks by the river, sometimes even around the tents."

The cook couldn't help but enjoy himself, and the more he repeated his stories, the more they became truer than the truth.

The police had come to investigate the crime and, in the cook's quarter, sent Biju's letters flying. . . .

"They had to do it," said the cook. "This is a serious matter."

The seriousness was proved when, one morning not long after Father Booty heard the news of his exile, the subdivisional officer arrived at Cho Oyu. The judge and Sai were on the lawn and he had to search to locate them within the camouflage of their own shadows and the shadows of leaves.

"The perpetrators are still absconding," said the SDO surrounded by three policemen with guns and *lathis*, "but please don't worry, sir. We will nip this in the bud. Crack down on antisocial elements.

"You know, my father was also a great shikari," he continued over tea. "If only he had been less adept, I told him, you would have left something for us as well! Isn't it so? Ha ha," he laughed, but his laugh would have registered bright pink on the litmus test. "Justice Sahib, you shikaris were too good, lions and leopards. . . . Now if you go into the forest and if you see a chicken that has escaped from somewhere, you are lucky, no?"

Silence. Had he gone too far?

"But no need to worry, we will catch the criminals. They are using the problems of Bhutan, Assam as an excuse to make trouble here. This country of ours is always being torn apart and it's sad for people like us, brought up with national feeling, and worst for you, sir, who struggled for our freedom. . . . These antinationals have no respect for anything or anyone, not even for themselves. . . . The whole economy is under threat."

"Do you know," he turned to Sai, "what are the three *T*s of the Darjeeling district? Can you tell me?" She shook her head. Disappointed in her, triumphant in himself, he intoned:

"Tea!

"Timber!

"Tourism!"

As he left, he stopped at a flowering creeper. "Beautiful blossom,

Justice Sahib. If you see such a sight, you will know there is a God." The passionflower was a glorious bizarre thing, each bloom lasting just a day, purple and white striped tentacles, half sea anemone, half flower—all by itself, it proffered enough reason for faith.

"I have become a keen gardener," said the SDO, "since I arrived in Kalimpong. I look after my plants exactly as if they were babies. Well, let me know if you have any more trouble. I think you won't, but no doubt this is a very touchy situation." He did up his shawl like a nationalist—Flap! Wrap! Things to do! No time to waste! Nation calls! And he got back into his jeep. The driver backed out of the gate, roared away.

"Let's see what he does," said the cook.

"They never find anyone," said the judge.

Sai didn't speak because she couldn't stop returning to the thought of Gyan avoiding her.

Some days later the police picked up a miserable drunk for the crime. The drunk was a customary sight lying oblivious to the world in a ditch by the side of the market road. Some passerby or the other would haul him up, smack his cheeks, and send him lurching home, crisscrossed with patterns of grasses, stars in his eyes.

Now, instead, the drunk was transported to the police station, where he sat on the floor, his hands and feet trussed. The policemen stood about looking bored. All of a sudden, though, triggered by something unapparent, they recovered from their malaise, jumped up, and began beating the man.

The more he screamed the harder they beat him; they reduced him to a pulp, bashed his head until blood streamed down his face, knocked out his teeth, kicked him until his ribs broke—

You could hear him up and down the hillside begging and screaming. The police watched with disgust. He was claiming his innocence: "I didn't steal guns from anybody, I didn't go to anyone's house, nothing, nothing, some mistake. . . ."

His were the first screams and they heralded the end of normal life on the hillside.

"I didn't do anything, but I am sorry." For hours they continued, the desperate shrieks tearing up the air, "I am sorry, I am sorry, I am sorry. . . ."

But the police were just practising their torture techniques, getting ready for what was coming. When the man crawled out on his knees, his eyes had been extinguished. They would heal into horizonless, flat blanks that would forever cause others to recoil in fear and disgust.

The only grace was that he wouldn't see them recoiling and would disappear entirely inside the alcohol that had always given him solace.

Thirty-six

It was Mr. Iype the newsagent who said offhandedly, waving a copy of *India Abroad*: "You're from Darjeeling side, no? Lot of trouble over there. . . ."

"Why?"

"Nepalis making trouble . . . very troublesome people. . . ."

"Strikes?"

"Much worse, *bhai*, not only strikes, the whole hillside is shut down."

"It is?"

"For many months this has been going on. Haven't you heard?"

"No. I haven't had any letters for a long time."

"Why do you think?"

Biju had blamed usual disruptions—bad weather, incompetance—for the break in his father's correspondence.

"They should kick the bastards back to Nepal," continued Mr. Iype. "Bangladeshis to Bangladesh, Afghans to Afghanistan, all Muslims to Pakistan, Tibetans, Bhutanese, why are they sitting in our country?"

"Why are we sitting here?"

"This country is different," he said without shame. "Without us what would they do?"

Biju went back to work.

Through the day, with gradually building momentum, he became convinced his father was dead. The judge wouldn't know how to find him if he would try to find him at all. His unease began to tighten.

By the next day he couldn't stand it anymore; he slipped out of the kitchen and purchased a twenty-five-dollar number from a bum who had a talent for learning numbers by lingering outside phone booths, overhearing people spell out their calling codes and recording them in his head. He had loitered behind one unsuspecting Mr. Onopolous making a phone call and charging it to his platinum—

"But be quick," he told Biju, "I'm not sure about this number, a couple of people have already used it. . . ."

The receiver was still moist and warm from the last intimacy it had conducted, and it breathed back at Biju, a dense tubercular crepitation. As there was no phone at Cho Oyu, Biju rang the number for the MetalBox guesthouse on Ringkingpong Road.

"Can you get my father? I will call again in two hours."

So, one evening, some weeks before the phone lines were cut, before the roads and bridges were bombed, and they descended into total madness, the MetalBox watchman came rattling the gate at Cho Oyu. The cook had a broth going with bones and green onions—

"La! Phone! La! Telephone! Telephone call from your son. La! From America. He will phone again in one hour. Come quick!"

The cook went immediately, leaving the rattling skeleton bones topped by dancing scrappy green, for Sai to watch—"Babyji!"

"Where are you going?" asked Sai, who had been pulling burrs from Mutt's pantaloons while thinking of Gyan's absence—

But the cook didn't reply. He was already out of the gate and running.

The phone sat squat in the drawing room of the guesthouse encircled by a lock and chain so the thieving servants might only receive phone calls and not make them. When it rang again, the watchman leapt at it, saying, "Phone, la! Phone! *La mai!*" and his whole family came running from their hut outside. Every time the phone rang, they ran with committed loyalty. Upkeepers of modern novelties, they would not, *would not,* let it fall to ordinariness.

"HELLO?"

"HELLO? HELLO?"

They gathered about the cook, giggling in delicious anticipation.

"HELLO?"

"HELLO? PITAJI??"

"BIJU?" By natural logic he raised his voice to cover the distance between them, sending his voice all the way to America.

"Biju, Biju," the watchman's family chorused, "it's Biju," they said to one another. "Oh, it's your son," they told the cook. "It's his son," they told one another. They watched for his expressions to change, for hints as to what was being said at the other end, wishing to insinuate themselves deeply into the conversation, to *become it,* in fact.

"HELLO HELLO????"

"???? HAH? I CAN'T HEAR. YOUR VOICE IS VERY FAR."

"I CAN'T HEAR. CAN YOU HEAR?"

"He can't hear."

"WHAT?"

"Still can't hear?" they asked the cook.

The atmosphere of Kalimpong reached Biju all the way in New York; it swelled densely on the line and he could feel the pulse of the forest, smell the humid air, the green-black lushness; he could imagine all its different textures, the plumage of banana, the stark spear of the cactus, the delicate gestures of ferns; he could hear the croak *trrrr whonk, wee wee butt ock butt ock* of frogs in the spinach, the rising note welding imperceptibly with the evening. . . .

"HELLO? HELLO?"

"Noise, noise," said the watchman's family, *"Can't hear?"*

The cook waved them away angrily, *"Shshshshsh,"* immediately terrified, then, at the loss of a precious second with his son. He turned back to the phone, still shooing them away from behind, almost sending his hand off with the vehemence of his gestures.

They retreated for a moment and then, growing accustomed to the dismissive motion, were no longer intimidated, and returned.

"HELLO?"

"KYA?"

"KYA?"

The shadow of their words was bigger than the substance. The echo of their own voices gulped the reply from across the world.

"THERE IS TOO MUCH NOISE."

The watchman's wife went outside and studied the precarious wire, the fragile connection trembling over ravines and over mountains, over Kanchenjunga smoking like a volcano or a cigar—a bird might have alighted upon it, a nightjar might have swooped through the shaky signal, the satellite in the firmament could have blipped—

"Too much wind, the wind is blowing," said the watchman's wife, "the line is swaying like this, like this"—her hand undulating.

The children climbed up the tree and tried to hold the line steady.

A gale of static inflicted itself on the space between father and son.

"WHAT HAPPENED?"—shrieking even louder—"EVERY-THING ALL RIGHT?!"

"WHAT DID YOU SAY?"

"Let it go," the wife said, plucking the children from the tree, "you're making it worse."

"WHAT IS HAPPENING? ARE THERE RIOTS? STRIKES?"

"NO TROUBLE NOW." (Better not worry him.) "NOT NOW!!"

"Is he going to come?" said the watchman.

"ARE YOU ALL RIGHT?" Biju shrieked on the New York street.

"DON'T WORRY ABOUT ME. DON'T WORRY ABOUT ANYTHING HERE. ARE THERE PROPER ARRANGEMENTS FOR EATING AT THE HOTEL? IS THE RESTAURANT GIVING YOU ACCOMMODATION? ARE THERE ANY OTHER PEOPLE FROM UTTAR PRADESH THERE?"

"Give accommodation. Free food. EVERYTHING FINE. BUT ARE YOU ALL RIGHT?" Biju asked again.

"EVERYTHING QUIET NOW."

"YOUR HEALTH IS ALL RIGHT?"

"YES. EVERYTHING ALL RIGHT."

"Ahh, everything all right," everyone said, nodding. "Everything all right? Everything all right."

Suddenly, after this there was nothing more to say, for while the emotion was there, the conversation was not; one had bloomed, not the other, and they fell abruptly into emptiness.

"When is he coming?" the watchman prompted.

"WHEN ARE YOU COMING?"

"I DON'T KNOW. I WILL TRY. . . ."

Biju wanted to weep.

"CAN'T YOU GET LEAVE?"

He hadn't even attained the decency of being granted a holiday now and then. He could not go home to see his father.

"WHEN WILL YOU GET LEAVE?"

"I DON'T KNOW. . . ."

"HELLO?"

"*La ma ma ma ma ma ma,* he can't get leave. Why not? Don't know, must be difficult there, make a lot of money, but one thing is certain, they have to work very hard for it. . . . Don't get something for nothing . . . nowhere in the world. . . ."

"HELLO? HELLO?"

"PITAJI, CAN YOU HEAR ME?"

They retreated from each other again—

Beep beep honk honk trr butt ock, the phone went dead and they were stranded in the distance that lay between them.

"HELLO? HELLO?"—into the rictus of the receiver.

"Hello? Hello? Hello? Hello?" they echoed back to themselves.

The cook put down the phone, trembling.

"He'll ring again," said the watchman.

But the phone remained mute.

Outside, the frogs said *tttt tttt,* as if they had swallowed the dial tone.

He tried to shake the gadget back into life, wishing for at least the customary words of good-bye. After all, even on clichéd phrases, you could hoist true emotion.

"There must be a problem with the line."

"Yes, yes, yes."

As always, the problem with the line.

"He will come back fat. I have heard they all come back fat," said the watchman's sister-in-law abruptly, trying to comfort the cook.

The call was over, and the emptiness Biju hoped to dispel was reinforced.

He could not talk to his father; there was nothing left between them but emergency sentences, clipped telegram lines shouted out as if in the midst of a war. They were no longer relevant to each other's lives except for the hope that they *would be* relevant. He stood with his head still in the phone booth studded with bits of stiff chewing gum and the usual *FuckShitCockDickPussyLove War,* swastikas, and hearts shot with arrows mingling in a dense graffiti garden, too sugary too angry too perverse—the sick sweet rotting mulch of the human heart.

If he continued his life in New York, he might never see his *pitaji* again. It happened all the time; ten years passed, fifteen, the telegram arrived, or the phone call, the parent was gone and the child was too late. Or they returned and found they'd missed the entire last quarter of a lifetime, their parents like photograph negatives. And there were worse tragedies. After the initial excitement was over, it often became obvious that the love was gone; for affection was only a habit after all, and people, they forgot, or they became accustomed to its absence. They returned and found just the facade; it had been eaten from inside, like Cho Oyu being gouged by termites from within.

They all grow fat there. . . .

The cook knew about them all growing fat there. It was one of the things everyone knew:

"Are you growing fat, *beta,* like everyone in America?" he had written to his son long ago, in a departure from their usual format.

"Yes, growing fat," Biju had written back, "when you see me next, I will be myself times ten." He laughed as he wrote the lines and the cook laughed very hard when he read them; he lay on his back and kicked his legs in the air like a cockroach.

"Yes," Biju had said, "I am growing fat—ten times myself," and was shocked when he went to the ninety-nine-cent store and found he had to buy his shirts at the children's rack. The shopkeeper, a man from Lahore, sat on a high ladder in the center and watched to make sure nobody stole anything, and his eyes clutched onto Biju as soon as he entered, making Biju sting with a feeling of culpability. But he had done nothing. Everyone could tell that he had, though, for his guilty look was there for all to see.

He missed Saeed. He wanted to look, once again, if briefly, at the country through the sanguine lens of his eyes.

Biju returned to the Gandhi Café where they had not noticed his absence.

"You all come and watch the cricket match, OK?" Harish-Harry had brought in a photo album to show his staff pictures of the New Jersey condominium for which he had just made a down payment. He had already mounted a giant satellite dish smack-bang in the middle of the front lawn despite the fact that the management of this select community insisted it be placed subtly to the side like a discreet ear; he had prevailed in his endeavor, having cleverly cried, "Racism! Racism! I am not getting good reception of Indian channels."

That left just his daughter to worry about. Their friend and competitor, Mr. Shah's wife, had hooked a bridegroom by making Galawati kebabs and Fed-Exing them overnight all the way to Oklahoma. "Some *dehati* family in the middle of the cornfield," Harish-Harry told his wife. "And you should see this fellow they are showing off about—what a *lutoo.* American size—he looks like something you would use to break down the door."

He told his daughter: "It used to be a matter of pride for a girl to have a pleasant personality. Act like a stupid now and you can regret later on for the rest of your life. . . . Then don't come crying to us, OK?"

Thirty-seven

The situation will improve, the SDO had said, but though they had begun to torture random people all over town, it didn't.

A series of strikes kept businesses closed.

A one-day strike.

A three-day strike.

Then a seven day.

When Lark's General Store opened briefly one morning, Lola fought a victorious battle with the Afghan princesses over the last jars and cans. Later that month the princesses could think of nothing but jam, furious about it, in the midst of murder and burning properties: "That thoroughly nasty woman!"

Lola gloated each day as she spread the Druk's marmalade thin so it would last.

A thirteen-day strike.

A twenty-one-day strike.

More strike than no strike.

More moisture in the air than air. It was hard to breathe and there was a feeling of being stifled in a place that was, after all, generous with space if nothing else.

Finally, the shops and offices didn't open at all—the Snow Lion Travel Agency and the STD booth, the shawl shop, the deaf tailors, Kanshi Nath & Sons Newsagents—everyone terrorized to keep their shutters down and not even poke their noses out of the windows. Roadblocks stopped traffic, prevented timber and stone trucks from leaving, halted tea from being transported. Nails were scattered on the road, Mobil oil spilled all about. The GNLF boys charged large sums of money if they let you through at all and coerced you to buy GNLF speeches on cassette tapes and Gorkhaland calendars.

Men arrived in trucks from Tindharia and Mahanadi, gathered outside the police station, and threw bricks and bottles. Tear gas didn't scatter them; neither did the *lathi* charge.

"Well, how much land do they want?" asked Lola gloomily.

Noni: "The subdivisions of Darjeeling, Kalimpong, and Kurseong, and extending to the foothills, parts of Jalpaiguri and Cooch Behar districts, from Bengal into Assam."

"No peace for the wicked," said Mrs. Sen, knitting needles going, for she was making a sweater for the prime minister out of sympathy for his troubles. Even in Delhi it gets cold . . . especially in those drafty bungalows in which they house top government officials. But she was not an accomplished knitter. Very slow. Unlike her mother, who, in the course of watching a movie, could knit a whole baby blanket.

"Who's wicked?" said Lola. "Not us. It's they who are wicked. And we are the ones who have no peace. No peace for the *not wicked*."

What was a country but the idea of it? She thought of India as a concept, a hope, or a desire. How often could you attack it before it crumbled? To undo something took practice; it was a dark art and they were perfecting it. With each argument the next would be easier, would become a compulsive act, and like wrecking a marriage, it would be impossible to keep away, to stop picking at wounds even if the wounds were your own.

They were done with their library books, but of course there was no question of returning them. One morning when the trim major who ran the Gymkhana Club arrived, he found the GNLF had scuttled out the librarians and desk clerks and were enjoying the most space and privacy they'd ever had in their lives, sleeping between the bookshelves, cavorting in the ladies' cloakroom, where, not so long ago, Lola had blown on her puff and delicately powdered her nose.

No tourists arrived from Calcutta in hilarious layers as if preparing for the Antarctic, weaving the cauterizing smell of mothballs through the town. No visitors came, with their rich city fat, to burden scabied nags on pony rides. This year the ponies were free.

Nobody came to the Himalayan Hotel and sat under the Roerich painting of a mountain lit up by the moon like a ghost in bedsheets, to "Experience a Quaint Return to Yesteryears" as the brochure suggested, to order Irish stew, and chew chew chew on the scrawny goats of Kalimpong.

The company guesthouses closed. The watchmen who always had to move at this time of year from their illicit occupation of the main houses during winter into their peripheral huts; who had to alter their expressions from dignity to *"Ji huzoor"* servitude; replace cupboard locks they had picked to disinter televisions and made-in-Japan electric heaters; this year, they found their comforts uninterrupted.

And while they stayed put, children were being plucked from boarding schools as parents opened the papers to read with horror of the salubrious climate of the hills being disturbed by separatist rebels and guerilla tactics. The mounting hysteria all around was perhaps to blame for the last group of boys at St. Xavier's disgracing themselves. When instructed to help with the preparation of dinner (cooks having vanished into the mist), they discovered that a chicken's head was best removed by twisting and popping it like a cork—much better than sawing away with a blunt knife. An orgy of blood and feathers ensued, a great skauwauking kerfuffle, headless birds running about spilling guts and excrement. The boys screamed until they cried with disgraceful laughter, their laughs drowning and struggling in sobs, and sobs bubbling and rising with laughter. The master in charge turned on the hosepipe to blast them into sense with cold water, but of course by now there was no water left in the tanks.

No gas either, or kerosene. They were all back to cooking on wood.

There was no water.

"Left the buckets out in the garden," said Lola to Noni, "to fill with rain. We better not flush the toilet anymore. Just add some Sunny Fresh to keep the smell down. For small jobs anyway."

There was no electricity, because the electricity department had been burned to protest arrests made at the roadblocks.

When the fridge shuddered silent the sisters were forced to cook all the perishable food at once. It was Kesang's day off.

Outside, rain was falling and it was almost time for curfew; drawn by the poignant smell of mutton cooking, a group of passing GNLF boys searching for shelter climbed through the kitchen window.

"Why your front door is locked, Aunty?"

The enormous locks that were usually on the tin trunks containing valuables had been moved to the front and back doors as extra precaution. Above their heads, in the attic, several objects of worth had been left vulnerable. Family *puja* silver from their preaetheist days; Bond Street baby cups with trowellike utensils that had once gathered and packed Farex into their own guppy mouths; a telescope made in Germany; their great-grandmother's pearly nose ring; bat eyeglasses from the sixties; silver marrow spoons (they had always been a great family for eating their marrow); damask napkins with a pocket sewn in to enfold triangles of cucumber sandwich—"Just a sprinkle of water, remember, to dampen the cloth before you set off for the picnic. . . ." Magpie things gleaned from a romantic version of the West and a fanciful version of the East that contained power enough to maintain dignity across the rotten offences between nations.

"What do you want?" Lola asked the boys and her face showed them that she had something to protect.

"We are selling calendars, Aunty, and cassettes for the movement."

"What calendars, cassettes?"

Balanced against the forced entry and their rebel camouflage attire was their disconcerting politeness.

The cassettes were recorded with the favorite washing-bloody-kukris-in-the-mother-waters-of-the-Teesta speech.

"Don't give them anything," hissed Lola in English, feeling faint, thinking they wouldn't understand. "Once you start, they'll keep coming back."

But they did understand. They understood her English and she didn't understand their Nepali.

"Any contribution to the effort for Gorkhaland is all right."

"All right for you, not all right for us."

"Shhh," Noni shushed her sister. "Don't be reckless," she gasped.

"We will issue you a receipt," said the boys, eyes on the food lying on the counter—intestinal-looking Essex Farm sausages; frozen salami with a furze of permafrost melting away.

"Nothing doing," said Lola.

"Shhhh," Noni said again. "Give us a calendar then."

"Only one, Aunty?"

"All right, well, two."

"But you know how we need money. . . ."

They invested in three calendars and two cassettes. Still the boys did not leave.

"Can we sleep on the floor? The police will never search for us here."

"No," said Lola.

"Fine, but please don't make any noise or trouble," said Noni.

The boys ate all the food before they slept.

Lola and Noni barricaded the door to their bedroom by moving the chest of drawers in front of it as quietly as they could. The boys heard and laughed loudly: "Don't worry. You are too old for us, you know."

The sisters spent the night awake, eyes aching against the dark. Mustafa sat rigid in Noni's arms, feeling his self-respect assaulted, the hole of his bottom a tight exclamation point of anger, his tail a straight and uncompromising line above it.

And Budhoo, their watchman?

They waited for him to arrive with his gun and scare the boys away, but Budhoo did not arrive.

"I told you. . . ." Lola said in a scorched whisper, "these Neps! Hand in hand. . . ."

"Maybe the boys threatened him," spat Noni.

"Oh, come on. He's probably uncle to one of them! We should have told them to go and now you've started this, Noni, they'll come all the time."

"What choice did we have? If we had said no, we would have paid for it. Don't be naïve."

"You're the one who is naïve: 'They have a point, they have poiii-intt, three-fourths of their point if not the whole poiiintt,' now look . . . *you stupid woman!*"

"Are you worried you'll be caught by the police," one of them asked with a smirk next morning, "for sheltering us? Is that what you're worried about? The police won't touch rich people, only people like us, but if you say anything we will be forced to take action against you."

"What action?"

"You'll find out, Aunty."

Still, their exquisite politeness.

They left with the rice and the soap, the oil, and the garden's annual output of five jars of tomato chutney, and as they climbed down the steps, they noticed what they hadn't seen in the darkness of their arrival—how nicely the property stretched into a lawn, then dropped into tiers below. There was quite enough land to accommodate a thin line of huts. Overhead, a grim leathern bobble of electrocuted bats hanging on wires strung between the trees indicated a powerful supply of electricity during peaceful times. The market was close; a beautiful tarred road was right in front; so they might walk to shops and schools in twenty minutes instead of two hours, three hours, each way. . . .

Not a month had passed before the sisters woke one morning to find that, under cover of night, a hut had come up like a mushroom on a newly cut gash at the bottom of the Mon Ami vegetable patch. They watched with horror as two boys calmly chopped down a bamboo from their property and carried it off right in front of their noses, a long taut drumstick, still cloudy and shivering with the push and pull, the contradiction between flexibility and contrariness, long enough to span an entire home of not-so-modest a size.

They rushed out: "This is our land!"

"It is not your land. It is free land," they countered, putting down the sentence, flatly, rudely.

"It is our land."

"It is unoccupied land."

"We'll call the police."

They shrugged, turned back, and kept on working.

Thirty-eight

It didn't come from nothing, even Lola knew, but from an old feeling of anger that couldn't be divorced from Kalimpong. It was part of every breath. It was in the eyes that waited, attached themselves to you as you approached, rode on your back as you walked on, with a muttered remark you couldn't catch in the moment of passing; it was in the snickering of those gathered at Thapa's Canteen, at Gompu's, at every unnamed roadside shack that sold eggs and matches.

These people could name them, recognize them—the few rich—but Lola and Noni could barely distinguish between the individuals making up the crowd of poor.

Only before, the sisters had never paid much attention for the simple reason that they didn't have to. It was natural they would incite envy, they supposed, and the laws of probability favored their slipping through life without anything more than muttered comments, but every now and then, somebody suffered the rotten luck of being in the exact wrong place at the exact wrong time when it all caught up—and generations worth of trouble settled on them. Just when Lola had thought it would continue, a hundred years like the one past—Trollope, BBC, a burst of hilarity at

Christmas—all of a sudden, all that they had claimed innocent, fun, funny, not really to matter, was proven wrong.

It *did* matter, buying tinned ham roll in a rice and dal country; it *did* matter to live in a big house and sit beside a heater in the evening, even one that sparked and shocked; it *did* matter to fly to London and return with chocolates filled with kirsch; it did matter that others could not. They had pretended it didn't, or had nothing to do with them, and suddenly it had everything to do with them. The wealth that seemed to protect them like a blanket was the very thing that left them exposed. They, amid extreme poverty, were baldly richer, and the statistics of difference were being broadcast over loudspeakers, written loudly across the walls. The anger had solidified into slogans and guns, and it turned out that they, *they*, Lola and Noni, were the unlucky ones who wouldn't slip through, who would pay the debt that should be shared with others over many generations.

Lola went to pay a visit to Pradhan, the flamboyant head of the Kalimpong wing of the GNLF, so as to complain about the illegal huts being built by his followers on Mon Ami property.

Pradhan said: "But I have to accommodate my men." He looked like a bandit teddy bear, with a great beard and a bandana around his head, gold earrings. Lola didn't know much about him, merely that he had been called the "maverick of Kalimpong" in the newspapers, renegade, fiery, unpredictable, a rebel, not a negotiator, who ran his wing of the GNLF like a king his kingdom, a robber his band. He was wilder, people said, and angrier than Ghising, the leader of the Darjeeling wing, who was the better politician and whose men were now occupying the Gymkhana Club. Ghising's résumé had appeared in the last *Indian Express* to get through the roadblocks: "Born on Manju tea estate; education, Singbuli tea estate; Ex–army Eighth Gorkha Rifles, action in Nagaland; actor in plays; author of prose works and poems [fifty-two books—could it be?]; bantamweight boxer; union man."

Behind Pradhan stood a soldier with a wooden stock rifle pointed out into the room. He looked, to Lola's eyes, like Budhoo's brother with Budhoo's gun.

"Side of road, my land." Lola, dressed in the widow's sari she had worn to the electric crematorium when Joydeep died, mumbled weakly in broken English, as if to pretend it was English she couldn't speak properly rather than illuminate the fact that it was Nepali she had never learned.

Pradhan's home was in a part of Kalimpong she had never visited before. On the outside walls, lengths of bamboo split in half had been filled with earth and planted with succulents. Porcupine and bearded cacti grew in Dalda tins and plastic bags lining the steps to the small rectangular house with a tin roof. The room was full of staring men, some standing, some seated on folding chairs, all crowded in as if at a doctor's waiting room. She could feel their intense desire to rid themselves of her as of an affliction. Another man with a favor had preceded Lola, a Marwari shopkeeper trying to bring a shipment of prayer lamps past the roadblocks. Strangely, Marwaris controlled the business of selling Tibetan objects of worship—lamps and bells, thunderbolts, the monks' plum robes and turmeric undershirts, buttons of brass each embossed with a lotus flower.

When the man was ushered in front of Pradhan, he began such a bending, bowing, writhing, that he would not even raise his eyes. He spewed flowery honorifics: "Respected Sir and *Huzoor* and Your Gracious Presence and Your Wish my Pleasure, Please Grant, Your Blessing Requested, Your Honorable Self, Your Beneficence, May the Blessings of God Rain upon You and Yours, Might Your Respected Gracious Self Prosper and Might You Grant Prosperity to Respectful Supplicants. . . ." He made an overabundant flower garden of speech, but to no avail, and finally, he backed out still scattering roses and pleas, prayers and blessings. . . .

Pradhan dismissed him: "No exceptions."

Then it had been Lola's turn.

"Sir, property is being encroached on."

"Name of property?"

"Mon Ami."

"What kind of name?"

"French name."

"I didn't know we live in France. Do we? Tell me, why don't I speak in French, then?"

He tried to send her away immediately, waving away the surveyor's plan and the property documents showing the measurements of the plot that she tried to unroll before him.

"My men must be accommodated," Pradhan stated.

"But our land. . . ."

"Along all roads, to a certain depth, it's government land, and that's the land we are taking."

The huts that had sprung up overnight were being populated by women, men, children, pigs, goats, dogs, chickens, cats, and cows. In a year, Lola could foresee, they would no longer be made of mud and bamboo but concrete and tiles.

"But it's our land. . . ."

"Do you use it?"

"For vegetables."

"You can grow them elsewhere. Put them on the side of your house."

"Have cut into the hill, land weak, landslide may occur," she muttered. "Very dangerous for your men. Landslides on road. . . ." She was trembling like a whisker from terror, although she insisted to herself that it was from rage.

"Landslide? They aren't building big houses like yours, Aunty, just little huts of bamboo. In fact, it's your house that might cause a landslide. Too heavy, no? Too big? Walls many feet wide? Stone, concrete? You are a rich woman? House-garden-servants!"

Here he began to smile.

"In fact," he said, "as you can see," he gestured out, "I am the raja of Kalimpong. A raja must have many queens." He jerked his head back to the sounds of the kitchen that came through the curtained door. "I have four, but would you," he looked Lola up and down, tipped his chair back, head at a comical angle, a coy naughty expression catching his face, "dear Aunty, would you like to be the fifth?"

The men in the room laughed so hard, "Ha Ha Ha." He had their loyalty. He knew the way to coax strength was to pretend it existed, so that it might grow to fit its reputation. . . . Lola, for one of the few times in her life, was the butt of the joke, detested, ridiculous, in the wrong part of town.

"And you know, you won't be bearing me any sons at your age so I will expect a big dowry. And you're not much to look at, nothing up"—he patted the front of his khaki shirt—"nothing down"—he patted his behind, which he twisted out of the chair—

"In fact, I have more of both!"

She could hear them laughing as she left.

How did her feet manage to walk? She would thank them all her life.

"Ah, fool," she heard someone say as she made her way down the steps.

The women were laughing at her from the kitchen window. "Look at her expression," one of them said.

They were beautiful girls with hair in silky loops and nose rings in sweet wrinkling noses. . . .

Mon Ami seemed like a supernatural dove of blue-white peace with a wreath of roses in its beak, Lola thought as she passed under the trellis over the gate.

"What happened, what did he say? Did you see him?" Noni asked.

But Lola couldn't manage to talk to Noni, who had been waiting for her sister to return.

But Lola went into the bathroom and sat trembling on the closed lid of the toilet.

"Joydeep," she screamed silently to her husband, dead so long ago, *"look at what you've done, you bloody fool!!!"*

Her lips stretched out and her mouth was enormous with the extent of her shame.

"Look at what you've left me to! Do you know how I have suffered, do you have any idea??? Where are you?! You and your piddling little life, and look what I have to deal with, just look. I don't even have my decency."

She held on to her ridiculed old woman's breasts and shook them. How could she and her sister leave now? If they left, the army would move in. Or squatters claiming squatters' rights would instigate a court case. They would lose the home that the two of them, Joydeep and Lola, had bought with such false ideas of retirement, sweet peas and mist, cat and books.

The silence rang in the pipes, reached an unbearable pitch, subsided, rose. She wrenched the tap open—not a drop fell—then she twisted the tap viciously shut as if wringing its neck.

Bastard! Never a chink in his certainty, his poise. Never the brains to buy a house in Calcutta—no. No. Not that Joydeep, with his romantic notions of countryside living; with his Wellington boots, binoculars, and bird-watching book; with his Yeats, his Rilke (in German), his Mandelstam (in Russian); in the purply mountains of Kalimpong with his bloody Talisker and his Burberry socks (memento from Scottish holiday of golf+smoked salmon+ distillery). Joydeep with his old-fashioned gentleman's charm. He had always walked as if the world were firm beneath his feet and he never suffered a doubt. He was a cartoon. *"You were a fool,"* she screamed at him.

But then,
in a moment,
quite suddenly,
she went weak.

"Your eyes are lovely, dark and deep."

He used to kiss those glistening orbs when he departed to work on his files.

"But I have promises to keep,"

First one eye then the other—

"And miles to go before I sleep—"

"And miles to go before you sleep?"

She would make a duet—

"And miles to go before I sleep."

He would echo.

To the end, and even beyond, he could resurrect the wit that had fired her love when they were not much more than children, after all. "Drink to me only with thine eyes," he had sung to her at their wedding reception, and then they had honeymooned in Europe.

Noni at the door: "Are you all right?"

Loudly, Lola said: "No, I'm not all right. Why don't you go away?"

"Why don't you open the door?"

"Go away I tell you, go join the boys in the street whom you are always defending."

"Lola, open the door."

"No."

"Open it."

"Bugger off," said Lola.

"Lola?" said Noni. "I made you a rum and *nimboo*."

"Bug off," Lola said.

"Well, sister, in any such situation atrocities are committed under cover of a legitimate cause—"

"Bosh."

"But if we forget there is some truth to what they are saying the problems will keep coming. Gorkhas have been used—"

"Cock and bull," she said crudely. "These people aren't good people. Gorkhas are mercenaries, that's what they are. Pay them and they are loyal to whatever. There's no principle involved, Noni. And what is this with the GOrkha? It was always GUrkha. AND then there aren't even many Gurkhas here—some of course, and some newly retired ones coming in from Hong Kong, but otherwise they are only sherpas, coolies—"

"Anglicized spelling. They're just changing it to—"

"My left toe! Why are they writing in English if they want to have Nepali taught in schools? These people are just louts, and that's the truth, Noni, you know it, we all know it."

"I don't know it."

"Then go and join them like I said. Leave your house, leave your books and your Ovaltine and your long johns. HA! I'd like to see you, *you liar and fake.*"

"I will."

"Go on, then. And after you are done with that, go end up in hell!"

"Hell?" Noni said, rattling the door on the other side of the bathroom door. *"Why hell?"*

"Because you'll be committing CRIME, that's why!" screeched Lola.

Noni returned to sit on the dragon cushions on the sofa. Oh, they had been wrong. The real place had evaded them. The two of them had been fools feeling they were doing something exciting just by occupying this picturesque cottage, by seducing themselves with those old travel books in the library, searching for a certain angled light with which to romance themselves, to locate what had been conjured only as a tale to tell before the Royal Geographic Society, when the author returned to give a talk accompanied by sherry and a scrolled certificate of honor spritzed with gold for an exploration of the far Himalayan kingdoms—but far from what? Exotic to whom? It was the center for the sisters, but they had never treated it as such.

Parallel lives were being led by those—Budhoo, Kesang—for whom there was no such doubleness or self-consciousness, while Lola and Noni indulged themselves in the pretense of it being a daily fight to keep up civilization in this place of towering, flickering green. They maintained their camping supplies, their flashlights, mosquito netting, raincoats, hot water bottles, brandy, radio, first-aid kit, Swiss army knife, book on poisonous snakes. These objects were talismans imbued with the task of transforming reality into something otherwise, supplies manufactured by a world that equated them with courage. But, really, they were equivalent to cowardice.

Noni tried to rouse herself. Maybe everyone felt this way at some point when one recognized there was a depth to one's life and emotions beyond one's own significance.

Thirty-nine

In the end what Sai and Gyan had excelled at was the first touch, so gentle, so infinitely so; they had touched each other as if they might break, and Sai couldn't forget that.

She remembered the ferocious look he had given her in Darjeeling, warning her to stay away.

One last time after refusing to acknowledge her, Gyan had come to Cho Oyu. He had sat at the table as if in chains.

A few months ago the ardent pursuit and now he behaved as if she had chased and trapped him, tail between his legs, into a cage!

What kind of man was this? she thought. She could not believe she had loved something so despicable. Her kiss had not turned him into a prince; he had morphed into a bloody frog.

"What kind of man are you?" she asked. "Is this any way to behave?"

"I'm confused," he said finally, reluctantly. "I'm only human and sometimes I'm weak. Sorry."

That "Sorry" unleashed a demoness of rage: "At whose expense are you weak and human! You'll never get anywhere in life, my friend," shouted Sai, "if this is what you think makes an excuse. A murderer could say the same and you think he would be let off the hook to hop in the spring?"

The usual thing happened, exactly what always happened in their fighting. He began to feel irritated, for, really, who was she to lecture him? "Gorkhaland for Gorkhas. We are the liberation army." He was a martyr, a man; a man, in fact, of ambition, principle.

"I don't have to listen to this," he said jumping up and storming off abruptly just as she was in powerful flow.

And Sai had cried, for it was the unjust truth.

Marooned during curfew, sick about Gyan, and sick with the desire to be desired, she still hoped for his return. She was bereft of her former skill at solitude.

She waited, read *Wuthering Heights* twice over, each time the potency of the writing imparting a wild animal feeling to her gut—and twice she read the last pages—still Gyan didn't come.

A stick insect as big as a small branch climbed the steps.

A beetle with an impolitic red behind.

A dead scorpion being dismantled by ants—first its Popeye arm went by, carried by a line of ant coolies, then the sting and, separately, the eye.

But no Gyan.

She went to visit Uncle Potty. "Ahoy there," he shouted to her from his veranda like a ship's deck.

But she smiled, he saw, only out of politeness, and he felt a flash of jealousy as do friends when they lose another to love, especially those who have understood that friendship is enough, steadier, healthier, easier on the heart. Something that always added and never took away.

Seeing her subtracted, Uncle Potty was scared and sang:

You're the tops
You're Nap-O-lean Brandy,
You're the tops
You're Ma-HAT-ma Gandy!

But her laugh was only another confectionary concocted for his sake, a pretense that their friendship was what it had been.

He had anticipated this and had tried to indicate to her long before how she must look at love; it was tapestry and art; the sorrow of it, the loss of it, should be part of the intelligence, and even a sad romance would be worth more than any simple bovine happiness. Years ago, as a student at Oxford, Uncle Potty had considered himself a lover of love. He looked up the word in the card catalog and brought back armfuls of books; he smoked cheroots, drank port and Madeira, read everything he could from psychology to science to pornography to poetry, Egyptian love letters, ninth century Tamilian erotica. . . . There was the joy of the chase and the joy of the fleeing, and when he set off on practical research trips, he had found pure love in the most sordid of spots, the wrong sides of town where the police didn't venture; medieval, tunneling streets so narrow you had to pass crabwise past the drug dealers and the whores; where, at night, men he never saw ladled their tongues into his mouth. There had been Louis and André, Guillermo, Rassoul, Johan and Yoshi, and "Humberto Santamaria," he had once shouted atop a mountain in the Lake District for an elegant amour. Some loved him while he didn't love them; others he loved madly, deeply, and they, they didn't love him at all. But Sai was up too close to appreciate his perspective.

Uncle Potty scratched his feet so the dead skin flew: "Once you start scratching, my dear, you cannot stop. . . ."

When Sai next went to Mon Ami, they laughed and guessed, glad for a bit of fun in the midst of trouble: "Who is the lucky boy? Tall and fair and handsome?"

"And rich?" Noni said. "Let's hope he's rich?"

Fortunately, though, a single bit of luck fell on Sai and shrouded this fall of her dignity. Her rescuer was the common domestic cold. Heroically, it caught her common domestic grief in the nick of time, muddled the origin of her streaming eyes and sore throat, shuffled the symptoms of virus and disgraceful fall from the tightrope of splendrous love. Shielded thus from simple diagnosis, she enveloped her face in the copious folds of a man's handkerchief. "A cold!" Whonk whonk. One part common cold to nine parts common grief. Lola and Noni prepared toddies of honey, lemon, rum, hot water.

"Sai, you look terrible, terrible."

Her eyes were red and raw, spilling over. Pressure weighed downward like a gestapo boot on her brain.

Back in Cho Oyu, the cook rummaged in the medicine drawer for the Coldrin and the Vicks Vaporub. He found a silk scarf for her throat, and Sai hung in the hot and cold excitement of Vicks, buffeted by arctic winds of eucalyptus, still feeling the perpetual gnawing urgency and intensity of waiting, of hope living on without sustenance. It must feed on itself. It would drive her mad.

Was her affection for Gyan just a habit? How on earth could she think of someone so much?

The more she did, the more she did, the more she did.

Summoning her strength, she spoke directly to her heart. "Oh why must you behave so badly?"

But it wouldn't soften its stance.

There was grace in forgetting and giving up, she reminded it; it was childish not to—everyone had to accept imperfection and loss in life.

The giant squid, the last dodo.

One morning, her cold on the wane, she realized her excuse would no longer hold. As curfew was lifted, in order to salvage her dignity, Sai started out on the undignified mission of searching for Gyan.

Forty

He wasn't anywhere in the market, not in the music and video shop where Rinzy and Tin Tin Dorji rented out exhausted tapes of Bruce Lee and Jackie Chan movies.

"No, haven't seen him," said Dawa Bhutia sticking his head out from the steam of cabbage cooking in the Chin Li Restaurant kitchen.

"Isn't in yet," said Tashi at the Snow Lion, who had closed down the travel side of the business, what with the lack of tourists, and set up a pool table. The posters still hung on the walls: "Experience the grandeur of the Raj; come to Sikkim, land of over two hundred monasteries." Locked at the back, he still had the treasures he took out to sell to the wealthier traveler: a rare *thangkha* of lamas sailing on magical sea beasts to spread the dharma to China; a nobleman's earring; a jade cup smuggled from a Tibetan monastery, so transparent the light shone through making a green and black stormy cloudscape. "Tragic what is happening in Tibet," the tourists would say, but their faces showed only glee in the booty. "Only twenty-five dollars!"

But now he was forced to depend on local currency. Tashi's retarded cousin was running back and forth carrying bottles between Gompu's and the pool table, so the men could continue drinking as they played and talked of the movement. A sud of vomit lay all around.

Sai walked by the deserted classrooms of Kalimpong college, dead insects bolled in piles against rimy windows, bees noosed by spiders' silk, blackboard still with its symbols and calculations. Here, in this chloroformed atmosphere, Gyan had studied. She walked around to the other side of the mountain that overlooked the Relli River and Bong Busti, where he lived. It was two hours downhill to his house in a poor part of Kalimpong quite foreign to her.

He had told her the story of his brave ancestors in the army, but why didn't he ever speak of his family here and now? In the back of her mind, Sai knew she should stay home, but she couldn't stop herself.

She walked by several churches: Jehovah's Witnesses, Adventists, Latter-day Saints, Baptists, Mormons, Pentecostals. The old English church stood at the town's heart, the Americans at the edge, but then the new ones had more money and more tambourine spirit, and they were catching up fast. Perfect practitioners, too, of the hide-behind-the-tree-and-pop-out technique to surprise those who might have run away; of the *salwar kameez* disguise (all the better to gobble you up, my dear . . .); and if you joined in a little harmless chat of language lessons (all the better to translate the Bible, my dear . . .), that was it—they were as hard to shake off as an amoeba.

But Sai walked by unmolested. The churches were dark; the missionaries always left in dangerous times to enjoy chocolate chip cookies and increase funds at home, until it was peaceful enough to venture forth again, that they might launch attack, renewed and fortified, against a weakened and desperate populace.

She passed by fields and small clusters of houses, became confused in a capillary web of paths that crisscrossed the mountains, perpendicular as creepers, dividing and petering into more paths leading to huts perched along eyebrow-width ledges in the thick bamboo. Tin roofs promised tetanus; outhouses gestured into the ether so that droppings would fall into the valley. Bamboo cleaved in half carried water to patches of corn and pumpkin, and wormlike tubes attached to pumps led from a stream to the shacks. They looked pretty in the sun, these little homes, babies crawling about with bottoms red through pants with the behinds cut out so they could do their *susu* and potty; fuschia and roses—for everyone in Kalimpong loved flowers and even amid botanical profusion added to it.

Sai knew that once the day failed, though, you wouldn't be able to ignore the poverty, and it would become obvious that in these homes it was cramped and wet, the smoke thick enough to choke you, the inhabitants eating meagerly in the candlelight too dim to see by, rats and snakes in the rafters fighting over insects and birds' eggs. You knew that rain collected down below and made the earth floor muddy, that all the men drank too much, reality skidding into nightmares, brawls, and beating.

A woman holding a baby passed by. The woman smelled of earth and smoke and an oversweet intense smell came from the baby, like corn boiling.

"Do you know where Gyan lives?" Sai asked.

She pointed at a house just ahead; there it stood and Sai felt a moment of shock.

It was a small, slime-slicked cube; the walls must have been made with cement corrupted by sand, because it came spilling forth from pockmarks as if from a punctured bag.

Crows' nests of electrical wiring hung from the corners of the structure, split into sections that disappeared into windows barred with thin jail grill. She could smell an open drain that told immediately of a sluggish plumbing system failing anew each day despite being so rudimentary. The drain ran from the house under a rough patchwork of stones and emptied over the property that was marked with barbed wire, and from under this wire came a perturbed harem of sulfurous hens being chased by a randy rooster.

The upper story of the house was unfinished, presumably abandoned for lack of funds, and, while waiting to stockpile enough to resume building, it had fallen into disrepair; no walls and no roof, just a few posts with iron rods sprouting from the top to provide a basic sketch of what was to have followed. An attempt had been made to save the rods from rust with upturned soda bottles, but they were bright orange anyway.

Still, she could tell it was someone's precious home. Marigolds and zinnias edged the veranda; the front door was ajar and she could see past its puckered veneer to a gilt clock and a poster of a bonneted golden-haired child against a moldering wall, just the kind of thing that Lola and Noni made merciless fun of.

There were houses like this everywhere, of course, common to those who had struggled to the far edge of the middle class—just to the edge, only just, holding on desperately—but were at every moment being undone, the house slipping back, not into the picturesque poverty that tourists liked to photograph but into something truly dismal—modernity proffered in its meanest form, brand-new one day, in ruin the next.

The house didn't match Gyan's talk, his English, his looks, his clothes, or his schooling. It didn't match his future. Every single thing his family had was going into him and it took ten of them to live like this to produce a boy, combed, educated, their best bet in the big world. Sisters' marriages, younger brother's studies, grandmother's teeth—all on hold, silenced, until he left, strove, sent something back.

Sai felt shame, then, for him. How he must have hoped his silence would be construed as dignity. Of course he had kept her far away. Of course he had never mentioned his father. The dilemmas and stresses that must exist within this house—how could he have let them out? And she felt distaste, then, for herself. How had she been linked to this enterprise, without her knowledge or consent?

She stood staring at the chickens, unsure of what to do.

Chickens, chickens, chickens bought to supplement a tiny income. The birds had never revealed themselves to her so clearly; a grotesque bunch, rape and violence being enacted, hens being hammered and pecked as they screamed and flapped, attempting escape from the rapist rooster.

Several minutes passed. Should she leave, should she stay?

The door was pushed open farther, and a girl of about ten came out of the house with a cooking pot to scrub out with mud and gravel at the outside tap.

"Does Gyan live here?" Sai asked despite herself.

Suspicion shadowed the girl's face. It was an old, unsurprised sureness of ulterior motives, a funny look in a child.

"He's my mathematics tutor."

Still looking as if someone like Sai could only mean trouble, she set down the pot and went back into the house as the rooster rushed forth to peck the grain stuck at the bottom, climbing right inside, giving the hens a reprieve.

At that moment, Gyan came out, caught her expression of distaste before she had a chance to disguise it, and was outraged. How dare she seek him out to find her indulgence in pity! He had been feeling guilty about his extended silence, was considering returning to see her, but now he knew he was quite right. The rooster climbed out of the pot and began to strut about. He was the only grand thing around, crowned, spurred, crowing like a colonial.

"What do you want?"

She saw his thoughts recast his eyes and mouth, remembered that he had abandoned her, not the other way around, and she was bitterly angry.

Dirty hypocrite.

Pretending one thing, living another. Nothing but lies through and through.

Farther away, she could see an outhouse made of four bamboo poles and threadbare sacking over an alarming drop.

Perhaps he'd hoped he'd wheedle his way into Cho Oyu; maybe his whole family could move in there, if he played his cards right, and use those capacious bathrooms, each as big as his entire home. Cho Oyu might be crumbling, but it had once been majestic; it had its past if not its future, and that might be enough—a gate of black lace, the name worked into imposing stone pillars with mossy cannonballs on top as in *To the Manor Born*.

The sister was looking at them curiously.

"What do you want?" Gyan's refrigerated voice repeated.

To think that she had come to call him *momo,* cosy scoop of minced mutton in charming dimpled wrapping, that she had come to climb into his lap, ask why he hadn't forgiven her as before at the Christmastime fight, but she wouldn't satisfy him by admitting any vulnerability now.

Instead she said she had come about Father Booty.

Her outrage at the injustice done to her friend returned to her in a rush. Dear Father Booty, who had been forced onto a jeep leaving for the Siliguri airport, having lost everything but his memories: the time he had given a lecture on how dairies might create a mini Swiss-style economy in Kalimpong and had been greeted with a standing ovation; his poem on a cow in the *Illustrated Weekly*; and "Nothing so sweet, dear friends"—evenings on Uncle Potty's veranda, when the music ended on a drawn-out note of honey, and the moon—it was whole—sailed upward, an alchemist's marvel of illuminated cheese. How fast the earth spun! It was all over.

How was he to live where, he despaired, he would be snipped into an elderly person supported by the state and packaged in a very clean box alongside other aged people with supposedly everything in common with him—

He had left his friend Uncle Potty in mourning, drinking, the world breaking in waves about him; chair going one way, the table and stove the other; the whole kitchen rocking back and forth.

"Look at what you people are doing," she accused Gyan.

"What am I doing? What have I to do with Father Booty?"

"Everything."

"Well, if that's what it will take, so be it. Should Nepalis sit miserably for another two hundred years so the police don't have an excuse to throw out Father Booty?" He came out of the gate, marched her away from his house.

"Yes," said Sai. "You, for one, are better gone than Father Booty. Think you're wonderful . . . well, you know what? *You're not!* He's done much more than you ever will for people on this hillside."

Gyan became seriously angry.

"In fact, good thing they kicked him out," he said, "who needs Swiss people here? For how many thousands of years have we produced our own milk?"

"Why don't you then? Why don't you make cheese?"

"We live in India, thank you very much. We don't want any cheese and the last thing we need is chocolate cigars."

"Ah, that same old thing again." She wished to claw him. She wanted to pluck out his eyes and kick him black-and-blue. The taste of blood, salty, dark—she could anticipate its flavor. "Civilization is important," she said.

"That is not civilization, you fool. Schools and hospitals. That is."

You fool—how dare he!

"But you have to set a standard. Or else everything will be brought down to the same low level as you and your family."

She was shocked at herself as she spoke, but in this moment she was willing to believe anything that lay on the other side of Gyan.

"I see, Swiss luxury sets a standard, chocolates and watches set the standard. . . . Yes, soothe your guilty conscience, stupid little girl, and hope someone doesn't burn down your house for the simple reason that you are a *fool*."

Again he was calling her *fool*—

"If this is what you've been thinking, why didn't you boycott the cheese instead of gobbling it down? Now you attack it? *Hypocrite!* But it was very nice to eat the cheese when you got a chance, no? All that cheese toast? Hundreds of pieces of cheese toast you must have eaten. Let alone the chocolate cigars. . . . So greedy, eating them like a fat pig. And tuna fish on toast and peanut butter biscuits!"

By now, with the conversation disintegrating, his sense of humor began to return to him, and Gyan began to giggle, his eyes to soften, and she could see his expression shift. They were falling back into familiarity, into common ground, into the dirty gray. Just ordinary humans in ordinary opaque boiled-egg light, without grace, without revelation, composite of contradictions, easy principles, arguing about what they half believed in or even what they didn't believe in at all, desiring comfort as much as raw austerity, authenticity as much as playacting, desiring coziness of family as much as to abandon it forever. Cheese and chocolate they wanted, but also to kick all these bloody foreign things out. A wild daring love to bicycle them into the sky, but also a rice and dal love blessed by the unexciting feel of everyday, its surprises safely enmeshed in something solidly familiar like marrying the daughter or son of your father's best friend and grumbling about the cost of potatoes, the cost of onions. Every single contradiction history or opportunity might make available to them, every contradiction they were heir to, they desired. But only as much, of course, as they desired purity and a lack of contradiction.

Sai began to laugh a bit as well.

"Momo?" she said, switching to a pleading tone.

Then, in a flash he veered back, was angry again. Remembered this was not a conversation he wished to end in laughter. The infantile nickname, the tender feel of her eyes—it aroused his ire. Her getting him to apologize, trying to smother him, swaddle him, drag him to drown in this pish pash mash, sicky sticky baby sweetieness . . . *eeeshhh*. . . .

He needed to be a man. He needed to stand tall and be rough. Dryness, space, good firm gestures. Not this fritter, flutter, this worming in sugar. . . .

Oh yes, how he needed to be strong—

For, if truth be told, as the weeks went by, he, Gyan, was scared—he who had thought there was no joy like screaming victory over oppression, he who had raised his fist to authority, who had found the fire of his college friends purifying, he who had claimed the hillside, enjoyed the thought of those Mon Ami sisters with their fake English accents blanching and trembling—he, who was hero for the homeland. . . .

He listened with growing trepidation as the conversation in Gompu's gained in fervor. When did shouting and strikes get you anywhere, they said, and talked of burning the circuit house, robbing the petrol pump.

When Chhang and Bhang, Gyan, Owl and Donkey had leaped into jeeps, filled up at the petrol station and driven off without paying, Gyan had been shaking just as much as the pump manager on the other side of the window, the muscles of his heart performing uncontrollable spasms.

There were those who were provoked by the challenge, but Gyan was finding that he wasn't one of these. He was angry that his family hadn't thought to ban him, keep him home. He hated his tragic father, his mother who looked to him for direction, had always looked to him for direction, even when he was a little boy, simply for being male. He spent the nights awake, worrying he couldn't live up to his proclamations.

But then, how could you have any self-respect knowing that you didn't believe in anything exactly? How did you embrace what was yours if you didn't leave something for it? How did you create a life of meaning and pride?

Yes, he owed much to his rejection of Sai.

The chink she had provided into another world gave him just enough room to kick; he could work against her, define the conflict in his life that he felt all along, but in a cotton-woolly way. In pushing her away, an energy was born, a purpose whittled. He wouldn't sweetly reconcile.

"You hate me," said Sai, as if she'd read his thoughts, "for big reasons, that have nothing to do with me. You aren't being fair."

"*What's fair? What's fair?* Do you have any *idea* of the world? Do you bother to *look?* Do you have any *understanding* of how justice operates or, rather, does NOT operate? You're not a baby anymore, you know. . . ."

"And how grown-up are you?! Too scared even to come for tuition because you know you've behaved nastily and you're too much of a coward to admit it! You're probably just sitting waiting for your mummy to arrange your marriage. Low-class family, uncultured, arranged-marriage types . . . they'll find you a silly fool to marry and you'll be delighted all your life to have a dummy. Why not admit it, Gyan??"

Coward! How dare she? Who would marry her!

"You think it's brave of me to sit on your veranda? I can't spend my life eating *cheese toast, can I?*"

"I didn't ask you to. You did it of your own free will, and pay us back for it, if that's what you think." She found a new attack and went after it even though she grew steadily more horrified by the vermin that coursed from her mouth, but it was as if she were on a stage; the role was more powerful than herself.

"Ate it for free . . . typical of you people, demand and take and then spit on what you've been given. There is exactly one reason why you will get nowhere—

"*Because you don't deserve to.* Why did you eat it if it was beneath you?"

"Not *beneath* me. Nothing to DO with me, YOU FOOL—"

"Don't call me FOOL. Through this whole conversation you've been repeating it, FOOL FOOL—"

Lunging at him with hands and nails, having learned something from the conduct of the common chicken some minutes ago, she scratched his arms in red streaks and—*"You told them about the guns, didn't you?"* she was shouting all of a sudden. *"You told them to come to Cho Oyu? You did, didn't you, DIDN'T YOU?"*

It all came bursting out although she hadn't considered this possibility before. Suddenly her anger, Gyan's absences, his ignoring her in Darjeeling—all came together.

His guilt hooked unawares, rose in his eye, disappeared reappeared. Wriggling leaping trying to get away like a caught fish. *"You're crazy."*

"I saw that," pounced Sai. Jumped to seize it from his eyes. But he caught her before she reached him and then threw her aside into the lantana bushes and beat about with a stick.

"Gyan *bhaiya?*" His sister's tentative voice as Sai managed to stand.

They both turned in horror. It had all been observed. He dropped the stick and told his sister: "Don't stick your nose here. Go back. Or I'll smack you hard."

And he shouted at Sai, "Never come here again." Oh, and now it would all be reported to his parents.

Sai screamed at the sister: "Good you saw, good that you heard. Go and tell your parents what your brother has been up to, telling me he loves me, making all kinds of promises and then sending robbers to our house. I'll go to the police and then let's see what happens to your family. Gyan will get his eyes pulled out, his head cut off, and then let's see when you all come crying to beg. . . . *Hah!*"

The sister was trying to hear but Gyan had her by the braids and was pulling her home. Sai had betrayed him, led him to betray others, his own people, his family. She had enticed him, sneaked up on him, spied on him, ruined him, caused him to behave badly. He couldn't wait for the day his mother would show him the photograph of the girl he was to marry, a charming girl, he hoped, with cheeks like two Simla apples, who hadn't allowed her mind to traverse the gutters and gray areas, and he would adore her for the miracle she was.

Sai was not miraculous; she was an uninspiring person, a reflection of all the contradictions around her, a mirror that showed him himself far too clearly for comfort.

Sai began to follow brother and sister but then stopped. Shame caught up with her. What had she done? It would be her they would laugh at, a desperate girl who had walked all this way for unrequited love. Gyan would be slapped on the back and cheered for his conquest. She would be humiliated. He had hit on the age-old trick that remade him into a hero, "the desired male". . . . The more he insulted her behind her back—"Oh, that crazy girl is following me . . ."—the more the men would cheer, the more his status would grow at Thapa's Canteen, the more Sai would be remade behind her back into a lunatic female, the more Gyan would fatten with pride. . . . She felt her own dignity departing, watched it from far away as Gyan and his sister walked down the path. As they turned into their house, it vanished as well.

She walked home very slowly, sick, sick. The mist was thickening, smoke adding to the dusk and the vapor. The smell of potatoes cooking came from *busti* houses all along the way, a smell that would surely connote comfort to souls across the world, but that couldn't comfort her. She felt none of the pity she'd felt earlier while contemplating this scene; even peasants could have love and happiness, but not her, not her . . .

When she arrived home she saw two people on the veranda talking to the cook and the judge.

A woman was pleading: "Who do you go to when you're poor? People like us have to suffer. All the *goondas* come out and the police go hand in hand with them."

"Who are you?"

It was the wife, begging for mercy, of the drunk the police had caught and questioned about the gun robbery and on whom they had practiced their new torture strategy. They, at Cho Oyu, had forgotten about this man, but the man's wife had traced the connection and she'd come with her father-in-law to see the judge, walking half a day from a village across the Relli River.

"What will we do?" she begged. "We are not even Nepalis, we are Lepchas. . . . He was innocent and the police have blinded him. He knew nothing about you, he was in the market as usual, everyone knows," sobbed the wife, looking to her father-in-law for help.

What use is it for a woman to protest and cry?

But her father-in-law was too scared. He said nothing at all, just stood there; his expression couldn't be told apart from his wrinkles. His son, when he was not drinking, had worked to rebuild the roads in the district, filling stones from the Teesta riverbed into contractors' trucks, unloading them at building sites, clearing landslides that tumbled over and over in the same eternal motion as the river coming down. His son's wife worked on the highways as well, but no work was being done now that the GNLF had closed down the roads.

"Why come to me? Go to the police. They are the ones who caught your husband, not I. It's not my fault," said the judge, alarmed into eloquence. "You had better leave from here."

"You can't send this woman to the police," said the cook, "they'll probably assault her."

The woman looked raped and beaten already. Her clothes were very soiled and her teeth resembled a row of rotten corn kernels, some of them missing, some blackened, and she was quite bent from carrying stone—

common sight, this sort of woman in the hills. Some foreigners had actually photographed her as proof of horror . . .

"George! . . . ! George!" said a shocked wife to her husband with a camera.

And he had leaned out of the car: Click! "Got it, babe . . . !"

"Help us," she begged.

The judge seemed suddenly to remember his personality, stiffened, and said nothing, set his mouth in a mask, would look neither left nor right, went back to his game of chess.

In this life, he remembered again, you must stop your thoughts if you wished to remain intact, or guilt and pity would take everything from you, even yourself from yourself. He was embarrassed by the attention that was being drawn to his humiliation yet again, the setting of the table with the tablecloth, the laughter, the robbery of the rifles that had never contributed to a fast-forward death ballet come duck season.

Now, typically, the mess had grown.

This was why he had retired. India was too messy for justice; it ended only in humiliation for the person in authority. He had done his duty as far as it was any citizen's duty to report problems to the police, and it was no longer his responsibility. Give these people a bit and one could find oneself supporting the whole family forever after, a constantly multiplying family, no doubt, because they might have no food, the husband might be blind and with broken legs, and the woman might be anemic and bent, but they'd still pop out an infant every nine months. If you let such people get an inch, they'd take everything you had—the families yoked together because of guilt on one side, and an unending greed and capacity for dependance on the other—and if they knew you were susceptible, everyone handed their guilt along so as to augment yours: old guilt, new guilt, any passed-on guilt whatever.

The cook looked at the man and woman and sighed.

They looked at Sai. *"Didi . . . ,"* the woman said. Her eyes were too devastated to look at directly.

Sai turned away and told herself she didn't care.

She was in no mood to be kind. If the gods had favored her she would, perhaps, but now, no, she would show them that if they did this to her, she would unleash evil on the earth in their own image, a perfect devilish student to the devil gods. . . .

It took a while for them to leave. They went and sat outside the gate, the cook forced to herd them out like cows, and then for a long while they squatted down on their haunches and didn't move, just stared emotionless, as if drained of hope and initiative.

They watched the judge taking Mutt for her walk and feeding her. He was angry and embarrassed that they were watching. Why didn't they *GO!*

"Tell them to leave or else we'll call the police," he told the cook.

"Jao, jao," the cook said, *"jao jao,"* through the gate, but they only retreated up the hill, behind the bushes and settled back down with the same blank look on their faces.

Sai climbed to her room, slammed the door, and flung herself at her reflection in the mirror:

What will happen to me?!

Gyan would find adulthood and purity in a quest for a homeland and she would be left forever adolescent, trapped in shameful dramatics. This was the history that sustained her: the family that never cared, the lover who forgot. . . .

She cried for a while, tears taking on their own momentum, but despite herself the image of the begging woman came back. She went downstairs and asked the cook: "Did you give them anything?"

"No," said the cook, also miserable. "What can you do," he said flatly, as if giving an answer, not asking a question.

Then he went back out with a sack of rice. *"Hss sss hsss?"* he hissed.

But by this time the pair had vanished.

Forty-one

The sky over Manhattan was messy, lots of stuff in it, branches and pigeons and choppy clouds lit with weird yellow light. The wind blew strongly and the pink pom-poms of the cherry trees in Riverside Park swished against the unsettled mix.

The unease that had followed Biju's phone call to Kalimpong was no longer something in the pit of his stomach; it had grown so big, *he was in its stomach.*

He had tried to telephone again the next day and the day after, but the line was quite dead now.

"More trouble," said Mr. Iype. "It will go on for a while. Very violent people. All those army types. . . ."

Along the Hudson, great waves of water were torn up and ripped forward, the wind propelling the gusts upriver.

"Look at that. It's getting *fucking Biblical,*" said someone next to him at the rails. *"Fucking Job. Why? Why?"*

Biju moved farther down the rails, but the man shifted down as well.

"You know what the name of this river *really* is?" Face fat from McDonald's, scant hair, he was like so many in this city, a mad and intelligent person camping out at the Barnes & Noble bookstore. The gale took his words and whipped them away; they reached Biju's ears strangely clipped, on their way to somewhere else. The man turned his face in toward Biju to save the wind from thus slicing their conversation. "Muhheakunnuk, *Muhheakunnuk*—the river that flows *both* ways," he added with significant eyebrows, "*both ways.* That is the *real fucking name.*" Sentences spilled out of the face along with juicy saliva. He was smiling and slavering over his information, gobbling and dispelling at the same time.

But what was the false name then? Biju possessed no name at all for this black water. It was not his history.

And then came *fucking Moby Dick*. The river full of *dead fucking whales.* The *fucking carcasses* were hauled up the river, *fucking pulverized* in the factories.

"*Oil,* you know," he said with intense internal frustration. "It's *always* been *fucking oil.* And *underwear.*"

Eyebrows and saliva spray.

"*Corsets!!*" he said suddenly.

"No speak English," said Biju through a tunnel made from his hands and began to walk quickly away.

"No speak English," he always said to mad people starting up conversations in this city, to the irascible ornery bums and Bible folk dressed in ornate bargain-basement suits and hats, waiting on street corners, getting their moral and physical exercise chasing after infidels. Devotees of the Church of Christ and the Holy Zion, born-agains handing out pamphlets that gave him up-to-date million-dollar news of the devil's activities: "SATAN IS WAITING TO BURN YOU ALIVE," screamed the headlines. "YOU DON'T HAVE A MOMENT TO LOSE."

Once, he had been accosted by a Lithuanian Hare Krishna, New York via Vilnius and Vrindavan. A reproachful veggie look accompanied the brochure to the former beef cook. Biju looked at him and had to avert his gaze as if from an obscenity. In its own way it was like a prostitute—it showed too much. The book in his hand had a cover of Krishna on the battlefield in lurid colors, the same ones used in movie posters.

What was India to these people? How many lived in the fake versions of their countries, in fake versions of other people's countries? Did their lives feel as unreal to them as his own did to him?

What was he doing and *why?*

It hadn't even been a question before he left. Of course, if you could *go,* you *went.* And if you *went,* of course, if you could, you *stayed.* . . .

The park lamps had come on by the time Biju climbed the urine-stinking stone steps to the street, and the lights were dissolving in the gloaming—to look at them made everyone feel like they were crying. In front of the stage-set night-light of the city, he saw the homeless man walking stiffly, as if on artificial legs, crossing with his grocery cart of rubbish to his plastic igloo where he would wait out the storm.

Biju walked back to the Gandhi Café, thinking he was emptying out. Year by year, his life wasn't amounting to anything at all; in a space that should have included family, friends, he was the only one displacing the air. And yet, another part of him had expanded: his self-consciousness, his self-pity—oh the tediousness of it. Clumsy in America, a giant-sized midget, a bigfat-sized helping of small. . . . Shouldn't he return to a life where he might slice his own importance, to where he might relinquish this overrated control over his own destiny and perhaps be subtracted from its determination altogether? He might even experience that greatest luxury of not noticing himself at all.

And if he continued on here? What would happen? Would he, like Harish-Harry, manufacture a fake version of himself and using what he had created as clues, understand himself backward? Life was not about life for him anymore, and death—what would even that mean to him? It would have nothing to do with death.

The proprietor of the newly opened Shangri-la Travel in the same block as the Gandhi Café ordered a "nonveg" lunch special each day: lamb curry, dal, vegetable pilau, and *kheer.* Mr. Kakkar was his name.

"*Arre,* Biju," he greeted him, for Biju had just been given the task of delivering his food. "Again you saved me from my wife's cooking, ha ha. We will throw her food down the toilet!"

"Why don't you give it to that dirty bum," said Biju trying to help the homeless man and insult him at the same time.

"Oh no," he said, "bitch-witch, she is the type, she will coming walking down the road on a surprise visit and catch him eating it, that kind of coincidence is always happening to her, and that will be the end of yours truly."

A minute later, "You are sure you want to go back??" he said alarmed, eyes popping. "You're making a big mistake. Thirty years in this country, hassle-free except for the bitch-witch, of course, and I have never gone back. Just even see the plumbing," he indicated the sound of the gurgling toilet behind him. "They should put their plumbing on their flag, just like we have the spinning wheel—top-class facility in this country.

"Going back?" he continued, "don't be completely crazy—all those relatives asking for money! Even strangers are asking for money—maybe they just try, you know, maybe you shit and dollars come out. I'm telling you, my friend, they will get you; if they won't, the robbers will; if the robbers won't, some disease will; if not some disease, the heat will; if not the heat, those mad Sardarjis will bring down your plane before you even arrive."

While Biju had been away, Indira Gandhi had been assassinated by the Sikhs in the name of their homeland; Rajiv Gandhi had taken over—

"Only a matter of time. Someone will get him, too," said Mr. Kakkar.

But Biju said: "I have to go. My father. . . ."

"Ah, soft feelings, they will get you nowhere. My father, so long as he was alive, he always told me, 'Good, stay away, don't come back to this shitty place.'"

Mr. Kakkar gnashed ice cubes with his teeth, lifting them from his Diet Coke with the help of his ballpoint pen, which had a plane modeled at its rear end.

Nevertheless, he sold Biju a ticket on Gulf Air: New York–London-Frankfurt–Abu Dhabi–Dubai-Bahrain-Karachi-Delhi-Calcutta. The cheapest they could find. It was like a bus in the sky.

"Don't say I didn't warn you."

Then he grew more thoughtful. "You know," he said, "America is in the process of buying up the world. Go back, you'll find they own the businesses. One day, you'll be working for an American company there or here. Think of your children. If you stay here, your son will earn a hundred thousand dollars for the same company he could be working for in India but making one thousand dollars. How, then, can you send your children to the best international college? You are making a big mistake. Still a world, my friend, where one side travels to be a servant, and the other side travels to be treated like a king. You want your son to be on this side or that side?

"Ah," he said, waggling his pen, "the minute you arrive, Biju, you will start to think of how to get the bloody hell out."

But Biju went to Jackson Heights, and from a store like a hangar he bought: a TV and VCR, a camera, sunglasses, baseball caps that said "NYC" and "Yankees" and "I Like My Beer Cold and My Women Hot," a digital two-time clock and radio and cassette player, waterproof watches, calculators, an electric razor, a toaster oven, a winter coat, nylon sweaters, polyester-cotton-blend shirts, a polyurethane quilt, a rain jacket, a folding umbrella, suede shoes, a leather wallet, a Japanese-made heater, a set of sharp knives, a hot water bottle, Fixodent, saffron, cashews and raisins, aftershave, T-shirts with "I love NY" and "Born in the USA" picked out in shiny stones, whiskey, and, after a moment of hesitation, a bottle of perfume called Windsong . . . who was that for? He didn't yet know her face.

While he shopped, he remembered that as a child he'd been part of a pack of boys who played so hard they'd come home exhausted. They'd thrown stones and slippers into trees to bring down *ber* and *jamun;* chased lizards until their tails fell off and tossed the leaping bits on little girls; they'd stolen *chooran* pellets from the shop, that looked like goat droppings but were so, so tasty with a bit of sandy crunch. He remembered bathing in the river, feeling his body against the cool firm river muscle, and sitting on a rock with his feet in the water, gnawing on sugarcane, working out the sweetness no matter how his jaw hurt, completely absorbed. He had played cricket cricket cricket. Biju found himself smiling at the memory of the time the whole village had watched India win a test match against Australia on a television running off a car battery because the transformer in the village had burned out. All over India the crops had been rotting in the fields, the nation's prostitutes complaining about lack of business because every male in the country had his eyes glued to the screen. He thought of samosas adjoining a spill of chutney coming by on a leaf plate. A place where he could never be the only one in a photograph.

Of course, he didn't go over his memories of the village school, of the schoolmaster who failed the children unless paid off by the parents. He didn't think of the roof that flew off each monsoon season or of the fact that not only his mother, but now also his grandmother, were dead. He didn't think of any of the things that had made him leave in the first place.

Forty-two

Despite her sweet succumb to bribery, the minute Gyan left the house, his little sister who had witnessed the fight between her brother and Sai switched allegiance to an unbearable urge to gossip, and when he returned, he found the whole household was aware of what had happened, expanded to theatrical dimensions. The talk of guns had the astonishing effect of waking his grandmother up out of a stupor (in fact, the savor of battles renewed was giving new life to the aged all over the hillside), and she crept over slowly with a rolled-up newspaper. Gyan saw her coming and wondered what she was doing. Then she reached him and smacked him hard on the head. "Take control of yourself. Running around like a fool, paying no attention to your studies! Where is this going to get you? In jail, that's where." She smacked him on his bottom as he tried to rush past. "Keep out of trouble, you understand," whacking again for good measure, "like a baby you will be crying."

"He may not have done anything," began his mother.

"Why would that girl come all the way then? For no reason? Stay away from those people," his grandmother growled, turning to Gyan. "What trouble you'll get yourself into . . . and we're a poor family . . . we will be at their mercy. . . . Gone crazy with your father away and your mother too weak to control you," she glowered at her daughter-in-law, glad of an excuse to do so. Locked Gyan up with a lock and key.

That day, when his friends came for him, at the sound of a jeep, his grandmother crawled outdoors, peering about with her rheumy eyes.

"At least tell them I'm not well. You'll ruin my reputation," Gyan screamed, his adolescent self coming to the forefront.

"He's sick," said the grandmother. "Very sick. Can't see you anymore."

"What's wrong?"

"He can't stop going to the bathroom doing *tatti*," she said. He groaned inside. "Must have eaten something overripe. He is like a tap turned on."

"Every family has to send a man to represent the household in our marches."

They were referring to the march the next day, a big one starting at the Mela Ground.

"The Indo-Nepal treaty is being burned tomorrow."

"If you want him doing *tatti* all over your march . . ."

They drove away and visited houses all over the hillside to remind everyone of the edict that each home must have a representative demonstrating the next day, although there were many who claimed digestive problems and heart conditions, sprained ankles, back pain . . . and tried to be excused with medical certificates: "Mr. Chatterjee must avoid exposure to anxiety and nervousness as he is a high-BP patient."

But they were not excused: "Then send someone else. Surely not everyone in the family is ill?"

An enormous decision removed, Gyan, after the initial protest, felt sweet peace settle on him, and though he pretended frustration, he was very relieved by this reprieve into childhood. He was young, no permanant harm had been done. Let the world carry on outside for a bit, and then when it was safe, he'd visit Sai and cajole her into being friends again. He wasn't a bad person. He didn't want to fight. The trouble was that he'd tried to be part of the larger questions, tried to become part of politics and history. Happiness had a smaller location, though this wasn't something to flaunt, of course; very few would stand up and announce, "Actually I'm a coward," but his timidity might be disguised, well, in a perfectly ordinary existence situated between meek contours. Saved from one humiliation by being horrible to Sai, he could now be serendipitously saved from another by claiming respect for his grandmother. Cowardice needed its facade, its reasoning, like anything else if it was to be his life's principle. Contentment was no easy matter. One had to situate it cannily, camouflage it, pretend it was something else.

He had a lot of time to think, and as the hours went by, he unearthed the grout from his belly button, the wax from his ears with a blunt lead pencil, listened to the radio and tested the cleanliness of the orifices against the music, tilting right, left: *"Chaandni raate, pyaar ki baate. . . ."* Then, sad to report, he picked some snot balls from his nose and fed them to a giant tiger-striped spider sitting in its web between the table and the wall. It pounced, couldn't believe its luck, and began slowly to eat. Gyan lay on his back and did languorous bicycling exercises with his legs.

Pleasures existed in the world—intense, tiny pleasures that nevertheless created a feeling of space on all sides.

But then, the guilt came back strong: how could he have told the boys about the guns? How? How could he have put Sai in such danger? His skin began to crawl and burn. He couldn't lie on the bed any longer. He got up and paced up and down. Could he ever be happy and innocent after what he had done?

So as Sai lay martyred in her room, and as Gyan first considered the joy of turning the wheels of a simple life and then sickened at the harm he had done to others, they missed the important protest, a defining moment of the conflict, when the Indo-Nepal treaty of 1950 was to be burned and the past consigned to the flames and destroyed.

"Someone will have to go . . . ," the cook said to the judge after the boys had come to Cho Oyu to make their demand of attendance at the march.

"Well, you had better go, then," said the judge.

Forty-three

27th July of 1986.

At night it rained and the cook prayed he wouldn't have to go, but by morning it had stopped and a bit of blue appeared, looking so fake and childish after the moody shades of monsoon, he felt it hollow his heart and lay in bed as long as he could, hoping it would get covered up. Then when he couldn't delay things any longer, he got up, put on his slippers, and went to the outhouse.

He met his friend the MetalBox watchman, and they walked together to the Mela Ground, through the entrance gate that was mounted with a statue of Gandhi to commemorate Indian Independence. Underneath, it read in Hindi, "Unity Love Service." Several thousand people were arriving, not only from Kalimpong, but from villages and towns all around, from Mirik, Pasumbang, Soureni Valley, Aloobari, Labong Valley, Kurseong and Peshok, Mungpootista Highway, and many other places besides. When they had all collected, they would march to the police station where they would set the documents on fire.

"The organizational skills of the GNLF are good," the cook said; he couldn't help but appreciate them, for this kind of order was a rare sight in Kalimpong.

They stood and waited as hours passed. Finally, when the sun was hot overhead and cast no shadow, a man blew a whistle and instructed them to move forward.

Waving kukris, the sickle blades high and flashing in the light, "*Jai* Gorkha," the men shouted. "*Jai* Gorkhaland! Gorkhaland for Gorkhas!"

"We should be finished in an hour," said the MetalBox watchman hopefully.

All was going according to plan, and they began to anticipate their lunch, since they were already hungry; but then, all of sudden when they reached the junction, an unexpected incident occurred. A volley of rocks and stones came pelting down from behind the post office, where the cook had waited for his letters from Biju and which, he noticed sadly, was barred and shut.

The stones hit the rooftops, BANG BANG BANG BANG; then they came flying with greater momentum, bounced down, and injured some of the people, who went reeling back.

Bruises. Blood.

It would never be uncovered who the culprits were, whose sinister plan this was—

Those hired by the police, said the marchers, so that the marchers might be goaded into returning the insult, throwing rocks back, thus giving the police an excuse to react.

Not true, said the police. The rioters, they claimed, had brought the stones with them to throw in the face of law and order.

However, all parties agreed that, in anger at this attack, the crowd began to throw the stones at the *jawans* all outfitted in their riot shields and batons. The missiles hit the police station roof, shattered the windows.

The police picked up the rocks and returned them. Who were they to be spiritually superior to the crowd?

And then, BAM BABAM, the air was full of stones and bottles and brickbats and screaming. The crowd began to collect rocks, raided a building site for more; the police began to chase the crowd; the stones came down; everyone was being hit, people, police; they jumped on one another, beating with sticks, bashing with rocks; began to slash with their sickles—a hand, a face, a nose, an ear.

A rumor spread that there were men among the protesters with guns. . . . Perhaps it was true. Perhaps it wasn't.

But the more adamant the protesters were, the more they fought back, the more they refused to scatter, the more certain the police were that they *were* armed. Defiance like this could surely not exist unless supported by weapons. So, they suspected.

In the end, the police couldn't bear the suspense of their suspicion and opened fire.

The marchers immediately to the front scattered, ran right and left—

Those who followed behind from beyond the Kanchan Cinema, pushed by the pushing of those still farther behind, were gunned down.

In a fast-forward blur, thirteen local boys were dead.

This was how history moved, the slow build, the quick burn, and in an incoherence, the leaping both backward and forward, swallowing the young into old hate. The space between life and death, in the end, too small to measure.

At this point, some of those running away turned back and relaunched themselves at the police, screaming vengeance. They pulled the guns from their hands, and the police, finding themselves suddenly, drastically, outnumbered, began to plead and whimper. One *jawan* was knifed to death, the arms of another were chopped off, a third was stabbed, and the heads of policemen came up on stakes before the station across from the bench under the plum tree, where the townspeople had rested themselves in more peaceful times and the cook sometimes read his letters. A beheaded body ran briefly down the street, blood fountaining from the neck, and they all saw the truth about living creatures—that after death, in final humiliation, the body defecates on itself.

The police ran backward like a film in reverse to get into the station but found that several of their colleagues, there before them, had locked the door and lay terrified on the floor, wouldn't let the others in, no matter how they hammered and pleaded. Chased by the mob, the police who were barred from shelter by their own men, ran into private homes.

Lola and Noni, who had again hosted the GNLF boys the night before, found three policemen hammering on the back door of Mon Ami. They sat whimpering in the drawing room as the ladies drew the curtains around them.

"Pathetic," Lola told them. "You are the police?!" Because now they were at her mercy and she wasn't at theirs. "Didn't help us all this time, and now see, need *our* help!"

"Ma," they called her, "Ma, please don't kick us out, we will do anything for you. We are as your sons."

"Hah! Now you're calling me Ma! Very fine and funny. This isn't how you were behaving a week ago. . . ."

In the bazaar they continued rioting. Jeeps were pushed into the ravine, buses were set on fire, the light from their burning reflected garishly on the settling mist of evening, and the fire spread to the jungles of bamboo. The air inside the hollow stems expanded and they burst and burned with the sound of renewed, magnified gunshot.

Everyone was running, the unwilling participants, the perpetrators, and the bashed-up police. They scattered into the side paths towards Bong Busti and to Teesta Bazaar. The cook ran alone because he'd lost the Metal-Box watchman, who had been torn away in another direction. He ran as fast as his lungs and legs would let him, his heart pounding painfully in his chest, ears, and throat, each breath poisonous. He managed to get some distance up the steep shortcut to Ringkingpong Road, and there he felt his legs collapse under him, they were trembling so hard. He sat above the bazaar among staffs of bamboo bearing white prayer flags, the script faded like the markings on a shell that's been washed by the ocean a long time. The Victorian tower of the Criminal Investigation Division was behind him and the dark bulk of Galingka, Tashiding, and Morgan House, dating to the British, but all company guesthouses now. A gardener squatted on the lawn of Morgan House still planted with the plants Mrs. Morgan had bought from England. He seemed unaware of what was going on; stared out without curiosity or ambition, without worry, developing a quality devoid of qualities to get him through this life.

The cook could see the fires burning below him and the men scattering. As they crossed the heat vapor of the flames, they seemed to ripple and blow like mirages. Above was Kanchenjunga, solid, extraordinary, a sight that for centuries had delivered men their freedom and thinned clogged human hearts to joy. But of course the cook couldn't feel this now and he didn't know if the sight of the mountain could ever be the same to him. Clawing at his heart as if it were a door was his panic—a scrabbling rodent creature.

How could anything be the same? The red of blood lay over the market road in slick pools mingled with a yellow spread of dal someone must have brought in anticipation of a picnic after the parade, and there were flies on it, left behind odd slippers, a sad pair of broken spectacles, even a tooth. It was rather like the government warning about safety that appeared in the cinema before the movie with the image of a man cycling to work, a poor man but with a wife who loved him, and she had sent his lunch with him in a tiffin container; then came a blowing of horns and a small, desperate cycle tinkle, and a messy blur clearing into the silent still image of a spread of food mingled with blood. Those mismatched colors, domesticity shuffled with death, sureness running into the unexpected, kindness replaced by the image of violence, always made the cook feel like throwing up and weeping both together.

Now he did and crying, continued crawling his way back to Cho Oyu, hiding in the bushes as he was passed by army tanks rolling down from the cantonment area into the town. Instead of foreign enemies, instead of the Chinese they had been preparing for, building their hatred against, they must fight their own people. . . .

This place, this market where he had bargained contentedly over potatoes, and insulted, yes *insulted*, the fruit *wallah* with happy impunity, enjoyed the rude words about decayed produce that flew from his lips; this place where he had with utter safety genuinely lost his temper with the deaf tailors, the inept plumber, the tardy baker with the cream horns; this place where he had resided secure in the knowledge that this was *basically* a civilized place where there was room for them all; where he had existed in what seemed a *sweetness* of crabbiness—was showing him now that he had been wrong. He wasn't wanted in Kalimpong and he didn't belong.

At this moment, a fear overtook him that he might never see his son again—

The letters that had come all these years were only his own hope writing to him. Biju was just a habit of thought. He didn't exist. Could he?

Forty-four

The incidents of horror grew, through the changing of the seasons, through winter and a flowery spring, summer, then rain and winter again. Roads were closed, there was curfew every night, and Kalimpong was trapped in its own madness. You couldn't leave the hillsides; nobody even left their houses if they could help it but stayed locked in and barricaded.

If you were a Nepali reluctant to join in, it was bad. The Metal-Box watchman had been beaten, forced to repeat "*Jai* Gorkha," and dragged to Mahakala Temple to swear an oath of loyalty to the cause.

If you weren't Nepali it was worse.

If you were Bengali, people who had known you your whole life wouldn't acknowledge you in the street.

Even the Biharis, Tibetans, Lepchas, and Sikkimese didn't acknowledge you. They, the unimportant shoals of a minority population, the small powerless numbers that might be caught up in either net, wanted to put the Bengalis on the other side of the argument from themselves, delineate them as the enemy.

"All these years," said Lola, "I've been buying eggs at that Tshering's shop down the road, and the other day he looked at me right in the face and said he had none. 'I see a basket of them right there,' I said, 'how can you tell me you have none?' 'They have been presold,' he said.

"Pem Pem," Lola had exclaimed on her way out, seeing her friend Mrs. Thondup's daughter come in. Just a few months ago Lola and Noni had partaken of fine civilities in her home that had harkened to another kind of life in another place, quail eggs with bamboo shoots, fat Tibetan carpets under their toes.

"Pem Pem??"

Pem Pem gave Lola a beseeching embarrassed look and rushed past.

"All of a sudden wrong side, no?" said Lola, "There is nobody who won't abandon you."

On the ledge below Mon Ami, among the row of illegal huts, the sisters had noticed a small temple flying a red and gold flag, ensuring that no matter what, into eternity, no official—police, government, nobody—would dare dispute the legitimacy of the landgrab. The gods themselves had blessed it now. Little shrines were springing up all over Kalimpong, adjoining constructions forbidden by the municipality—squatter genius. And the trespassers were tapping phone lines, water pipes, electric lines in jumbles of illegal connections. The trees that provided Lola and Noni with pears, so many that they had cursed it, "Stewed pears and cream, stewed pears and cream every damn day!" had been stripped overnight. The broccoli patch was gone, the area near the gate was being used as a bathroom. Little children lined up in rows to spit at Lola and Noni as they walked by, and when Kesang, their maid, was bitten by one of the sqatter's dogs, she screamed away, "Look your dog has bitten me, now you must put oil and turmeric on the wound so I don't die from an infection."

But they just laughed.

The GNLF boys had burned down the government rest house by the river, beyond the bridge where Father Booty had photographed the polka-dotted butterfly. In fact, forest inspection bungalows all over the district were burning, upon whose verandas generations of ICS men had stood and admired the serenity, the hovering, angelic peace of dawn and dusk in the mountains.

The circuit house was burned, and the house of the chief minister's niece. Detonators set off landslides as negotiations went nowhere. Kalimpong was transformed into a ghost town, the wind tumbling around the melancholy streets, garbage flying by unhindered. Whatever point the GNLF might have had, it was severely out of hand; even one man's anger, in those days, seemed enough to set the hillside alight.

Women rushed by on the roads. The men trembled at home for fear of being picked up, being tortured on any kind of flimsy excuse, the GNLF accusing them of being police informers, the police accusing them of being militants. It was dangerous to drive even for those who might, for a car was just a trap; vehicles were being surrounded and stolen; they could be more nimble on their feet, hide in the jungle at the sound of trouble, wade through the *jhoras* and make their way home on footpaths. Anyway, after a while, there was no more fuel because the GNLF boys had siphoned off the last of it, and the pumps were closed.

The cook tried to calm himself by repeating, "It will be all right, everything goes through a bad time, the world goes in a cycle, bad things happen, pass, and things are once again good . . ." But his voice had more pleading in it than conviction, more hope than wisdom.

After this—after the gun robbery and after the parade, after his seeing the frailty of his life here as a non-Nepali—he couldn't manage to compose himself properly; there was nobody, nothing—but a sinister presence loomed—he was sure something even worse stood around the corner. Where was Biju, where was he? He leaped at every shadow.

So, it was usually Sai who walked to the shuttered market searching for a shop with a half open back door signaling quick secret business, or a cardboard sign propped at the window of a hut of someone selling a handful of peanuts or a few eggs.

Excepting these meager purchases Sai made, the garden was feeding them almost entirely. For the first time, they in Cho Oyu were eating the real food of the hillside. *Dalda saag,* pink-flowered, flat-leafed; *bhutiya dhaniya* growing copiously around the cook's quarter; the new tendrils of squash or pumpkin vine; curled *ningro* fiddleheads, *churbi* cheese and bamboo shoots sold by women who appeared from behind bushes on forest paths with the cheese wrapped in ferns and the yellow slices of bamboo shoots in buckets of water. After the rains, mushrooms pushed their way up, sweet as chicken and glorious as Kanchenjunga, so big, fanning out. People collected the oyster mushrooms in Father Booty's abandoned garden. For a while the smell of them cooking gave the town the surprising air of wealth and comfort.

One day, when Sai arrived home with a kilo of damp *atta* and some potatoes, she found two figures, familiar from a previous occasion, on the veranda, pleading with the cook and judge.

"Please, sahib. . . ." It was the same wife and father of the tortured man.

"Oh no," the cook had said in horror when he saw them, "oh no, *baap re,* what are you coming here for?" although he knew.

It was the impoverished who walked the line so thin it was questionable if it existed, an imaginary line between the insurgents and the law, between being robbed (who would listen to them if they went to the police?) and being hunted by the police as scapegoats for the crimes of others.

They were hungriest.

"Why are you coming here making trouble? We already told you we had nothing to do with the police picking up your husband. We were hardly the ones to accuse him or beat him. . . . Had they told us, we would have gone at once and said this is not the man . . . we were not informed. . . . What do we owe you?" said the cook. But he was giving them the *atta* Sai had brought back . . . when the judge barked, "Don't give them anything," and continued his chess game.

"Please, sahib," they begged with hands folded, heads bent. "Who comes to our help? Can we live on no food at all? We will be your servants forever . . . God will repay you . . . God will reward you. . . ."

But the judge was adamant.

Again, herded out, they sat outside the gate.

"Tell them to go," he told the cook.

"Jao jao," said the cook, although he was concerned that they might need to rest before having to walk another five to six hours through the forest to their village.

Again they moved and sat farther up so as not to give offense. Again they saw Mutt. She was attached by her snout to her favorite whiffy spot, unaware of anything else. The woman suddenly brightened and said to the man, "Sell that kind of dog and you can get a lot of money. . . ." Mutt didn't budge from the smell for a long, long time. If the judge hadn't been there, they could have reached out—and grabbed her.

Some days later, when they at Cho Oyu had again forgotten these two unimportant if upsetting people, they returned.

But they didn't come to the gate; they secreted themselves immediately in the *jhora* ravine and waited for Mutt, that connoisseur of smells, to appear for her daily round of the property. Rediscovering scents and enhancing them was an ever evolving art form. She was involved with an old favorite, grown better with age, that brought forth certain depths and facets of her personality. She was wholly absorbed, didn't notice the intruders who crept up to her and pounced!

Startled, she yelped, but immediately they clamped her muzzle with hands strong from physical labor.

The judge was having his bucket bath, the cook was churning butter, Sai was in her bed whispering venomously, "Gyan, you bastard, you think I'm going to cry over you?" They didn't see or hear a thing.

The trespassers lifted Mutt up, bound her with rope, and put her in a sack. The man slung the sack over his shoulders, and they carried her through town without drawing any attention to themselves. They walked around the mountainside, then all the way down and across the Relli and over three ridges that billowed like blue-green ocean, to a small hamlet that was far from any paved road.

"You don't think they'll find us?" the father asked his daughter-in-law.

"They won't walk so far and they can't drive here. They don't know our names, they don't know our village, they asked us no questions."

She was right.

Even the police hadn't bothered to find out the name of the man they had beaten and blinded. They would hardly bother to look for a dog.

Mutt was healthy, they noticed, when they pinched her through the sack; fat and ready to make them a little money. "Or maybe we can use her to breed and then we can sell the puppies. . . ." (They didn't know, of course, that she had been fixed long ago by a visiting vet when she was beginning to attract love from all kinds of scurrilous loafers on the hillside, wheedling strays, conniving gentleman dogs. . . .)

"Should we take her out of the sack?"

"Better leave her in for now. She'll just start barking. . . ."

Forty-five

Like a failing bus laboring through the sky, the Gulf Air plane seemed barely to be managing, though most of the passengers felt immediately comfortable with this lack of oomph. Oh yes, they were going home, knees cramped, ceiling level at their heads, sweat-gluey, fate-resigned, but happy.

The first stop was Heathrow and they crawled out at the far end that hadn't been renovated for the new days of globalization but lingered back in the old age of colonization.

All the third-world flights docked here, families waiting days for their connections, squatting on the floor in big bacterial clumps, and it was a long trek to where the European–North American travelers came and went, making those brisk no-nonsense flights with extra leg-room and private TV, whizzing over for a single meeting in such a manner that it was truly hard to imagine they were shitting-peeing, bleeding-weeping humans at all. Silk and cashmere, bleached teeth, Prozac, laptops, and a sandwich for their lunch named The Milano.

Frankfurt. The planeload spent the night in a similar quarantined zone, a thousand souls stretched out as if occupying a morgue, even their faces covered to block the buzzing tube lights.

Like a bus, New York–London-Frankfurt–Abu Dhabi–Dubai-Bahrain-Karachi-Delhi-Calcutta, the plane stopped again to allow men from the Gulf countries to clamber on. They came racing—Quick! Quick! . . . Quick!!—unzipping their carry-ons for the Scotch, drinking straight from the bottle's mouth. Crooked little ice crystals formed on the plane window. Inside, it was hot. Biju ate his tray of chicken curry, spinach and rice, strawberry ice cream, rinsed his mouth into the empty ice-cream cup, then tried to get another dinner. "As it is we are short," the stewardesses said, harassed by the men, drunk and hooting, pinching them as they passed, calling them by name, "Sheila! Raveena! Kusum! Nandita!"

Added to the smell of sweat, there was now the thick odor of food and cigarettes, the recycled breathing of an entire plane, the growing fetor of the bathroom.

In the mirror of this bathroom, Biju saluted himself. Here he was, on his way home, without name or knowledge of the American president, without the name of the river on whose bank he had lingered, without even hearing about any of the tourist sights—no Statue of Liberty, Macy's, Little Italy, Brooklyn Bridge, Museum of Immigration; no bialy at Barney Greengrass, soupy dumpling at Jimmy's Shanghai, no gospel churches of Harlem tour. He returned over the lonely ocean and he thought that this kind of perspective could only make you sad. Now, he promised himself, he would forget the insight, begin anew. He would buy a taxi. His savings were small, collected in his shoe, his sock, his underwear, through all these years, but he thought he could manage it. He'd drive up and down the mountainside on market days, gold tinsel, gods above the dashboard, a comical horn, *PAWpumPOM paw* or *TWEE-deee-deee DEE-TWEE-deee-deee*. And he'd build a house with solid walls, a roof that wouldn't fly off every monsoon season. Biju played the scene of meeting his father again and again like a movie in his head, wept a bit at the thought of so much happiness and emotion. They'd sit out in the evenings, drink *chhang,* tell jokes of the kind he had overheard on the plane being exchanged by drunk men:

So one day Santa Singh and Banta Singh are doing nothing, passing the time, staring at the sky, and all of a sudden an airforce plane flies by, men parachute out of it, get into military jeeps waiting for them in the fields, and go home. '*Arre, sala,* this is the life,' says Santa to Banta, 'what a way to make your money.' So off they go to the recruitment agency and a few months later, there they are in the plane. '*Wahe Guruji Ka Khalsa, Wahe*

Guruji Ki Fateh,' says Santa and jumps. *'Wahe Guruji Ka Khalsa, Wahe Guruji Ki Fateh,'* says Banta and jumps.

"'*Arre,* Banta,' says Santa, a second later, 'this *sala* parachute is not opening.'

"'Ai Santa," says Banta, "neither does mine. Typical government *intezaam,* just you wait and see, when we get to the bottom, the *bhenchoot* jeep won't be there.'"

Forty-six

Sai looked out of her window and couldn't tell what all the noise was about.

The judge was shouting: "Mutt, Mutt." It was her stew time and the cook had boiled soy Nutrinuggets with pumpkin and a Maggi soup cube. It worried the judge that she should have to eat like this, but she'd already had the last of the meat; the judge had barred himself and Sai from it, and the cook, of course, never had the luxury of eating meat in the first place. There was still some peanut butter, though, for Mutt's chapatis, and powdered milk.

But Mutt wouldn't answer.

"Mutty, Mutt, stew. . . ." The judge walked around the garden, out of the gate, and walked up and down the road.

"Stew stew—

"Mutty Mutt? MUTT?" His voice became anxious.

The afternoon turned into evening, the mist swept down, but Mutt didn't appear.

He remembered the boys in their guerilla outfits arriving for the guns. Mutt had barked, the boys had screamed like a bunch of schoolgirls, retreated down the steps to cower behind the bushes. But Mutt had been scared, too; she wasn't the brave dog they imagined.

"MUTT-MUTT MUTTY-MUTTMUTTYMUTTMUTT?!"

She hadn't arrived by the time darkness settled in.

He felt more keenly than ever that at nightfall in Kalimpong, there was a real ceding of power. You couldn't rise against such a powerful dark, so enormous, without a chink. He went out with the biggest flashlight they had, shone it uselessly into the jungle; listened for jackals; waited on the veranda all night; watched the invisible mountainsides opposite as the falling lanterns of drunks plummeted like shooting stars. By the time dawn showed, he was frantic. He ventured to the small *busti* houses to ask if they had seen her; he asked the milkman and the baker, who was now at home with his battered tin trunk, which contained the *khari* biscuits and milk rusks Mutt so enjoyed.

"No, have not seen the *kutti*."

The judge was angry at hearing her referred to as a "*kutti*" but restrained himself because he couldn't afford to shout at those whose help he might now need.

He asked the plumber, the electrician. Uselessly, he gestured at the deaf tailors who had made Mutt a winter coat out of a blanket, with a buckle at the belly.

He received blank faces, some angry laughter. "*Saala Machoot* . . . what does he think? We're going to look for his dog?" People were insulted. "At a time like this. We can't even eat!"

He knocked on the doors of Mrs. Thondup, Lola and Noni, anyone who might be kind, if not on his behalf, then for Mutt, or for the sake of their profession, position, religion. (He missed the missionaries—they would have understood and would have been duty-bound to help.) Everyone he called on responded with immediate doom. Was this a hopeful time? They were already reconciled to Mutt's fate, and the judge wished to strangle them as they spoke.

Mrs. Thondup: "Was she expensive?"

The judge never thought of her that way, but yes, she had been expensive, delivered from a Calcutta kennel specializing in red setters. A certificate of pedigree had accompanied her: "Sire: Cecil. Dam: Ophelia."

"*La ma ma ma ma,* must have been stolen, Justice," Mrs. Thondup said. "Our dogs, Ping and Ting—we brought them all the way from Lhasa, and when we got here, Ping vanished. The robber kept him captive to breed pups, mated and mated him. Good source of income, no? Just go to thirteenth mile, you'll see watered down versions of Ping running about everywhere. Finally he broke away and escaped, but his whole personality had changed." She pointed out the victim, drooling out of his old man's mouth, glaring at the judge.

Uncle Potty: "Somebody must be out to rob you, Justice Sahib—getting rid of obstacles. That Gobbo, he poisoned my Kutta Sahib, years ago now."

"But we were just robbed."

"Someone else must have decided to do the same. . . ."

Afghan princesses: "Our dog, Afghan hound, you know, we were traveling with our father and one day she went missing. She was eaten by the Nagas, yes, they eat dogs—they ate Frisky. Even our slaves—yes, we had slaves—we threatened them with their lives, but still they didn't manage to rescue her in time."

Lola: "The trouble with us Indians is that we have no love of animals. A dog, a cat is there just to kick. We can't resist—beat, stone, torment, we don't rest until the creature is dead and then we feel very content—good! Put it down! Destroyed it! All gone!—we feel satisfaction in this."

What had he done? He hadn't been fair to her. He had put Mutt in a place where she could never survive, a rough, mad place. Bhutia hill dogs—battle-scarred mastiffs, grins disfigured by violence, ears stiff from having been bloodied over and over—might have torn her to bits. Nightshade grew in every ravine, flowers crisp and white as the pope's robes, but hallucinogenic—she might have imbibed the poisonous sap. The cobras—husband-wife, wide as the biscuit jar, living in the bank behind Cho Oyu—might have bitten her. Rabid, hallucinating jackals, unable to drink, unable to swallow, might have come from the forest, thirsty, so thirsty. . . . Just two years ago, when they had brought a rabies epidemic into town, the judge had taken Mutt for a vaccine most people could not afford. He had saved her while stray dogs were rounded up and slaughtered by the truckful (mistaking the only ride of their lives for a new life of luxury smiling and wagging away) and whole families too penniless to pay for the three-thousand-rupee vaccine died; the hospital staff had been ordered to say they had no medicine for fear of riots. In between the madness of rabies came moments of lucidity, so the victims knew exactly what was happening to them, exactly what lunacy looked like, felt like. . . .

He had thought his vigilance would protect his dog from all possible harm.

The price of such arrogance had been great.

He went to see the subdivisional officer who had visited Cho Oyu after the robbery, but trouble had upset the SDO's good nature. He was no longer the gardening enthusiast who had complimented the judge's passionflower.

"My dear sir," he said to the judge, "I am fond of animals myself, but in these times . . . it's a luxury we can't afford—"

He had given up his special cherry tobacco, as well—it seemed an embarrassment at a time like this. One always felt compelled to go back to Gandhian-style austerity when the integrity of the nation was being threatened, rice-dal, roti-*namak*, over and over. It was just horrible. . . .

The judge persisted, "But can't you do anything . . ." and he became angry, threw up his hands.

"A dog! Justice, just listen to yourself. People are being killed. What can I do? Of course I have such high regard. . . . I have made time despite worry of being accused of favoritism . . . but we are in an emergency situation. In Calcutta, in Delhi, there is great concern about this severe deterioration of law and order, and in the end that's what we must think of, isn't it so? Our country. We must suffer inconvenience and I don't need to tell someone of your experience this. . . ." The SDO fixed the judge with a certain gluey look that convinced him he meant to be rude.

The judge went on to the police station where the sound of a man's screaming issued from the inner chamber on purpose, the judge thought, to intimidate him, to extract a bribe.

He looked at the policemen in front of him. They looked insolently back.

They were waiting in the front room, biding time until they would all go in and give the man a final lesson he couldn't unlearn. They began to snigger. "Ha, ha, ha. Come about his dog! Dog? Ha, ha ha ha ha. . . . *Madman!*" They became angry halfway through their humor. "Don't waste our time," they said. "Get out."

Did they perhaps know the name of the person they had picked up after the gun robbery? The judge persisted. He wondered, just a thought, could he be responsible?

Which person?

The one whom they had accused of stealing his guns . . . he wasn't blaming the police in any way, but the man's wife and father had visited him and seemed upset. . . . There was no such person, they said, what was he talking about? Now, would he stop wasting their time and *get out?* The sound of the victim screaming in the back intensified as if on cue to give the judge a not so subtle message.

He couldn't conceive of punishment great enough for humanity. A man wasn't equal to an animal, not one particle of him. Human life was stinking, corrupt, and meanwhile there were beautiful creatures who lived with delicacy on the earth without doing anyone any harm. "*We* should be dying," the judge almost wept.

The world had failed Mutt. It had failed beauty; it had failed grace. But by having forsaken this world, for having held himself apart, Mutt would suffer.

The judge had lost his clout. . . . A bit of "sir sahib *huzoor*" for politeness' sake, but that was just residual veneer now; he knew what they really thought of him.

He remembered all of a sudden why he had gone to England and joined the ICS; it was clearer than ever why—but now that position of power was gone, frittered away in years of misanthropy and cynicism.

"Biscuit, pooch, din din, milkie, khana, ishtoo, porridge, dalia, chalo, car, pom-pom, doo-doo, walkie"—

He shouted all the language that was between Mutt and himself, sending nursery words of love flying over the Himalayas, rattled her leash so it clinked the way that made her jump—whoop!—up on all four legs together, as if on a pogo stick.

"Walkie, baba, muffin. . . .

"Mutt, mutton, little chop . . ." he cried, then, "forgive me, my little dog. . . . Please let her go whoever you are. . . ."

He kept burning the image of Mutt, how she sometimes lay on her back with all four legs in the air, warming her tummy as she snoozed in the sun. How he'd recently tempted her to eat her lousy pumpkin stew by running around the garden making buzzing noises as if the vegetable were a strange insect, and then he'd popped the cube into her wide-open-with-surprise mouth, and in amazement she'd hastily swallowed.

He pictured the two of them cozy in bed: good night, good morning.

The army came out at dusk to make sure curfew was strictly enforced.

"You must return, sir," said a soldier.

"Get out of my way," he said in a British accent to make the man back away, but the soldier continued to follow at a safe distance until the judge turned angrily toward home while pretending not to be hurried.

Please come home, my dear, my lovely girl,
Princess Duchess Queen,
Soo-soo, Poo-poo, Cuckoo, good good smelly smell,
Naughty girl,
Treat-treat, dinnertime,
Diamond Pearl,
Teatime! Biscuit!
Sweetheart! Chicki!
Catch the bone!

How ridiculous it all sounded without a dog to receive the words.

The soldier followed meekly, surprised at what was coming from the judge's mouth.

Something was wrong, he told his wife back in the quarters for married servicemen, concrete blocks defacing the wilderness.

Something indecent was happening.

"What?" she said, newly married, absolutely delighted by her modern plumbing and cooking gadgets.

"God knows what happens, these senile men and their animals . . . you know," he said, "all kinds of strange things. . . ."

Then they forgot the conversation, because the army was still being well fed and the wife informed her husband that they had been allotted so much butter that they could share it with their extended family, even though this was against the law, and that while a broiler chicken was usually between six hundred and eight hundred grams, the chicken they had been delivered was almost double the weight: was the army poultry supplier injecting the birds with water?

Forty-seven

In the meantime, in the aftermath of the parade, the police had been reinforced and were hunting down the GNLF boys, combing remote hamlets, trying to weed Gorkhaland supporters from the Marxists, from the Congress supporters, from those who didn't care either way. They raided tea gardens as they were closing down; managers recalling the attacks by rebels on plantation owners in Assam left on private planes for Calcutta.

Wanted men, on the run, were dodging the police, sleeping in the homes of the wealthier people in town—Lola and Noni, the doctor, the Afghan princesses, retired officials, Bengalis, outsiders, anyone whose home would not be searched.

There were reports of comings and goings over the Nepal and Sikkim border, of retired army men controlling the movement, offering quick training on how to wire bombs, ambush the police, blow up the bridges. But anyone could see they were still mostly just boys, taking their style from Rambo, heads full up with kung fu and karate chops, roaring around on stolen motorcycles, stolen jeeps, having a fantastic time. Money and guns in their pockets. They were living the movies. By the time they were done, they would defeat their fictions and the new films would be based on them. . . .

They arrived with masks in the night, climbed over gates, ransacked houses. Seeing a woman walking home bundled in a shawl, they made her unwrap it and took the rice and the bit of sugar she'd concealed.

On the road to the market, the trees were hung with the limbs of enemies—which side and whose enemy? This was the time to make anyone you didn't like disappear, to avenge ancient family vendettas. Screams continued from the police station though a bottle of Black Label could save your life. Injured men, their spilling guts wrapped in chicken skins to keep them fresh, were rushed on bamboo stretchers to the doctor to be stitched up; a man was found buried in the sewage tank, every inch of his body slashed with a knife, his eyes gouged out. . . .

But while the residents were shocked by the violence, they were also often surprised by the mundaneness of it all. Discovered the extent of perversity that the heart is capable of as they sat at home with nothing to do, and found that it was possible, faced with the stench of unimaginable evil, for a human being to grow bored, yawn, be absorbed by the problem of a missing sock, by neighborly irritations, to feel hunger skipping like a little mouse inside a tummy and return, once again, to the pressing matter of what to eat. . . . There they were, the most commonplace of them, those quite mismatched with the larger-than-life questions, caught up in the mythic battles of past vs. present, justice vs. injustice—the most ordinary swept up in extraordinary hatred, because extraordinary hatred was, after all, a commonplace event.

Forty-eight

After Delhi, the Gulf Air flight landed in Calcutta's Dum Dum airport. Biju smelled again, the distinctive smell of a floor being disinfected with phenyl by a sweeper woman both destitute and with a talent for being exceedingly irritating. Eyes lowered and swatting bare feet with a filthy rag, she introduced some visitors for the first time to that potent mixture of intense sympathy and intense annoyance.

There was an unruly crowd around the luggage conveyer belts because several planes were in at the same time and even more varieties of Indians than the ones showcased on Gulf Air were on display, back in the common soup after deliberate evolution into available niches abroad. There was the yuppie who had taken lessons on wine, those who were still maintaining their culture and going to the temple in Bern, or wherever. The funky Bhangra boy with earring and baggy pants. The hippie who had hit on the fact that you could escape from being a drab immigrant and have a fantastic time as an Indian among the tie-dyed, spout all kinds of Hindu-mantra-Tantra-Mother-Earth–native-peoples–single-energy–organic-*Shakti*-ganja-crystal-shaman-intuition stuff. There were computer boys who'd made a million. Taxi drivers, toilet cleaners, and young straight-laced businessmen who tried to be cool by having friends over for "some really hot curry, man, how spicy can you take it?"

Indians who lived abroad, Indians who traveled abroad, richest and poorest, the back-and-forth ones maintaining green cards. The Indian student bringing back a bright blonde, pretending it was nothing, trying to be easy, but every molecule tense and self-conscious: "Come on, yaar, love has no color. . . ." He had *just happened to stumble into the stereotype;* he was the genuine thing that *just happened to be the cliché. . . .*

Behind him a pair of Indian girls made vomity faces.

"Must have got off the plane and run for an American dame so he could get his green card and didn't care if she looked like a horse or no. *Which she does!!!!*"

"Our ladies are the most beautiful in the world," said one man earnestly to the Indian girls, perhaps worried they would feel hurt, but it sounded as if he were trying to console himself.

"Yes, our women are the best in the world," said another woman, and our men are the absolute worst *gadhas* in the whole wide world."

"Dadi Amma!" everyone shouting. "Dadi Amma!" A granny, sari hitched high for action, showing limp, flesh-colored socks and hairy legs, was racing about with the luggage trolley, whacking into ankles, clambering over the luggage belt.

Two men with disdain on their faces, off the Air France flight, had sought each other out, "Where are you from, man?" hanging aloof.

"Ohio."

"Columbus?"

"No, a little outside."

"Where?"

"Small town, you wouldn't know."

"?"

"Paris, Ohio." He said this a little defensively. "You?"

"South Dakota."

He brightened. "Just look at this," he said, gesturing outward, relieving them both of pressure, "each time you come back you think something must have changed, but it's always the same."

"That's right," said the other man. "You don't like to say it, but you have to. Some countries don't get ahead for a reason. . . ."

They were waiting for their suitcases, but they didn't arrive.

Many bags didn't arrive and Biju overheard a fight at the Air France counter where the passengers had to fill out lost-luggage forms:

"They are only giving compensation to nonresident Indians and foreigners, not to Indian nationals, WHY?" All the Indian nationals were screaming, "Unfair unfair UNFAIR UNFAIR!"

"This is Air France airline policy sir," said the official, trying to calm them, "Foreigners need money for hotel/toothbrush—"

"So, our family is in Jalpaiguri, we are traveling on" said one woman, "and now we have to stay overnight and wait for our suitcases. . . . What kind of argument are you giving us? We are paying as much as the other fellow. Foreigners get more and Indians get less. Treating people from a rich country well and people from a poor country badly. It's a disgrace. Why this lopsided policy against your own people??"

"It *IS* Air France policy, madam," he repeated. As if throwing out the words *Paris* or *Europe* would immediately intimidate, assure non-corruption, and silence opposition.

"How am I supposed to travel to Jalpaiguri in my dirty underwear? As it is I am smelling so badly, I am ashamed even to go near anyone," the same lady said, holding her own nose with an anguished expression to show how she was ashamed even to be near herself.

All the NRIs holding their green cards and passports, looked complacent and civilized. That's just how it was, wasn't it? Fortune piled on more good fortune. They had more money and because they had more money, they would get more money. It was easy for them to stand in line, and they stood patiently, displaying how they didn't have to fight anymore; their manners proved just how well taken care of they were. And they couldn't wait for the shopping—"Shopping *ke liye jaenge, bhel puri khaenge* . . . dollars me *kamaenge, pum pum pum*. "Only eight rupees to the tailor, only twenty-two cents!" they would say, triumphantly translating everything into American currency; and while the shopping was converted into dollars, tips to the servants could be calculated in local currency: "Fifteen hundred rupees, is he mad? Give him one hundred, even that's too much."

A Calcutta sister accompanying a Chicago sister "getting value for her daaller, getting value for her daaller," discovering the first germ of leprous, all-consuming hatred that would in time rot the families irreversibly from within.

American, British, and Indian passports were all navy-blue, and the NRIs tried to make sure the right sides were turned up, so airline officials could see the name of the country and know right away whom to treat with respect.

There was a drawback, though, in this, for though the staff of Air France might be instructed differently, somewhere along the line—immigration, luggage check, security—you might get the resentful or nationalist kind of employee who would take pains to slow-torture you under any excuse. "Ah jealousy, jealousy"—they inoculated themselves in advance so no criticism would get through during the visit—"ah just jealous, jealous, jealous of our daallars."

"Well, hope you make it out alive, man," said the Ohio man to the South Dakota man after they had filled out their claims, feeling double happy, once for the Air France money, twice to have it all reconfirmed: "Oh ho ho, incompetent India, you've got to be expecting this, *typical, typical!*"

They passed by Biju who was inspecting his luggage that had finally arrived, and had arrived intact.

"But the problem occurred in *France,*" said someone, "not here. They didn't load the suitcases *there.*"

But the men were too gratified to pay attention.

"Good luck," they said to each other with a slap on the back, and the Ohio man left, glad to be bolstered by the story of the lost bag—ammunition against his father, because he knew his father was not proud of him. How could he not be? But he wasn't.

He knew what his father thought: that immigration, so often presented as a heroic act, could just as easily be the opposite; that it was cowardice that led many to America; fear marked the journey, not bravery; a cockroachy desire to scuttle to where you never saw poverty, not really, never had to suffer a tug to your conscience; where you never heard the demands of servants, beggars, bankrupt relatives, and where your generosity would never be openly claimed; where by merely looking after your own wife-child-dog-yard you could feel virtuous. Experience the relief of being an unknown transplant to the locals and hide the perspective granted by journey. Ohio was the first place he loved, for there he had at last been able to acquire a poise—

But then his father looked at him, sitting in his pajama kurta working away at his teeth with his toothpick, and he knew that his father thought it was the sureness that comes from putting yourself in a small place. And the son wouldn't be able to contain his anger: Jealous, jealous, even of your own son, he would think, jealousy, third-world chip on the shoulder—

Once, his father came to the States, and he had not been impressed, even by the size of the house:

"What is the point? All that space lying there useless, waste of water, waste of electricity, waste of heating, air-conditioning, not very intelligent is it? And you have to drive half an hour to the market! They call this the first world??? *Ekdum bekaar!*"

The father on the hot dog: "The sausage is bad, the bun is bad, the ketchup is bad, even the mustard is bad. And this an American institution! You can get a better sausage in Calcutta!"

Now the son had the lost-luggage story.

Biju stepped out of the airport into the Calcutta night, warm, mammalian. His feet sank into dust winnowed to softness at his feet, and he felt an unbearable feeling, sad and tender, old and sweet like the memory of falling asleep, a baby on his mother's lap. Thousands of people were out though it was almost eleven. He saw a pair of elegant bearded goats in a rickshaw, riding to slaughter. A conference of old men with elegant goat faces, smoking bidis. A mosque and minarets lit magic green in the night with a group of women rushing by in burkas, bangles clinking under the black and a big psychedelic mess of color from a sweet shop. Rotis flew through the air as in a juggling act, polka-dotting the sky high over a restaurant that bore the slogan "Good food makes good mood." Biju stood there in that dusty tepid soft sari night. Sweet drabness of home—he felt everything shifting and clicking into place around him, felt himself slowly shrink back to size, the enormous anxiety of being a foreigner ebbing—that unbearable arrogance and shame of the immigrant. Nobody paid attention to him here, and if they said anything at all, their words were easy, unconcerned. He looked about and for the first time in God knows how long, his vision unblurred and he found that he could see clearly.

Forty-nine

The judge got down on his knees, and he prayed to God, he, Jemubhai Popatlal the agnostic, who had made a long hard journey to jettison his family's prayers; he who had refused to throw the coconut into the water and bless his own voyage all those years ago on the deck of the SS *Strathnaver.*

"If you return Mutt, I will acknowledge you in public, *I will never deny you again,* I will tell the world that I believe in you—you—if you return Mutt—"

Then he got up. He was undoing his education, retreating to the superstitious man making bargains, offering sacrifices, gambling with fate, cajoling, daring whatever was out there—

Show me if you exist!

Or else I will know you are nothing.

Nothing! Nothing!—taunting it.

But by night, the thought reentered his mind—

Was this faith that he had turned away, was it paying him back?

For sins he had committed that no court in the world could take on. But that fact, he knew, didn't lessen the weight they placed on the scale, didn't render them nothing. . . . But who could be paying him back? He didn't believe in angered divinity, in a scale of balance. Of course not. The universe wasn't in the business of justice. That had simply been his own human conceit—until he learned better.

Yet he thought of his family that he had abandoned.

He thought of his father, whose strength and hope and love he had fed on, only to turn around to spit in his face. Then he thought of how he had returned his wife, Nimi. By this time, Bomanbhai Patel of the delicately carved *haveli* was dead, and an uncle had usurped the throne, the one misfortune of Bomanbhai—all daughters, no son—playing out its curse beyond his existence.

The judge's mind returned to why exactly he had sent his wife home. It hinged on one particular incident.

Early one morning in Bonda, a car stopped and a whole group of ladies came flowering out, passionate Congresswoman Mrs. Mohan at the wheel. She had spotted Nimi by the gate of Jemubhai's residence: "Oh, Mrs. Patel, come along with us—why always no? This time I won't take no for an answer! Let's go and have some fun. You must get out of the house now and then."

Half happy, half scared, she had found herself on the wide lap of a stranger in the car. They had driven to the station and had to park far away, for thousands of people had gathered to scream and demonstrate: "British raj *murdabad!*" They had stopped for a while, then followed a procession of cars to a house.

Nimi was handed a plate with scrambled eggs and toast, but she didn't eat because there was too much commotion, too many people, all shouting and arguing. She tried to smile at a baby, who remembered how to work the muscles well after the moment and smiled back when it was too late.

Finally, a voice said, "Hurry up, the train is about to leave, we'd better get to the station," and most of the crowd poured out of the house again. One of the people left behind had dropped her at her home and that was that.

"We're part of history being made, Mrs. Patel. Today you saw one of the greatest men in India."

Which was the one? She couldn't tell.

The judge, returning from tour—five partridge, two quail, one deer, recorded in his hunting diary—had been summoned by the district commissioner on his return and been given the astonishing news that his wife had been part of the Nehru welcoming committee at the Cantonment Railway Station. She had partaken of scrambled eggs and toast with top members of the Congress Party.

It wasn't the black mark that had been registered against Jemubhai, blocking his promotion, that was of concern to the commissioner, but the embarrassment that would be suffered by the commissioner himself and by the entire civil service that had, he brought down his fist, "A reputation, goddamn it!"

"It couldn't be true, sir. My wife is a very traditional lady. She is too reserved, as you know, to attend the club. In fact, she never leaves the house."

"She did this time, oh yes, she did. It's the traditional types that you have to watch out for, Mr. Patel. Not quite as shy as you would like to claim—it serves as a decoy. I think you will find this trip impossible to disprove, since we have corroboration of it from more than one person. I trust that no member of your family," he paused, "will do anything to compromise your career again. I'm warning you, Patel, as a friend."

Unfriendly face. Mr. Singh hated Jemubhai and he hated Gujaratis and, in particular, he hated Patels, always out to seek their own advantage, like jackals.

Jemubhai drove home along the canal road. He knew the efficiency of the spies they employed, but his jaw had clenched and unclenched: How could it be?

"Out of kindness I invited her," Mrs. Mohan had said when confronted by Jemubhai.

"Out of diabolic slyness," Jemubhai fumed.

"Out of naughtiness," Mr. Mohan said, placing a *mithai* in Mrs. Mohan's mouth to congratulate his politically astute wife.

But what would Nimi say?

His back was to her as she entered. Slowly he fixed himself a drink, poured a cruel shimmer of Scotch, picked up ice cubes with silver pincers in the shape of claws, dropped them into his glass. The ice cracked and smoked.

"What is it?" he asked, swiveling the cubes and turning around, an expression on his face as if he were holding court, preparing to follow a careful rational process.

He swallowed and the whiskey half paralyzed his esophagus. Then the numbness dissipated in a delicious release of heat.

He counted on the fingers of his free hand:

1. "Are you just a country bumpkin?"

Pause.

2. "Are you a liar?"

Pause.

3. "Are you playing foolish female games?"

Pause.

4. "Are you trying deliberately to make me angry?"

Long long pause.

Then, a venomous spat-out sentence:

5. "Or are you just incredibly stupid?"

When she said nothing, he waited.

"Which of the above? We are not ending this conversation until you reply."

Longer wait.

"Which? Are you bloody stupid, I ask you?!"

Silence.

"Well, I will have to conclude that it is all of the above. Is it all of the above??"

With fear that grew as she spoke the words, summoning up the same spirit of the powder-puff night, she defied him. To his amazed ears and her own shocked ears, as if waking up to a moment of clarity before death, she said: *"You are the one who is stupid."*

For the first time he hit her, although he had wanted to before and fought the urge for some time. He emptied his glass on her head, sent a jug of water swinging into the face he no longer found beautiful, filled her ears with leaping soda water. Then, when this wasn't enough to assuage his rage, he hammered down with his fists, raising his arms to bring them down on her again and again, rhythmically, until his own hands were exhausted and his shoulders next day were strained sore as if from chopping wood. He even limped a bit, his leg hurting from kicking her.

"Stupid bitch, dirty bitch!" The more he swore, the harder he found he could hit.

Blotchy bruises showed the next morning in disastrous contrast to the sight of contented civilization—eggs in eggcups, tea cozy on the pot, newspaper. The bruises didn't fade for weeks. Ten blue and black fingerprints clamped on her arm, a thunder-dark cloud loomed up on her side where he had pushed her into the wall—a surprisingly diffuse cloud for that one hard precise push.

The anger, once released, like a genie from a bottle, could never again be curtailed. The quieter she was, the louder he shouted, and if she protested, it was worse. She soon realized that whatever she did or didn't do, the outcome was much the same. His hatred was its own creature; it rose and burned out, reappeared of its own accord, and in her he sought only its justification, its perfection. In its purest moments he could imagine himself killing her.

At this point he grew circumspect, meticulous in every other area of his life—his work, his bath, his hair-combing—uneasy with the realization of how simple it would really be for him to skid from control and jeopardize his career to commit a final violent act.

Spring came to Bonda in milk-swilled colors and newly hatched caterpillars, lizards, and frogs hopped and crawled about in adorable baby size. He could bear her face no longer, bought her a ticket, and returned her to Gujarat.

"I can't go," Nimi said, waking from her stupor. She could take it for herself—in fact it would be like a balm, a dark place to hide herself—but for her family—well, the thought of their shame on her behalf was too much to bear.

"If I don't send you back," he had said to her at this point, in a tone almost kind, "I will kill you. And I don't want to be blamed for such a crime, so you have to go."

Six months later a telegram arrived in Bonda to announce the arrival of a baby.

Jemubhai got drunk that night and not out of joy. Without seeing his child, he was sure what it would look like: red as a blister, going off like a kettle, spilling liquids, waves of heat and anger emanating from it.

Far away, Nimi was staring at her daughter. She was fast asleep, and in those early months of life, peace seemed to be deeply anchored in her nature.

"Your wife is ready to return. She is rested," wrote the uncle in the *haveli,* hopefully. He had mistaken the reason for Nimi's arrival home and attributed it to Jemubhai's concern for his wife's health, because it was appropriate, after all, to have a daughter return for the birth of a first child. They hoped this baby would bring the father back to their community. He was influential now—he might help them all.

Jemu sent money with a letter. "It will not be suitable," he replied. "My work is such. No schools. Constant travel. . . ."

The uncle turned his niece from the door. "You are your husband's responsibility," he said angrily. "Go back. Your father gave a dowry when you married—you got your share and it is not for daughters to come claiming anything thereafter. If you have made your husband angry, go ask for forgiveness."

Please come home, my dear, my lovely girl.

She had lived the rest of her life with a sister who had not married as successfully, as high up, as Nimi. Her brother-in-law resented every bite that entered Nimi's mouth. He watched for signs that she was growing fat under his generous care.

Jemubhai's father arrived to plead.

"Our family honor is gone. We are lucky Bomanbhai is dead, thank God. It's the scandal of the town."

"Why are you talking like this?" he said to his father. "You're following the script of a village idiot. She is unsuitable to be my wife."

"It was a mistake to send you away. You have become like a stranger to us."

"You are the one who sent me and now you come and say it was a mistake! A fine thing." He had been recruited to bring his countrymen into the modern age, but he could only make it himself by cutting them off entirely, or they would show up reproachful, pointing out to him the lie he had become.

His father stayed only two nights. They didn't talk much after the first conversation, and Jemubhai asked no questions about anyone in Piphit, since he realized that it would have been a mockery to do so. But when his father left, Jemubhai tried to give him some money, shabbily trying to transfer it between hands. He wouldn't take it, turned his face, and climbed into the car. The judge felt he should call him back, was about to, the words began in his throat—but then he didn't say anything and the driver took his father back to the station where, not so long ago, Nimi had, unknown to herself, seen Nehru.

War broke out in Europe and India, even in the villages, and the news of the country disintegrating filled the newspapers; almost a million were dead in riots, three to four million in the Bengal famine, thirteen million were evicted from their homes; the birth of the nation was all in shadow. It seemed appropriate.

The judge worked harder than ever. The departure of the British left such a vacuum of power, all Indian members of the ICS rose to the very top, no matter what side they had taken in the independence movement, no matter their talents or expertise.

Somewhere, in the course of those dusky years, a second telegram arrived, the telegram that preceded the telegram about Sai's impending arrival at Cho Oyu.

A woman had caught fire over a stove.

Oh, this country, people exclaimed, glad to fall into the usual sentences, where human life was cheap, where standards were shoddy, where stoves were badly made and cheap saris caught fire as easily—

—as a woman you wanted dead or—

—well, as a woman who wanted to kill herself—

—without a witness, without a case—

—so simple, a single movement of the hand—

—and for the police, a case so simple, just another quick movement of the hand—

—the rupees made an oiled movement between palms—

"Oh thank you, sir," said a policeman.

"Nothing to thank me for," said the brother-in-law.

And in a blink of an eye you could have missed the entire thing.

The judge chose to believe it was an accident.

Ashes have no weight, they tell no secrets, they rise too lightly for guilt; too lightly for gravity, they float upward and, thankfully, disappear.

These years were blurry for many, and when they came out of them, exhausted, the whole world had changed, there were gaps in everything—what had happened in their own families, what had happened elsewhere, what filth had occurred like an epidemic everywhere in a world that was now full of unmarked graves—they didn't look, because they couldn't afford to examine the past. They had to grasp the future with everything they had.

One true thing Jemubhai learned: a human can be transformed into anything. It was possible to forget and sometimes essential to do so.

Now Jemubhai wondered if he had killed his wife for the sake of false ideals. Stolen her dignity, shamed his family, shamed hers, turned her into the embodiment of their humiliation. Even they couldn't accept her then, and her life could only be useless after that, and his daughter could only be useless and absurd. He had condemmed the girl to convent boarding schools, relieved when she reached a new height of uselessness and absurdity by eloping with a man who had grown up in an orphanage. Not even the relatives expected him to pay any attention to her again—

He hadn't liked his wife, but that was no excuse, was it?

Then he remembered a moment long ago when he had indeed liked her. He was twenty, she fourteen. The place was Piphit and they were on a bicycle, traversing gloriously down a slope through cow pats.

Sai had arrived so many years later, and though he had never properly admitted the fact to himself, he knew he hoped an unacknowledged system of justice was beginning to erase his debts.

"Mutt," his voice splintered. "My funny love. My naughty love. My funny naughty love." Over the mountains he went searching.

. . . Joined by Sai and the cook.

When Mutt went missing, Sai, who had hidden her loss of Gyan first in a cold and then in the madness of the hillside, found a disguise so perfect, even she was confused as to the origin of her misery. "Mutt Mutty Mutton chop," she yodeled wildly, in a way she could never ever have publicly proclaimed her own unhappiness. She felt grateful for the greatness of this landscape, walked on trying to recover the horizon—for it felt as if the space bequeathed her at the end of a romance that had promised a wide vista—well, it was nonexistent. Sadness was so claustrophobic.

The cook was walking, too, shouting, "MUTTY," his worry over his son gloved in Mutt's vanishing, "MUTTY." He was talking to his fate—his hand was out, his palm was open, the letter, it had not come.

Fifty

"No bus to Kalimpong."

"Why not?"

It was in the newspaper, wasn't it? The man at the Siliguri bus station had been surprised at Biju's ignorance. On TV? In every conversation? In the air?

Then the problems were continuing?

Worsening. How could he not know? Where had he come from?

From America. No newspaper, no phone. . . .

He nodded, then, in sympathy.

But: "No vehicles going to Kalimpong. Things are very tense, *bhai*. There was shooting there. Everyone has gone crazy."

Biju became insistent. "I have to go. My father is there. . . ."

"Can't go. There's no way. There's an emergency situation and they've put up roadblocks, spread Mobil oil and nails all over the streets—roads are completely closed."

Biju sat on his belongings in the bus station until the man finally took pity on him.

"Listen," he said, "go to Panitunk and you might find some vehicle from there, but it's very dangerous. You will have to beg the GNLF men."

Biju waited there for four days until a GNLF jeep was leaving. They were renting extra seats for extortionary amounts.

"No room," the men told him.

He opened his new wallet to dollars.

He paid. Abraham Lincoln, in God we trust. . . . The men had never seen American money, passed the bills around and studied them.

"But you can't take so much luggage."

He paid some more, they piled his cases onto the roof and banded them with rope, and then they left, riding high on the thin road above the flooded fields, through the incandescence of young rice and banana, through a wildlife sanctuary with giant signs, "DO NOT DISTURB THE WILD ANIMALS," hammered onto the trees. He felt so lighthearted to be back, even this journey with these men didn't unsettle him. He poked his head out and looked up at his bags to make sure they were still properly fastened.

The road tilted, barely a ledge over the Teesta, an insane river, he remembered, leaping both backward and forward within each moment. Biju hung on to the metal frame of the jeep as it maneuvered through ridged gullies and ruts and over rocks—there were more holes in the road than there was road and everything from his liver to his blood was getting a good shake. He looked down over at oblivion, hurried his vision back to the gouged bank. Death was so close—he had forgotten this in his eternal existence in America—this constant proximity of one's nearest destination.

So, hanging tightly on to the metal carapace, they twisted uphill. There were many butterflies of myriad varieties, and when it rained a bit, the butterflies disappeared. The rain stopped and they returned; another little spasm, and they vanished again. Clouds blew in and out of the jeep, obscuring the men from one another every now and again. All along, the frogs sang lustily. There were at least a dozen landslides on the road between Siliguri and Kalimpong, and as they waited for them to be cleared, vendors came by offering *momos* in buckets, coconuts cut into triangle slices. This was where his father lived and where he had visited him and where they had hatched the plot to send him to America, and Biju had, in his innocence, done just what his father had, in his own innocence, told him to do. What could his father have known? This way of leaving your family for work had condemned them over several generations to have their hearts always in other places, their minds thinking about people elsewhere; they could never be in a single existence at one time. How wonderful it was going to be to have things otherwise.

Fifty-one

The judge, exhausted from waiting, fell asleep and dreamed that Mutt was dying—for a moment she came out of a delirium, gave him a familiar look, wagged with a heroic effort, and then, in a second it was gone, the soul behind the eyes.

"Mutt?" The judge bent toward her, searching for a flicker.

"No," said the cook, also in the judge's dream, "she's dead, look," he insisted with an air of finality, and he lifted one of Mutt's legs and let it go. It didn't snap back. It settled slowly. She was stiffening, and he flicked her with his nails, but she didn't flinch.

"Don't touch her! I'll kill you!" screamed the judge aloud, waking himself up, convinced by the logic of his dream.

The next day when he came back from another fruitless search, he repeated the words. "If you don't find her RIGHT NOW," he said, shrilly, to the cook, "I'LL KILL YOU. That's it. I've had enough. It's your fault. It was your responsibility to watch her when I went for my bath."

Here was the difference: the cook had been fond of Mutt. He had taken her for walks, made toast for her breakfast with an egg in the wintertime, made her stew, called to her, "Mutty, Ishtu, Ishtoo," but it was clear, always, that she was just an animal to him.

The judge and his cook had lived together for more years than they had with anyone else, practically in the same room, closer to each other than to any other human being and—nothing, zero, no understanding.

It was so long since Mutt had gone missing. She would be dead now if she'd been bitten by a snake or she'd have starved to death if lost or injured far away.

"But FIND OUT," he told the cook. "FIND HER. RIGHT NOW."

"How, how can I, sahib?" He begged. . . . "I am trying, I have tried. . . ."

"FIND HER. It's your fault. Mutt was in your care! I will *KILL YOU*. Wait and see. You didn't do your duty. You didn't watch over her. It was your duty and you let her be stolen. How dare you? How *dare* you??"

The cook wondered if he *had* done something wrong and his guilt began to grow. Had he indeed been negligent? He had failed in his duty, *hadn't he?* He hadn't looked hard enough. He hadn't shown respect. He should have been watching the dog the day she went missing. . . .

He began to weep without looking at anyone or anything and disappeared into the forest.

It occurred to him as he stumbled about that he'd done something so awful, he'd be paid back by fate and something even more awful would happen—

Sai now walked up and down the path shouting into the trees for the cook: "Come home, it's all right, he doesn't mean it, he is so sad he's crazy, he doesn't know what he's saying. . . ."

The judge was drinking on the veranda and telling himself he felt no remorse, he was perfectly justified in what he had said to the cook. . . . Of course he was! I'll kill you!

"Where are you?" called Sai, walking under the Milky Way, which, she had read in *My Vanishing Tribe*, the Lepchas called Zo-lungming, "world of rice."

Uncle Potty called out—"Did you find the dog?"

"No, and now the cook has also gone."

"He'll be back. Join me for a tipple?"

But she continued.

The cook didn't hear her because he had stumbled into Thapa's Canteen, full of men drinking, spending the dregs of their money. He told them what had happened and it made them laugh, a bit of humor in these frightening days. Dog died! The hilarity spread. They could barely stop laughing. In a place where people died without being given any attention. They died of TB, hepatitis, leprosy, plain old fever. . . . And no jobs, no work, nothing to eat—this commotion over a dog! Ha ha ha ha ha ha.

"It's not something funny," said the cook, but he laughed a bit, too, out of relief that this was clearly humorous, but then he felt worse, doubly guilty, and he resumed his mewling. He had ignored his duty. . . . Why hadn't he watched that *kutti*. . . .

In a corner of Thapa's Canteen was Gyan, who had been let out of the house again. He wasn't laughing. Oh, that awful day when he had told the boys about the judge's guns. What, after all, had Sai done to him? The guilt took over again and he felt dizzy and nauseous. When the cook left, he went out after him.

"I haven't been coming for tuition because of all this trouble. . . . How is Sai?" he mumbled.

"She is very worried about the dog. She is crying all the time."

"Tell her that I will look for Mutt."

"How will you?"

"Tell her that I promise. I will find the dog. Don't worry at all. Be sure and tell her. I will find Mutt and bring her to the house."

He uttered this sentence with a conviction that had nothing to do with Mutt or his ability to find her.

The cook looked at him suspiciously. He hadn't been impressed by Gyan's capabilities. In fact, Sai herself had told the cook that her tutor was not very bright.

But again Gyan nodded his assurance. Next time he saw Sai, he would have a present for her.

Fifty-two

Biju hadn't seen such vastness in a long time—the sheer, overwhelming enormity of mountainside and scree coming down the flank of it. In places, the entire mountain had simply fallen out of itself, spread like a glacier with boulders, uprooted trees. Across the destruction, the precarious ant trail of the road was washed away. He felt exhilarated by the immensity of wilderness, by the lunatic creepers, the shooting hooting abundance of green, the great caterwauling vulgarity of frogs that was like the sound of the earth and the air itself. But the problems of the road were tedious. So, feeling patient in the way one feels before the greatness of nature, impatient in the way one feels with human details, he waited to see his father. The work of recarving a path through this ruin was, of course, usually contracted to teams of hunchbacked midget men and women, rebuilding things stone by stone, putting it all together again each time their work was rent apart, carrying rocks and mud in wicker baskets attached to bands around their foreheads, staggering loony with the weight, pounding on hulking river boulders over and over for hours with hammers and chisels until a bit chipped off, then another bit. They laid out the stones and the surface was tarred again—Biju remembered how, as a child, his father had always made him walk across newly spread pitch whenever they encountered some, in order to reinforce, he said, the thin soles of Biju's shoes. Now that the government had suspended repairs, the GNLF men in the jeep were forced to clamber out themselves and roll boulders aside, remove fallen tree trunks, shovel clods of earth. . . . They went through seven landslides. At the eighth they kept getting mired in the mud, the jeep rolling back down.

They backed up, needing space to rev up the engine and gather enough momentum to get over the ruts and the unmade soil and drove forward again at high speed. Again and again the engine stalled and shut off and they rolled back down. Backed up and went *whroom whroom whrooming!* . . .

They got out again, all of them except the driver, untied the luggage, and piled it on the mud. Finally, on the eleventh try, backing up a good long way and rushing, engine surging—the jeep went flustering over, and they applauded with relief, piled up the bags again, clambered in, and went on. They were almost a whole day into a journey that should have taken two hours. Surely they would soon arrive.

Then they veered off onto a smaller road, even harder to traverse.

"Is this the Kalimpong road?" Biju asked, bewildered.

"We have to drop some men off first. . . . Detour."

Hours passed. . . . The ninth landslide and the tenth.

"But when will we reach Kalimpong?" asked Biju. "Will we reach it by night?"

"Calm down, *bhai*." They didn't seem worried, although the sun was sinking fast and a cool damp darkness spilled from the jungle.

It was late evening by the time they reached a few small huts along a dirt track of churned mud and deep puddles of water. The men got out and took down all their belongings, including Biju's boxes and cases.

"How long are we staying?"

"This is as far as we are going. You can walk up to Kalimpong by yourself," they said and pointed at a path through the trees. "Shortcut."

Panic lurched in him. "How will I take my things?"

"Leave them here. Safekeeping." They laughed. "We'll send them to you later."

"No," said Biju, terrified by the realization that he was being robbed.

"Go!" They pointed.

He stood there. The foliage loomed in a single mass; the sound of frogs swelled into the same tone that had expanded in Biju's ear through the phone that day when he called his father from the streets of New York.

Up above, the mountains stretched—

Below, they dropped straight down, as in a nightmare, all the way to the Teesta.

"Go, will you?! *Bhago,*" a man said, pointing now with his rifle.

Biju turned.

"But give us your wallet and remove your shoes before you go."

He turned around again.

"His belt is also nice," said another of the men, eyeing the leather. "Such nice clothes you get in America. The quality is very good."

Biju handed over his wallet. He took off his belt.

"You're forgetting your shoes."

He took them off. Under fake soles were his savings.

"Your jacket." And when his denim jacket was off, they decided even his jeans and T-shirt were desirable.

Biju began to quake, and fumbling, tripping, he took off the last items of clothing, stood in his white underpants.

By this time, dogs from all over the *busti* had arrived galloping. They were battered and balding from fights and disease, but they, like their masters, had the air of outlaws. They surrounded Biju with gangster swagger, tails curved up over them like flags, growling and barking.

Children and women peered from the shadows.

"Let me go," he begged.

One of the men, laughing wildly, pulled a nightgown off a hedge where it was drying. "No, no, don't give that to him," squealed a toothless crone, clearly the owner of the garment. "Let him have it, we'll buy you another. He's come from America. How can he go and see his family naked?"

They laughed.

And Biju ran—

He ran into the jungle chased by the dogs, who also seemed in on the joke, grinning and snapping.

Finally, when Biju had passed what the dogs deemed their line of control, they tired of him and wandered back.

Darkness fell and he sat right in the middle of the path—without his baggage, without his savings, worst of all, without his pride. Back from America with far less than he'd ever had.

He put on the nightgown. It had large, faded pink flowers and yellow, puffy sleeves, ruffles at the neck and hem. It must have been carefully picked from a pile at the bazaar.

Why had he left? Why had he left? He'd been a fool. He thought of Harish-Harry—"Go for a rest and then return." Mr. Kakkar, the travel agent, who had warned him—"My friend, I am telling you, you are making a big mistake."

He thought of Saeed Saeed.

One last time, Biju had run into him.

"Biju, man, I see this girl, Lutfi's sister, she is visiting from Zanzibar, and the MINUTE I see her, I say to Lutfi, 'I think she is the ONE, man.'"

"You're already married."

"But in four years I get my green card and . . . *fsshht* . . . out of there. . . . I get divorced and I marry for real. Now we are only going to have a ceremony in the mosque. . . . This girl . . . she is. . . ."

Biju waited.

Saeed exploded with amazement: "SO. . . ."

Biju waited.

"CLEAN!! She smell . . . SO NICE! And size fourteen. BEST SIZE!"

Saeed showed him with his hands apart what a sweet handful his second wife was.

"But when I meet her, I don't even touch her. Not even like this—" He stuck out his finger like a coy snail from a shell. "I behave myself. We will buy a house in New Jersey. I'm taking a course in airplane maintenance."

Biju sat there in terror of what he'd done, of being alone in the forest, and of the men coming after him again. He couldn't stop thinking of all that he'd bought and lost. Of the money he'd hidden under fake soles in his shoes. Of his wallet. Suddenly, he felt an old throbbing of the knee that he had hurt slipping on Harish-Harry's floor.

Fifty-three

At Cho Oyu, the frogs were croaking in the jhora, in the bed of spinach, and high in the water tank above the trees. Late into the night, the cook made his way through the nightshade and knocked on the judge's door.

"What is it?" asked the judge.

The cook opened the door wrapped in such a haze of alcohol, it watered his own eyes like an onion. After his stop at Thapa's Canteen and all the drinking he'd done there, he'd returned to his own supply of *chhang* and imbibed that as well.

"If I have been disobedient," he slurred, approaching the foot of the judge's bed with unfocused eyes, "beat me."

"What?" said the judge, sitting up in bed and switching on the light, drunk himself. He on whiskey.

"What?"

"I'm a bad man," cried the cook, "I'm a bad man, beat me, sahib, punish me."

How dare he—

How dare he lose Mutt how dare he not find her how dare he presume to come and disturb the judge—

"*WHAT ARE YOU SAYING????!!!*" the judge yelled.

"Sahib, beat me—

"If it will make you feel better," said the judge, "all right."

"I'm a wicked man, a weak man. I'd be better dead than alive."

The judge got out of bed. In bed he was heavy; standing he was light. He had to keep moving. . . . If he didn't extend himself into action, he would fall. He smacked the cook over the head with his slipper. "If this is what you want!"

Then the cook fell at his feet, clasping one of them and weeping for mercy. "I'm a bad man, forgive me, forgive me. . . ."

"Leave," said the judge, repulsed, trying to wrench his foot free. *"Leave."*

The cook would not. He held tighter. He wept and slobbered on it. Slime came from his nose, tears from his eyes.

The judge began to beat him harder and harder to get him to let go. He kicked out and hit.

"Sahib. I drink. I'm a bad man. Beat me. Beat me."

Smacking him, beating him, beating him—

"I've been bad," the cook said, "I've been drinking I ate the same rice as you not the servant's rice but the Dehradun rice I ate the meat and lied I ate out of the same pot I stole liquor from the army I made *chhang* I did the accounts differently for years I have cheated you in the accounts each and every day my money was dirty it was false sometimes I kicked Mutt I didn't take her for walks just sat by the side of the road smoked a bidi and came home I'm a bad man I watched out for nobody and nothing but myself—*Beat me!*"

The surge of anger was familiar to the judge.

He said, "You filth, you hypocrite. If you want punishment I'll give it to you!"

"Yes," wept the cook, "that is right. It's your duty to discipline me. It's as it should be."

Sai came rushing from her room, hearing the thuds. "What is happening??? Stop. Stop it immediately. Stop it!" she screamed, "Stop it!"

"Let him," the cook said. "Let him. He wants to *kill me. Let* him kill me. What is my life? It's nothing. Better that it's gone. It's useless to everyone. It's useless to you and to me. Kill me! Maybe that will give you satisfaction. It will give me satisfaction. Go on!"

"I'll kill you! I'll kill you!"

"Kill me."

"I'll kill you."

The cook didn't mention his son . . . he had none . . . he'd never had one . . . it was just his hope writing to him . . . Biju was nonexistent. . . .

The judge was beating with all the force of his sagging, puckering flesh, flecks of saliva flying from his slack muscled mouth, and his chin wobbled uncontrollably. Yet that arm, from which the flesh hung already dead, came down, bringing the slipper upon the cook's head.

"There's something filthy going on," Sai wept and covered her ears, her eyes. "Don't you know? Can't you tell? Something filthy is going on."

But they didn't stop.

She fled outside. Stood in the rich humus dark in her white cotton pajamas and felt the empty burden of the day, her own small heart, her disgust at the cook, at his pleading, her hatred of the judge, her pitiful selfish sadness, her pitiful selfish pointless love. . . .

The sound followed her, though, the muffled thuds and cries of the men inside, of the judge beating the cook. Could it really be for Mutt's sake . . . ?

And Mutt? Where was Mutt?

Sold to a family that couldn't love her in a village beyond Kurseong, an ordinary family, paying hard for modernity, receiving a sham. They wouldn't care for Mutt. She was just a concept. They were striving toward an idea of something, toward what it meant to have a fancy dog. She disappointed them just as modern life did, and they tied her to a tree, kicked her . . .

Sai thought of crossing the *jhora* and escaping to Uncle Potty—

Who would be thinking of Father Booty—

Wobbling across the bridge, through the bamboo, with a wheel of cheese fastened to the backseat of his bicycle.

One day soon, the GNLF men would arrive again—

Don't mind me, love—just shut the door behind you when you leave, don't want the rowdies getting you—

When Uncle Potty woke, he would realize he'd signed away his property and Father Booty's, as well, to new owners. . . .

And Mrs. Sen—she would knit the sweater that Rajiv Gandhi would never wear and that Lola and Noni said would not have matched his Kashmiri pundit, peaches 'n' cream complexion anyway. His destiny would be interwoven with a female Tamil Tiger in more intimate fashion than anything Mrs. Sen with her yellow sweater could have dreamed of.

And Lola and Noni would commit annual massacres at this time of year with Baygon, mosquito coils, and swatters. Every two years Lola would visit London, come back with Knorr soup packets and Marks and Spencer underwear. Pixie would marry an Englishman and Lola would almost die with delight. "Everyone in England wants an Indian girl these days!"

And Gyan? Where was Gyan? Sai didn't know that he missed her—

She stood in the dark and it began to rain as it so often did on an August night. The electricity went off, as always, and the televisions frizzed and the BBC was diced by storm. Lantern light came on in homes. Plunk, ping, piddle, drips fell into the pots and pans placed under leaks—

Sai stood in the wet. The rain boxed the leaves, fell in jubilant dung-like plops into the *jhora*. The rain slapped, anthem-singing frogs exulted in their millions, from the Teesta up to Cho Oyu, high into the Deolo and Singalila Mountains. Drowned the sound of the judge hitting the cook.

"What is this all about?" asked Sai, but her mouth couldn't address her ear in the tumult; her heart lying in pieces, didn't seem able to address her mind; her mind couldn't talk to her heart. "Shame on myself . . ." she said. . . . Who was she . . . she with her self-importance, her demand for happiness, yelling it at fate, at the deaf heavens, screaming for her joy to be brought forth . . . ?

How dare. . . . How dare you not . . . ?

Why shouldn't I have . . . ? . . . How dare. . . . I deserve. . . . Her small greedy soul. . . . Her tantrums and fits. . . . Her mean tears. . . . Her crying, enough for all the sadness in the world, was only for herself. Life wasn't single in its purpose . . . or even in its direction. . . . The simplicity of what she'd been taught wouldn't hold. Never again could she think there was but one narrative and that this narrative belonged only to herself, that she might create her own tiny happiness and live safely within it.

But what would happen at Cho Oyu?

The cook would hobble back to his quarter—

The judge would return to his room—

All night it would rain. It would continue, off and on, on and off, with a savagery matched only by the ferocity with which the earth responded to the onslaught. Uncivilized voluptuous green would be unleashed; the town would slide down the hill. Slowly, painstakingly, like ants, men would make their paths and civilization and their wars once again, only to have it wash away again. . . .

The new morning would hatch, black or blue, clear or smothered. Breakfast, lunch. The judge would sit at his chessboard, and at 4:30, without thinking, from mere habit, he would open his mouth and say, as he always said, "Panna Lal, bring the tea."

And always there would have to be something sweet and something salty—

Sai stood there—

She thought of her father and the space program. She thought of all the *National Geographic*s and books she had read. Of the judge's journey, of the cook's journey, of Biju's. Of the globe twirling on its axis.

And she felt a glimmer of strength. Of resolve. She must leave.

The congress of hopeful frogs continued to sing, even as a weak whiskey light showed in the east as the rain slowed.

Behind Sai, Cho Oyu was still full of shadow. She could no longer hear the men inside. The judge lay exhausted in his bed. The cook sat hunched in the kitchen, his face still in the grip of a nightmare.

Sai, dizzy from lack of sleep, turned to go inside. But then, just as she did, she became conscious of a tiny dot of a figure laboring up the slope through the clouds that were still sunk in the valley. She stopped to look. The dot vanished into the trees, reappeared, vanished again, came around the bend in the mountain. It made a pink and yellow patch of color slowly growing bigger—striving through bushy detonations of wild cardamom—

Gyan? she thought with a burst of hope. A message: I will love you after all.

Someone who had found Mutt? Right here. . . . She's right here, alive and well! Plumper than ever!

The figure persisted. Someone else. A bent-over woman dragging one leg onerously. She must be on her way elsewhere.

Sai went inside to the kitchen. "I'll make you tea," she told the cook, who was covered in slipper marks.

She put on the kettle, struggled with a soggy match. Finally it flared and she lit the balled newspaper under the sticks.

Then they heard the gate being rattled. Oh dear, thought Sai with dread, perhaps it was the same begging woman again, the one whose husband had been blinded.

Again the gate rattled.

"I'll go," said the cook and he got up slowly, dusted himself off.

He walked through the drenched weeds to the gate.

At the gate, peeping through the black lace wrought iron, between the mossy canonballs, was the figure in a nightgown.

"Pitaji?" said the figure, all ruffles and colors.

Kanchenjunga appeared above the parting clouds, as it did only very early in the morning during this season.

"Biju?" whispered the cook—

"Biju!" he yelled, demented—

Sai looked out and saw two figures leaping at each other as the gate swung open.

The five peaks of Kanchenjunga turned golden with the kind of luminous light that made you feel, if briefly, that truth was apparent.

All you needed to do was to reach out and pluck it.

My Salaams

To my editor, Joan Bingham, and my agent, Michael Carlisle, for their unstinting enthusiasm and generosity regarding everything to do with *The Inheritance of Loss*. Also, to Rose Marie Morse, David Davidar, David Godwin, Simon Prosser and Ravi Singh. To Adelaide Docx for additional editing help.

To the Santa Maddalena Foundation, the Eastern Frontier Society, to Bunny Gupta and Doma Rai of *Sukhtara*, each for a desk with a view during three vital stages in the writing of this book.